RECEIVE

ᨪ THE ᨪ

GIFT

LOUISE MARLEY

ACE BOOKS, NEW YORK

This book is an Ace original edition,
and has never been previously published

RECEIVE THE GIFT

An Ace Book / published by arrangement with
the author

PRINTING HISTORY
Ace edition / November 1997

All rights reserved.
Copyright © 1997 by Louise Marley.
Cover art by Bob Eggleton.
This book may not be reproduced in whole or in part,
by mimeograph or any other means, without permission.
For information address: The Berkley Publishing Group,
a member of Penguin Putnam Inc.,
200 Madison Avenue, New York, New York 10016.

The Putnam Berkley World Wide Web site address is
http://www.berkley.com

Make sure to check our *PB Plug*,
the science fiction/fantasy newsletter, at
http://www.pbplug.com

ISBN: 0-441-00486-5

ACE®
Ace Books are published by The Berkley Publishing Group,
a member of Penguin Putnam Inc.,
200 Madison Avenue, New York, New York 10016.
ACE and the "A" design are trademarks
belonging to Charter Communications, Inc.

PRINTED IN THE UNITED STATES OF AMERICA

10 9 8 7 6 5 4 3 2 1

For Brian, Cathy, Dave, Jeralee, and Niven:
without whom nothing

PROLOGUE

✹ MREEN'S SMALL FINGERS DANCED ACROSS THE STOPS OF her little *filla,* and her *Aiodu* melody bubbled up to resonate merrily against the stone walls. Sira listened and watched, her chin propped on one long, narrow hand, her elbow on the ironwood table between them. She did not interrupt until Mreen began to embellish her tune.

No, no, Mreen, Sira sent then. *You must stay in the mode, or make a modulation to the next.*

Mreen's eyes flashed green. *Why, Cantrix Sira?* she sent. She put down the *filla,* and kicked her short legs against the chair. *Why must I?*

Sira regarded her gravely. Mreen was redheaded, dimpled, and plump. She was, in fact, very like her mother. But Isbel had never been as willful as her daughter, except once.

It is unmusical, Sira sent to her. *It jars on the ear.*

Not on my ear! Mreen responded. Tiny sparks, born of her temper, appeared in the air around her. They glinted on her hair, and lifted little tendrils of it to waft around her face.

Sira raised one long forefinger. All of her students knew

1

that warning finger very well. Mreen's pink lip pouted, but the disturbance in her tiny *quiru* subsided at once.

When you are a full Cantrix, and have mastered your art, Sira sent, *you will undoubtedly forget all I have said and embellish however you like. But for now, please follow my instruction. When you play in* Aiodu, *you must not leap to* Doryu *without preparation. I will show you.*

Sira lifted her own ironwood *filla*, *obis*-carved at the House of Soren just as Mreen's had been. She repeated the notes and rhythms of Mreen's melody exactly, but after the first statement her modulation to *Doryu* was smooth and sweet, like a tidbit of dried fruit melting on the tongue. Mreen caught her breath at the beauty of it.

Sira stopped playing and gazed at her student with her eyebrow lifted high, the slash of white just at the apex of the arch. This, too, was familiar to her students.

Mreen squirmed and giggled. She was, after all, not yet five years old.

All right, Cantrix Sira, she sent. She dimpled at her teacher as she picked up her own instrument. *I will try.*

Sira leaned her chin on her hand once again, and listened. She thought of Isbel, her old friend, Mreen's mother. She could almost see her behind her daughter, a hazy familiar figure, an apparition of memory reaching out a soft hand to stroke the childish curls. A wave of remembered grief swept Sira, and she shook her head sharply to banish both the image and the emotion.

Abruptly, Mreen stopped playing. Her eyes glistened with welling tears; like the needles of the ironwood trees curling in on themselves in the deep cold season, they turned dark, a black green for which there was no name.

Oh, Mreen, Sira sent swiftly. *It was not you. I only . . . I thought of something, that is all.*

I know what you thought. The tears, shining faintly yellow in the light of the *quiru*, spilled over Mreen's smooth cheeks.

Sira stared at her. *You know?*

The little girl dashed away the tears with her fingers. *I always know. I see the pictures.*

Sira looked down at her *filla,* turning it in her fingers. Sometimes she hardly knew what to say to this child, who even now was two years younger than the youngest student ever to attend Conservatory. Mreen's Gift was so intense that she went about Observatory wrapped in a little cloud of light that only faded when she lay down on her cot to sleep. Her moods brought sparks flying about her, or small shadows shifting through the light. And she was silent, always.

Gifted students never spoke aloud in Sira's presence, in order to practice their sending and listening, to sharpen their mental skills. But with their families, and with other House members, they chattered as freely and volubly as any other children. Only Mreen did not speak at all, not to her Gifted friends, not to her teachers, not even to her unGifted father and stepmother. She had never cried as a baby, nor made any of the usual infant sounds. She was utterly and entirely a creature of the Gift.

Who is the lady? Mreen asked. *The one you saw? Why does she make you sad?*

Sira indulged herself by reaching out her long arm to gently stroke away the last tear from Mreen's face. The thought that Mreen could see the image in her mind, and yet not recognize it, was exquisitely painful. Sira took the child's small hand in her own.

She was your mother, Mreen, she sent gently. *She loved you very much.*

The little girl sat still for a long time, looking down at her own hand in Sira's. When she raised her eyes, the look in them made Sira's scalp prickle under her short-cropped hair.

I thought so, Mreen sent. *I have seen her.*

How? How could you have seen her?

Mreen turned her little hand over and pressed it into Sira's. *Cantrix Sira . . . when I touch things, certain things . . . I know about them, about the other people who touched them.*

Sira listened, and watched. There seemed to be an old, old woman behind the child's eyes.

Kai, my father, that is . . . gave me my mother's brushes. When I hold them in my hand, I can see her.

Perhaps you only imagine that, Mreen. It would be natural.

Mreen shook her head firmly, her red curls bouncing, and she let go of Sira's hand. *No, Cantrix Sira. I can see her. She had red hair, like me!*

That is right, Mreen. She was beautiful.

Was she your friend?

Sira nodded slowly, thinking of the years that had passed since she and Isbel had been girls together at Conservatory.

Was she a Singer, Cantrix Sira?

Sira hesitated. This was the hard part, and she had hoped not to have to touch upon it for some time yet. The child was so precocious—there were no rules to follow in teaching her.

Your mother was a full Cantrix. Cantrix Isbel v'Amric.

Mreen was still for a moment, thinking. When she looked back at Sira, the old woman looked out again from behind the childish features.

But Cantrixes do not have babies.

That is right, Mreen. But to your mother— Sira remembered Isbel, caressing the swell of her stomach, smiling up at Kai. *To your mother, you were more important than being a Cantrix.*

Mreen sighed and shook her head. *I think I am too young to understand.*

That is a very wise observation.

They sat in silence for a time, each with her own thoughts. Sira asked, *Will you play once more?*

Mreen dimpled, and reached for her *filla. I will play again. I will modulate!*

Sira smiled a little, and sat back to listen, but her heart ached. A strange and heavy Gift had been laid upon the child. As Mreen began her melody, Sira reflected that there was only one place where Mreen could realize her full potential. She needed the structure, the discipline, and the safety of a House entirely devoted to the Gift and to the Gifted. She needed Conservatory.

It would not be easy to send Mreen away, to let others take charge of her training, of the molding and direction of her Gift. Her father and her stepmother would miss her terribly, and so, Sira knew, would she herself. But like every Cantor and Cantrix on the Continent, Sira was accustomed to sacrifice. She would not shirk this one. She would do what she must.

CHAPTER ONE

✦ THE SNOW OF THE DEEP COLD SEASON LAY THICKLY ON the peaks and valleys around Amric. Ironwood trees drooped under its weight and the road leading away from the House was blankly white, undisturbed by any footstep of man or *hruss*. When Cantor Zakri v'Amric looked out through the rippled lime-glass window of his private apartment, cold sunlight sparkled on the snowpack and dazzled his eyes. He turned his gaze upward to the wide vivid sky. It infected him with restiveness, with longing for the outside. He had remained here at Amric, working in its Cantoris, for three solid years. He had not been outside its walls since the day Cantrix Sira had left the House in his care and departed for Observatory. Not since his early childhood had he spent so long a time in one place.

Idly, Zakri stretched out a lazy fibril of his thought and tweaked one of the ironwood branches overhanging the courtyard, just to see the snow fall from it in a glittering cascade. He chuckled, leaning into the window to watch the little pile of white snow drop to the clean-swept gray of the cobblestones. At least he could still do it. Three years of Cantoris discipline had not dulled his special talent!

The *quirunha* had been performed an hour before, and the warmth and light of the House *quiru* enveloped even the edges of the courtyard, spilling over onto the snow beyond. Cantor Ovan and Cantor Gavn, Zakri's senior and junior respectively, had flanked him on the dais in the Cantoris as they did each day. Their combined psi, borne on the music of *filhata* and voice, made Amric's *quiru* one of the strongest and warmest on the Continent, behind only those of Lamdon and Conservatory. Magister Edrus was justifiably proud of his three Cantors.

Zakri sighed again, and turned away from the window to brush and retie his long hair. He patted his tunic to make sure his *filla* was there before he went out of his apartment and down the broad carved staircase to return to the Cantoris. Cantor Gavn was already seated, and a short line of people in brightly dyed tunics waited in front of him.

Not many today, Cantor Zakri, Gavn sent.

Zakri stepped up on the dais and sat down next to his junior. Indeed, their duties would be light. *You could handle this all by yourself,* he sent to Gavn with a wink.

Gavn's answering smile was shy. He was only slightly younger than Zakri, but his Conservatory upbringing, his lack of experience, made him seem tender and unformed. Even his features were babyish, his mouth full and soft, his cheeks smooth. Zakri shielded the thought, sure that Gavn would not appreciate it. Gavn had four summers, after all, and would have five before long, Spirit willing. He had to be at least twenty-two years old.

Zakri was not sure of his own age; his parents, like so many itinerants and working people, had measured their children's ages only in summers. With five years between summers, the system was no more than a general one, and there was great variety in its accuracy.

I could handle these, I think, Gavn sent now, *but they would only ask for you in any case!*

Zakri's mouth curled in amusement. *If they only knew!* he responded. *Perhaps I should stay away and let them find out what you can do.* He turned to nod to the small group of people seeking healing. The first of them stepped forward, and Zakri took his *filla* out of his tunic, ready to begin.

He had barely opened his mouth to ask the Houseman what was troubling him when a clatter of *hruss* hooves sounded from the courtyard, and a voice called loudly and hoarsely from the steps leading to the House. Every head in the Cantoris turned. Even Gavn murmured aloud, "Travelers!"

The Housemen and women chattered excitedly to each other, and turned about, torn between their turn at Cantoris hours and wanting to see who had come. Very few travelers had been seen at Amric during the past months, and in recent weeks, none at all. A face at the evening meal, bearing fresh news and perhaps some gossip, would be welcome.

Amric's Housekeeper, Cael, burst into the Cantoris, hurrying up the aisle between the ironwood benches. His face was pale, his expression grim. As Zakri rose to meet him, he felt a chill of premonition creep across his shoulders.

Cael bowed very briefly. Zakri nodded in return. "Housekeeper?" he said.

"Cantor Zakri, you are needed in the great room," Cael murmured.

Without hesitating, knowing in his bones that something grave was happening, Zakri tucked his *filla* back into his tunic and stepped down from the dais. To Gavn he sent, *You will have to care for these people alone, after all.*

Yes, Cantor Zakri, Gavn responded. *Shall I join you then?*

Good idea. As Zakri followed Cael out of the Cantoris, he heard Gavn speaking to the House members, his voice soothing and assured. He did not sound a bit shy.

The double doors to the great room were closed. Cael opened one of them for Zakri to slip through, and then shut it firmly again, forestalling several curious House members who lingered in the hall, trying to see inside.

The great room was empty except for two men, both still heavily swathed in traveling furs, collapsed into one of the deep window seats. One looked up at Zakri with desperate eyes. The other sprawled in the seat with his legs dangling to the floor. He did not move at all.

Zakri's steps slowed as he approached them, and his premonition solidified into dread. A tiny cold cell of fear and anger was born just under his heart. He knew already whose face he would see when he pulled back the *caeru*-fur hood of the unconscious man. And he knew the man was beyond any help he could give.

He tried just the same. He got out his *filla* and played, searching for a spark, for any glimmer of life in his old friend and master, but there was none to be found. He played on, frantically. His psi probed and prodded relentlessly, refusing to give up, but there was no consciousness to awaken, no pulse, however weak, to encourage. The people of Amric believed Zakri to be the greatest healer on the Continent, but there was nothing he could do for the Singer Iban.

Iban had been his mentor, his master, his teacher. Any healing Zakri knew, he had learned from Iban. But Iban was gone, gone now with the Spirit beyond the stars.

"What happened?" he demanded of Iban's companion. The man slumped beside his dead comrade, his face sagging with fatigue and fright. "Who are you?" Zakri snapped.

The man turned pale eyes to Zakri, and then looked swiftly away. "I'm Clive v'Trevi. Iban's sister's mate. We were coming to you . . . you're Cantor Zakri, aren't you?"

He looked up to see Zakri's nod, and then averted his gaze again. "We were coming to you, to tell you—" He broke off, looking around the circle of faces bending over the three of them, but meeting no one's eyes. "Iban wanted to see you."

"But what happened?" Zakri repeated. He spoke harshly, his voice rough with grief and shock and anger. The air around him shifted and darkened, as if his emotions were a cloud before the sun. He took a sharp breath, concentrating on his control, and the light returned. This was no time for an undisciplined display. It would do no honor to Iban's memory to lose control of his Gift.

"I don't know," Clive muttered. "We were hurrying, traveling as fast as we could in the deep cold . . . and then last night, just after the *quiru* was up, he cried out, like he'd seen something or heard something . . . and then no more." Now he did look up at Zakri, and Zakri believed him to be telling the truth. "I couldn't wake him up, not then or since. As soon as morning came, I just followed the road here. I was so afraid. . . ."

Clive v'Trevi hung his head, and Zakri and those around him were silent. They were Nevyans, and they understood perfectly. Of course he had been afraid. He was no Singer, who could call up a *quiru* whenever he needed it. Had Clive not reached Amric before dark, his own death would have been as certain as Iban's.

"Where were you riding from?"

This was a new voice, a deep and commanding one. Clive's eyes darted up in search of the speaker, and then away again. He hesitated a long time, and the hard spot of cold under Zakri's heart spread wider, filling the space between his ribs.

"Soren," Clive finally whispered. Zakri looked up at Berk, who had asked the question. The Gifted Cantor and the unGifted courier stared at each other until Berk gave a sharp gesture with his head.

Zakri turned back to Iban's body, directing the Housemen to lift it and transport it to his own rooms. In the background he heard Berk speaking to the Magister, and he heard Cantor Gavn come into the great room. Housekeeper Cael led Clive away to bathe and eat, and Zakri heard Berk telling him to be in the Magister's apartment within the hour. There would be little rest for Clive v'Trevi, at least not until all the truth of the disastrous journey were known.

Gavn came to Zakri and stood before him, biting his full lower lip. *Are you all right, Cantor?*

Zakri shook his head. *Something terrible has happened,* he sent.

What is it? Who was that man?

That was my master.

Gavn sucked in a noisy breath, and his blue eyes were

wide and shocked. *Not the Singer Iban! From your itinerant days?*

My itinerant days, thought Zakri. They had not lasted long, but they had changed him forever, changed everything. For a moment he missed them with a longing so fierce that he saw Gavn step back suddenly, and knew he had not shielded himself enough. *I am sorry,* he sent. *It is just that . . . without Iban . . . I would not be here today. Or perhaps anywhere!*

The two Cantors walked slowly out of the great room, and started up the wide staircase to the upper level of the House.

Can I do anything to help? Gavn asked.

I do not know yet.

Too many Singers had died in recent years. No Nevyan Singer's death would ever be lightly dismissed, but in this case, Zakri swore to himself, he would have answers . . . or else. What else, he could not have said at that moment. But the coldness under his heart wound itself into a frigid knot of fury. He felt it when he breathed, when he moved. It demanded release. It demanded revenge.

"The rumors from Soren have been around for a long time," Berk said heavily. His body dwarfed the carved ironwood chair he sat in. His long legs barely fit beneath the table in the Magister's apartment. Berk's grizzled hair and beard were always neatly combed, but despite his years of service to the upper levels of the House, he retained the weather-beaten, travel-hardened look of a rider. And so he had been in his youth, as Zakri well knew.

"For too long," Zakri said. "It is time something was done."

Magister Edrus leaned forward. "But what will you do, Cantor Zakri?" he asked. "If you and Berk go riding into Soren, your own safety may be at risk!"

Zakri shrugged. He was spending a good deal of his energy simply controlling his psi so as not to darken and disturb the *quiru* light in the room, and he could feel Gavn staring at him, wondering.

Edrus pressed him. "What injury did you find in Singer Iban?"

Zakri took a deep, shuddering breath. "I found no injury at all, Magister," he said slowly. "No injury to his body, that is."

Berk turned in Clive's direction. The smaller man cowered in misery at one end of the table. "Houseman! Are you sure you heard nothing last night, no *hruss* or men behind you?"

Clive's eyes flickered up at the others, and slid away again. He shook his head. Zakri saw that his hands trembled, and that he grasped his elbows to stop them. Berk looked at Zakri, his eyebrows up and his lips pursed beneath his beard. Zakri knew what Berk wanted.

Carefully, as Berk and the Magister discussed possible actions to take, Zakri extended his psi, reaching ever so cautiously into Clive's mind. He had to be very subtle. If Cantor Gavn, who had been so carefully trained in discretion at Conservatory, were to catch him trespassing, he would never understand. And Cantrix Sira would have objected, of course . . . or perhaps not, if she had seen Singer Iban lying dead in the great room, his mobile features stilled forever. That thought made Zakri set his jaw. Trying to keep his face impassive, he strengthened his touch, delving more boldly into Clive's thoughts.

It was little use. Clive had no Gift at all. Zakri read only a confusion of fear, and a cloud of fatigue brought about by his sleepless night and frantic ride from the last night's campsite. Zakri withdrew his psi, and gave Berk a small shake of his head. Gavn's eyes were on him again, and he shielded himself carefully.

"I want to go home, to Trevi," Clive whined. "I've told you all I know! How can I know what's wrong at Soren, anyway? I'm no itinerant!"

Berk turned an unsympathetic face to the man. "It's too bad you're not," he growled. "We've not seen an itinerant here for weeks. There's no one to escort you."

Clive's eyes flickered away again. Zakri watched him

closely, sensing something, some slight deception, some hidden fear.

"Clive," Zakri said slowly. "You said Singer Iban went to Soren with goods from Trevi." Clive nodded, not looking into Zakri's face. "What were the goods, what was he carrying?"

Clive looked out the window, at the floor, anywhere but at the three other men. "It was . . . it was food and cloth. We make felted cloth at Trevi, you know, and we grow the oaten grain no one else does, so they wanted . . . they sent . . ." His voice trailed off, and Zakri clenched a fist in irritation.

"What?" Berk pressed. "They sent what?"

"They sent us an itinerant."

The three Amric men stared at the traveler in amazement.

"They had nothing else?" Magister Edrus blurted.

Clive blinked. "Nothing else we wanted, I'd guess."

"Has this happened before?" Magister Edrus wanted to know.

"Once or twice. They've sent an itinerant for our Magister to use for a trip or two, and then we sent him back loaded up with supplies. Only this time . . ."

"Yes?"

"They said they needed the grain quickly, and since Singer Iban was at home, and the Magister wanted the itinerant for something else, Iban and I took the shipment to Soren." He blinked again, looking either innocent or stupid.

"Something happened at Soren. That's what we need to know," Berk said firmly.

A silence stretched around the room. The Amric men did not look at Clive, but they waited, letting him shift and squirm in his seat. The scent of fear grew sharp around him, but Zakri and the others did not relent.

Clive perspired freely now, although he had shed his heavy *caeru* furs in the great room. "I don't know what you want!" he cried.

Zakri stared at him. "I think you do."

"But if I . . ."

"Yes?"

"Do you know what they're doing to people there?" Clive burst out in a panic. "I have a family, children. . . ."

"Singer Iban had a family!" Zakri rapped, and the air around him glimmered angrily. "And friends!"

Clive sagged in his chair, looking down at his hands twisting together before him. More moments of silence passed, while Zakri gritted his teeth until his jaw ached. At length Clive looked up.

"There was a man . . . he used to be a Singer, an itinerant. Karl v'Perl." Clive struggled for courage. "He sits at meals in the great room at Soren, like . . . like a warning. A threat. His mind is gone, and he just sits there, staring. He—" Clive shuddered. "He drools. And he shakes. He—he soils himself. His mate has to do everything for him."

Cantor Gavn sucked in his breath, shocked.

Clive cast him a look, and then stammered on. "When they took Iban up the stairs, up to Cho's rooms—"

"Cho?" asked Magister Edrus.

"Cho—he's an *obis*-carver, or he was. But something has happened to the Magister at Soren, and Cho's in charge, or seems to be. He sits at the center table."

"What about their Cantors?"

Clive shook his head, pale and beaten looking. "I never saw them," he whispered. "The place is full of Singers, but they're all itinerants. And they took Iban up to Cho, and when he came back, he wouldn't tell me anything. He said it was better I didn't know! We left in a hurry, sneaked away, really, just before dawn."

"We must report to Lamdon," Magister Edrus said to Berk and to Zakri. "They need to know what's happening, take some sort of action." He turned back to Clive. "It's true that there are no itinerants in the House. We can't send you home at the moment."

Clive nodded. "I know. It was the same at Trevi. No itinerants."

Berk thumped a big fist on the table. "That's their weapon, then," he said. "Control the itinerant Singers and you control the Continent."

Edrus nodded. "The people are trapped. Prisoners in their own Houses."

Zakri's voice shook when he spoke. "Iban refused to join them," he said bitterly, "and so they killed him. By the Six Stars! They will pay for this."

Clive held up a shaking hand. "Cantor Zakri, be careful! You don't know—you didn't see that man, that awful man, slobbering and mindless. She has to feed him, has to hold his head and . . . put the spoon in his mouth . . . it's awful!"

Zakri shoved back his chair and stood. "They will pay for that, too." He nodded to Gavn. "Magister, Gavn and Ovan can manage for a time without me. I must go to to Soren. I must see what is happening for myself, and find out what happened to Iban."

Magister Edrus regarded him for several moments. "I suppose, Cantor Gavn, that you and Cantor Ovan can handle the Cantoris?"

Gavn's round, smooth chin stuck out. "Of course, Magister."

Good for you! Zakri sent to him, and Gavn sent back, *I hope.*

Berk rose and looked down at Zakri. "I'm coming with you."

"It may not be safe," Zakri warned.

Berk chuckled. "Less for you than for me, Cantor," he said. "And you and I are old road comrades, in any case."

"So we are," Zakri said. He stood, keeping his expression blank. His face felt as stiff as a piece of *caeru* leather left in the cold. He wanted to weep, or rage about in a tantrum as he would have before Cantrix Sira and Singer Iban had taught him to harness his wild Gift. He took a deep, slow breath, and bowed deeply to Magister Edrus, and to his junior.

"By your leave, then, Magister." He nodded to Berk. "And thank you, Berk. We will ride in the morning."

He strode from the room. In his mind, he heard, *Good luck, Cantor Zakri. Take care.*

And you, Cantor Gavn.

All will be well until you return.

Zakri felt a sudden homesickness that he would not have credited earlier in the day. But there was no time for doubts now. The task at hand was too important.

CHAPTER
TWO

SIRA WATCHED FROM THE DAIS AS Observatory's House members took their seats. Anyone who could be spared from their duties was present today in the Cantoris. Theo sat on the nearest bench with the students clustered around him. He had cut his blond hair for the coming journey, and it curled vigorously around his ears. It made him look younger than his eight summers. Mreen knelt beside him on the bench to have a good view. Her small round face was solemn in its nimbus of light. The other student Singers, Yve and Jule and Arry, fidgeted on Theo's left, their short legs dangling, their fingers in their mouths or their noses. They were even younger than Mreen, and had hardly begun their studies. At Theo's insistence, they spent most of their time with their families still. Sira made no argument; Theo's instincts were unerring. And they were being proved right once again; another Gifted babe had been born at Observatory, assisted into the world with Theo's help. There had not been such an abundance of the Gift on the Continent in a hundred summers.

Magister Pol leaned against the back wall of the Cantoris,

his powerful arms folded across his chest. His blunt features were impassive, but Sira sensed his mood clearly. Indeed, this was a great day, and Pol was right to feel pride in his House, and his Cantoris; next to Sira on the dais, now tuning the precious and ancient *filhata*, was Sira's and Theo's very first student, Trisa. Today she would perform her first *quirunha*, with Sira as her senior. Her mother and stepfather, seated with the assembly, watched her every movement as she adjusted the central C and tuned the other strings to it.

Only the Spirit, Sira thought, could have wrought such change as Observatory had seen in the past two summers. The House glowed with light and warmth; its nursery gardens thrived, as did its people. Their clothes were simple and their tools either well-worn or make-do, but the people were healthy, and safe from the cold.

It was time. The Singers on the dais stood, and the assembly stood with them. They bowed formally. Trisa looked at Sira, and then sat on her stool, the *filhata* across her lap. She closed her eyes, took a deep breath, and began to pluck the strings of the *filhata*. She played a melody in *Iridu* that she had practiced over and over in the past months, so often that at one time she cried out that she never wanted to hear it again! But Sira had been taught by her own teachers to begin with the familiar and expand upon it, and so she taught Trisa and Mreen. She knew that today, with her nerves charged and everyone watching, Trisa would be grateful for the hours she had spent on this particular piece.

Trisa's work was not the changeable, virtuosic music that Mreen would surely one day play; but she was consistent and steady, very like Theo himself. Her fingers were nimble, and her voice, when she began to sing, floated nicely on the breath, without tension or pressure. Her transition to *Aiodu* was perhaps a little rushed, but that was to be expected. Sira joined in when the new mode was established, enriching the texture of the music with a counterpoint on her own instrument, supporting the melodic line with her dark, even voice. After today, it would be Sira leading, or Theo, and Trisa following. But this, by tradition, was Trisa's *quirunha,* and she must demonstrate her ability to direct it.

The light and warmth swelled from the dais, a wave of energy that broke only on the barrier of deep cold beyond the House. Theo's psi was joined to theirs, but he stayed behind, beneath, there only to encourage Trisa should she falter.

Sira could no longer count the *quirunha* she and Theo had peformed together. She often felt they were as one person, she and Theo, two halves that were whole only when their psi was joined. She had healed her wounds, here at Observatory with Theo; and she dreaded being alone again, even for a short time.

The *quiru* was secure, the *quirunha* complete. Trisa stilled her *filhata* with the palm of her hand laid flat on the strings, and waited for a moment, eyes still closed, listening to the last notes fade against the high ceiling. When she opened her eyes, she looked first to her teacher.

Well done, Singer Trisa, Sira sent. *Your first modulation was a bit hurried, but all in all, a fine* quirunha. She stood and bowed formally to the new Singer.

For years Trisa had been working toward this moment. She bowed in return, carefully proper, but her eyes shone and her smile stretched so wide Sira thought it must hurt. She turned out into the Cantoris to find her mother. Brnwen's cheeks were wet, and she leaned happily toward Kai, her mate, whispering to him as she watched her daughter accept the bows of the Housemen and women.

Everyone present chanted together:

> SMILE ON US,
> O SPIRIT OF STARS,
> SEND US THE SUMMER TO WARM THE WORLD,
> UNTIL THE SUNS WILL SHINE ALWAYS TOGETHER.

The moment the formal prayer was finished, Trisa leaped off the dais, fourteen-year-old dignity forgotten, and danced up the aisle to her parents. Sira saw, though, that although the girl chattered excitedly to Brnwen, they did not touch.

That discipline, at least, she had absorbed at Conservatory. She would not be a full Cantrix for some time yet—there was still much for her to learn—but she was officially Singer Trisa from this moment, and there were formalities associated with her new title. Sira approved of her observance of them. It set a good example for the other students.

Theo came to Sira as she stepped down from the dais. *Congratulations,* he sent.

And to you, she answered. The people swirled around them, the parents of Yve and Arry and Jule coming to fetch them, bowing respectfully to Sira and Theo. Only Mreen stood alone, a tiny figure encircled by light.

Theo nodded toward the new Singer where she stood surrounded by well-wishers. He grinned at Sira. *Well, it seems the two of you will manage perfectly without me,* he sent.

Sira touched his hand very lightly, a brief and fleeting contact. She felt an urge to smooth back his thick curls, a thing she would never dream of actually doing. *We will manage,* she told him, *but never perfectly. We will miss you greatly.*

Then I had better hurry back, he sent. He winked at Mreen. *But this one is in a terrific hurry, are you not, little one?*

So I am, Cantor Theo!

Theo chuckled. *The* ferrel *chick can hardly wait to tumble from its mother's nest.*

The three of them turned to go up the aisle. Kai, Mreen's father, waited a few steps away, and Mreen went to him, reaching up to take his hand. Kai looked down at his little daughter with a sad pride. He was not troubled by the faint glow that always surrounded her; it was her silence that disturbed him, although he had stopped asking about it. Mreen was all he had left of Isbel . . . and now Mreen would leave him, too, very probably never to return. Sira thanked the Spirit that he had Brnwen and Trisa to comfort him.

And Mreen—Mreen would have Conservatory. Sira was surprised to feel a tiny flame of envy flicker in her heart. Despite all that had happened, she still missed it. At her

farewell ceremony—how long ago? Three summers?—
Magister Mkel had said that every Singer's true home was
Conservatory. Perhaps, she thought, in her deepest heart she
believed him.

Pol stepped forward to meet them. His bow was stiff and
awkward still, but most definitely a bow. "Congratulations,
Cantrix Sira," he said gruffly, "and Cantor Theo. A fine
debut for your student. A fine day for Observatory."

Theo bowed, too, in the elegant way of a big man who is
also graceful. "So it is," he said. "Your Cantoris is multi-
plying like a softwood grove in the summer, Pol!"

"Just don't forget that it still needs you, Cantor Theo,"
Pol growled.

Theo's eyes were on Sira as he spoke. "I will not forget."
His eyes were the deep blue of summer, the rare and
precious summer when both suns rose to wheel across
Nevya's skies. "This is my home," he said.

When Theo spoke the word *home,* Sira felt a whisper of
premonition tickle in her mind. She bit her lip. She knew
better than to ignore the call of her Gift. But what could
this be, this slight breath of warning? What did it mean?
Surely, before summer came, they would both be here
again, together. Home.

All the supplies necessary for travel were laid out on the
floor and on the long workbench in Observatory's stables.
Morys, the guide, pointed them out to Theo, who handled
each one, making sure everything was in good repair and
sturdy enough for the long journey. Mreen stood on tiptoe
beside him, trying to see what was on the workbench. There
were two saddles only, since Mreen would ride behind
Theo. The saddle packs were clean and ready to be filled
with grain and dried meat and herbs for the *keftet.* There was
an ironwood cooking pot, much dented and black with many
summers of use, but whole; and carved ironwood cups,
bowls, and spoons, three of each. A bundle of softwood,
gathered from the slopes of Observatory's mountain and
then dried and cut into lengths for the cookfire, filled the
room with a summery fragrance. Yellow-white bedfurs had

been neatly rolled and tied. And, at the end of the table, a tiny *caeru*-leather pouch, set aside especially for this journey.

Morys pointed to the little bag, and Theo picked it up and poured its contents into his hand.

"We've been saving that," Morys said proudly, as if it had come from his own cupboards. "Not much metal at Observatory, but this should be enough for supplies to get us home."

Mreen reached out her hand, and Theo dropped one of the bits into her palm. It shone, catching the light, and Mreen gasped.

What is this, Cantor Theo? she sent with intensity.

It is only a bit of metal, Mreen, he answered. *It is what I used to be paid, when I was an itinerant Singer. It has been quite some time since I saw any.*

She stared at the metal for long moments. Her eyes were wide, and as she looked at the metal, they grew glazed and glassy. Theo frowned and stepped closer.

I see . . . I see so many hands, she sent. *Hands, and then more hands . . .* The light around her dimmed and rippled. Theo touched her shoulder, then knelt beside her. Her small body was tense, and her face strained and white. She seemed to be struggling with some idea, some concept, too big for her.

So many hands, and . . . something . . .

What is it, Mreen? Theo asked. Her hand, holding the bit of metal, trembled now. Gently, he uncurled her fingers and took the metal away. Her eyes focused again, and her color returned, but her little *quiru* was still faded.

What a strange thing, she sent to him. *I do not understand what I saw, Cantor Theo!*

Theo smiled at her, and she leaned against his shoulder. He sent, *I do not know, Mreen. I do not see the pictures as you do.*

She stared at him. *But you have been a Singer all your life! Why am I different?*

You will have to ask the Spirit that one, Theo sent, and he chuckled. *I have eight summers, but I have few answers!*

Mreen smiled suddenly, making her dimples flash. *You are so old, Cantor Theo!*

Indeed.

What does it feel like to be so old?

Theo laughed aloud. *Like one of those ironwood trees down the mountain,* he told her. *Tall and broad and hard, and like I can see a long way.*

Then I am like a softwood tree?

A good comparison. You are certainly soft! He tousled her red hair, and she giggled without making a sound.

How many summers do I have, Cantor Theo?

Theo got to his feet and looked down at her. He was almost as tall as Sira herself, and Mreen had to tip her head far back to see into his face.

You are an unusual case, Mreen, he told her. *You were born just before the summer, so you already have one, but it hardly counts!*

And how long until I have two?

Until the Visitor comes.

How long until the Visitor comes?

One more year. Five years between summers, remember?

I remember that! It is easy! Much easier than remembering how to modulate from Aiodu *to* Doryu!

So it is, Mreen, so it is. Theo turned back to Morys and their preparations. When he chanced to look down again, he saw Mreen's eyes fixed upon the little leather pouch, and her curiosity was like a fire burning under a cooking pot, bright and hot.

Cantor Theo, she sent. *Where does the metal come from?*

I do not have the answer to that, either.

"I don't see the point of this," Pol rasped, but he stood back, holding the door, and Sira bowed slightly and stepped in to his apartment. Theo followed behind, with Mreen at his side.

The room was large, dominated by a long, polished table and a number of chairs arranged around it. Pol ran his House differently from any Magister Sira had known. In his rooms, all sorts of work took place. Cupboards lined the walls, and here and there some unfinished task waited, an open ledger book or a stack of arrows needing furring. Otherwise the apartment was austere and bare. In truth, there were very few objects anywhere at Observatory that were anything but functional. Sira thought of the lovely bits of *obis*-carving she had seen in her travels. Perhaps when Theo returned, he might bring just one example, some small bit of art like those from Soren, where the *obis*-carvers lived and worked. Not for herself alone, but for the House members to appreciate.

The three Singers sat at one end of the table, and Pol, still standing, regarded Mreen intently. She looked back at him with a clear and innocent gaze, the air around her faintly but clearly brighter than the rest of the room.

"Don't talk, do you?" Pol said abruptly.

Mreen shook her head slowly. Sira saw Theo put his fingers over his lips to hide a smile. "But you want to see our metal?" Pol went on. "Do you understand what it is?"

Mreen shook her head again.

"When we told her of it, she asked to touch it," Sira said, "to try to understand. In the stables, she held a bit of metal in her hand—"

"Metal generously provided by you for our journey," Theo put in.

Pol waved his hand rather grandly. "Observatory is proud to send one of our Gifted children to Conservatory."

Theo grinned openly at that. "Even the Glacier itself can change direction," he murmured.

Pol shot him a hard look. "It will not hurt the Houses of the Continent to be reminded of what we have here," he said. He stuck out his chin as if he faced the Magister of Lamdon himself. "It has been many summers since the Committee has had real news of Observatory."

May I see it now? Mreen sent. Sira lifted her scarred eyebrow at Pol.

"Mreen is ready," she said. Years before, a lifetime of experience before, as it seemed, she had seen this treasured artifact, once and once only. She had been unable to understand its nature. Pol, of course, believed he understood it perfectly. He was fanatic about it, in fact. Sira resisted such unsupported beliefs. Indeed, despite her years at Observatory, she resisted virtually all of their philosophy, but she admitted to a vague hope that Mreen's odd ability might dispel this one mystery.

Pol moved very deliberately, in the manner of performing a ritual. He walked to a tall cupboard at the end of the room and opened it. It was empty except for one long, slender, heavily wrapped object, which he bore with much care to the table. He laid it on the polished wood and carefully, layer by layer, put back the folds of soft leather.

Sira became aware of Theo's tension beside her, and realized that he had never seen this. It had perhaps not been laid open to the light since Pol had shown it to her to settle their argument years before.

They had never resolved the argument. Nor were they likely to do so, Sira thought. But she caught her breath again as the smooth, shining surface of the great metal slab was revealed.

Incredible . . . Theo's sending was almost involuntary. He bent far forward, to touch with one finger the black, glazed piece that lay before them. Its markings were strangely carved into it, shining up from below the surface as if from below some thick, dark, but translucent ice. Its edges were uneven, looking almost torn, but smoothly surfaced, as if they had melted away. *I have never seen anything like it. Surely such a large piece cannot be metal!*

But what else could it be? Sira asked. Theo shook his head. Pol stood over the artifact, triumphant in the silence. *He believes it is evidence, proof of their beliefs,* Sira added. *He says it is the reason they Watch.*

Mreen left her chair, and came closer to the object. She put her hands on the edge of the table, to lift herself up enough to see clearly. She waited for the space of a heartbeat, and then she reached out one small hand and laid it on the shining surface of the strange thing. She squeezed her eyes shut. Sira closed her own eyes and followed her.

I am here with you, Mreen, she sent reassuringly. *Right here.*

I am fine, Cantrix Sira, Mreen sent. *I—*

She broke off abruptly, and Sira felt as if in herself the trembling of Mreen's hand on the metal, the waves of sensation that came through her fingers and into her mind. There was an impression of spinning, and of speed, a feeling so intense that Sira gripped the arms of her own chair to keep from falling. Everything around her—around Mreen—was a deep, empty blackness, with pinpoints of light—stars, perhaps?—in strange and unfamiliar patterns. It was profoundly beautiful, spacious and peaceful, until, with a suddenness that snatched Sira's breath from her lungs, terror filled the emptiness, and there was a flood of fear and grief. The speed became a dreadful thing, an overwhelming sensation of falling, of impending impact, as if she had tumbled from the cliff road and were plunging into the chasm below.

It was all Sira could do to stay with Mreen, to keep from closing her own mind, until she felt Theo's hand on her own, and realized that they were together, the three of them. The sensation of falling grew worse, more frightening, and Sira did not know where it would lead.

It was Theo who broke the spell. Very sharply, he sent, *That is enough, Mreen. Lift your hand from the metal,* and she obeyed. The vision, the impression, faded almost instantly.

The three Gifted ones stared at one another, and Pol's small, hard eyes watched them, waiting, until he could bear it no more. He burst out, "What happened?"

Neither Sira nor Mreen could find words for what they had experienced. Theo spoke, haltingly.

"It would be very difficult to describe," he said. "I am not so sensitive as Cantrix Sira, or Mreen, but there was an impression of blackness, and speed . . . and points of light, little flames, or stars. Then a falling, as if from one of these great cliffs around us. And fear. Terrible fear."

Pol gave a short, sharp laugh that grated on Sira's nerves. "The Ship!" he cried.

Sira looked up at him, shaking her head. "I do not know," she said slowly. "Perhaps. But it was not a pleasant thing."

Theo went to stand behind Mreen, who looked up at him with solemn eyes. *Were you afraid, little one?* he asked gently.

She shook her head. *No, Cantor Theo. But someone was. Very afraid.*

But you do not know who?

No. The picture is . . . sort of faded. Dim. It was—I think it was too long ago. It is too old. She looked up at the object on the table, and she took a quick step backward.

Sira stood. "Thank you, Magister," she said.

Pol bowed, and went to the door behind them. "You can tell them at Conservatory," he said to Theo. "And they can tell Lamdon. Tell them it is still here."

"I will, if you like," Theo answered doubtfully. "But I am not sure even now what it is."

"They know," Pol said with assurance. "They have always known!"

CHAPTER
THREE

"IT IS WICKED," ZAKRI TOLD BERK, AS THEY MADE THEIR first camp in the Mariks east of Amric, "how good it feels to be out in the open again."

Berk laughed. "Please, Cantor Zakri, make your *quiru* before you indulge in your feelings! It's mightily cold in these mountains today."

Zakri pulled his *filla* from his tunic, but he stole one more moment to look out into the gathering twilight. Nevya's sky darkened swiftly to violet, presaging the purple of the long night. As he watched, a lone star began to beckon in the south. Conservatory's star, the itinerants called it. Iban had pointed it out to him on their first trip together. When Conservatory's star begins to shine, he had said, you'd better have your *filla* in your hand or it'll be too late.

I remember, Zakri called silently after his master's departed spirit. I remember. When he put his *filla* to his lips he played an itinerant's melody, a melody Iban would have approved, direct and brief and simple, and the *quiru* sprang up swiftly around them.

Berk said, "That's more like it." Even the *hruss* shifted

their feet and gave throaty growls as the circle of light swelled around them. "*Hruss* don't like the dark any more than I do!" Berk chuckled.

"Silly beasts," Zakri murmured, "and they were born to it!" But he tucked away his *filla* and went to pull off their saddles and set out their feed. He patted the shaggy broad heads and tugged their drooping ears, making them whuff and push their heads into his chest, asking for more. He gave each of them one last rub. "Later, you foolish things. I would like my own meal!"

Berk had already put flint to stone and a little cooking fire crackled invitingly in the center of the *quiru*. Zakri pulled the cooking pot and *keftet* makings from his saddle pack.

"I can do that," Berk said, reaching for the pot. "You're Cantor Zakri now, after all."

Zakri laughed, and pushed back his *caeru* hood. "You see this?" he said. He passed his hand over his head. Only wisps of fine hair met his fingers now at the back of his neck. "I am an itinerant once again, shorn hair and all. Singer Zakri!" He began to slice the dried *caeru* meat while Berk melted some snow in the pot to soak it. Zakri added, "In truth, if we go to Soren I had best be simply Singer. It may not be healthy to be a Cantor in that company."

"If you're going to be Singer, you'd better do something about the way you talk," Berk told him.

Zakri protested, "What about the way I talk? I was raised with itinerants!"

"Yes, but you've come to sound just like Cantor Ovan and Cantor Gavn. Like all the Conservatory-trained. Like you'd rather be sending than speaking aloud."

Zakri stirred the *caeru* meat in the pot and found it soft enough. He dropped in the grain and the spicy herbs, again as Iban had taught him. "I did not realize," he began, and then stopped, surprised. "I didn't realize that. I have not . . . I mean, I haven't thought about it."

"That's better." Berk chuckled. "But you'd better practice."

Zakri sat back on his heels to look up through the glow of his *quiru* into the wide starry sky. The ironwood trees groaned as the deep cold settled over them, and the wind sighed through the branches. It was easy to believe himself an itinerant once again. If he had not been so grieved over Iban's death, he could have enjoyed the respite from the pressures of the Cantoris, of caring for the sick, of knowing that each day, no matter his inclination, the work must go on.

The two men ate their *keftet* as experienced travelers, leaving no scrap of meat or grain behind. They brewed and drank tea, and then went together out of the *quiru* to relieve themselves before rolling into their bedfurs. Berk banked the little fire. It glowed softly within the brighter light of the *quiru*. Zakri lay awake watching it for a long time, relishing the freedom of the mountains and the stars.

It seemed only yesterday, yet a lifetime ago, that he had traveled with Iban. Iban had been patient, funny, strict . . . the perfect master for a boy who had had no master for too long. Zakri's two teachers—Sira and Iban—had saved his life, helped him to discipline and harness his untamed Gift. It was hard to accept that Singer Iban would no longer come riding up to Amric, would no longer tease Zakri the Cantor about Zakri the itinerant Singer. The days of their journeys together seemed shining and perfect now in memory.

Yes, Zakri thought, there was much to be said for the itinerant life, but it had not been his to choose. The Gift had always had him in its grasp, and the Gift would not be denied. Even Iban had known that.

The journey to Soren from Amric was a long one. It took eight days of riding, with Berk and Zakri pressing the pace, and the *hruss* needing more and more rest as they worked their way to the southeast. Zakri had not ridden in three years, and his thighs and backside ached on the second and third day, but the saddlesoreness disappeared as they rode on. They saw *caeru*, grown thin and wary from the long years of winter. They came upon tracks of *tkir*, and were thankful not to see the beast itself. A *ferrel* scream disturbed their sleep once or twice, but otherwise the nights were peaceful. Several wild *hruss* raised their heads from foraging as they passed. Zakri called to them in a low tone, but these beasts were not accustomed to people, and their liquid dark eyes rolled as they made their throaty growls and flicked their ears nervously back and forth. That made Zakri laugh. *Hruss* raised in stables could hardly bear to be out of the sight of humans, and if an itinerant Singer did not make his *quiru* big enough to include them, the *hruss* would trample the travelers rather than be left outside the light.

Since Berk had decided they should avoid Ogre Pass, and Bariken as well, they took the most direct possible route south, and they saw no other people during the journey. Zakri had never actually been to Soren, but Iban had described all the Houses and the landmarks and roads that led to them. As part of his apprenticeship, Zakri had carefully committed them to memory.

As they rode down into the Southern Timberlands, the air softened and grew warmer. Ironwood suckers, thick and numerous, crisscrossed the open country beneath the snowpack. In places softwood trees still stood in little groves here and there, but they were black and shriveled by the cold. Mists clouded the ground in the early morning hours, and they often broke camp with wisps of fog swirling around the thick legs of the *hruss*.

There was no danger of missing the last turn to Soren; Zakri had never seen such a well-traveled road. The snowpack was trampled and dirty, and *hruss* prints and the marks of *pukuru* runners were everywhere.

"Busy place," was Berk's comment.

Zakri grunted agreement. He was concentrating, keeping his mind open, listening for anything that might give him a clue, or a warning. They rode two more hours before they saw the glow of a *quiru* shining among the hills. Then one last rise, and the House lay before them, a great ancient sprawl of stone and ironwood cupped in a shallow valley.

Soren's walls were weathered to the soft blue gray of the morning mists. Its unswept courtyard was as trampled and dirty as the road leading down to it, and its circle of light was dimmer, more ragged than any House *quiru* Zakri had ever seen. The chill of presentiment prickled his skin again.

He could well believe that Soren's Cantor and Cantrix were already lost.

"Look at that," he said to Berk. "Their nursery gardens must be in terrible shape. I do not—I mean, I don't see how they can grow anything in a *quiru* like that."

Berk muttered, "It looks bad enough." They rode on into the courtyard, and waited for a moment before the steps, but no one came to open the doors. They dismounted and turned away from the front, leading their *hruss* instead to the back of the House. Zakri kept his mind open, listening, but he heard only muddled echoes, half-formed, unfocused. It was like peering into cloud, seeing nothing but shapes and shadows. Berk raised questioning eyebrows at him, and he shook his head.

"Nothing," he murmured. "Not even their Cantors."

A stableman feeding grain to several *hruss* in loose boxes looked up with a frown when they appeared at the stable door. "Not more beasts to feed!" was his greeting. "How does Cho think I can manage that?"

Berk stood tall and glared at the man with snow-reddened eyes. "Is that your welcome? We have been traveling eight days! Since when does any House on the Continent treat travelers so?"

The stableman, who was about Berk's own age, put his hands on his hips and stared at them both. "This House is full of nothing but travelers," he said. "Problem is, they come, but they don't go. Look at this crowd!" He waved his hand at the stables around them, where *hruss* looked curiously out of every stall, their long ears turning back and forth. In truth, Zakri had never seen so many *hruss* in one place before.

He had the reins of both their beasts in his hand as he stepped up to face the stableman. "Look, Houseman," he said. "This is Berk v'Amric. He's courier for Magister Edrus, and I'm his Singer! You'd better fetch somebody to take him up the stairs, and do it quick."

The man smiled nastily at Zakri. "You think Singers are special here?" he said. "You'll see before long." He gestured to the stalls. "Well, I'm not turning you away, in any case.

If you can squeeze your beasts into one of the stalls, you're welcome to. Tack room is over there"—he pointed—"and kitchens the other direction. Although I hope you're not too hungry. Nothing much but meat on our tables these days."

The stableman went back inside, and they heard him calling for someone. "Better do this the usual way," Berk said. "I'll go up alone." Zakri nodded.

"Yes, Houseman," he said mildly. "I'll no doubt meet you in the kitchens, or the *ubanyor*."

They parted, Berk to go in search of his escort to the upper levels, and Zakri to unsaddle and curry the *hruss*. He debated simply leaving them outside the stables, knowing they wouldn't leave the circle of light. But the state of the *quiru* gave him no confidence, and he decided against it. He found a stall with only one beast, and crowded his two in with it. The tack room, where he went to hang their saddles, was also full, crammed to the rafters with bridles and ropes, stacks of bows and furred arrows, empty saddle packs. Zakri shook his head, looking at the clutter. It must be true. Soren was overflowing with itinerant Singers.

Alone, Zakri wandered in the direction of the kitchens. Soren, by long tradition a House dedicated to *obis*-carvers, was richly adorned with objects, some useful and others only decorative, lining every wall, filling every corner. Open shelves were laden with bowls, vases, boxes, and implements, and closed cupboards, Zakri was sure, held even more. He stopped to examine some of the things, impressed by their intricacy, and in some, true beauty. Occasionally the mark of the *obis*-knife, the metal blade wielded with psi, could still be seen on the ironwood. More commonly the psi-carving was so smooth and skilled that the ironwood, which would yield to a bone or stone implement only when used with great strength, seemed to have been smoothed with a miraculous hand, as if it were no harder to shape than the gray clay found in summer above the cliffs of Arren.

What was bizarre about the House was its *quiru*. It was quite warm in places, and then utterly frigid in random spots, as if it had gaps, rifts in it. It was like the water of the *ubanyor* or *ubanyix*, improperly heated by some careless junior Cantor, with icy currents left flowing beneath a warm surface. And the House itself appeared untidy, as if its care was as random as the warmth of its *quiru*. Zakri guarded his mind, hiding his surprise, as he walked on to the kitchens. He felt like a *caeru* pup that had stumbled into an *urbear* den, and he meant to watch his step at every moment.

"Well, here's another new face!" The woman who spoke was wrinkled and cross looking. "And where did they get you from, Houseman?"

Zakri bowed to her, and to the three or four Housewomen laboring at the sinks and the ovens. Their glances were cursory, but he smiled politely at them. "I have—I've come from Amric," he said. "I'm Singer Zakri," he added, and bowed again to the whole group.

The woman snorted. "Another one! Well, you're probably hungry and thirsty. I'm Mura, and these are my kitchens, so you'll not be helping yourself without permission."

Zakri smiled as winningly as he knew how, and bowed again to Mura. "I wouldn't think of it," he murmured sweetly.

"Hmm." Mura's sour expression did not improve. "Sook!" she called, and a young girl hurried forward, wiping her hands on a bit of towel. Her hair, bound back with a strip of soft *caeru* leather, was as black as the stone of the ovens, but glossy as ice. She had great dark eyes that slanted upward at their outer corners. She nodded to Zakri, and smiled at him, the first friendly gesture he had received at Soren.

Mura pointed to a long scarred table. "Sook will find you a bite and you can have a sip of wine, since you've just arrived. Sit over there."

Zakri did as he was bid, but he said quickly to Sook, "I'd rather just have tea, if you have some." The girl turned to the huge fireplace and reached for a large kettle resting on the hob.

Mura snorted again. "What itinerant refuses wine when it's offered?"

Of course, no itinerant Zakri knew would refuse, but he

could hardly tell her that. "We—we're not much for wine at Amric," he said. He only hoped Amric was so distant that these women knew nothing at all about it. "But you're very generous, Housewoman," he added. "It's good to be sitting down in a nice warm kitchen."

"Just don't sit too long," Mura snapped. "We've work to do." She turned her back to him and took up a great knife carved from ironwood. She was cutting a hunk of cured *caeru* meat into chunks with rapid, sure slices with the knife.

Sook smiled again at Zakri as she brought him a loaf of nutbread and a small knife, and a bowl of quickly heated *keftet*. She poured the tea into a finely carved teacup that was so thin it was almost translucent. The kettle she left within his reach. He watched her work, admiring her long eyes.

"Sook," he mused. "Now that's a name I've never heard."

"It's a traditional name here," she answered as she handed him a spoon. "It was my grandmother's, and her grandmother's, summers past remembering."

"It's lovely." Zakri took a spoonful of the *keftet*. He and Berk had eaten better in their campsites. As the stableman had said, there was too much meat and not enough grain. The bit of fish that flavored it was welcome, though. He had not tasted fish since his days at Arren. He drank two cups of tea, quickly, and then stood and carried his dishes to where Sook was scrubbing pots at the sink, her small hands red with water and strong soap.

"I thank you," he said.

She took the dishes from his hands before he could put them down. As she did so, her wet fingers brushed his hands. Before he could catch himself, he flinched away from her touch. The carved teacup slipped between them, and fell toward the floor, where it would no doubt have shattered into a dozen pieces. Reflexively, Zakri's psi flicked out, a quick tap of energy that lifted the cup back into Sook's fingers. Her eyes went wide, and she looked from him to the cup, unsure of what had happened. She opened her mouth, but he shook his head slightly, and she closed it again.

He knew he must be more careful. He had not realized how accustomed he had become to the discipline of the Cantoris. When had anyone except his own Houseman last touched him? It must be almost a summer ago.

He smiled at Sook, and she smiled back, but warily. He cursed himself as he left the kitchens to go in search of the *ubanyor*. Surely, he scolded himself, you can manage yourself better than this. One would think he was a wild boy again!

Soren was indeed full of itinerant Singers. When Zakri found the *ubanyor*, its big tub was half-full of them, lounging about in the water, laughing and joking together. From the *ubanyix* down the hall, similar loud conversations and laughter sounded in the higher registers. He stripped, dropping his soiled tunic and trousers in a corner, and slipped under the water with a groan of pleasure. At least, with so many Singers about, the water was decently warm. His skin tingled with it, and he ducked under the surface to soak his hair.

A heavy man slid over next to him, making the ironwood of the tub creak as he moved. "You're the courier's Singer, hmm?"

Zakri looked out from under the lather he was rubbing into his scalp. "So I am," he said. "Zakri v'Amric."

The man was dark and looked to have eight or nine summers. The arm he rested on the edge of the tub was thick and covered in black hair. He pointed vaguely upward with his chin, at the upper levels of the House. "I'd drop the Amric part of that, if I were you. Cho won't like it."

Another man came closer on Zakri's other side. "It's true, Singer. We're all v'Soren, now. All of us." He gestured around the *ubanyor*. "Every man in here is an itinerant."

Zakri leaned back to rinse the soap from his hair, and scrubbed his face with his fingers to give himself time to think.

When he took his hands away, he contrived as innocent a

look as he could. "Amric is a long way from Soren," he said.

"So that means you haven't heard?"

"Heard what?"

The second man peered at Zakri. His red hair was faded, and his complexion roughened by sun and weather. His face and body were narrow as a *wezel's*. "You'd best come talk to Cho," he said.

"Cho?" Zakri kept his mind blank and empty, just in case, but he felt no tickle of probing psi. More than likely, these itinerants, like most, could not hear his thoughts. It was unusual for any but the Conservatory-trained to be able to listen and send, but he himself was an exception, and there might be others.

"Cho. He's the one in charge here."

"But what about your Magister?"

The man's eyes became mere slits, and he stood, dripping water on Zakri. "I'll take you to Cho. He'll explain how things are."

The first man put a heavy hand on Zakri's shoulder, and Zakri whirled, water flying from his hair as he turned away from the touch, his bare hide scraping against the ironwood of the tub. The man cried out, "By the Spirit, Zakri! I didn't mean to scare you! Listen, all Singers are safe here. It's elsewhere you have to worry."

Zakri drew a deep breath. "Sorry, Singer," he said. "I—I've been on the road awhile. I'm jumpy."

The heavy man nodded, as if he understood perfectly. "Sure you are. That close to the Glacier . . . *tkir,* even *urbear* once in a while, I hear."

Zakri grinned, as casually as he could manage. "*Urbear* come off the Glacier once in a while," he agreed. "It's the *tkir* that scare me."

"Down here we have mostly *carwal,* and they hardly move out of the water." The man patted his belly. "My mate tells me I look just like one!" He laughed.

The red-haired man climbed out of the tub, and he gestured to Zakri. "If you're ready," he said as he reached for a towel from a lopsided stack. "We can get in to see Cho before the evening meal."

Zakri followed, and accepted a towel to dry himself.

The dark man lifted a hand in farewell to Zakri. "See you in the great room," he said. "By the way, I'm Shiro, and that's Klas. I was born right here at Soren, so you can come to me if you have questions."

"Good to meet you, Singer Shiro." Zakri bowed shallowly above his towel.

"You can drop the Singer." Klas laughed. "There's so many of us here, it's hard to find somebody who isn't a Singer!"

Zakri dried as quickly as he could, and had to dress in his soiled clothes, with only a change of linen from his pack. He followed Klas down a long corridor and up a staircase. As they went, he listened. There was a great deal of psi about, but none trained as his own had been, at least none that he could detect. Where on the Continent, he wondered, were the Cantor and Cantrix of Soren?

CHAPTER FOUR

ZAKRI SHOULDERED HIS SADDLE PACK AND HURRIED after Klas. The older man scurried down the corridor, reminding Zakri of a *wezel* fleeing from the hunters. His pale eyes darted back from time to time to make sure Zakri was following. The patchy *quiru* made irregular shadows, and Zakri's shoulders prickled each time he walked through a little pocket of darkness; it was against all his instincts to leave them unrepaired, and it disturbed him to think that there might be no one in the entire House who could do it. How did the House members live with such a *quiru*?

Only once did he see a bit of *quiru* that was intact, strong and evenly bright from the stone floor to the ironwood ceiling. It was just beneath the main staircase, a narrow hall that led toward the back of the House. He fell behind Klas as he peered into it, trying to discern the origin of the light. Klas already had one foot on the stairs when he saw that Zakri had stopped. He flapped his hand in the direction of the hall.

"Carvery," he said, and then he hurried on. Zakri had to leap up the stairs two at a time to catch up with him.

The banister of the staircase felt strange under his hand, and when he looked down at it, his progress slowed yet again. There were banisters on every staircase on the Continent, of course, but this one was beautiful, *obis*-carved into a design of whorls and spirals that seemed almost to move, to writhe under his fingers. Its pattern drew his hand upward as if the carver's Gift still haunted the ironwood. When he reached the top, his fingers lifted from it with reluctance. His guide appeared not to notice any of it, neither the beauty of that piece nor of any of the others that met their eyes at every turn.

Klas scuttled on to the very end of the upper hallway. More laden shelves and cupboards lined the walls, but Zakri had to pass them with no more than a brief glance. Klas was already bobbing his head to several men squatting over a game of stone-and-bone. A woman leaned in bored fashion near a door, watching the throw of the game pieces. All of them, the men and the woman, wore the leather tunics of itinerants, and their hair was cropped short around weathered faces. They looked Zakri up and down in a moment of idle curiosity, and then turned back to their game.

"So who's winning?" Zakri asked. No one answered.

Klas pointed at Zakri with his red-stubbled chin, and said, "We need to see Cho. This one just came today."

The woman straightened to push open the door. "Take him in, then," she said. She eyed Zakri briefly as he passed, then turned back to the game. He was only one more Singer in a House full of Singers, hardly worth her interest.

Zakri had been in more than one Magisterial apartment, and the room he and Klas entered was exactly that. It was spacious, with elegant and generously proportioned furnishings, everything gracefully carved in what he already thought of as Soren fashion. A long table dominated the room, with chairs drawn up to it in formal ranks.

But there was no Magister here. The thin dark man pacing past the window wore the dark tunic of the upper levels, but Zakri had no doubt it was an affectation. A man and a woman, also dressed in somber colors, sat at the table. The woman had a large account book before her, her arms curled around it as if to protect her responsibility. The man held a *ferrel*-quill pen in his hand, poised above a single sheet of Clare's heavy paper. They were watching the man pace, their eyes hooded, their faces drawn. When the dark man whirled to see who had entered, both of them stiffened.

Berk glowered from one end of the table. He had not yet bathed. His gray hair was coming out of its binding, his beard was matted, and he scowled indiscriminately at everyone in the room.

Klas cleared his throat. "Cho, here's an itinerant who just rode in today. Thought you'd want to meet him . . ." His voice trailed away as the man's eyes, long, dark eyes, like those of the girl Sook, fixed upon him. Klas stiffened like the others, and Zakri heard the click of his throat as he tried to swallow.

When Cho's eyes shifted to Zakri they narrowed suddenly. Instinctively, Zakri shielded his mind, and not a moment too soon.

At first it was only an intrusion, much like being prodded with a rude finger. But when the finger met resistance, the psi became a knife that thrust and sliced at Zakri's mind without regard for any harm it might do. It was clumsy and obvious, but it was powerful. It was very, very dangerous. Zakri struggled to keep his face innocent as he closed his mind firmly against it.

Cho's eyes flickered. Zakri tried to disguise his shields behind a cloud of muffled thoughts like those he heard around him. Perspiration trickled down his ribs under his tunic. He made his eyes round, and he produced a foolish smile as he bowed.

"Are you the one I thank for the nice hot bath?" he asked.

The flicker left Cho's eyes, leaving them the flat black of charred ironwood. "No," he said. "I have better things to do than warm the *ubanyor*. Who are you?" His voice was light, the pitch rather high, without resonance or inflection.

Klas put his hand on Zakri's shoulder, and Zakri held himself still, suppressing his discomfort at the touch.

"This is Zakri," Klas said.

"My itinerant," Berk growled. His eyes met Zakri's

briefly, and then turned back to Cho. "We'll be on our way first light tomorrow," he said.

Cho leaned against the window casing with his head tipped back, looking down his thin, hooked nose. He wore an *obis* knife strapped around his waist in a finely tooled scabbard. His black hair was long, braided into a plait that hung over his shoulder almost to his waist. He drew it through his fingers, again and again, as he regarded the newcomers. "And what if your—" He emphasized the possessive, a slight smile curling his lips. "If your itinerant would rather not?"

"It's hardly his choice, is it?" Berk snapped. "My Magister hired him. He's been paid."

Zakri tried to look as guileless as possible. "That's right," he said brightly. "Magister Edrus keeps me very busy at Amric, actually. If it's not travelers, it's hunting parties. I never have to go looking for work."

Cho straightened, and tossed the braid back over his shoulder. "Well, it's time their precious Cantors and Cantrixes did some of that work!" he said. "Real work. Let them get their own hands dirty, instead of yours." His eyelids lowered until none of the white showed at all. He strolled to the chair at the center of the table and sat in it, leaning to the side with his arm draped lazily over the high carved back. "Young Zakri is welcome to join us here," he said to the room at large. "We'll have plenty of work for him, if work is what he wants."

Berk sat back heavily against his own chair, scraping its legs against the stone floor. He glared at Cho.

"Um, well," Zakri stammered. "Um—Houseman Cho—Singer Cho?"

"Not Singer," Cho said, very quietly. "Carver." He took his arm from the chair back and leaned forward, angling his body menacingly across the table at Berk. "I wasn't good enough for Conservatory, you see," he went on. "My Gift was only good enough for the carvery!" Louder, he added, "And good enough to gather every itinerant on the Continent into my service!"

Berk still stared, his arms folded. Zakri cleared his throat.

"Well, then, Carver . . . Cho. You see, I really need to get Houseman Berk, here, back to Amric. How else will he go? And my family, you know . . . they'll be expecting me." He shrugged, and shuffled his feet like a boy of three summers.

"Ah." Cho's black eyes measured Zakri, up and down. Klas, standing beside him, drew a sharp breath and took a sudden step back, as if trying to get out of the way. Again, and without warning, Zakri felt the bludgeon of Cho's psi, the crude attack against his shields. He had never felt a mind like it; there was an animal essence about it, a brute aggressive force like that of a hunting beast. Even in the early days, when his own psi had been out of control, Zakri felt certain it had never been so ugly, so—vulgar, was the word that came to his mind. At another time, he could have laughed at himself, the upstart itinerant who had become Cantor! Was he now as refined as any Conservatory-trained Singer? But Cho was trying to force him to reveal who and what he was, and such an invasion of uncontrolled psi could be lethal. Turning it aside took all his attention.

Thank the Spirit that Sira's instruction had been thorough. Zakri thickened the fog in the forepart of his mind, and hid behind it. It was difficult. The trickle of perspiration became a flood, but he held his silly grin in place, and endured. Behind him he heard Klas groan slightly, and he knew the itinerant felt the effects of Cho's psi. He remembered well the nauseating sensation that inadequate shielding could cause, and he marveled at the strength and reach of Cho's mind.

Then, suddenly, it seemed that his disguised shields had done their job. Cho lost interest all at once, glancing around the room at the others, and then back at Zakri.

"If you know what's good for you," Cho said lazily, his lip-curling smile returning. "You'll stay right here. This is where it's going to happen."

"Um . . . what would that be, that's going to happen?"

"Never mind!" Berk ordered. He stood suddenly, towering over the other people in the room. The two at the table, the unGifted ones, had watched everything in tense silence, and Zakri was sharply aware, through his shields, of their fear. Berk stamped to the door and pulled it open. "Let's go, Singer," he said.

Zakri turned obediently to the doorway. The heavy door, as if it had taken on life of its own, flew abruptly from Berk's hand and slammed into its frame with a bang that echoed in the high-ceilinged room. Zakri whirled to look at Cho.

Cho still held his negligent pose, but his effort had brought beads of sweat to his forehead. "That's a taste, Houseman," he sneered. "No one leaves until I permit it."

Berk said deliberately, "Would that be the room, or the House?"

Cho said, "Both," and laughed.

Zakri said innocently to Berk, "Houseman, I don't understand. What's happening here?"

Berk lifted his hand, palm up, toward Cho in an elegant, very upper-level gesture. "Perhaps, Carver, you'd like to explain to Zakri," he said. "And while you're at it, you can tell him what's going to happen when Lamdon gets word of all this!" This time he succeeded in making his exit. Klas stood pale and sweating by the door, looking longingly at it as it closed behind Berk.

Zakri turned slowly to face Cho once more. The cold knot of anger under his breastbone had drawn painfully tight. His Gift raged within him, and he concentrated on his control as he never had before. His back felt like Glacier ice, stiff and unyielding.

"You won't be leaving here just now," Cho said. His tone was almost casual. "If I let you go, it spoils the effect."

"Effect?"

Cho's lips lifted, just the outer corners. The Housewoman at the table began, "Cho . . ." but he silenced her with a hand.

"All the itinerants have banded together," he said, "right here at Soren. This is a new day for Nevya, a new day for Singers. We have more of the Gift under this roof than any House on the Continent—even Conservatory!"

Zakri looked about him, keeping his eyes wide and his

expression naive. He could not resist. "Then why is the *quiru* such a mess?" he asked.

The Housewoman's eyes came up to his face quickly, and then slid away. The Houseman sat with his shoulders rigid, his gaze locked on the paper before him. There was a small thump behind Zakri as Klas stepped right against the wall, as far away as he could get.

Cho stood and leaned forward, his fists on the table, his eyes black and cold. "Do you see anyone freezing?" he hissed. "Anyone suffering? There is more than one way, more than Conservatory's way, to keep a House warm! We'll teach it to you." He waved a hand at the door. "Now go on, Klas will find you a room. Might as well make yourself comfortable. You'll be here awhile."

"But—" Zakri began.

The blow of psi came again, but Zakri was prepared this time. He turned it away with a parry of his own, a reactive feint of energy. He stopped short of actually striking at the other man's mind, but just the same Cho frowned, sensing the resistance. Zakri smiled and shrugged, as if it was little matter to him if he stayed or not, and as if he had not felt Cho's psi at all.

Cho raised his long arm and pointed at the door. Klas hastened to throw it open and make his escape.

Zakri followed, but he looked back over his shoulder to see Cho snatch the account book from the Housewoman's hands with unnecessary roughness. The Houseman slumped over his piece of paper, his pen idle in his hand.

Zakri reached back with his psi and tugged at the chair behind Cho just as the carver was about to resume his seat. The heavy chair crashed satisfyingly against the floor, and a spate of curses rang out as Zakri closed the door. The players squatting in the corridor raised their heads at the noise. Zakri grinned cheerfully down at them.

"Did you hear something?" he asked brightly. They looked from his foolish grin to the closed door, but they kept a prudent silence.

By the time Zakri reached the staircase, though, the pleasure of his small prank had faded, and as he followed

Klas downstairs he had to repress a shower of sparks that bloomed about him like little rebellious flowers.

Klas took him to a room already crowded with three other itinerants and their possessions. Before he left, Klas asked, "Didn't you feel that, feel Cho's psi? It just about knocked me over, and it wasn't even me he was after!"

Zakri turned away the question with one of his own. "Why would you want to work for a man like that? What is . . . what's the point?"

Klas shrugged, and his pale eyes shifted. "It's because we're tired of being used, of having nothing. Why should the Cantors and Cantrixes have all the privileges? We're Gifted, too!"

Zakri stared at him, wanting to argue, to dispute such idiocy. He sensed the other's resentment, but it seemed compounded as much of fear and confusion as real indignation. He reflected that any discussion with such a person would be pointless, and would only arouse suspicion. He answered Klas's shrug with one of his own, and another boyish grin, and carried his pack into the overcrowded room.

Cho sat in the Magister's seat at the evening meal, at the exact center of the great room, with several itinerant Singers about him, the same ones Zakri had seen upstairs. The Singers were noisy, talking and laughing, all but one. That one sat limply in his carved chair, his head lolling against the shoulder of the woman next to him. His mouth was slack, his hands useless on the table. The woman was spooning *keftet* into his mouth. Most of it fell back out, and patiently she scooped it up and tried again, over and over. Zakri remembered Clive's horror as he described this man, the drooling mindless man that was Cho's example. Clive had not exaggerated. The man's empty eyes made Zakri's skin crawl.

Cho leaned against the arm of his chair, toying with his braid, looking about the room and eating little. Several upper-level House members, in their dark tunics, sat far from the center at a table in a corner. The working

Housemen and women clustered near them, avoiding the tables dominated by itinerant Singers. Zakri would rather have sat with the Housemen, but he was squeezed between Klas's wiry frame and Shiro's large one. Berk was at the corner table.

Berk raised his brows, but Zakri shook his head. Tomorrow he would find a safer time. Tonight, he was certain he was at risk, and he dared not open his mind enough to try to listen to others' thoughts. Cho's psi was too dangerous, and it was possible that there might be others willing, and able, to misuse the Gift as he did.

Shiro elbowed Zakri and pointed with his spoon to a quiet group near the windows, perhaps eight men and women. They looked somber, even grim, but with none of the sinister intensity of Cho. "Those are the other carvers," he said, through a mouthful of *keftet*. "They keep to themselves, even now."

Zakri said, "I would—I'd sure like to see the carvery."

Shiro made a grandiose gesture. "I could show you—after the morning meal. Been there a hundred times." He dug his spoon into his bowl again, shaking his head. "Right now it's the warmest place in the House."

"Better watch what you say," Klas muttered. "He hears more every day."

Shiro scraped the spoon against the bowl, gathering every bit of grain that was left. "Ship! I didn't say anything everybody doesn't already know," he complained.

"Just warning our young friend here," Klas said.

Zakri finished his *keftet* and pushed his bowl away. It was Sook who saw, and came to his table to take it from him.

"More *keftet*, Singer?" she asked.

He shook his head, and she smiled down at him as she picked up the bowl. Shiro asked loudly, "No bread tonight, Housewoman?"

"Not tonight," she answered, and turned to leave.

Shiro shocked Zakri by reaching out to pinch the girl's arm between a meaty thumb and forefinger. She snatched her arm away with a little gasp. Zakri was sure the pinch had hurt.

"Are you sure, little Sook? Just a bite of bread for one of the Gifted?"

Her face flushed, and she rubbed at her arm with her free hand. With asperity she said, "No bread for the Gifted or the unGifted!" As she spoke she moved back, putting distance between herself and Shiro. The Singers at the next table noticed the exchange, and one of them reached over and tweaked her tunic, just above her slender hips.

"So, why not, little Housewoman?" that one cried, and laughed when she jumped.

"You explain it, why don't you?" she snapped. "The grain hardly grows anymore!"

"Ship and stars, she's a nice little piece!" Shiro said, and he reached to take hold of her arm once again.

Zakri took a deep breath to control his seething temper, but somehow one small fibril of psi escaped him. It nipped out, just one little lash of energy that collided with Shiro's teacup and flipped it over, spilling steaming tea into his lap. Shiro cried out in pain and leaped to his feet to hold his hot trousers away from his skin. The Singers hooted with joy at this new target, pointing and calling out insults. Sook seized her opportunity and fled the great room.

Zakri dared not speak. He thrust back his chair and stalked away from the table, struggling to manage the energy that welled from him like a fountain, cold and hot at the same time. Berk followed, and caught up with him in the corridor beyond the kitchens.

Zakri relaxed somewhat when they were alone in the halls, but the air around him glimmered.

"They may not let us go, in truth," Berk told him quietly. They walked with a casual manner toward the stables, as if going to check on their *hruss* or their tack, but they kept a sharp eye about them.

"When we are ready, we will go," Zakri answered through tight lips. "But I want to know exactly what is happening here first. Will you be safe, Berk?"

"I am more worried about you," the big man said. "No one is saying much, but the Gift has been used in some terrible ways in this House. And to top it all off, there is a

Gifted child, ready and wishing to go to Conservatory, but Cho has refused to allow it."

"But that is outrageous! How can he stop it?"

Berk's face was bleak, and Zakri was sure the big man was no less angry than he. "Everyone in this House is terrified of Cho. Did you see the man in the great room, there at the center table?"

"I did."

"It's revolting."

"He has tried his psi already on me," Zakri said. "But I can handle it."

"Are you sure?"

Zakri rubbed his hand over the soft wisps of his brown hair. His shoulders prickled again, and he took a deep breath and released. "I will be all right, Berk. Let us pretend that we are resigned to staying for a time. But it will be a short time!"

"Be on your guard at every moment, Cantor Zakri."

"I will, Berk. By the Spirit, I will!"

CHAPTER
FIVE

★ ZAKRI, HAVING BEEN FOR SOME TIME USED TO SLEEPING alone, spent a poor night listening to the chatter and then the snores of the three itinerant Singers whose room he had to share. He gave up trying to sleep eventually, and left his bed long before the morning meal to wander the corridors of Soren, feeling the sting of the cold floor even through his fur boots. After a time, the sounds and smells of cooking drew him to the kitchens. At Amric his Houseman brought tea to Cantor Zakri before he was even awake. No such luxury for an itinerant Singer, and most certainly not at Soren! Cautiously, he put his head around the kitchen door, wary of Mura's sharp tongue.

Mura was frowning over a younger Housewoman as she stirred the *caeru* stew that bubbled cheerily on the huge stove. Sook, her cheeks pink with the heat of the cookfire, was slicing loaves of hot nutbread at the table, stopping occasionally to blow on her fingertips. The scarlet of her tunic made her the brightest spot in the room, and Zakri smiled to see her. Behind her, the big kettle steamed gently on the hob. It was a shame, he thought, that those who dwelled in the upper levels of the House—any House—would rarely come upon this charming scene.

He waited to call to Sook until Mura had turned away to one of the grain barrels in a corner, and even then he kept his voice low.

"Sook! Good morning to you. What's the chance of some tea?"

She looked up and smiled, then put her finger to her lips. "Shhh! Mura will scold you!" She glanced at Mura's back, and then sidelong back at Zakri, her great eyes gleaming, catching the firelight. "Wait there," she murmured.

Zakri hastily withdrew, and lounged against the wall by the kitchen door. Only a few moments passed before Sook slipped out with one of the beautifully carved teacups in her hand, and a little slice of fragrant nutbread on a scrap of cloth.

"You're an early riser, Zakri," she said. She held out her offering. Tendrils of black hair clung to her damp cheeks, and she brushed them back after he took the teacup from her hand.

"So I am," he agreed. "I thank you for the tea, Sook. It is—it's always good to have a friend among the cooks!"

She laughed, and opened her mouth to speak, but a cry from the kitchen forestalled her. Quickly, she pulled the door open and looked back inside. "Oh, no—Eun has burned herself!"

Zakri followed her back into the kitchen. Eun, a woman of perhaps eight or nine summers, stood over the sink, closing her eyes tightly, grimacing with pain. The burn had left a broad stripe against her palm, already blistering, and Zakri knew it must be viciously painful.

Mura poured cool water over the burn, her hands gentle and careful, all the while cursing steadily under her breath. Zakri forgot everything but the injury, stepping up beside the burned woman and leaning over her to see clearly.

"This cannot wait until Cantoris hours," he said with authority. Mura and Sook both looked at him strangely. Suddenly remembering, he shook his head sharply. "What I

mean is, she won't be able to stand the pain," he amended.
"Someone should call your Cantor or Cantrix now."

The women glanced at each other, and then back at him
without responding. He knew without their saying it that
there would be no Cantor to treat this burn. Eun sobbed.
"It's not fair," she whispered.

There was risk in this, but the healer in Zakri could not
turn away. He handed his teacup and nutbread back to Sook,
and reached into his tunic for his *filla*.

"Well, now, Housewoman," he said lightly. "Just between
us, don't you think itinerants are the best healers anyway?"

Mura snapped, "So Cho would say! In any case, it's all
we have, and in abundance."

"Oh, do be cautious, Mura!" cried Eun, fearful even in
her distress.

Sook cast Zakri a grateful glance, and led Eun to a chair.
The woman leaned back against it, holding out her burned
palm as if it might hurt less if it were farther away. Zakri
knelt beside her, and played a quick fragment of melody in
Doryu, soothing the heat of the burn, easing the pressure
beneath it that made the skin blister. The palm was a
sensitive place, he well knew. It was the seat of feeling and
the root of touch. Iban had taught him that.

He modulated to *Iridu* to help Eun relax, something else
Iban had taught him. He did not hurry, but played for several
minutes while the other Housewomen stood by, listening.
Sook kept a sympathetic hand on Eun's shoulder, but her
eyes never left Zakri's face. Mura leaned against the
ironwood table, creasing her apron with her fingers. She,
too, watched Zakri closely, her wrinkles deepening and her
eyes bright and quick as a *ferrel*'s.

When Zakri stopped playing and put his *filla* down on the
table, it was Mura who handed him a clean strip of felted
cloth for a bandage. He wrapped it around the burned hand,
securing it with a bit of quill Mura fetched from a drawer.
Eun opened her eyes then, but their lids drooped and she
yawned. "She should rest now," Zakri said quietly. "She
could sleep for a little, and that would be good."

"I'll take her to her apartment," Sook offered. Zakri

nodded agreement. Mura still observed him with fierce attention.

Another of the Housewomen came to help. "Take her arm, Nori," Sook said. Together, careful of the bandaged hand, they lifted Eun to her feet, and supported her between them. Slowly, they made their way out of the kitchen.

Mura eyed Zakri in speculative silence. He could only give her his best grin and a helpless gesture with his two hands. "Better put me to work, Housewoman!" he said. "I am—I'm more used to the stables, but I'm willing."

"I wonder about that, Singer," she said.

"About what?" he asked. He got to his feet, picking up his *filla* to tuck it away in his tunic, and sipped at the tea that had grown cold as he worked.

"I wonder about you and the stables," Mura said flatly.

He looked up and met her eyes, and his smile faded. Mura's was an intelligent face, a face made hard by experience, and by suffering. He had no wish to lie to her. "It is true about the stables," he said, "I assure you of that. I have worked many hours with *hruss*."

"Not many itinerants play the way you do, although I grant you they're sometimes fine healers. Who taught you?"

"The Singer Iban taught me, for one," Zakri ventured.

Mura caught her breath and bit her lip. She looked about to speak, but then turned quickly away as if to stop herself. She hesitated, her back to Zakri. Then abruptly she pointed at the loaves of nutbread on the table. "If you want to help, you can get started on those," she muttered. She did not turn back again.

It felt strange to Zakri to be loitering about with nothing to do at mid-day. He helped Sook and Mura in the kitchen, and then he bathed, but still he felt restless and idle as the traditional hour for the *quirunha* approached. Curious, he wandered toward the Cantoris.

The doors to the Cantoris stood open, but the room was empty. One or two people in bright tunics passed Zakri as they came to and from the great room. They looked at him without curiosity. Only the Housemen and women seemed to have much to do. He peeked in past the double doors of the great room, and saw that the tables were being laid for the mid-day meal, just as in any other House on the Continent.

An itinerant Singer wandered down the corridor and went into the Cantoris alone, his *filla* in his hand. Another Singer, her body stocky and strong in leather trousers, took up a position just outside the great room. A third, a man not much older than himself, came past, going to stand in the great room among the tables. A Houseman who was still working there quickly disappeared, glancing at Zakri as he hurried away toward the kitchens.

Each of the Singers began to play his own *filla* in the mode and the melody of his choice, as if to call up the small *quiru* of traveling parties. They made no effort to coordinate the music. They played at will, each in his own fashion. Zakri watched and listened in amazement.

From the corridors, from the *ubanyor* and *ubanyix,* from the staircase, from the upper levels, he heard the jangling discord of a dozen *filla* sounding independently. Circles of light and warmth grew, and touched, and blended together where they overlapped. The colors were oddly disparate, and the shapes of the *quiru* were strange, too, some circular and wide, others slender, taller, reaching up toward the ceiling. Some were ragged, like those made by apprentices still learning the craft. The result was a patchwork of shades of light throughout the House. It reminded Zakri of a snowfield dappled with shadow.

He had never seen a more infuriating and wasteful exercise. Berk came out of the *ubanyor* and found him, and they stood together in the corridor watching the bits of *quiru* bloom. Berk was openmouthed with surprise. Zakri was fuming.

He thought his anger would burst from his chest in a scalding fountain. The Gift was poured out in this place as if it were no more than the contents of a chamber pot dumped into the waste drop! Where were Soren's Cantor and Cantrix? Who would accept this excuse for a *quirunha* if it was not necessary?

A thought came to him suddenly, and he tried to check his anger. This was the moment to listen, surely. Every Singer in the House, it seemed, was occupied in trying to cobble together a House *quiru*. Could Cho detect one mind open and vulnerable among so many? Zakri hoped not.

He signaled to Berk, a lift of his hand and quirk of his eyebrow, and then he went to a chair in the hallway. He sat in it, vaguely aware of the intricacy of its carved arms and back, no doubt the life's work of some long-gone carver. He leaned his head back against it, and closed his eyes while Berk stood nearby, keeping watch.

The mental noise was almost unbearable as Zakri opened his mind. He relaxed his shields gradually, bit by bit. With each barrier that he lowered, the clamor poured in. Not since his early days, before Sira had taught him the skill of effective shielding, had he allowed such invasion, and he was no longer accustomed to it. He gripped the arms of the chair as he opened himself further. His stomach turned and he reeled under a flood tide of thoughts and feelings and fears.

For several moments he simply let it all wash over him. It did not get easier to bear, but he began to be able to distinguish some of what he heard. The Gifted minds of the Singers, although unfocused, were like eddies in the torrent, set apart from the unGifted minds. There were others, which Zakri guessed must be the carvers, whose Gifts were different, yet still clearly delineated from the unGifted. There was one dark, strong force, some distance away. It had a shape, looming, fearsome. There was a space of silence around it, a chasm of fear between it and all the others. Zakri knew it to be Cho, and he skirted it carefully as he searched through the flood.

And then, at last, he found what he was seeking. He heard her through the noise, through the distraction. She was far from him, he guessed at the very top of the House, and her mind was dim with fatigue and despair, but she was alive.

Cantrix Elnor? Zakri sent very carefully. *Can you hear me?*

He sensed her sudden attention, and the intensity of her fear. Then, after a cautious interval, came an answer.

I can hear you. Who are you?

It is safer for both of us if I do not tell you that, Zakri answered, trying to send clearly without being detected.

Where are you?

I am here, he responded simply. *In the House.*

Can you help me? Can you get help?

I am going to try. I wanted to know if you were here, if you were safe.

Cantrix Elnor's thoughts came again, very clearly. *I am here, but not safe. My senior is dead. Killed.*

The horror of that flat statement made Zakri's throat close, but there was little time for sympathy.

Do you know where your Magister is? And his family?

They went to Lamdon, but never returned. I can only hope that they reached it.

Zakri felt Berk move closer, warning him, and he sent quickly, *I will send to you again soon. Be patient. Be careful.*

And you, she answered. *Be watchful at every moment. They hate all who come from Conservatory.*

Zakri had not come from Conservatory, of course, but it was far too complicated to explain to her now. He doubted Cho and the itinerants would appreciate the difference in any case. He broke the contact with Cantrix Elnor, and threw up his shields with immense relief.

When he opened his eyes, Berk was standing as close to him as he could without actually touching him. The Singers had ceased playing, and the odd, fragmented *quiru,* warm and bright in spots, shady and cold in others, was as complete as it was going to get. Zakri rose, shaky with nerves and still feeling a faint nausea. He watched the Singers put away their instruments and amble by twos and threes into the great room for the mid-day meal. He was too tired at the moment to be angry, but Berk was not.

"Preposterous," he growled. "Cho has filled the House with fools!"

"Better keep that thought to yourself," Zakri whispered.

"Come on, let us go to the stables, and I will tell you what I heard."

Before they got far, however, Sook came running after them, calling to them to wait.

"Zakri," she said, almost but not quite bowing. "Mura asks if you would come to the carvery for a moment."

Zakri met Berk's eyes, and hesitated. Sook, seeing, said softly, "It's all right. It's safe there." Her dark eyes flashed about her, from one side to the other, making certain no one else had heard.

The two men turned to follow her. House members and Singers streamed past them into the great room for their meal, talking and laughing together. Sook fell in behind the crowd, and then, when no one was watching, she turned right, down the corridor beneath the staircase, instead of left to the great room.

It was pleasant to walk into the even brightness and warmth of the carvery. The fragrance of newly cut ironwood wafted from the open door, a clean, pungent odor that made Zakri sniff appreciatively. He had never smelled it before; only a psi-Gifted *obis* carver, equipped with an *obis* knife, could actually cut into and through the rock-hard wood of the ancient trees. Even the suckers by which the great trees propagated, and which stretched in tangled patterns all over the Continent, were almost as hard as the knives themselves.

The *obis* knives were what Zakri saw first when he entered the carvery. They hung in gleaming rows within easy reach of the carvers, meticulously clean and shining with rendered and purified *caeru* oil. They were dark and mysterious, sharp, flexible, virtually unbreakable. Their ironwood handles were almost as black as the metal of the knives, oiled and worn to glossy smoothness.

Eight carvers sat idle at their workbenches as Sook led Zakri and Berk into the carvery. Half-finished pieces rested before each of them, but no one was working now. Mura stood with her hand on the shoulder of a young man who looked very like her. He was strongly built, with long black hair bound neatly behind his head. One of the other carvers stood and closed the door firmly.

"Zakri," Mura said quickly, in a low tone. "This is my son, Yul. The carvers have something to say to you."

Zakri bowed slightly, and waited. He felt Berk's wary presence behind him. It was like having a big boulder at his back, solid and immovable. Zakri was glad he was there.

Yul bowed to them, and gestured to the group around him. "We want to know if my mother is right. She has guessed you're not interested in joining Cho, and we've been hoping, expecting someone, from somewhere, to come. We're taking a terrible risk in asking, but Sook thinks you can be trusted. Is that true?"

Berk gave a low rumble in his throat, a warning sound. Zakri heard him, and flicked him a look of assent. He opened his mind again, briefly, to scan the room.

It was interesting, touching these minds. Zakri had begun his life with itinerants, and then had spent his youth in seclusion, his own Gift dangerously out of control. Very late, when he already had almost four summers, he had been taught to hear and send safely by Cantrix Sira, and since then he had listened to the highly disciplined thoughts of the Conservatory-trained on a daily basis. But these Gifted men and women, the *obis*-carvers, were different. They were not able to send and listen, as Cantors and Cantrixes were; but their minds were clear and practical, disciplined in another way. Their application of the Gift, the intensity with which they had to focus their psi to carve the unforgiving iron-wood, gave their minds a sharpness, a definition, that had great appeal to Zakri. And at this moment, more to the point, he sensed no deception or sinister intent. He doubted they would have been capable of hiding any.

He nodded now to Yul. "I was an itinerant," he said, including all the carvers in his glance. "But I do other work now, for Amric." He sensed Berk's approval, his relief that he did not reveal everything. He intended to use absolute caution in this House, lest some questing mind guess his true status. But he felt confidence here. He liked these artisans.

Sook smiled brilliantly at Zakri. He supposed it to be hope that made her dark eyes glow. Mura gave a sharp little sound of satisfaction, but she had another question. "Him?" she asked shortly, pointing a work-hardened finger at Berk.

Berk chuckled. "I'm a courier for Amric, Housewoman," he said. "I have been so for seven summers. I've grown these gray hairs in the service of my House and my Magister. I would hardly change my course this far along."

"That's good enough for me," she said.

"Well, then, Houseman," said Yul slowly, "and Singer," inclining his head to Zakri. "You've seen how it is here, I think."

"We have," Berk said.

"We've had no choice in these matters. Our Magister and his family went off to consult with Lamdon when it first began, and they never returned." Yul's eyes glittered in the bright light of the carvery as he looked back and forth between them. "But their itinerants did," he said in a flat voice. "Their Singers came back only four days after they left the House."

Zakri swallowed hard. Four days. Lamdon was at least eight days' ride from Soren, more probably ten or twelve, with a large traveling party. There was no hope for Soren's Magister.

"There were children?" he whispered.

Yul's eyes were bleak as he answered. "Two little ones," he said. "The Magister's mate was afraid to leave them behind."

"Has no one tried to resist?" Berk asked, his voice a mere scrape in the deepest register. Zakri knew how this story would affect the courier. Berk loved his grandchildren with a fierceness that was sometimes comical; at this moment it was tragic.

Another carver stood and spoke. "Yes," he said bitterly. "This is—was—a fine House, a brave House. But everyone who confronted Cho either died or ended up like that Singer at the center table in the great room, mindless, helpless. Even our senior Cantor is dead, although everyone pretends it was just age, or sickness. The itinerants stand between Cho and the rest of the House, and even those Singers who would rather be free are afraid to oppose him. His reach is long, and his power is growing."

Sook put in nervously, "We'd better get to the meal, or someone will get suspicious."

Mura moved quickly to the door. "We will talk again. We just wanted you to know." She slipped out into the corridor.

Berk followed, with Sook behind him. Zakri looked around at the carvers once more, being sure to record their faces in his memory. It would be good to know who might be allies in this awful business.

He wished Sira were with him. Her strength and her courage would be an enormous asset to them all. He and Berk could hardly save the situation alone. Yul, and Mura, and Sook—they would all be helpful. But they were dealing with a Gift gone bad, its genius perverted. Anyone who opposed it would put himself in the greatest danger.

Well, with the help of the Spirit, Zakri thought, I will try to imagine what Sira would have done . . . and then do it. But I wish she were here!

CHAPTER
SIX

★ THE JOURNEY TO CONSERVATORY HAD BEEN PLANNED FOR the turn of the seasons, when the changing weather hinted at the end of the deep cold. Mreen drove her parents wild with her impatience, going again and again to Observatory's thick windows during the endless days of white weather, pressing her face to the glass, trying to see through the snow that fell so thickly the sky was indistinguishable from the ground. The white weather preceded the change, and when it was over, the milder season would at last begin. There would still be half a year before the Visitor rolled up over the eastern horizon to add its feeble warmth to the sun's and bring the summer, and by that time Mreen would already have begun her new life as a first-level student at Conservatory.

The white weather passed in its time, and the day was at hand. The night before the journey, Theo and Sira walked in the nursery gardens. They breathed the steamy rich air and felt the fronds of growing things, plants that could not tolerate the cold of outside, brushing at their cheeks and hands. Other House members strolled past them, but they left the Cantor and Cantrix strictly alone. Sira sometimes stroked a leaf or a bud, using her right hand, the one without calluses, to feel the textures on her fingertips. *I have had the same dream three times,* she sent.

Tell me.

All dreams were significant, and they respected them. But any that came more than once were a call from the Gift, and received special attention.

It is odd, she sent. *In the dream, I see a tiny quiru. It is small, but very bright, and all by itself out in the open, as if on the Glacier, or . . . I do not know where, really, but alone. And there is a* tkir—*I think it is a* tkir—*approaching the quiru, and not afraid of it as they are supposed to be. There is no fire, no people . . . just the glow of the quiru shining above the snow. The* tkir *circles the light, around and around, and somehow I know it wants to put out the light, to jump on it, to smother it. The beast, whatever it is, makes a terrible sound, like growling, but not a natural noise, and it tenses, ready to spring. I am too far away, and I cannot do anything, but it seems important that the quiru hold. Then, just before the beast actually leaps, I waken.*

And what do you think it means?

She traced her scarred eyebrow with her forefinger. *It seems a warning.* The angles of her face were sharply drawn, her eyes fierce with concentration. *Be on your guard, Theo. Beware of everything, and especially . . .*

I know, he sent back. *Especially Mreen.*

She touched his shoulder with her palm, briefly, very lightly. For them, it was an intimate gesture. *Especially Mreen,* she agreed. *The little quiru—the light—it could be Mreen. But why should she be in any danger?*

I wish you could come with us, Theo sent.

Sira had not traveled outside the walls of the House for three years, yet her hair was cropped as short as any itinerant's, shorter even than Theo's was now. He had always seen it as a symbol of her restlessness, her feeling of never truly belonging.

It is too soon, she answered him. *Trisa is far too young to manage the Cantoris alone.*

I know. Theo was always less shy of physical contact than she. He reached for her hand and caught it between his. *I will be on my guard. I promise you.*

She returned the pressure of his hand for a moment before pulling her own away. Theo gave her the lopsided smile that made merry creases around his eyes, the expression she loved, and she had to return it despite her worry. Their minds were one, their least thought, their most intimate concern, open to the other.

She had often wondered if the unGifted, who mated and then lived in physical closeness all their lives, could ever comprehend the intense communion there was between herself and Theo. She loved him as she loved the Gift, with reverence, joy, and gratitude. When he was gone, she knew she would feel as if part of her very being were missing; and this was the only thought she shielded from him.

Go with the Spirit, my dear, she sent. *And come back swiftly.*

Mreen and Morys and Theo mounted their two *hruss* on a gray and cloudy morning. The beasts were laden and outfitted as if by Lamdon itself; Pol had spared nothing that might enhance the reputation of his House. Kai found no words to bid his little daughter farewell; he knelt and embraced her, his cheeks wet and his mouth twisted. His pain was such that the Gifted ones around him had to strengthen their shields. Brnwen, too, kissing her step-daughter for the last time, wept openly. Mreen's own eyes were red and swollen with tears and with indignant surprise that after waiting so long, and so impatiently, she should now grieve at leaving her parents.

It will pass, Mreen, Sira sent to her gently. *You will always miss them, but the pain will pass.*

Kai and Brnwen stood in misery on the steps, with Trisa beside them sending her silent goodbyes to her stepsister. Theo and Sira had made their farewells; Theo nodded to Morys that he was ready. He wanted to go quickly, and not prolong the scene. Pol stood proudly on the top step, nodding and smiling as if he had caused it all to happen.

Theo bowed, and lifted his hand, and turned his *hruss* away from the House. Mreen clutched at his waist, hiding her face against his back, wetting his furs with her tears as they rode off after Morys.

Theo had been an itinerant since he had three summers. He knew the roads and passes of the Continent as well as any. But no one, except those who had been born there, knew the road that led to Observatory. It had been a long time since Theo had been on it, and he was amazed again at its tortuousness, at the sheerness of the cliffs that loomed to the north, at the towering boulders that obstructed the way and promised to confound any who tried to find the way to Observatory—or from it—on their own.

Mreen clung to him, a speck of warmth and silence behind him. Once they started down the canyon road, where the chasm gaped to their left and the icy rocks made the *hruss* step slowly, she took one look into the dark void and hid her face once more against his back. She sent nothing during the slow hours of riding, until the *hruss* squeezed through a narrow slit in the cliff, and the path opened out onto a valley of sparse irontrees. The trees, smaller than those lower on the Continent, leaned to the north, their roots dry and crooked against the rocky ground.

Mreen, Theo sent gently. *We have left the cliff road.*

Her grip loosened as she lifted her head and looked around at their surroundings. Over his shoulder, he saw her faint glow brighten, and he smiled. She was as changeable as light itself, a sprite of energy, of emotion. Conservatory would have their hands full with this Gift!

Morys called back over his shoulder, "Was your little one there afraid? It's a scary road, all right."

Mreen cuddled against Theo's back again. *I just thought about Conservatory,* she sent happily. *I told myself I could only go to Conservatory if I could ride down that road!*

Theo laughed. "She will make a fine traveler, Morys."

Around them the day was as gray as old snow, the clouds hanging heavily above their heads and the rimed rocks dull and dark. The brilliance of the sky in the deep cold season was gone, but Theo knew that to be a good thing. The sun in a clear sky could make tender skin flame. He himself had not been out on the roads since first going to Observatory— how long ago? Could it possibly be eight years? Indeed, he would soon have nine summers!

He threw back his head and breathed deeply of the fresh air. The peaks of Observatory's mountains loomed above them in strange, tumbled spikes of rock and snow, higher than any of those on the Continent. It was no wonder Observatory had been isolated for so long. It was not only their beliefs, the Watching for the Ship every single night at the top of the House, that separated them from the rest of Nevya; whoever had chosen the site for their House, summers past remembering, must have intended them to be separate, different. But now, with the sending of Mreen to Conservatory, a connection would be made. Observatory would be part of Nevya despite their differences. The Gift willed it so.

Morys wanted to be down in Ogre Pass before the end of the daylight, and so they ate a quick mid-day meal in the saddle, handing bits of nutbread and dried *caeru* strips back and forth, taking snow in their mouths to quench their thirst. Once or twice they stopped to relieve themselves, but otherwise they pressed on. Theo looked back during one of these brief rests, and saw that the road they had traversed was already invisible. The giant rocks were scattered everywhere, as if by the hand of the Spirit itself, to disguise the way.

When they could just see the Pass through breaks in the landscape, Theo heard Sira faintly in his mind.

Theo?

Yes, he answered, as strongly as he could. His reach was not nearly so great as hers. *All is well. We are in the Pass.*

And Mreen?

Fine.

He could not understand her last message, but he caught the sense of it. He wished he could have heard it more clearly; he would not hear her voice again for a long time. He sent back to her as strongly as he was able, and could only hope that perhaps she could hear although he no longer could. Then Morys was leading them down the last slope, and pointing to a campsite, a level spot protected by a stand of giant trees, encircled by their suckers. The Pass stretched before them, its road wide and clear as if scraped out with a gigantic *obis* knife, running from the northwest to the southeast. They dismounted, and Theo lifted Mreen down. She stretched her arms over her head and did a little dance of freedom, then dashed about the campsite with all the energy of a five-year-old who has been restrained for too many hours.

Morys laughed. "Doesn't say much, does she?"

Theo was taking out his *filla* to call up his first camp *quiru* in years. "She does not say anything, my friend," he answered. "Not a word."

Morys stared at the child. "I'd heard that, but I thought it was exaggerated—you know, stories about the Gifted." He began the unsaddling of the *hruss*. "Why doesn't she speak, Cantor Theo?"

Theo turned his *filla* absently in his hand, and looked to the northeast, over the snowy reaches of the Pass. "We are not exactly certain. Perhaps it is because her stepsister sent to her since her babyhood, or perhaps it is simply her nature."

"Does she always have that light around her like that?"

Theo looked over at Mreen, who was plunging her fingers into the snow and scattering it around her in a pale shower. "Yes, Morys, she does." He laughed, filled with pleasure at the calm evening and the carefree play of the child. "She will never be cold, that one!"

"Lucky," Morys said.

Theo hoped he was right.

Mreen was fascinated by the darkness outside the *quiru*. Theo took her out once, briefly, to relieve herself, and then had to insist that she hurry back into the safety of the light and warmth.

I want to look at the stars! she protested.

You can see them from the quiru, he answered. *It is not safe to stay outside in the cold.*

Why? I do not feel cold!

You could feel it, though, very soon, and by the time you felt it, it might be too late.

Why?

For answer, Theo scooped up the squirming girl and carried her back to her bedfurs, dropping her in a giggling pile. Morys was laughing, but Theo looked somber.

Mreen, he sent.

She looked up at him, giggles subsiding, her eyes suddenly round, the deep green of ironwood needles. *Yes, Cantor Theo.*

I have no wish to frighten you, Mreen, but riding on the Continent is a very serious thing. When it comes to the cold, and the danger, you must no longer be a child. Your Gift is precious, and it is your duty to protect it.

Mreen pointed to the saddle they had ridden during the long day. *I know,* she answered. *There are many pictures with that.*

Are there? Theo knelt beside her, helping her off with her bulky furs, tucking her into her bed for the night.

Yes. I know people can die of the cold, and of other things.

It is true, Mreen. It is our lifework—we Singers—to try to keep that from happening.

I will remember.

Mreen yawned and snuggled into the yellow-white depths of her bedfurs. Morys had already banked the fire, and rolled into his own bed. The two *hruss,* grumbling in their throats, stood hipshot, broad heads hanging low, to rest the night. Theo went to his own bedfurs, and sat down to pull off his boots.

Mreen's eyes were already closed, her thick auburn lashes making delicate half circles on her plump cheeks.

Cantor Theo.

Yes, Mreen?

Mreen sighed, almost asleep. *Cantrix Sira sends good night.*

Theo looked up. He had heard nothing, not so much as a tickle in his mind. He stared at Mreen, and tried hard to push down the thought that he would have preferred to hear Sira's voice himself. If his Gift was not strong enough, there was nothing to be done about it.

He looked up at his *quiru* and found it steady and strong in the vast darkness. The embers of the fire glowed dully under the banked softwood. All was well.

He rolled himself into his furs, and pulled them up under his chin. Before he slept, the deep and rewarding sleep that came after a day in the open, he gave thanks to the Spirit, with passionate sincerity, for his Gift and its training.

CHAPTER SEVEN

FAR INTO THE LONG NIGHT HOURS, ZAKRI STARTED UP suddenly from an uneasy sleep. A rhythmic sound had invaded his dreams, and it persisted when he was fully awake, a light tapping at the door of his room that paused and then came again. The other occupants of his room slept on undisturbed. Zakri extended a cautious fibril of psi to find who came knocking at such an hour. When he recognized her, he hurried to the door, wearing only his trousers.

Sook stood in the hall, her eyes wide and glistening in the *quiru* light. Her black hair hung in long tangles, as if she, too, had just risen from her bed. "Oh, Singer, thank the Spirit it's you!" she whispered. "Could you please come, please? And hurry!"

Zakri answered without hesitating. "Of course." As a Cantor, he was somewhat used to calls that came in the middle of the night. He stepped back into the crowded room to retrieve his tunic and boots. He pulled them on in the hallway and tucked his *filla* into his tunic while Sook shifted from foot to foot beside him.

"What has happened?" Zakri asked as he followed her

quick steps down the corridor. He kept his voice low, and his thoughts as well. Shielding his mind every waking moment was tiring him; even as he tried to sleep, he must stay half-alert, on guard.

"It's Nori," she said breathlessly. She led him around a corner and down a long corridor to the back of the House, where large family apartments flanked the nursery gardens and the carvery. "She's bleeding. . . ." Her eyes were enormous, tear-washed and frightened. "We don't know what it is, and she won't say anything. . . ."

They did not have far to go. The apartment was near the *ubanyor*. Sook opened the door without knocking, and went in with Zakri close behind her. Several white, strained faces turned up to them. Zakri recognized Mura, but he had no time to speak to her before Sook seized his hand.

With a strength that surprised him, she tugged him into another room, an inner bedroom. It was small and dim, furnished with a cot and a chair, and a carved table cluttered with a young woman's small possessions, brushes, hair bindings, quill pens in an ironwood jar. Nori lay on the narrow bed with her knees drawn up, bedfurs clutched tightly to her breast. Her eyelids and her lips were clenched and pale. She was surely no older than Sook; Zakri doubted she had four summers, but her pain aged her, making deep furrows in her smooth skin.

Zakri had to lower his shields to assess the girl's agony, the wrenching spasms that made her moan wretchedly. He scanned her body with his psi, briefly, his *filla* still in his hand, before he knelt beside the bed. Then, before beginning to work, he spoke quietly to Sook.

"Have you attended childbirths?"

Sook protested, "This can't be a childbirth, Singer!" Her eyes flashed in the half darkness. "Nori's not mated!"

"She is having a miscarriage, nevertheless," Zakri said, completely forgetting to watch his speech patterns. "We will need towels, and water, and if you are too upset to help her, then you must find an older woman who has some experience."

"No! I'll do it!"

She put her head outside the bedroom door to ask for the supplies, and was back almost immediately, hovering over Zakri, touching Nori's hand and forehead.

Zakri played in *Lidya* first, to relax the suffering girl. He was certain that her fear and the tension it caused made her pains worse. He had helped several Housewomen at Amric to give birth. It was a powerful and natural process that usually needed little assistance. Laboring women had been grateful for his soothing melodies and for his special talent, the gentle touches of psi here and there that gently urged the babes on their way. But there was nothing Zakri could do for Nori's babe; he knew as soon as he touched her with his psi that her child was dead before it was even formed.

It was Mura who brought clean towels, and a heavy pitcher brimming with water. "What is it?" she whispered to Sook. "What's wrong with Nori?"

"The Singer says it's a miscarriage," Sook answered as she lifted the towels from Mura's arm. Mura set the pitcher beside the foot of the cot. Zakri went on with his melody, aware of Sook lifting the fur that covered her friend to place a thick pad of towels beneath her. She replaced the blanket and then knelt beside Zakri. He sensed her gaze on him, felt the pressure of her trust and hope.

Nori's body needed to shed its burden, and because of that Zakri dared not stop her bleeding completely. He was worried about the risk of her losing too much blood, growing too weak. He tried not to think of the tragic circumstances of Cantrix Isbel's giving birth to her babe; surely this girl need not suffer the same fate as Mreen's mother had.

Moments passed as the *Lidya* melody flowed on; Zakri transformed the lowered third of *Lidya* into the second degree of *Mu-Lidya,* a subtle variation that was rewarded as Nori's tight fists relaxed, and her eyelids smoothed and fluttered slightly. A sighing breath escaped her. Only then did Zakri modulate to *Aiodu,* the second mode, to sweep her body once again with his psi.

He hoped no one was listening at this moment. His mind must be generously opened; this was Iban's legacy, this understanding that to sense the precise functioning of Nori's body, to touch her thoughts, to feel what had gone wrong and to find what he might be able to put right . . . to do all these things, the Singer's mind must not be shielded. He must allow the pain and misery to register in himself. It was the flaw in Conservatory's rigid training, the weakness that made Cantors and Cantrixes superficial healers. Sira had not allowed Zakri to learn it, although it still plagued her own healing.

He touched Nori's mind now, gently, searching for a reason, a cause. She was unGifted, of course, but her feelings were very strong. She was so frightened, and hurt. . . . Zakri's melody died as he sucked in a sudden breath. The sharp hiss made Mura and Sook jump.

In Nori's mind was an unspeakable deed, a vile image. . . . Zakri had to put down his *filla*, pull away from the awful picture in her mind.

Nori knew exactly what had happened to her, and the understanding of it exaggerated her fear and her pain, made her afraid to speak, even to her friends and her family.

Zakri had tasted the memory of what had happened to the girl. Her body and her babe had been deliberately hurt. The life that had taken root in her had been extinguished, pinched out as deliberately and carelessly as one might pinch out an annoying ember that fell from the cooking fire. With his carver's psi, he had severed the cord that nourished the growing babe in her womb. No doubt he had convinced her that he could kill her just as easily . . . and perhaps he could.

Zakri reeled under the shock of it, the violence, the enormity of the evil that inspired it. He lost the iron grip he kept on his Gift, and behind him a brush and a quill rolled and fell from the table, and the empty chair scraped noisily on the floor as if someone had pushed it. Sook gasped, and Mura cried out.

Zakri leaned forward, pressing his forehead into his hands, striving for control.

O Spirit! he thought. How is it possible for the Gift to be used in such a way?

In his mind he heard a flashing warning. *Be careful, friend. He will hear you.*

Zakri closed his mind sharply, suddenly, and sat back on his heels. He trembled, and perspiration stung his eyes when he opened them. Sook was staring at him.

"What is it?" she begged. "Singer! What is it?"

Zakri shook his head back and forth, slowly. "It was he," he said wearily. "Cho did this."

He had been angry already, over Iban's death, but he was now filled with a deep revulsion as well. Not only was Cho dangerously powerful, but he must be a man without remorse, without even the semblance of control. What sane person could have done such a thing? Everyone in this House was in peril. Zakri felt the knot in his breast turn to stone.

Are you all right, Singer?

It was the same voice that had warned him, the same person who had heard him in his shock. *I am all right,* he sent back. *Were you following?*

Yes.

Can he hear us?

There was a pause before the imprisoned Cantrix answered, and her sending when it came was careful and wary. *It seems he hears very strong thoughts, although he is not able to understand more subtle ones. But he is easily angered, and very dangerous, especially for us . . . and probably for you. Beware any mention of Conservatory.*

There was no time to explain everything now, to reveal the truth. Clearly, Cantrix Elnor believed Zakri to have come from her own tradition; and in a way, of course, he had. He only sent, *Thank you,* before he broke the contact.

The girl on the cot moaned as a fresh spasm began, and Zakri resumed his melody, trying to ease her. Sook replaced the blood-soaked towels with fresh ones. Mura came with the broth, and when Nori was able to drink, they spooned a bit into her mouth. The night passed slowly, and the morning found them all exhausted, but Nori was stronger, her burden shed, the bleeding stopped.

Before she fell into a healing sleep, Nori clutched Mura's

hand. She made a pitiful sight. Her eyes were red and swollen, her hair tangled around her. With a sob, she said, "You have to know—I thought he meant to make me his mate. I believed him!"

Mura tried to shush her, putting her rough hand against her cheek, but Nori shook her head sharply.

"No, Mura, it's true! Cho . . . I thought he cared about me, that he . . ." She sobbed again, and her voice went high with the strain. "But when I told him about the babe . . ."

Mura smoothed Nori's hair. "There," she murmured, "it doesn't matter, and he isn't worth it. It doesn't matter. There will be other babes for you. Sleep, now."

Sook was weeping, too, silently, but Zakri sensed her tears were more from anger than sorrow. When they left the bedroom, she seized his arm with sharp strength, and her eyes blazed.

"Singer," she said in a tense whisper. "I thank you for healing Nori. We have to do something about Cho!"

"I must find Berk," Zakri said. "We will go to Lamdon at once. They will have to take action."

Mura heard this, and she spoke from behind him, where she had been reassuring Nori's family. "Cho won't let you leave," she said. "No Singer is allowed to leave this House except under his orders."

Zakri clenched his fists, and saw the telltale sparks fly up around him. He quelled them quickly. He was at risk of letting these brave women learn his secret. And in this House, knowledge was dangerous.

"We need a distraction," he muttered. "Some noisy event to keep Cho occupied."

Sook stared at him for a long moment, her eyes brilliant in her weary face. "When can you be ready, Singer Zakri?"

"Sook!" Mura cried. "What are you thinking?"

Sook began to gather the long strands of her hair into a fresh binding. "I'm thinking of the carvery," she said, "and the carvers. They can be very noisy sometimes."

Before Zakri could answer, the door to the apartment was abruptly opened from the outside. The three of them were caught by surprise, openmouthed and off guard. The members of Nori's family clung together in fear.

It was Cho himself who had opened the door, and he stood now in the doorway, his long arms braced on the frame, the thin braid of his hair swinging gently against his chest. His narrow eyes fastened on Zakri. "What business could you have in this apartment, Singer?" he murmured. His tone was light, almost casual.

Mura stepped forward. "Nori, one of my kitchen girls, was taken ill in the night," she said quickly. "This Singer was about, so I called on him to help."

"Why, whatever could be the matter with our little Nori?" Cho asked. He stepped inside the apartment. One of the itinerants from upstairs followed close behind, not speaking, watching Cho's every movement. Cho's glance took in Nori's family, then turned to the closed door to the bedroom. "Is she in there?" He took a step toward it. "I'll just see if she's feeling better."

"She's asleep," Mura said hastily.

Cho chuckled, a sinister, light sound. "I won't disturb her a bit."

As Cho moved toward the bedroom, Sook stepped forward as if to intercept him. Zakri caught her eye and shook his head. Her eyes flashed, but she stopped, and stood with her hands on her hips, watching Cho open the bedroom door.

Zakri closed his eyes. Controlling his temper was taking a great deal of his energy, and he was following Cho with his mind at a careful distance, ready to act if Cho threatened Nori any further. He listened as the man went in to her and bent over the cot. Tension made Zakri's shoulders hard, his neck stiff. He breathed deeply, trying to release it. He felt eyes on him, and he opened his eyes to see Cho's man staring at him. Still he watched over the sleeping Nori with his Gift, his physical eyes open but unfocused. He knew when Cho bent over her, touched her body with his own, cruder psi, and then withdrew it.

Cho smiled as he came out of the bedroom. "Nori looks fine to me," he said to Nori's family. "When she wakes up, you can tell her I was here, and that I'm sorry she had a bad night. No doubt that will make her feel better."

Mura looked murderous, and Sook stood beside her, her chin lifted, her great eyes glittering.

Cho laughed, a sound like the slither of claws on stone. "Oh, yes, I look out for all my House members," he said lightly. He tipped his head to one side and his eyes moved over Sook, up and down, and then again. "All of them," he repeated. "Remember that, won't you?"

Cho's man pulled the door closed behind them as they left. Zakri released his breath in a rush, and Sook gave a little sound of relief. Mura stood in the center of the room, her arms folded tightly, looking after Cho.

"I could poison that man!" she hissed.

"Be careful, Housewoman," Zakri told her. "It is possible he could hear that thought."

"Yes, I know," she answered. "But at this moment I hardly care. No one is safe here!"

"That is perfectly true," Zakri agreed wearily. "But we will do what we can." His eyes burned with fatigue. It was time for the morning meal, but he wanted only his bed.

"Well, Sook," Mura said, "we'd better get to work."

"But you must be exhausted!" Zakri said. "I am—I'm worn out!"

"Well, you did all the work, Singer," Sook said, with a pat on his shoulder. "We only helped."

"Yes, go to your bed," Mura urged him. She did not smile, but the wrinkles of her face were a little softer as she looked at him. "When you waken, come to the kitchens. We'll save you some *keftet*."

Zakri bowed slightly in thanks, and raised a hand in farewell to the other House members before he left the apartment.

He was in the hall when he heard footsteps behind him. He looked over his shoulder to see that Mura had followed him out, and he waited for her to catch up.

"Singer," she murmured, "perhaps you yourself should have been a carver. Did you ever think of it?"

"I—I beg your pardon?"

Her eyes were canny and sharp as she looked up at him. "I saw what happened, there in Nori's room. I saw the things move, the brush and so forth, the chair. Your psi is strong, isn't it?"

Zakri ducked his head and laughed, trying to look as if he had been caught out. "Well, sometimes it is, yes. I try to control it, but . . ." He lifted one shoulder, and spread his hands. "It gets away from me."

"Hmm." Mura looked at him one more time, hard. Zakri knew she had no Gift, but he felt as if her eyes saw to his very center, and he had to avert his own. "Well. Have a good rest, Singer."

"Thank you, thanks, Mura. I—I'll see you later." He bowed to her and hurried away, down the corridor. He hated deceiving Mura. He must be more careful! She saw far more than was good for her. He did not want either Mura or Sook to be endangered by knowing his secret.

CHAPTER
EIGHT

✦ ZAKRI AND BERK MADE SURREPTITIOUS PREPARATIONS. They filled their saddle packs with generous provisions from Mura's stores, everything she could spare, and Zakri made sure their *hruss* were clean and well fed, ready to ride. Sook promised them a signal. Zakri fretted about her safety, but she cast him a sidelong look from her wonderful eyes and assured him she could take care of herself.

"It's you who has to be careful, Singer Zakri," she said. "And I . . . we'll be waiting for you to come back!"

She put her small, warm hand on his. He controlled his impulse to pull away, as much not to hurt her feelings as to hide his secret. He admired her spirit. Any House could be proud of such a member.

They waited three days. Then, at the mid-day meal, Berk found a badly cracked cup at his place, one that would clearly leak if tea were poured in it. He lifted it up and said loudly, "This is broken!"

Sook was hovering nearby, watchful. "Oh, I'm sorry, Houseman," she exclaimed. "Let me get you another!" She hurried out of the great room, wending her way deftly between the long tables. Zakri heard the exchange from his usual seat between Klas and Shiro, and he saw Berk's nod in his direction.

It was the agreed-upon sign. Berk rose and left, while Zakri sat on, pretending to be part of the conversation around him. The carvers and Sook had planned well. Only a very few minutes passed before the uproar began.

There was little doubt it came from the carvery. Shouts and crashes rolled from the corridor behind the stairs, and a flood of psi came with them, a wave of it that Zakri was sure would deafen anyone who tried to listen through it. He threw up his own shields before it could reach him.

Cho cursed. He and his henchmen leaped up from the center table and hurried toward the carvery. Zakri and several other Singers followed them out, but once they reached the corridor, Zakri turned in the opposite direction, only glancing behind him to see that no one noticed. The noise increased, a din of raised voices and the slam of ironwood against the stone floor. The racket followed him as he made haste down the hall.

He saw the stableman running toward him, drawn by the commotion, and he ducked into the linen room until the man passed. Then Zakri fled, his fur boots quiet on the stone, to the stables.

"By the Spirit!" Berk muttered. "What are they doing in there?" He was hastily saddling his own *hruss*. He had already saddled Zakri's and it waited patiently beside him, all saddle packs tied on, bedfurs secured with their thongs. The stable doors stood open to the morning.

"I believe they are fighting, Houseman," Zakri answered with a grin.

"Over what?"

"Why, what do men fight over?" Zakri responded. He put his foot in the wooden stirrup and swung quickly up into the high-cantled saddle. "They fight over women, do they not?"

He tried not to think of Sook in the middle of the melee, of Sook drawing Cho's attention to herself. At least, he thought, she was not Gifted. Cho's interest in her should be short-lived. All of them—Mura, Sook, Yul, and Zakri—were counting on it.

Berk settled into his own saddle, and they urged their beasts out of the stable. *Hruss* rarely galloped, or indeed moved at any pace faster than a heavy, swinging trot, and it took some time to work them up even to that. Zakri watched nervously over his shoulder as they rode around the House to the front, where the road led away up the slope.

Even outside, they could hear the shouting from the carvery. Zakri wished desperately to know what was happening, but he dared not open his mind. The carvers had planned a barrage of their special psi, the same psi that powered the *obis* knives. He could feel it beyond his shields, just as they had promised, a storm of it beating against the barricade he kept in place, protecting himself. It would be foolhardy to allow that bedlam to touch him. It should effectively cover their escape.

He sincerely hoped it gave Cho a stinker of a headache.

Sook shrank against the wall of the carvery, beaten back by the turmoil around her. She knew there was more in the air than just the shouts and banging, but she was deaf to it, and glad to be so.

When Cho came in, the carvers, who had divided themselves into two groups beforehand, bellowed and shook fists at each other. One daring pair shoved each other back and forth, making the workbenches rock. The two Singers who always accompanied Cho went immediately pale. In a moment one staggered, his hands over his sweating face, and Sook knew the psi being randomly thrown about the room was too much for him. One carver's psi could not have done it; but their concerted efforts created a strong enough wave to affect a Singer. When Cho saw that, he suddenly thrust up his long arm, his black eyes snapping.

"Stop!" he cried.

Sook was not sure it was enough time. Yul, Mura's son, caught her eye, and she shook her head just a little, to indicate that Zakri and the courier needed more, a little longer. They would hardly be out of the courtyard yet.

Yul took her cue. He picked up a half-carved chunk of ironwood and held it over his head with a yell, as if he were about to throw it, and someone immediately howled back at him. The din worsened. The black *obis* knives rattled on their hooks, and the half-carved pieces of ironwood on the worktables danced under the force of the kinesthetic psi that flashed around the room.

The other itinerant Singer also felt the effects now, hunching his shoulders and lurching to the door. A number of House members clustered there, peering in, trying to see what was happening. In his disorientation the Singer could not get past them.

Cho stepped to the middle of the room, both arms lifted above his head, and he turned his dark gaze on Yul. Sook held her breath.

The ironwood dropped suddenly from Yul's hands, and the carver pitched forward to the stone floor, nerveless. All the noise ceased abruptly as the carvers stared at their fallen comrade, and the sudden silence made Sook's ears ring. A moment passed before she could hear the gentle clicking the *obis* knives made as they swung back and forth, bumping against each other. She cried out, and ran to kneel by Yul.

"So," Cho said, his voice no more than a murmur. He pointed at Sook. "Is this the cause?"

One of the other carvers stepped forward, fearful, but holding his ground. "There aren't enough of them anymore," he said stoutly, following the line Sook and Mura had invented. "Girls, I mean! This House is full of men. There are hardly any women, and this one was promised to me!"

Sook met the man's eyes, and kept silent. They had planned this carefully, hoping to trivialize the incident in Cho's mind. They hadn't thought Cho would actually attack a fellow carver—she could hardly believe even now that he had. She thought of the drooling man at the center table in the great room and she shuddered.

Two of the other carvers offered comment, weakly, trying

to keep up the pretense of argument. The sight of Yul sprawled on the floor restrained them. Sook knew the courage required to face up to Cho, and she prayed she would have it, too.

Cho's eyes, assessing her, were stone-hard. "Ah—it's you again," he said smoothly. "You're Nori's friend . . . Sook, isn't it? Maybe you'd better come with me. Looks like you're the one to answer for my meal being interrupted."

Someone had run to fetch Mura from the kitchen, and she came rushing in now to crouch beside her son. She threw a vicious glance up at Cho.

"If he doesn't recover," she hissed, "you'd better watch what you eat, Carver!"

Several of the carvers gasped at her daring, but Cho laughed. "So I will, Housewoman!" he exclaimed. "So I will! But don't worry . . . he'll recover. It was just the tiniest slap. A warning. Next time perhaps he'll heed me when I speak!"

In truth, Yul's eyes were already opening, and his ashen face began to color again. Sook chafed his wrists while Mura gently stroked his temples. Yul turned his hand to grip Sook's, and she breathed a sigh of relief; he was telling her he was all right. She gave Mura the smallest nod of reassurance.

Cho stooped to say in her ear, "I think you and I will have a little talk . . . upstairs."

Sook felt a chill in her veins, and she cringed before she could stop herself. Cho took her arm just above the elbow. He was strong, and his grip hurt when she tried to pull away.

"Let her be," Mura snapped.

Cho only laughed again, softer this time. "Mind your son, there, Housewoman," he said. "I'm just going to get an explanation from our little troublemaker, here."

Sook had to get to her feet, or be dragged up bodily. She stood up, and when she wrenched her arm from Cho's long fingers she knew she would have a nasty bruise by evening. His eyes were glittering, half-shut, as he leaned over her.

"Don't ever do that again," he whispered, so close to her

face that his breath stirred the loose tendrils of her hair. "Do you think only the Gifted are vulnerable to me?"

The room was deadly silent now. Even the *obis* knives hung still on their hooks; no psi buffeted the air, and all eyes were on Cho and Sook. Cho was far taller than she, and he gripped her chin and tipped her head back, forcing her to look into his eyes. She wished she dared spit in his face. She felt small and alone—who would stand against him if he wanted to harm her?

Zakri and Berk were surely far enough away by now, she thought. She let her eyes drop. "Just leave me alone," she said, affecting a small voice. "I didn't mean to cause any trouble."

Cho hesitated. Then he snorted derisively and released her. "My friends," he said, addressing them all. "We have more important things to do than fight over women." He chuckled as he turned to the man who had spoken before. "Don't worry, Carver. There will be plenty of these to go around before we're done."

He lifted his hand to his two itinerants, now recovered, and went to the open door. The Singer Shiro met him there.

"Cho! They're gone!" he cried. "The Singer Zakri and his courier! *Hruss,* tack, everything, gone!"

Sook's heart thumped suddenly in her breast, and she kept her eyes down, staring at the floor.

Very slowly, Cho turned back from the door. Sook watched, holding her breath, as his fur-booted feet came to stand before her once again.

"What have you done, little Sook?" he said, his voice no more than a whisper. "You think you can play grown-up games? Do you want to play with me?"

He seized her arm again, only this time there was no pulling away. He held it tightly, at the same time deliberately pressing the back of his hard hand into the softness of her breast. Sook looked up into his face, and a wave of revulsion swept her that was stronger than her fear. He laughed, and she knew he had felt it, read it from her. Her skin prickled as she realized that he liked it.

"Cho!" Mura spoke up boldly, but Sook heard the tremor

in her voice. "It's my fault—it was my idea!" the older woman insisted.

"It doesn't matter." Cho didn't even turn his head as he answered her. "Little Sook here will help me understand . . . she'll be telling me all about it!" He propelled Sook forward, toward the door.

One of his itinerants stepped forward, blocking his path. He said uneasily, "Cho, don't you think . . . couldn't you . . ."

Cho paused for the barest moment. His eyes narrowed and his chin rose as he looked down his nose at the man. He didn't speak.

The itinerant stumbled back, and fell hard to his knees. His fellow Singer jumped to his side, catching him before he could collapse all the way. Without aid, he would surely have struck his head against the side of the workbench. Cho thrust Sook forward then, through the door, past the watching, silent House members. She threw a last look over her shoulder at the itinerant. He was utterly unconscious, his body limp, his features slack.

Mura ran after them, crying, "Cho! Let her go!"

She caught up with them in the corridor, and took hold of Cho's sleeve. He stopped once more, the last time. With a jerk that Sook felt, too, he pulled his arm free of Mura's hand.

"Woman," he said flatly, "if you ever touch me again, I'll kill that halfwit son of yours."

Mura stepped back, haltingly, turning helpless eyes to Sook. Sook turned her face away to hide her own terror. "It's all right, Mura," she heard herself say. "I'll be all right." Some part of her marveled. Where did the courage come from? It was for Zakri, that was the answer. She had done it for Zakri.

It was all she had time for. Cho dragged her up the broad staircase and down the long corridor to the Magister's apartment. Several itinerants in the hall watched dumbly as he pulled her inside, and kicked the door shut behind them.

* * *

In the Timberlands that night, in the mouth of Ogre Pass, Zakri woke trembling and sweating in his bedfurs, driven from sleep by an awful dream. He had seen an *urbear* dragging Sook off across the Great Glacier. She screamed for his help, and he tried to run to her, feet dragging in the heavy snow, but he could not reach her.

Sira had taught him that the dreams of the Gifted are never to be ignored. But what could he do about this one? O Spirit, he prayed, please, please watch over Sook. Keep her safe until I can return.

CHAPTER
NINE

★ IN THE EIGHT YEARS THAT HAD PASSED SINCE THEO'S LAST visit to Conservatory, Magister Mkel seemed to have aged four summers. Theo bowed low to him, hiding his concern at Mkel's appearance. Of course he knew that Mkel's shielding, that strict barrier that had been so difficult for Sira to overcome in herself, would shut out all but the strongest emotions. Just the same, Theo had no wish to offend.

Mreen and Theo had come directly to the Magister's apartment on their arrival, leaving Morys to stable the *hruss*. Mreen, suddenly bashful, hid herself behind Theo as he greeted Mkel and his mate, Cathrin.

Mkel's gray hair had grown white, and so thin that his scalp showed; the skin of his face sagged, and was darkened in patches as if he, whose duties rarely allowed for travel outside his House, had been riding in the cold and sun. Cathrin was still plump and pink-cheeked, her white hair thick and beautifully bound. She stood close to her mate, one hand on the back of his chair as if she could support him through the ironwood.

"Magister Mkel," Theo said formally, speaking aloud for Cathrin's sake. "Observatory sends you greetings, and a student for Conservatory."

Mreen peeked around Theo's leg, showing only one green eye and a tumble of hair mussed into an auburn cloud by her *caeru* hood.

Cathrin smiled down at her. "Welcome to our House, dear. Won't you come and say hello?"

Mreen vanished immediately behind Theo, her small hands clutching at his trousers, her face buried in the furs he still wore.

Mkel spoke slowly, as if he did not quite understand. "Observatory sends a student?" His voice was cracked and hoarse, and Theo was certain he must be ill. But this was Conservatory! Surely someone here could heal him.

Theo bowed once again. "It is true, Magister." He stepped aside so that Mreen was visible, and he urged her forward with a gentle hand. The *quiru* at Conservatory was bright, but still Mreen's little halo shone distinctly, darkling now in places because of her shyness. Cathrin took a small sharp breath.

"My goodness," she murmured. "What is this, Singer?"

Mreen tipped her round face up to Theo. *Why does she call you Singer?* she demanded. *Does she not know you are a Cantor?*

When I was last here, I was only Singer, Theo sent back to her.

Mkel said, "Cantor? What does she mean?"

"Who?" Cathrin asked.

"It is this child, Cathrin," Mkel told her. "She wants us to call Theo Cantor."

Cathrin held up her hands, confused. She was used to silent conversations flowing around her, exchanges she could not hear, but this was too much. "Please," she complained. "Will one of you tell me what's happening? Surely the child doesn't already send?"

Mreen did not release her grip on Theo, but her usual ebullience was returning, and her eyes shone brightly up at the old couple. *Theo is Cantor,* she sent firmly, and very clearly, as if perhaps Mkel could not hear so well. *He has been Cantor Theo v'Observatory these five years! Did you not know?*

The heavy lines of Mkel's face lifted, and Theo recognized a bit of the spirit and good nature he remembered.

Mkel said, "No, child, I did not know." He leaned forward in his chair to meet Mreen's eyes. "I do not know you, either. What is your name?"

Mreen frowned up at Theo. *Cantor Theo, can he not send?*

Before Theo could respond Mkel sent firmly, *Of course I can! But my mate, Cathrin, is not Gifted. Can you not speak?*

Mreen shook her curly head. *No.*

"Excuse me, Magister," Theo hastened to say. "And Cathrin. I had better explain. It is rather complicated."

"So it must be," Cathrin said. "Well, it's been a long time since I heard one of your stories, Singer . . . Theo! Oh, I hardly know what to call you." She bustled about, bringing chairs forward, signaling to a Housewoman to bring refreshments. "At least sit down, and have something to drink and to eat."

The Housewoman brought a tray with tidbits of nuts encased in dried fruit, and Cathrin held it out to Mreen. "Do try something, child," she said with a smile. "And don't worry—we're going to work it all out."

Mreen happily seized a sweet morsel, and wriggled up into a chair to sit cross-legged, munching. When Theo was also settled with a cup of tea in his hand, Cathrin herself sat down. Mkel watched Mreen throughout all the preparations, his eyebrows rising as her little cloud of light brightened and shifted with her mood, wisps of curly hair wafting about her face.

"I have never seen such a one," he murmured.

Carefully, knowing how affecting his news would be, Theo said, "Magister Mkel . . . this is Mreen. She is Isbel's daughter."

Cathrin put her hand to her breast, and then to her cheek. Mreen saw her, and caught her mood. The light around her darkened, and a shadow seemed to float through it, crossing her face. Cathrin bit her lip, and reached for the tray of fruit again, holding it out to Mreen. "Never mind, child," she said gently. "It is past." The little girl dimpled at Cathrin as she took another sweet.

"Mreen came to Observatory with Cantrix Sira in the last summer," Theo went on. "I know you have reservations about what we have done there, Magister"— with a polite nod— "but we have done what we must. I am not Conservatory-trained, although I would have liked to be; but I serve now as Cantor in Observatory's Cantoris, and we—Sira and I—are teaching four other Gifted children there."

"So many!" Cathrin breathed.

"Indeed. And one, Trisa, has already performed her first *quirunha*."

Mkel leaned on one arm of his chair, his chin cupped in his hand, and regarded Mreen. Theo kept his mind respectfully shielded, but his shields were not what Mkel's were, and the older man's emotions seeped through. Sadness, regret, and self-reproach had been dragging at Mkel for a long time, and they had aged him, had worn him down like the waves of the Frozen Sea wear away the rocks of the coast.

"Theo—Cantor Theo," he said slowly. Theo knew what a great effort it was for Mkel to use the title. All his precepts, all the discipline by which he had lived his life, were challenged by it. Theo sensed his attempt to find a footing, to choose a path that would reconcile his past and this present. All the ground beneath him must seem to be shifting and crumbling like talus at the foot of a cliff.

Theo said quietly, "At least at Observatory I am Cantor Theo."

"Of course," Mkel answered. He straightened in his chair. "And so you should be here. Cantor Theo, I failed Cantrix Isbel, and I can never forget it. I failed Cantrix Sira, as well. I am hard put to understand why Observatory should have so much of the Gift and the Houses of the Continent so little."

"It is what we are all trying to understand," Theo said tactfully.

"But Sira seems to know—she was so sure!"

"Sira has insights that only the Gift can explain," Theo murmured. He wished he could say more to ease Mkel's self-reproach, but, he thought ruefully, the insights were mostly Sira's.

Mreen had eaten her fill of sweets. She knelt in the chair that was too big for her, diffidence forgotten, and gazed intensely at Mkel. *Why do you have a mate, and the other Gifted do not?*

It is tradition, he answered her. *The Magister of Conservatory takes a mate, because he has no Cantoris of his own, and because his mate acts as mother to all the children who come here to study.*

Theo was impressed by the immediacy and directness of the answer, but Mreen seemed to take it quite for granted. *And so I will never have a mate?*

Do you wish to be a full Cantrix, and play the filhata *on the dais, to perform the* quirunha?

The little girl squirmed, and her halo of light glittered joyously. *So I do! Oh, so I do!*

Mkel smiled once more, but Theo felt his weariness like a stone in his mind. Mkel's shoulders were bowed by the weight of it, his body tired by what his mind could not push away.

Cathrin leaned toward Mreen. "Are you full now, dear? Would you like to bathe?"

Mreen nodded.

"Can you not answer me, Mreen?" Cathrin asked, not yet understanding.

Mreen shook her head, very deliberately.

Cathrin's eyes filled with bright tears. "Oh, Theo," she said softly. "She can't talk at all? Not a word?"

"No, Cathrin," he responded. "She has never spoken aloud in her life, or cried, or laughed."

The tears spilled over Cathrin's pink cheeks, and Mreen jumped down from her chair and ran to stand beside her. She patted Cathrin's hand, then looked over her shoulder at Theo.

Cantor Theo, she sent, *please tell the lady not to be sad, because I am not. Tell her about my Gift, and tell her not to cry!*

"Cathrin," Theo said quickly, "Mreen sends that she is not unhappy, nor should you be. Her Gift is very strong, and that is why she is here. She wanted this very much, to come here to study."

"Will she sing?" Mkel asked.

"We think not. But, as you see . . ." Theo had to grin at Mreen's small figure and its nimbus of light that now glowed with sympathy as she gazed up at Cathrin. "She has no difficulty making *quiru.*"

Cathrin, the mate of the Magister of Conservatory, held a unique position on Nevya. She was the one unGifted person on the Continent whose life was surrounded and saturated by the Gift. She gave a pragmatic sigh now, and held out her hand to Mreen.

"Wait for just a moment, Cathrin," Mkel said. With difficulty, he stood and shuffled to a cabinet nearby. The others watched and waited as he dug in it, reaching far to the back for something. In a moment he returned to his chair, sitting down heavily, with a little grunt as if the effort had tired him still further. He held a leather-wrapped object in his hand, something small and narrow.

Mreen? he sent, smiling a little at the child. *Will you come here to me?*

Mreen glanced up at Cathrin and then gently freed her hand and walked slowly to Mkel.

Mkel held out the little package. *I would like you to have this, child,* he sent. He leaned back wearily in his chair to watch her unwrap the folds of soft *caeru* hide.

A *filla* lay inside. It was small, inset with tiny bits of metal at each stop. It was worn to shiny smoothness by generations of fingers. Mreen wrapped her fingers around it and lifted it. She closed her eyes, and Theo held his breath.

After a moment she opened her eyes and looked hard at Mkel. *It is a very old* filla, she sent to him.

Indeed it is, Mreen, he answered. *I would like you to have it.*

She looked to Theo as if for permission. He could only lift one shoulder. *Mreen, I believe this is between you and Magister Mkel.*

She turned back to Mkel and dimpled. *Thank you,* she sent simply. *I like it much better than my own. I will send mine back to Observatory, and I will play this one!*

Mkel smiled. *It has not been played in a very long time,* he sent. *Not since I became Magister of Conservatory.*

But why do you not play?

Mkel leaned his head tiredly against the back of his chair. *I am a Magister instead of a Singer,* he answered. He closed his eyes, and Theo looked at Mreen and put his finger to his lips. Mreen trotted to the door and took Cathrin's hand once again.

"Well, that's nice, isn't it," Cathrin said. "And now you'll bathe, and then we'll go to the dormitory, where there are nine other children just like you."

Mreen looked over her shoulder again. *Just like me, Cantor Theo?*

He winked at her. *There is no one just like you, Mreen.*

Will I see you again?

Of course. I promise.

Mkel opened his eyes to watch them leave, and when the door had closed behind them, he gave a heavy sigh.

"Are there only nine in the newest class, then, Magister?" Theo asked.

"Only nine. Ten, now, with your little one. We have been very worried . . . some think we should force all itinerants, by law, to send their children here for training. Had this been done before, you might have come to Conservatory as a child."

"But how could the itinerants be forced?"

"Lamdon could take away their privileges, their freedom, even deny them their homes. As you know, itinerants are always welcome, in all the Houses, fed and given beds as they need them. I hate the idea of denying them that. But I do not know what will happen to us all if the Gift does not return to us."

"Magister Mkel . . . Sira and I both believe that the Gift flourishes at Observatory because of the welcome it receives. You remember Trisa, do you not?"

"Yes, I remember her very well. She ran away from us, and Amric refused to send her back. They have paid a high price for that."

Theo rubbed the back of his neck, suddenly feeling very weary himself. He had not yet bathed; his muscles ached, and he was hungry.

"Do you know, Magister Mkel, Trisa is doing very well at Observatory. Her first *quirunha* was not brilliant, but it was nothing to be ashamed of. The three others are all showing every indication of a good strong Gift—"

"But they speak, surely?"

Theo laughed. "Indeed they do! They have to be reminded often to keep their lips closed and their minds open!" He sobered as he looked at the door through which Mreen had passed. "It is only Mreen who is this way," he said softly. "Her Gift is so strong, and so unusual . . . it must have some special purpose. We are convinced that only Conservatory can prepare her properly."

"Cantor Theo," Mkel said slowly. "How is Sira? In truth?"

Theo smiled at the older man, and opened his mind so that Mkel would understand fully. *Sira is well, and happy,* he sent. *She sends you her best regards.*

Has she forgiven me, then?

I am certain she would say there is nothing to forgive.

Mkel passed his hand over his eyes, a gesture so weary that Theo wanted to touch the man's hand, to clasp his shoulder as Cathrin did. He shielded his feelings of sympathy.

There is much for which I need forgiveness, I am afraid, Mkel sent. *She asked me for help, tried to explain. . . . I should have listened to her, heard her out. But it cannot be undone now. All I can do . . .* He, too, looked at the doorway where Mreen, wrapped in her cloud of light, had gone hand in hand with Cathrin. *I will do my best for the child. Isbel's child.*

That will be a great deal, Magister.

Perhaps.

A silence stretched between them, and Theo waited. After some moments Mkel shook himself. "Now," he said aloud, striving for a matter-of-fact tone. "Now you must bathe, and eat. I am sure you are tired."

"So I am," Theo agreed. The Magister's Houseman came forward, and Theo bowed to Mkel and took his leave.

The man led him down the stairs to the *ubanyor,* and as he always had, Theo admired Conservatory's spare elegance, its polished archways, its high ceilings and broad unadorned corridors. Strains of music floated through the House from the student wing. Theo smiled, remembering the envy those sounds had caused for him years before. Even now he knew he could never be one of the elite, one of the Conservatory-trained Cantors with their refined techniques and sophisticated musicality; but his Gift was fully realized, thanks to Sira, and he had no need to be jealous any longer.

As he sank into the hot water of the *ubanyor,* feeling the warmth caress his tired muscles, it came to him that Conservatory might be ready at last to hear Sira's message. It would mean change, and many would resist. But Mreen's very existence was powerful evidence that there could be another way, perhaps a better way.

Probably, he thought, Sira should have made this journey with Mreen, and I should have remained behind.

He stretched under the water, and dropped his head back to soak his hair. On the benches of the *ubanyor* were piles of thick towels, and sweet-smelling bars of soap filled the niches in the carved tub. Fresh linens waited, left by the Houseman, and a meal was even now being warmed for him in the kitchen.

It had been Sira's decision to stay at Observatory. She could have been the one to make this trip, certainly. He chuckled. At this moment, luxuriating in the comforts of Conservatory, he was glad she had not.

CHAPTER
TEN

Zakri and Berk rode as far into the twilight as they dared. They pushed their *hruss* until the beasts grumbled, but they kept them at the quick pace. It was their second night out from Soren, and they were well into Ogre Pass, their road now flat and broad, the familiar steep mountainsides rising to the east and west of them. Only when the men had begun to shiver dangerously did they stop to make their camp.

Zakri sat his *hruss,* and kept his *filla* inside his hood as he played, not letting his face or more than the tips of his fingers be exposed to the frigid evening air until the *quiru* bloomed about them and its warmth crept in through their furs.

Berk put back his hood to feel the heat on his grizzled cheeks, and took a grateful sniff of fresh air. He dismounted, grunting as he stretched stiff muscles. "It's almost too much for these old bones," he growled. "Any colder and they wouldn't move at all. But I doubt anyone from Soren would dare ride this late!"

"We took a bit of a chance," Zakri said. To the east he saw

Conservatory's star glinting above the horizon. "But Iban taught me a trick or two about quick *quiru*. And I believe you are right—no one will come after us now."

He looked up through the *quiru* to see the stars coming to life above the Continent. Shreds of flat cloud, luminescent in the reflected light of the snowpack, crept across the sky. "How long till the summer, do you think?" he mused.

Berk squatted with his saddle pack at hand, laying out softwood for the cookfire. He chuckled. "Are you going to be like the children, Cantor?" he said. "Asking how long? How long?"

Zakri laughed down at him. "So I am," he said. "How long?"

Berk struck the flint and stone and sat back on his heels as the little fire began to crackle. He squinted up into the night. "Let's see," he mused. "The deep cold passed—oh, a quarter of a year ago. And that leaves half a year, so—it should be a quarter of a year more before the Visitor shows up."

"Not soon enough," Zakri commented, soberly now.

"No," Berk agreed, "not for Soren." He sliced dried *caeru* meat into the cooking pot, and threw in a double handful of snow. "By then they'll have nothing to eat but meat."

"Yet the itinerants think they can keep the nursery gardens going on their own, with those overlapped *quiru* they waste so much energy on!"

Berk eyed Zakri. "That makes you angrier than anything else, I think."

Zakri shook himself, and let out a gusty breath. "No, not really, Berk. But it is insane—they have a Cantrix right there in the House, and they keep her locked in an attic! What is the point of that?"

"The point is that Cho fears her. You were able to shield yourself from his psi, and she might be strong enough to resist him, too. He's surrounded himself with people he knows he can control."

"And gotten rid of any others."

"Yes."

"But I still do not know what he did to Iban. Or how he

made it happen!" Zakri went to his *hruss,* as he had so often in his youth, for comfort. He leaned his forehead against the rough long hair, and pulled at the beast's ears. It rumbled and nudged him with its broad head.

Berk went on stirring the *keftet,* adding the green and yellow herbs, crumbling in bits of the salted fish Mura had sent along as a treat. Zakri unsaddled the *hruss,* and as he waited for the meal to be ready, he curried them both thoroughly, tired though he was. He had pushed aside his worry about Sook all day, but now, with the idleness of the night, it rose in him again. He dreaded his dreams.

"Come and eat, Cantor," Berk said. Zakri obeyed, coming to sit close to the fire, his rolled bedfurs at his back. Berk handed him a full bowl and a spoon, and they both made quick work of the meal, eating every scrap, and following the *keftet* with strong tea. When they were finished, and their bowls scrubbed with handfuls of snow, they sat watching the cookfire burn down and listening to the vast silence around them. The quiet was punctuated once by the long scream of a hunting *ferrel.* Zakri lifted his head when he heard it.

"That is strange," he said.

"What is?"

"Iban told me animals rarely hunt near the Pass. Too many humans travel through it, too often, and scare them off."

Berk snorted. "Cho's seen to that, though, hasn't he? No one's doing much traveling these days."

The silence stretched again, until Zakri asked, "What do you think Lamdon will do about it, Berk? What can they do?"

Berk stood up to unroll his bedfurs, looming over Zakri like one of the irontrees on the ridge above them. "I think it's a job for the senior Cantor," he said heavily, "although I doubt, in these times, they'll be able to pry him out of his nice warm House."

"By the Ship, Berk, one would think you did not approve of Lamdon!"

"I've been a courier a long time, Cantor Zakri—a

lifetime, as my bones are telling me tonight. And I've seen a lot. Sometimes I think Lamdon treats the Continent, and the Houses, like they were pieces in a game of knuckle and bone!"

His bedfurs were ready, but Berk stood looking out into the purple night as it folded down over the frosty white landscape.

"You know, there's an old story . . . it's not as if our Cho v'Soren was the first Gifted ever to go bad.

"Summers and summers ago, before my own father was even born, or his father . . . there was a Cantrix at Perl. The story goes that she was listening to everything around her, eavesdropping on the thoughts of anyone she pleased, and she got hold of some information—she found out the Housekeeper there was selling this and that for bits of metal, things that weren't his, and then there were other things, some secret of her senior's he didn't want known. Generally, she just caused a lot of trouble for everyone.

"In the end, the senior Cantor of Lamdon went to Perl and confronted her, disciplined her. He faced her right in her own Cantoris, and they had it out, psi and all. That's the part that people remember, the two of them going at it in the Cantoris, and things falling around them, the *quiru* disturbed and the other Gifted in the House hardly able to think for the noise."

"What happened to the Cantrix?"

Berk shrugged. "I expect she settled down and did her job! It used to be that the senior Cantor was a powerful presence on the Continent."

"But not now?"

"Well, now the Gift is in such short supply . . . everything seems different. Not since Cantrix Sharn made her tour of the Houses a few years ago have we seen any Cantor leave Lamdon's courtyard, to say nothing of the senior."

Zakri smoothed out his own bedfurs, and sat to pull off his heavy boots, sighing with pleasure as he wiggled his bare toes in the fresh air. "You know, Berk, it could be that even the senior Cantor is no match for Cho. His is a weird

Gift, a dark one, as if it is turned inside out, the opposite of what the Gift is meant to be. We use the Gift to build, or to create—but his talent is for destruction." Zakri leaned back on his elbows and stared up into the stars. "My own Gift could have been like that, if not for Cantrix Sira."

"But you would never have used it in that way," Berk said with confidence.

"No," Zakri said. He rolled into his bedfurs, and pillowed his head on his arm, looking up at the distant stars. "No, that would not be in my nature." Very softly, he added, "But I might have used it on myself."

"We at Amric thank the Spirit you did not, Cantor," Berk said warmly.

Zakri smiled at him, touched by the affection in his voice, and even more by Berk's faith. "Better thank Cantrix Sira, while you are at it."

"So I will, when I see her!"

Berk lay down in the soft pile of his furs, and drew them around him. Silence fell across the campsite, broken only by the panting of the *hruss* and the occasional rustle of a gentle breeze through the tops of the irontrees. It was a precious moment of peace that Zakri treasured before he fell asleep. It did not last. His dreams were terrible, fearful ones, with Sook suffering at the center of them. He woke in a sweat, tangled in his furs and breathing hard. But there was nothing at all he could do.

Zakri had been an itinerant, apprenticed to Iban, on his earlier visit to Lamdon. Even then he had been stunned by the profligate way in which they spent their Singer energies, the warmth which caused the House members to wear thin sleeveless tunics and the lightest of boots, and the rare, short-lived nursery flowers that were cut from their stems and set to languish briefly in *obis*-carved vases.

On this visit, he was greeted warily, as if the Housekeeper hardly knew how to regard him; he was certainly no longer an itinerant, but no one outside of Amric recognized him as full Cantor, either. Zakri tried not to laugh as he watched the Housekeeper struggle delicately with his status. He was assigned a Houseman and led to a room reserved for visiting Cantors, but otherwise the Housekeeper maintained an ambivalent stance. She avoided his title, and her bows were equivocal, neither deep nor shallow, not too brief, but not too long.

The senior Cantor of Lamdon had no doubts, however.

"Amric's courier tells me I must address you as Cantor," he said. They met for the first time in the Committee chamber, as the other Cantors and Committee members were gathering. The senior Cantor, Abram, bowed to Zakri in a way that implied both disdain and disapproval. He spoke aloud, as well, which Zakri knew was intended to be a deliberate insult.

"In truth," Abram proclaimed, "why should the House of Amric need three Cantors, and why should one of them be an itinerant? I fail to see it."

"Do you, Cantor Abram?" Zakri blinked innocently and leaned toward the older man. Abram was plump and dark, and considerably shorter than he. He smiled sweetly at him. "Shall I explain it to you, then? It is really quite a simple thing. . . ."

The man bristled like a *wezel* in the cold, but his response was interrupted by the arrival of Lamdon's Magister and his entourage of Housemen and women. Everyone around the large table rose and bowed. Berk winked at Zakri from his place near the Committee members, and Zakri grinned and gave him a cheerful wave. He knew Abram was watching him, but he was surprised when he felt the exploratory tickle in his mind. The senior Cantor was listening to his thoughts! It was unbelievably rude, an utter breach of courtesy. It was, in fact, the same offense Zakri himself practiced whenever he deemed it necessary.

Zakri turned the probe aside. He had no doubt that his shields were equal to those of any Conservatory-trained Singer . . . Sira had seen to that. But he wished he dared stretch out a playful finger of psi, perhaps tweak one of the flowers out of the elaborate arrangement in the center of the table, or flick all the *ferrel*-quill pens onto the floor. He knew Sira would have heard his thought, and she would have raised her long forefinger, warning him to discipline himself. The image made him chuckle, and Abram frowned harder.

"Are we amusing you?"

Zakri looked into the other man's eyes, and saw the anger and resentment that festered there. With insight born of his own miserable youth, he understood that Abram's feelings arose from his fear, and he felt a twinge of sympathy. "I remembered something funny, Cantor Abram," he murmured. "Nothing more."

"I find nothing amusing in the present crisis," Abram snapped.

"No, of course not," Zakri said mildly. He glanced at the other side of the table, and saw Berk shake his head. Zakri lifted one deprecating shoulder, and sat down in his chair with his hands folded before him, the very picture of a dignified and mature Cantor. Abram sat next to him, directly across from the Magister.

All of Lamdon's eight Singers were present; besides Abram, there were six Cantors and one Cantrix. The Committee members were also present, with a number of Housemen and women. It was an impressive gathering. Magister Gowan gave a formal greeting, and the Cantors and Committee members sat down with their servants standing behind them.

Zakri stared at Magister Gowan. He had never seen such a fat man, nor one so pale. Skin, hair, shining fingernails . . . he was white all over. His long hair was twisted into an intricate binding, and the skin of his neck spilled over in folds against the black fabric of his tunic. Even his eyes were light, the color of blue ice, and they were almost lost in the thick flesh of his face.

"The courier from Amric," the Magister began, "tells me there is a situation at Soren that must be addressed." He nodded to Berk. "Apparently a number of itinerants have gathered there, and are causing a good deal of mischief."

Zakri unfolded his hands abruptly, and they became fists on his knees. "Mischief?" he repeated in amazement.

"It can hardly be more than that, can it?" Cantor Abram

asked. He waved a dismissive hand. "They are only itinerants, after all."

Zakri drew breath to speak again, but Berk, sensing an explosion, spoke more quickly.

"You understand, Magister Gowan, that Cho is not an itinerant. He was a carver, who very nearly qualified for Conservatory—"

"Yes, yes, I remember that, Berk," the Magister interrupted him. As he nodded his head, the flesh of his neck rippled like the hide of a fat *caeru*. "Cantor Abram," he went on, "I do think we'll have to send a party to Soren. Sort this out as quickly as possible."

Abram shifted uneasily in his chair. He opened his mouth, but then closed it again without speaking.

"Beware, Magister," Berk said bluntly. "Cho's a dangerous man, and he's surrounded himself with itinerants who—"

"You needn't worry," Magister Gowan said. "I'm sure we can handle one rebellious carver."

Zakri could restrain himself no longer. "Do you realize," he demanded, "that Cho has killed several people, and rendered at least one mindless? That he imprisons the Cantrix of Soren in an attic?"

Magister Gowan's pale eyes flicked toward Zakri and then to Abram. "I'm sure the senior Cantor will have the situation well in hand before the summer comes. Won't you, Cantor?"

Abram's dark eyes moved to the Magister, to Zakri, and away again. His fear was as palpable to Zakri as if he had trembled, although he did not. He answered the Magister, "Of course." There were nods of approval around the group.

Zakri sent urgently to Abram, *Cantor, anyone who confronts Cho must have very strong shielding! You must be on your guard at every moment. His Gift is lethal, crude but very powerful, and he . . .*

Abram stiffened in his chair, and his face grew dark. Zakri realized that he was using anger to disguise his fear.

"Cantor Zakri," he snarled, with a nasty inflection on the title. "Were you not taught that you do not send to your seniors unless invited?" He held up his hands and addressed the entire gathering, his voice rising to shrillness. "This is what comes of allowing half-trained Singers to step into the Cantoris! We must take steps, see that this sort of corruption does not happen again."

"Cantor—" Berk began, but Abram ignored him.

"I urge the members of the Committee to take note, and when the present crisis is past, to seriously consider passing the laws we have proposed. That will settle the problem of the Gift and its training once and for all. Cantor Zakri, here"—again the emphasis on the title—"might possibly have become a very fine Cantor if he had had proper training. Conservatory training."

Zakri sighed and rolled his eyes. He stood up slowly, and put his fists on the table, leaning forward to look down at Abram.

"Zakri!" Berk implored, without effect.

"With all respect," Zakri said. "With all respect, Cantor . . ." He spoke the title lazily, drawing it out. "You know nothing of me or my work, or the need of the Cantoris in which I sing. But more to the point, you are completely ignorant of what is happening at Soren, and how serious it is!"

Abram leaped to his feet. "How dare you?" he hissed. "I am the senior Cantor of Nevya! How dare you speak to me so?" He turned to the group at large. "Do you see? Do you see the kind of thing we have to deal with? There is no respect anymore, no discipline!"

Berk stood then, too, and looked across the table from his great height. "Cantor Abram, Magister Gowan," he said. "Whatever you may think of our arrangements at Amric, Cantor Zakri's right. What's happening at Soren is bad, for both the House members there, and for all of us. They've got every itinerant on the Continent gathered there, willingly or unwillingly, and those they couldn't persuade to join them they've killed. Singer Iban, for example—"

Abram snapped, "An itinerant! Their shields are a mess, their control is sloppy. Have no doubt, Berk, we will send someone fully—" He glared at Zakri, and repeated the word. "Fully qualified."

Zakri folded his arms, and closed his mouth firmly. *And are you sure your shields are better, Cantor Abram?* he sent.

Of course they are, the Cantor answered.

Zakri's chin rose. *Then shield this.* His psi whipped out, a quick slash that separated the binding that restrained Abram's long hair. Abram gasped, feeling it snap apart. He reached back for it, but too late. His hair tumbled freely down his back, and the ruined binding fell to the floor.

How dare you? he sent, and his psi fluttered at Zakri, as if to answer in kind. Zakri parried it effortlessly.

Do you see, Cantor Abram? he sent. *When you go to meet Cho, you had better be ready!*

He broke the contact, and became aware that around him angry voices were raised, fists thumping on the table and chairs scraping as men leaned forward to shout at him and at each other. Berk was begging for calm, for rational thought. No one listened.

Zakri cast one scornful glance around the table, at the well-fed and elegant people who sat in judgment on the business of the Continent. Cantor Abram was trying to retie his hair, snapping at his Houseman, who was struggling to help him with the broken binding. Magister Gowan was barking commands that no one heard.

Zakri gave a short laugh. He would have better luck with the cooks at Soren, he thought. He turned his back and strode out of the Committee chamber, much as Sira had done years before. Only the faint, flashing glitter of the air showed where he had been standing, and soon it, too, faded.

CHAPTER
ELEVEN

✦ MREEN'S NIMBUS SPARKLED IN THE MORNING SUNLIGHT, setting her apart from her classmates. She glowed like a small sun among stars. Her hands expressed her every thought, and her eyes danced with them, making her a vivid, if silent, figure. The children around her were noisier, filling gaps in their sending with spoken words, but they would grow quieter and quieter as their skills grew.

Mreen felt Theo's gaze and turned to look across the great room, to find him where he sat with the Magister and Cathrin at the center table. *Is it today, Cantor Theo?*

It is, Mreen.

The light around her dimmed. She nodded solemnly.

I will miss you.

And I will miss you, Theo answered. He smiled at her. *We all will.*

But Cantrix Sira is waiting for you. And Yve and Jule and Arry.

Yes. So they are. Theo winked at Mreen, and then he rose from the table. "Cathrin," he said with a bow, "and Magister

Mkel. It is time once again to say farewell. I thank you for your hospitality these past days."

Cathrin had to help Mkel struggle to his feet, and the Housekeeper came to his aid, as well. Theo felt a painful twinge of premonition as he watched the Magister straighten, leaning heavily on the back of his chair. Mkel gestured to the Housekeeper, who in turn signaled a Houseman waiting by the doors of the great room.

"Cantor Theo," Mkel said. "It has been a pleasure having you here again, even for so brief a visit. And now there are some things we would like you to carry to Observatory for us." The Houseman stepped forward to lay several neatly wrapped packages on the table before Theo.

Cathrin smiled warmly at him, and rested her hand on one of the bundles. "Here are some seeds, and root cuttings from our own gardens," she said. "They're for plants you may not have at Observatory. And there are a few small things— clothes, and one or two toys, and three *filla*—for the children. For the Gifted ones you and Cantrix Sira are teaching."

It was like a benediction. In a way, it was Conservatory's formal blessing of Observatory's tiny school. Theo was overwhelmed with emotion, with thanksgiving; he thought of what these gifts would signify to Sira, the joy they would bring her, and he could have glowed like Mreen. He bowed again, deeply. "On behalf of my House, I thank you."

The Housekeeper added, "When you come again, Cantor, if you will bring a *pukuru,* we will send other things, the bigger things you need, rolls of cloth and cooking pots. Perhaps you could bring a list."

Mkel said, "In the meantime, with your permission . . ." He held out a small pouch for Theo to accept. "We understand how remote Observatory is, and how difficult it must be for your House members to buy what they need."

"Magister Mkel . . . this is very generous of you," Theo said. He lifted the little leather bag in his palm, appreciating its weight. "Magister Pol will be grateful."

What is that, Cantor Theo?

Mreen had crossed the great room and come to stand

beside him. She gazed with intensity at the leather pouch, and Theo put the bag in her hand.

Mreen's eyes went wide. She did not open the bag at first, but she stared up at Theo. *Oh,* she sent, *it is metal. Many little pieces!*

Yes, Mreen. This bag holds bits of metal for Observatory, to buy things like spoons and brushes, or perhaps a strong pukuru *to haul things up the mountain.*

Mreen opened the pouch and peered inside. She plunged in her hand, and pulled out one of the pieces, a shining black oblong that glittered in her small palm. She gave the bag back to Theo, and examined the bit of metal in her hand closely, turning it over and over, tracing with her short finger the mysterious marks that lay beneath its surface.

Theo smiled at Mkel and Cathrin. "Magister Mkel, you are most considerate, and Sira will be touched. There are many things—"

"Why, Theo, what is the matter with the child?" Cathrin exclaimed.

Theo looked down at Mreen to see that her eyes were glassy, fastened on some faraway point. The bit of metal was clutched in her fist, and the fist pressed to her cheek.

Mreen? Theo sent. *Mreen, what is it? What do you see?*

Now a small hand, Mreen's free hand, crept into his. *I am all right, Theo . . . but the pictures are wonderful! The hands, and now that I have seen the big metal, I see the stars, too, and the wind. . . . It is beautiful.*

It is not frightening this time?

Mreen sighed, and blinked, and turned her face up to Theo. *The piece is too small,* she sent pragmatically. *The big piece shows me more pictures.*

Mkel was staring at the two of them. *The big piece?*

Theo said aloud, for Cathrin's sake, "Observatory has a very strange . . . object, stowed away in a cupboard."

Mkel and Cathrin exchanged a glance. Mkel's expression was guarded as he looked back at Theo. *We will not speak of it aloud,* he sent carefully.

Theo stared at Mkel. He remembered Pol's words, on that day in his apartment when he had unwrapped the metal slab to show them. They know, Pol had said, they have always known.

"But—" Theo began aloud, and then caught himself. *But why?* he finished.

Tell me first why the child knows of it, Mkel sent carefully. *What does she mean when she talks of pictures?*

Theo still held Mreen's hand in his. He squeezed it gently. *Mreen, can you explain to the Magister?*

Mreen bit her lip, looking across the table at Magister Mkel. Around them, the morning meal went on, lively talk amid the clatter of ironwood dishes and cups. Cathrin stood close behind Mkel, forced to wait until he had the opportunity to explain to her what had happened. The Housekeeper also stood helplessly watching, and Morys had come up beside him.

Magister, I will show you, Mreen sent suddenly. She surprised everyone by ducking under the long table. She wriggled between the chairs, and Theo chuckled to see her emerge on the other side like a *caeru* pup darting among irontree suckers. Having found the quickest path to his side, she now stood very close to Mkel, holding out the bit of metal on her palm.

If I concentrate, I see pictures, she sent, looking up at him with solemn eyes. *Would you like to see them?*

Mkel, too, was smiling. He sat down again in his chair, his eyes on Mreen's earnest face, and he nodded. *Yes, Mreen, with your permission I will follow you.*

You should close your eyes, Mreen instructed, and Mkel obeyed. Mreen closed her hand over the metal, and put her other hand on Mkel's. Her eyelids did not close, but they wavered, half covering her eyes. Her expression grew distant and vague, like someone lost in thought, or in a dream. For some moments the two of them, the old man and the tiny girl, were isolated in silence, as Theo and Cathrin and the others watched and waited. After a time Mkel opened his eyes and blinked as if to clear his vision. Mreen gave his hand a little pat before she bent down to thread her way back under the table.

When she reappeared next to Theo, she returned the bit of

metal to him. *Thank you, Cantor Theo*. Blithely, she waved at Mkel and Cathrin, and scampered back across the great room to the table where her classmates sat finishing their meal.

Cathrin could bear it no longer. "Mkel, what is it? What was happening?"

Her mate shook his head heavily. "I hardly know how to tell you, my dear." He reached to take her hand, and held it as he spoke. "I have never seen such a Gift, nor heard of one."

"Mreen sees pictures, Cathrin," Theo said quietly. "Certain objects, when she touches them, seem to speak to her of those who have touched them before."

Morys, who knew of this phenomenon, swelled with pride at the rare talent Observatory had produced. The Housekeeper stood in silent amazement.

"And did you see the pictures, then, Mkel?"

Mkel sighed. "I did," he answered. "But only because she showed them to me."

Magister, Theo sent carefully. *Is it true, then, that Lamdon and Conservatory know of the big piece of metal?*

Mkel looked up at him thoughtfully. *It is something of an open secret, Cantor Theo. No one speaks of it, and some no longer believe in it.* He shrugged. *We do not know what it is, and we would not want other Houses to follow Observatory's strange customs . . . and so we have relegated it to one of those stories with no ending. Mostly because no one knows the ending.*

Slowly, Mkel rose from his chair. "Do you know, Cantor Theo," he said aloud, "I hope you have done the right thing, bringing Mreen to Conservatory. We are delighted to have her among us, but I wonder whether we know any more about how to train her Gift than you or Cantrix Sira."

"I think her Gift will find its own way," Theo said.

"If the Spirit wills," Mkel said softly. "But I wonder if Sira herself should not be teaching her."

"Sira thought she needed Conservatory," Theo repeated.

Mkel sighed and said sadly, "It would be best if she had both."

Cathrin looked across the great room. Mreen glowed among her friends, a tiny, smiling, haloed sprite. "Poor little thing," she murmured. "I'm afraid for her."

Premonition tingled in Theo once again. O Spirit, he prayed, keep her safe. Watch over Isbel's child.

It was all he could do. Even if he spent every moment guarding Mreen, he could not shield her from the strength, and the import, of her birthright.

The Gift had them all in its grasp, and they could only go where it sent them.

CHAPTER
TWELVE

★ "WE CAN RIDE NORTH, THROUGH FORGOTTEN PASS," Zakri suggested. "In this season, it should not be too cold, should it?"

He and Berk strolled together through Lamdon's long, hot corridors toward the stables. They planned to leave early the next morning, at first light. Zakri was sure he could wheedle some bread and fruit from the kitchen to take along, so they would not have to wait for the morning meal to be served in the great room.

"Forgotten Pass is always cold," Berk answered. His knowledge of the roads and passes was as thorough as any itinerant's. "But it will do. Windy Pass is easier, but it takes longer. I'd like to get home before my grandchildren grow up!"

They had decided to go straight to Amric. Zakri missed his Cantoris, and Berk wanted to report to Magister Edrus. Zakri wished he could put the whole mess of Soren behind him; he tried to believe that because they had turned the situation over to Lamdon, to authority, he could be finished with Cho v'Soren and his rebels.

But he still had no answers about Iban. And, worse, Sook still worried his dreams. In his latest, she had been calling to him, crying out for help. She teetered on the brink of a precipice, with no one to catch her. He had tried to go to her, slipping and skidding across slick ice, and had found Cho standing in his way, a thin dark figure with glittering eyes that seemed to grow taller as he struggled to approach. Zakri woke in a fiery sweat of fury and frustration, his legs aching from straining against the furs of his bed.

When they reached the stables, Zakri led the way in, turning left toward the loose box where they had left their *hruss*.

The stables were alive with noise and bustle. People, stablemen and Housemen, were calling orders and questions to each other, and handing gear back and forth, bridles and harness and saddle packs. In one corner several Housemen were packing a large *pukuru*.

Six *hruss* were being curried and fitted with saddles, and a seventh with harness for the *pukuru*. An enormous pile of bedfurs blocked the door, with the Housekeeper herself frowning over the stack. Pointing to one of the bedfurs, she made a Housewoman pull it out and unroll it to check its thickness. Then she gave instructions as the woman redid the roll and tied it.

Two of Lamdon's Singers stood against the far wall, watching the proceedings. Their faces were carefully blank, but even without hearing their thoughts, Zakri felt their unease. They were both young. Cantrix Jana, Zakri knew, had been a classmate of Sira's, and Cantor Izak appeared to be no more than a summer older than she. Zakri himself, of course, was even younger, but he thought of himself as aged by experience.

Zakri and Berk sidled past the clutter and made their way to the loose box. Berk pulled open its half gate and Zakri went in to pull the *hruss*'s ears and stroke their shaggy necks. He picked up their feet, one by one, and inspected their wide hooves. While he occupied his hands, he listened.

Izak, do you know anything about traveling? I do not even know how to get there! This was Cantrix Jana, standing with her hands folded tightly together. Her features were rigid and unreadable, as if carved of ice. Izak affected a fierce look of concentration as he surveyed the preparations.

Nor do I, but we will have four experienced travelers with us. He answered bravely, but Zakri knew it took effort.

But no itinerants? Not even one?

Jana, there is not one in the House—it is as the Singer from Amric said. All the itinerants have been gathered at Soren.

But what will we be able to do, you and I?

We will have to do as Cantor Abram says—reason with them, but shield ourselves carefully. Strongly. We will have Magister Gowan's courier with us, and he is experienced in this sort of negotiation. The main thing is to get their Cantrix back in the Cantoris where she belongs, and to help her establish the quiru.

Jana was silent then, watching the bedfurs and packs being tied to the saddles. The *hruss* were put in their stalls, the saddles laid in a neat row before them, ready for the morning.

Zakri whispered to Berk, "They are sending their youngest and least experienced Cantors," he said. "And both are scared to death."

"So they should be," Berk muttered. He leaned on the stable door, ostensibly supervising Zakri's work, but casting a skeptical eye on the hubbub behind him.

"These two know nothing of travel, and even less of Cho and what he is capable of," Zakri said softly. "Ship and Stars! It is like offering newborn *caeru* up for the *ferrel* to find. They will not last a day at Soren."

A long moment passed. Zakri sighed heavily, thinking, and Berk met his eyes. "It's your decision, Cantor," he said. "I'm only the courier here."

Zakri leaned wearily against the nearest *hruss,* and closed his eyes for a moment. He thought of his Cantoris, of Cantor Gavn coping with Cantor Ovan. He thought of his dream of Sook calling to him, begging for help. And always, underlying everything, was the vivid image of Iban, dead in his arms. There was really no choice in the matter, and he knew it.

"We will have to follow them," he said. "Amric will have to wait a bit longer."

"It will still be there," Berk said calmly. "Although my mate won't recognize me when I finally make it home."

Zakri managed a tired chuckle. "Are you sure she has noticed your absence?"

Berk laughed. "You make a good point, Cantor Zakri. In any case, the Spirit has me by the ear, and it hurts too much to tug it free."

"Let us keep our plans to ourselves, though," Zakri said. "I doubt Lamdon's courier wants us along. Although—" He was quiet for a moment, listening again. "Although I have no doubt that a certain Cantor and Cantrix would be much relieved to have our company."

"Perhaps you could ease their minds a bit, just tell them we're not far behind."

Zakri thought about that for a moment. He picked up the currycomb, and began working tangles out of his *hruss*'s thick coat, and as he did so he dared a stronger probe. Gently, so as not to be detected, he tested the minds of the two Singers, just a brief touching that gave him a sense of their natures, their characters. It was done deftly, subtly, and he flattered himself that even the great Cantrix Sira—had she been able to bring herself to try it—could not have done it more smoothly.

He shook his head. "I think it is best I do not," he said. "They are both—naive, I think is the best word. They are unused to keeping secrets, and even less to having to shield themselves at every moment. They are frightened, but perhaps that will save them."

"Perhaps," Berk said. He looked over his shoulder at the young man and woman standing stiff and silent amid the commotion. "But perhaps not."

Since there was only one route from Lamdon to Soren, the same Zakri and Berk had ridden only days before, it was easy to follow the Lamdon party without being seen. There was no fear of being left behind. Zakri and Berk watched the elaborate farewell ceremony for Cantrix Jana and Cantor Izak from the window seats in the great room. They would make their own departure, without formalities, an hour later.

The Magister's white hair shone brilliantly in the morning sun. Clouds waited on the western horizon, and Zakri knew they would stretch across the sky by noon, and was glad; he wondered if anyone had warned Jana and Izak they should protect their faces and their hands. Their skin was soft and pale as only the skin of those who spent all their lives within doors could be. Behind Jana and Izak four other riders waited, and an extra *hruss* was harnessed to the large *pukuru*. The bone runners of the sled pressed deeply into the snow, weighed down by the heavy load.

As the Magister, and the senior Cantor, gave short speeches, Zakri watched how the Cantrix shrank back into her furs, hiding her fear, and how Cantor Izak sat straight, imitating courage if not able to feel it. Zakri admired his nerve; it could not be easy for Izak, as it had not been for his own junior, Gavn, to face uncertainty after years of Conservatory, where every step was planned, every decision dictated by tradition.

The ceremony went on too long, wasting daylight, making Zakri fidget and groan. He wanted to do something to hurry things along, tweak a *hruss* tail or tug on a rein.

"Never mind, Cantor," Berk muttered to him. "One more day won't make that much difference."

But Zakri's dreams had been haunted again the night before. Now the decision had been made, he longed to be off, to hurry to Soren to face down the danger, to prove to himself that Sook was safe. But their progress would be limited by the speed of Lamdon's party, and it did not look as if it would be an efficient trip. The *pukuru* alone would force them to a slower pace.

He sighed, restraining himself; it would be so easy to spank the nearest *hruss,* just a light slap of psi to hurry things along, get them all moving. But then, he supposed it would be like trying to hurry the Glacier in its slow progress across the Continent. He said to Berk, "I hope you are right," and strove to be patient.

It was harder even than they had expected to match their pace to that of the Lamdon party. The first night, they almost rode right into Lamdon's camp. With still an hour of light left, Jana and Izak and their Housemen had made their camp right in the middle of the broad road of Ogre Pass. Someone had created an enormous *quiru,* the largest Zakri had ever seen out of doors. Its light extended far beyond the perimeter of their camp, almost reaching from one side of the Pass to the other, and stretched up past the irontrees on the slope, its outer edge paling from yellow to a faint green against the early twilight. A large cooking fire blazed, tended by one of the Housemen. Only the size of the *quiru* warned Berk and Zakri; they saw it above the irontrees, and backtracked until they were certain their own more modest *quiru* would not be visible.

"At this rate, it will be summer before we get there," Zakri fumed.

Berk chuckled. "Perhaps we should just ride right up and join them, then," he said.

Zakri bit his lip, thinking. "Do you think perhaps we should?" he asked.

Berk shook his head. "No, I don't," he answered firmly. "I think a party of that size will have Cho and his Singers on the attack all too soon. They will lose the opportunity to negotiate, and you and I will be easy targets." He gave a short laugh as he pulled softwood out of his saddle pack. "I doubt we're Cho's favorite people just now!"

The night seemed interminable. They had been forced to stop at least an hour too early, and they could not break camp until Lamdon left theirs; it felt to Zakri like mid-morning when he finally mounted his *hruss.* Until then there was nothing to do but watch. He sat on a huge irontree sucker, his back against the trunk of its great parent tree. He was shielded by enormous boughs that drooped under their burden of snow. The Lamdon travelers rolled and stowed their bedfurs, laboriously refilled their saddle packs, which they had for some reason completely emptied the night before, and at length, at last, saddled their *hruss* and departed. Zakri tried to listen, but at such a distance, he heard only fragments of thought. Sira, he knew very well, could have heard everything, and she could have sent to them as well, as effortlessly as if they were in the next room. He grinned, thinking how good Sira was at eavesdropping, when she had had so little practice; he himself should have been the expert!

The trip south to Soren took half again as long as Zakri and Berk had spent riding north. Their *hruss* grew lazy and lethargic, ambling through Ogre Pass, resting too long at night. Snow fell, the fat slow flakes of very late winter, and the heavy clouds only parted in the early mornings. For most of the day the landscape was a dull, monotonous gray. Zakri was still anxious about Sook, and he worried about his Cantoris, but mostly he was bored and restive. He itched for action, and he managed to blame Cho for the tedium of this slow journey. In his mind, he planned a hundred maneuvers against his enemy, but every scenario he devised ended the same way: his own strength against Cho's. Even in his imagination, he shied away from that. He had serious doubts of his ability to deal with Cho alone. But he had even less confidence in the strength of Cantrix Jana or Cantor Izak against Carver Cho.

On the night before they would finally leave the Pass, Zakri asked Berk, "Do you think they will find the right turning to Soren?"

"So I do," was Berk's answer. "I know Bran—he's Lamdon's courier. I'm sure this slow pace is not his choice! He's traveled as much as I have—we're of an age, I think."

"And what age would that be, Berk?" Zakri asked.

Berk combed his beard with his fingers and looked past the *quiru,* where the irontrees loomed behind veils of drifting snowflakes. "I served our Magister's father," he said thoughtfully, "for five summers. I've served his son for two. I was almost five summers when I became courier for Amric—and I believe all of that gives me twelve summers." He raised his eyebrows and laughed aloud. "That makes me sixty years old, give or take a year! Six Stars, but that's a great number!"

"Berk, I will ask the Spirit to make me just like you when I have twelve summers," Zakri said sincerely. "You are all that is fine and strong in a Houseman."

Berk inclined his head to Zakri. "You're kind," he said. "But it's not hard to serve well when the House is Amric."

"That is true," Zakri agreed. "It is a fine House, with a fine Magister. It will be good to go home again."

A silence fell between them as they each thought of Amric and their own concerns there. Zakri had surprised himself by speaking the truth—he had come to regard Amric as home. He had been without a home for too many years; then, when Sira had come for him, home had been wherever she and Iban were. But now, truly, he felt as if he belonged at Amric. Odd that he should come to understand that only when he was at such a distance from it.

When he rolled into his bedfurs that night, Zakri prayed to the Spirit that he might go home again, in time . . . once it was all over, with Cho defeated, Sook safe, and Iban avenged. In the back of his mind, very far back, behind a door he dared not open, there lurked a fear as dark as the shadowed trees around their camp. If Cho were to win, then he, Zakri, would be the defeated one. That could mean only death. He had hoped to hand over this duty to Lamdon, but the Spirit had other plans. He had no choice but to follow this through to the end, whatever that might be.

But he kept the thought shut away, hidden from his conscious mind. He had to put his trust in the Spirit, and in the Gift. He would waste no energy in being afraid.

Soon they would be riding down the road to Soren. Even the Lamdon party could not stretch out the last bit of road past two days. The two Cantors from Lamdon would ride right into the heart of danger, and Cantor Zakri v'Amric would be as close behind them as he dared.

CHAPTER
THIRTEEN

ZAKRI AND BERK WATCHED FROM BEHIND A TOWERING boulder on the hill above Soren as the Lamdon travelers took up a position in front of the house, just beyond its cobbled courtyard. Izak and Jana played their *filla* together, seated side by side on stools, as formally as if they were in their own Cantoris. Their *quiru* bloomed high and wide, its light spilling over the cobblestones and the trampled snow beyond, a circle that shone brilliantly against the grayness of late winter. It was as unblemished and steady as the walls of Conservatory itself, and the ragged *quiru* that was all Soren had wavered and trembled, looking abashed by its neighbor's perfection.

The Lamdon Housemen busied themselves with the bedfurs and cooking pots and saddle packs. They unloaded rugs and mats to set them on. Even a small table emerged from the *pukuru,* and when all these things were arranged there was still room to spare in the *quiru.* The campsite looked like the inside of an upper-level apartment.

The courier Bran bowed to the two Singers and walked

slowly up across the courtyard to the double doors of Soren. They opened immediately to admit him.

Zakri could hear nothing; he was too far away. But he and Berk could see faces in Soren's windows, faces that changed as the House members took turns peering out at the great *quiru* and the people inside it.

"I'd have thought Bran was wiser than that," Berk grumbled.

"Yes, I wish they had done something different, but they still do not understand," Zakri answered gloomily. He pulled his furs tighter against the cold. "All that display only makes Cho's point."

The hour of the *quirunha* came while they still huddled beneath the great rock. Soren's *quiru* grew marginally brighter, but it was no less ragged. Cantor Izak and Cantrix Jana sat stiffly on their stools, waiting. Their own sphere of light glowed with unwavering warmth around them and the Housemen standing nearby.

"I think we had better get closer," Zakri said. "I can hear nothing, and I doubt I can do anything at this distance. I fear that—"

The double doors to Soren opened once again. Bran came out and crossed the courtyard to go into the *quiru,* where he bowed once again and stood talking for a moment. Cantor Izak rose and stepped out of the *quiru* then, his back very straight, and crossed the courtyard with the courier at his heels. Cantrix Jana stood to watch them go. When the doors closed behind Izak she stayed where she was, a solitary figure.

Zakri and Berk mounted their *hruss* and hurried down the last distance into the valley. As he rode, Zakri stretched his mind outward, trying to hear something, anything. The difficulty of it surprised him. He had suffered terribly from the random thoughts and feelings of others, and had worked hard building shields to protect himself. Now when he needed to be open, his every instinct rebelled. He felt exposed and vulnerable, but he persisted, refusing to let his shields spring up. The lack of them was a sensation of chill against his forehead, as if he had forgotten to pull his hood around his face. As they rode closer, fragments of thought reached him, but nothing from Cantor Izak, nor from Cho's brutish Gift. Perhaps he had been wrong, and Lamdon truly did know how to negotiate with a rebellious carver!

"Do you see those trees, just to the north of their camp?" Zakri asked. "That might be close enough."

Berk grunted assent, and they turned their *hruss*.

The Southern Timberlands were named for their thickly forested hills. Away from the traveled road, the irontrees grew closely together in tangled, impenetrable groves that blocked their passage. Suckers swelled in great woody coils above the ground, too high for the *hruss* to step over. They were forced to turn and backtrack again and again.

It took too long, but they finally reached the spot Zakri had chosen. He dismounted and leaned against the trunk of the nearest irontree to close his eyes and concentrate. He cast about, sampling the fragments of thought that reached him, but with caution. Cantrix Elnor had said that Cho was capable of hearing thoughts if they were very strong. Zakri did not want to be detected before he knew what was happening inside the House. Behind him Berk stood quietly, holding the *hruss* reins.

Zakri whispered, "Cantrix Elnor is still there, she is sending to Izak! He is answering her, but I am afraid—it is too loud—Izak is not used to shielding—" He fell silent, straining to hear.

"What is it?" Berk asked softly.

"I do not know. It broke off." Zakri straightened, his eyes fixed on the House as if he could see through its stone walls. Sook was in there, somewhere.

The doors opened, and Cantor Izak walked away across the courtyard, his steps deliberate, neither quick nor slow. He was alone. Jana came to the edge of their *quiru* to meet him, and he lifted his hand to her as he approached. There was something in his hand, some small object that flashed briefly in the sun. Behind him, a tall, dark figure appeared in the doorway, flanked by two shorter ones.

Zakri threw up his shields immediately, and expanded them, trying to put them between Izak and that dark figure.

He drew an enormous breath and clenched his fists, throwing all the strength he had into an extended barrier, knowing it would be thin and fragile, but hoping at least to dilute what was coming, to weaken it, trying with all his might to reach past the limit of his power. . . .

Izak fell at the edge of the cobblestones, just short of the Lamdon *quiru*. He crumpled as if the impulses that connected mind and body simply ceased to be, all at once. His body lay sprawled in an ungainly position, his legs at a ghastly angle, awkward, wrong. He did not move.

Zakri heard the cries of Cantrix Elnor in his mind, *Cantor! Cantor Izak, are you all right? O Spirit* . . . And then Jana was crying out, too, silently.

Izak! Izak! Send something . . . oh, who will help us?

Zakri ran. His fur boots slipped in the snow as he raced toward the Lamdon *quiru,* propelled by Jana's desperation. He felt, at the edges of his mind, the darkness that was Cho, and he drew in his shields around himself, thickening and strengthening them. The calls of the other Singers were shut out, but it was necessary.

He parried Cho's battering strikes even as he ran toward the camp. Jana, unprepared, reeled and fell to her knees, clutching her head between her hands. Zakri called out aloud to her.

"Shield yourself! Cantrix, close your mind, or he will injure you!"

The face she turned to him was ashen and distorted with fear and shock. She recognized him, though, he could see that, and he felt her shields go up in a firm, Conservatory-trained wall, a thin, brittle barrier. Cho's waves of angry energy skittered away from it like drops of water on a hot stone. He nodded to her.

"Yes! Keep it up!" He ran to Izak, and knelt beside him.

Between the open doors of Soren, Cho raised his long arms, his hands in claws, his face dark and furious. The two itinerants beside him each took a step back, forced away by his rage.

Behind Zakri Jana cried out. Cho's brute force was too much for her.

Her sobs made Zakri grit his teeth. Cho's eyes glittered from the shadows of the House, and Zakri let the cold flame of his own anger burn high. The distance across the courtyard seemed to shrink to nothing as he gathered his resources for a furious, reckless wave of psi. Cho staggered slightly under its impact, and Zakri grinned fiercely, showing his teeth. For the moment he did not feel like Cantor Zakri; he felt like Zakri the hunter, like a *tkir* or a *ferrel* with his blood high and his prey in sight.

He was tempted to throw caution aside, to indulge in the savage joy of open battle. He could strike again, could try for the weakness in Cho's defenses, without regard for the consequences. It would be a relief, a blessed release from the tension, to pit his own strength against the carver's without a thought for the risk, for what might come later. His psi flexed within him like a muscle craving exercise.

It was the sound of Jana crying, a woman's tears, that held him back; Sook might be weeping, also, in that cursed House.

Cho's kinetic abilities were strong, stronger even than Zakri's. A lifetime of wielding an *obis* knife had honed and strengthened them, and he was unrestrained by any integrity, any empathy. His response to Zakri's attack was a vicious, lethal swamping of psi that cut off even Jana's sobs. Zakri was saved from Izak's fate only by those shields he had worked so hard to develop.

Zakri felt as if he and Cho were two *hruss* butting their heads together, kicking with their great hooves, biting, striving for domination. Neither would go down. The struggle could drain away the last drop of life from both combatants if one of them did not surrender.

And abruptly, as if he realized exactly that, Cho ceased his attack.

Zakri sat back on his heels by the fallen Cantor's head. He trembled, and his tunic was soaked with sweat under his furs. How close, he wondered, had he been to breaking? In his fury, he had lost his sense of vulnerability. Now, when it had ceased, he was appalled at the risk he had been ready to take.

Cho recovered quickly. His itinerants had disappeared, unable to bear the proximity of the psi battle, but Cho leaned casually against the doorjamb, a sardonic figure, fingering his narrow braid. He contrived to look as if their struggle had been only a game, an amusement, something to while away a dull afternoon.

"Singer," he called. "Welcome back." His light, high-pitched voice carried clearly across the stones of the courtyard.

Zakri thought irrelevantly that Cho might have made a good Singer after all. It would have been better for them all if he had. He bent to lift Izak's body from the cobblestones.

"Leave him there!" Cho commanded. His psi, dark and ominous, began to gather again, like thunderheads rising, threatening a storm.

Zakri paused with his hands under Izak's shoulders. "If I leave him, he will die in the cold," he snapped at Cho. "How will that help your cause?"

"He is dead anyway," Cho said in an offhanded manner.

Cantrix Jana gasped, and sent, *Izak! Izak?*

Zakri looked down at the unconscious Cantor. The breath still moved in his chest, and a pulse throbbed in his forehead. He still held the little object in his hand, and Zakri saw now that it was a bit of carving, a small ironwood panel of some kind. "He is not dead," Zakri told Cho.

But when Zakri tried to lift Izak, Cho attacked again, and he needed all his energy, both mental and physical, to protect himself. He lowered Izak gently to the cobblestones. Even then, because his strength was divided, Zakri felt shaky and sick from the effects of Cho's psi. He turned to face Cho one more time.

Taking a deep breath, Zakri concentrated everything he had, or hoped he had, into one blow, a sharply focused blast of psi that would have devasted any Singer. Cho dropped the offensive, and there was a sudden, and shocking, mental silence. Zakri felt dizzy and weak with exhaustion, and took satisfaction in assuring himself Cho felt the same. They were at an impasse.

"I will not leave him here," he said when some of his strength returned.

Cho laughed, and lifted his narrow head to look down his nose. "I always leave an example behind me," he snarled. "That way the next one thinks twice before crossing me."

Izak groaned, and moved slightly, but from his mind there was nothing. Zakri got slowly to his feet and went into the *quiru* to stand before Cantrix Jana.

We must do this together, he sent. Her eyes were wide with fear, but she met his gaze steadily. *Together we can make a shield strong enough, I think, and then I will bring Izak here, where he will at least be warm.*

He cast a quick glance at the sky. Twilight was not far off, and the deep cold right behind it. Even now Izak was in danger of freezing. Zakri knew all too well what would happen if he lay too long on those icy stones.

Tell me what to do, Jana sent.

Join your shields with mine, he told her. *Follow me closely, and we will combine our strength.*

He meant only that they should combine their psi, but when he returned to Izak's side, and bent to lift the fallen Singer, the Cantrix followed him, putting her hands under Izak's shoulders to help support his weight.

Cho stood with his head tilted back against the doorjamb, as if nothing that happened were of any concern to him. But when they lifted Izak between them, the cutting edge of his psi sliced at them. It was a different attack from the brute, undirected blows they had felt before. It was as precise a strike, Zakri was sure, as Cho was capable of, and it was as lethal as the highly honed blade of an *obis* knife.

Jana sucked in her breath, but she held. *I am here,* she sent to Zakri, and he felt the polished discipline of Conservatory in her effort. Her skills were born of years of training and unrelenting practice, and despite her fear, for herself and for Izak, the refined precision of her shielding, added to his own, made them doubly strong. And, thank the Spirit, Cho was weakened and tired. They turned aside the attack, and together they raised Izak upright. The injured Singer's feet shuffled and stumbled, seeking purchase on the cold stones. He still gripped the bit of ironwood tightly, mindlessly. It seemed only the muscles of that hand were still fully in his control.

Supporting the Cantor between them, they backed away from the courtyard and over the much-trampled snow to the camp. Inside the *quiru* the Housemen hovered about them, unwilling to touch one of the Gifted, but not wanting Izak to fall again. Zakri and Jana stretched him gently on a pallet of bedfurs, where he lay with his head falling back, his legs nerveless. He was safe, at least for the moment. Zakri looked back at the House.

Cho called, "He will not thank you. He will wish you had left him to die!"

Jana had been bending over Izak, covering him, pillowing his head. Now she came to stand beside Zakri. *What does that man want?* she sent. *And what has he done to Izak?*

Cho turned and stalked into the hall behind him. He did not touch the great double doors, but they slammed shut behind him with a great crash that made everyone jump.

He did that, Zakri sent to Jana. *He did that to Izak's mind.*

O Spirit, she sent shakily. *Will he recover? He will not die, will he?*

Zakri wished he could reassure her. *I do not know, Cantrix,* he answered. *I will do what I can, and you must, too. But I do not know.*

Damn Cantor Abram! she exclaimed unexpectedly.

Zakri raised his eyebrows, looking down at her.

He sent us because he was afraid to come himself, she sent. *I know it as surely as I know anything. If Izak does not recover, I will denounce him!*

Is that such a strong punishment? Zakri asked.

Jana went back to Izak's pallet and knelt beside him. *For a Cantor, it is the only punishment,* she sent slowly. *And for the senior Cantor of Lamdon . . . well, perhaps not. But it is all we have.*

Zakri sank down on Izak's other side, and he pulled his *filla* out of his tunic. *For now,* he sent, *let us see if we can help Cantor Izak.*

Jana brought out her own *filla* and prepared to follow Zakri. Exhausted as he was, he smiled at her.

I think your senior Cantor would be surprised by the courage of his junior Cantrix.

She answered with a lift of her chin. *I thank you. I know he would be surprised by Amric's Cantor! I can hardly wait to tell him.*

Berk joined the Lamdon camp before dark. He turned their two *hruss* in with the other beasts just as the last light was fading to the west, the sky shading from violet to purple. The Housemen cooked and served a generous meal of *keftet*, dried fruit, nutbread, and tea, while the House members of Soren crowded the windows to watch. Zakri and Jana worked over Izak for an hour, then rested, ate, and worked again.

Dark came, and with it the bite of cold beyond the *quiru*. Zakri and Jana lay down on their bedfurs, too exhausted to do more. The Housemen were preparing to sleep when a sound from the House brought them all to their feet.

The big doors opened, which was in itself a shocking thing in the hours of the night. There was a moment of suspense before Bran, the courier, stumbled into their sight, staggering as if he had been pushed.

No doubt, Zakri thought, he had been pushed. No Nevyan fully in his right mind willingly leaves House or *quiru* after dark. The courier caught his balance, and looked back at the House as if hoping for a change of heart.

"Bran!" Berk called. "We're here, man!"

Bran whirled to see that the camp *quiru* was intact, and he hurried across the courtyard to rush into its warmth and light.

"Thank the Spirit!" he breathed as he stepped inside. "They would have left me out here to die, without a thought!"

He looked down at Izak, who lay pale and unmoving as if his spirit had already gone beyond the stars. Bran recognized Zakri, and bowed briefly. "Is he dead?" he blurted.

Zakri and Jana exchanged a glance.

"He is not dead," Jana said, "but he would have been had Cantor Zakri not been here. He extended his own shields, risking himself, and because of that, Cantor Izak may recover the full use of his mind. Without Cantor Zakri's aid, Cantor Izak would surely have died, and most probably I would, too."

She did not go on, but the Housemen and Bran looked at each other, wide-eyed. The deaths of their Singers meant the deaths of them all. Bran rubbed his eyes, and then he collapsed on a nearby stool.

"I could not persuade them," he said wearily. "There were no negotiations, only a list of demands."

"What are they? Who gave them to you?" Jana asked.

"They want food, clothes, other supplies—even metal. They want higher pay for itinerants, more privileges. As for who made the demands—" His face was bleak as he looked up at the group. "They have no Magister. This carver, this Cho—he acts as Magister, and claims their own Magister came to Lamdon, but of course we never saw him there. And Cho says he now speaks for every itinerant on the Continent."

"We've already told you all of this," Berk said roughly. "Why did it take Cantor Izak being hurt to make the Committee listen?"

Bran shook his head and shrugged. A Houseman began stoking up the cookfire to make tea, and Bran watched him for a moment before he spoke.

"Our Magister has never been outside the doors of Lamdon in his life, nor has our senior Cantor, since he came there. They—to be honest, I, too—had no idea that such evil was possible, that anyone would use the Gift this way!"

"And why, why would he do it?" Jana cried.

"Cho was tested for Conservatory, years ago," Zakri told her. "He failed his testing, and I believe he has never forgotten. And he has gathered other malcontents around him, Singers who are willing to hurt anyone in their path."

"I wonder that he failed," Jana said slowly. "His Gift must be very strong."

"Strength is not the only criterion, though, is it?" Zakri answered, Zakri who had never been tested except during Sira's rigorous training of him. "There is the question of discipline, of control, of character. Someone must have sensed that Cho would never make a Cantor. But such power—By the Ship! Surely it could have been channeled somehow."

"And now what? How do we fight him?"

It was the question no one wanted to ask. It echoed in every mind, but received no answer.

The cookfire blazed, and tea was made. When Bran had been served a restorative cup, each of them took one, and they sat on into the night, watching the stars, waiting for the dawn. Sometime mid-night, Jana lay down to sleep while Zakri kept watch over Izak.

Berk lay down as well, and the Housemen rolled into their bedfurs. Only Bran sat up with Zakri, too agitated by the events of the day, and his own failure, to sleep. When the others had closed their eyes, Zakri asked him quietly, "Did you see a girl in the House, a young woman with great dark eyes and black hair? Her name is Sook."

Bran turned slowly to look at Zakri. "Is she a friend of yours, Cantor?"

Tension closed Zakri's throat, and he only nodded.

Bran sighed. "He keeps her in his apartment," he said heavily. He did not explain who he meant, but Zakri understood all too well. "I saw her once."

"Is she all right?"

"I don't know," was the answer. "She never spoke."

"Did you hear any word of Cantrix Elnor?"

The courier shook his head.

There was nothing more to say. Bran bent forward, his elbows on his knees, his face in his hands. He didn't look up to see the flashing of the air around Cantor Zakri, the fury that sparked and burned. Zakri sat on through the night, close by the injured man, his hands clenched into fists and his mouth a bitter line.

CHAPTER
FOURTEEN

★ Mreen and her class listened as Maestro Nikei played a short study in the third mode, *Doryu*. It was only an exercise, but Nikei's technique was limpid, perfect; he played as if support and intonation and tempo were as effortless as the breath he took to begin. Mreen wriggled in her chair with the sheer pleasure of it. The teacher played it twice through, and then each of the students attempted it in their turn.

Mreen barely waited for the boy next to her to finish before she put her own *filla* to her lips. The pattern was as clear in her mind as if she had always known it. The notes swirled in precise and graceful shapes, organized by the rhythm into a sharply defined pattern. She repeated the exercise exactly. Maestro Nikei smiled at her when she was done, but he spoke only to the others, pointing out their errors, asking them to try again.

Mreen's nimbus clouded about her, and she kicked her feet against the legs of her chair until the teacher turned to her.

Mreen, why are you angry?

I played the study perfectly!

Nikei folded his arms and regarded her calmly. *Yes, you did.*

But you did not say so!

Why should I point out what you already know?

Mreen's mouth opened in surprise. Someone giggled and she snapped her mouth shut and glared at him. *Be quiet, Palo,* she sent. *You cannot even play the first-mode studies yet!*

Palo wailed, "That's not fair! Maestro—"

Nikei sighed. *Palo, please do not speak aloud in class. Send your thoughts.*

But she— the boy began.

The teacher held up his hand. *Enough,* he sent sternly. *Mreen, please go to the third practice room, with your* filla, *and wait for me there.*

Mreen was indignant. *Why?* She jumped to her feet, and stood looking up at Nikei with her hands on her hips.

He was not a tall man, but she was small. Nikei's mouth pursed as he looked down at her, making deep grooves in his face. Mreen was sure he had at least twelve summers, maybe thirteen. His hair was gray, and the skin around his eyes and mouth was wrinkled and thin. But his voice, and his music, were as fresh as new snow.

Mreen, he sent clearly, *do as I ask. Now.*

All the children could feel Nikei's temper rising, although no telltale shimmers appeared around him. His control, of course, was absolute. Mreen hung her head in humiliation as she left the classroom. Her feet dragged, and she wandered slowly down the hall to the practice room. Behind her she heard Palo trying the *Doryu* study once again, missing half the notes and making a mess of the rhythm. Mreen stamped her foot in frustration. She gave the practice-room door an angry bang when she went in.

She stood with her back to the wall, her *filla* dangling in her fingers. They were all so slow, so stupid! It was boring—boring!—waiting for everyone else to catch up.

She nursed those thoughts, building up a good case of temper, planning revenges on Palo that she knew she would never complete. After a time that, too, got boring. Then she turned around and around in the practice room, looking for something to do.

There was nothing, of course. The practice rooms were small and bare, cubicles furnished with one stool, meant for only one thing. Time passed. The tedium made Mreen yawn, but she could not even lie down, unless she lay on the cold stone floor. At last she sat on the stool. The only diversion she had was her *filla*.

The *Doryu* exercise was still as clear to her as if it was painted on the bare wall of the practice room. Its simplicity made it perfect. How could the others not see? The scale shaped itself if you only played the right rhythm, and the lowered fourth degree melted down to the third in the most logical, natural way.

She played it again, and it reminded her of a similar study in *Aiodu*. They could be combined, she thought, if she allowed the fourth degree of *Doryu* to become the seventh of *Aiodu*—oh, yes! And then, if you added quarter tones to fill in the interval . . .

The little practice room was as bright as summer sunshine when Maestro Nikei came looking for her at last. Mreen had forgotten all about pouting.

Listen, Maestro Nikei, she sent, the moment he appeared. *Listen to this, this works, do you not think?*

He leaned against the wall, and she played her new creation for him. He nodded when she finished. *Try the cadence again,* he sent. *Retard the ending, like this. . . .* He demonstrated on his own instrument, and then listened as she imitated.

Yes, that is better, Mreen agreed. She dimpled and swung her short legs. *I like this better than class. Could we not just work together, you and I?*

Nikei kept her waiting for a response while he tucked his *filla* away, and then folded his arms, gazing down at her. *You must think, Mreen.*

Mreen sat very still. *You are angry with me.*

No, I am not angry, but I want you to think about what you came here to do.

I came here to learn to be a Singer!

Yes, and so did your classmates. They are slower than you, and they knew less when they arrived, but they want to be Singers just as you do. You must not impede their studies.

Mreen pondered that. She thought of Palo, and Emly, and the twins who had cried for their mother for weeks after they arrived at Conservatory. She thought of the first-level students, too, Corin and Sith, who would soon go into their own Cantorises, and who had known her own mother, her real mother, when she was a first-level student here and they had been third level, like herself. Thoughts of her mother led her to Sira, and Theo, and she began to see the pattern. It was a design, and it had shape, like the *Doryu* study, with a rhythm that was defined by Nevya's seasons, by its history, by the Gift. This pattern was too great, too complex, for her to hold in her mind all at once, but she saw it was there. And she knew, looking up at Nikei, that he was helping her to see it.

Nikei followed her thoughts. *Yes. You are part of a great tradition. Some are quick, and some are not, but we all serve together. We each make our sacrifices for the Gift—yours is to be patient.*

She sighed, and looked down at her *filla. I am sorry, Maestro Nikei.* She looked around at the brilliance of the light in the practice room, and she knew that poor Palo would never make such warmth, and she felt sorry for him. She stood and bowed to her teacher. *I will remember. May I come back to class, now?*

Please.

It took Zakri and Berk eight days of travel to reach Conservatory with Cantrix Jana and Cantor Izak. Their pace was slow, because Izak had to ride in the *pukuru,* well padded with bedfurs. They jettisoned all unnecessary supplies, leaving them lying outside Soren's courtyard. They were hardly out of sight over the hill before the House members were out, retrieving everything for use in the House.

Izak had not regained enough strength to ride *hruss,*

although he was improving. Zakri and Jana worked over him every night and every morning, trying to repair the bonds that had broken under Cho's attack. Little by little, the sparks that joined his mind and his body grew in brightness and strength. Zakri feared for his Gift, but he was alive, and for brief periods he could stand and move about, with help. He had not spoken, nor would he release the bit of carving from Soren. When anyone tried to take it from him, he whimpered and pulled away. In the end, they all thought it best to let him keep it.

Unheralded, they rode into Conservatory's courtyard. One of the Housemen pounded on the doors, and the Housekeeper of Conservatory came out onto the steps.

"Cantrix Jana!" he exclaimed, appalled. "We had no— why, what is all this?"

Jana dismounted with the help of one of the Housemen, and walked slowly up the steps to Conservatory. "This is Cantor Zakri v'Amric," she said, with a gesture. "And in that *pukuru* is Cantor Izak, badly hurt. We have come directly from Soren."

The Housekeeper paled, and stared at Zakri. Then, without a word, he whirled and hurried into the House.

Several Housemen and women came out immediately, taking the reins of the *hruss,* two big men bringing a litter for Izak. They carefully moved him into it, and carried him indoors. Everyone else followed, and the Housekeeper led them immediately up the stairs, except for Izak. Zakri looked back to see the litter set gently down in a room just beneath the foot of the staircase, near the Cantoris.

The Housekeeper had summoned the Singers of Conservatory with remarkable speed. They were already gathered in Magister Mkel's apartment, taking seats around the big table, their faces grim.

They were all new faces to Zakri. Maestro Nikei, Maestra Lisvet, Maestra Magret, the others. He struggled to keep their names straight. It seemed Conservatory was full of gray-haired Singers, and he did not have the advantage of having known their names beforehand. He knew they must think him very strange; he was introduced as Cantor Zakri, and yet none of these people, the people who trained Nevya's Cantors, had ever met him.

Bran hastened to explain what had happened. "You know of the problems at Soren, I'm sure," he said to Magister Mkel. "Cantor Abram sent Cantrix Jana and Cantor Izak and myself to negotiate with this Cho, try to bring him to some understanding." He shrugged eloquently. "There's no use talking to that one. He's got a House full of frightened people, and a bunch of itinerants who do everything he tells them."

"But what does he want?" asked Maestro Nikei. "What will satisfy him?"

"He says he wants equality," Bran said flatly. "For all the Gifted. I think he just wants power, and Spirit knows he's got plenty of that. In truth, I'm sure he likes things just the way they are."

"And the carvers?" Magister Mkel asked. His appearance concerned Zakri; he was gray of skin and his hands trembled where he rested them on the table. "Do they want the same?"

Bran could only shake his head. "I don't know about the carvers," he said. "I didn't see them."

"Did Cantor Izak?"

"No," Bran answered. "We were together. We met with Cho, but he laughed at everything we had to say. It was—I'm afraid Cantor Izak had no patience. He was angry, I don't blame him for that. Cho was insulting. It was a nasty argument, all about duty, and responsibility to the people, and the Committee—Cantor Izak said everything Cantor Abram and Magister Gowan told him to say. Then he told Cho he could see why he had not been admitted to Conservatory. He said if he'd had a decent Gift he'd have been a Cantor like himself, and as it was, he'd have to let the fully Gifted rule the Continent—and then he walked out. He just turned his back and left. I liked his spirit! But Cho followed him. I didn't know—" Bran gulped and spread his hands. "I didn't know what he could do."

The Housekeeper raised one more question. "If Cantor

Izak never went to the carvery, where did he get that piece of carving he's holding so tightly in his hand?"

"Cho gave it to him—threw it at him, more like," Bran replied. "Cho said, 'Look at what my Gift can do! Where would you be without that?' and tossed that bit at Cantor Izak. I don't know why he kept it."

"He will not let it go," Zakri put in. "Of course, for the moment his mind is not whole—Cho is capable of terrible violence, especially to the Gifted. But for Cantor Izak—perhaps it feels to him as if, keeping that bit of carving, he can understand what has happened to him."

"What is it?" the Housekeeper asked.

"It is a panel for a *filhata*," Jana said miserably. "The section that fronts the soundboard. He has not let it leave his hand since it happened."

Zakri looked at her with sympathy. She had been blaming herself, ever since the confrontation at Soren, for not going into the House with Izak. She believed she could have helped him to keep his temper. Zakri was certain it would have made no difference.

Magister Mkel looked around the room, into each face. "What are we to do?" he asked slowly. "How can we risk any more Singers? We have so few to spare. And yet, Cantrix Elnor is trapped, and Soren's House members are being held hostage. I hardly know where to turn next."

A heavy silence settled over the room. Zakri had held a vain hope that here, at Conservatory, he would find the answer, the weapon they needed to deal with Cho. He feared now that they would be no further ahead than they had been. O Spirit, he thought, what are we to do?

There was no knock, or any audible footstep outside the Magister's apartment, but the door swung open, making a small click in the stillness. Every head turned.

A small child, no more than five or six, stood alone in the doorway. She was wrapped in a halo of light that made her red hair shine, and that moved with her as she stepped into the room. Her eyes were the color of softwood leaves in summer, but they were glazed now, round and unfocused.

Four years had passed since Zakri had seen her, but he

guessed immediately who she was, even before Cathrin exclaimed, "Mreen!"

Mreen? Zakri sent.

Her eyes found his, but they seemed to look at him through a thick fog. *Are you Cantor Zakri?*

Yes, I am.

You play my mother's filhata?

Yes.

We must go after Cantor Theo, she sent immediately. *He is too far away for me to call him, but we will need him.* Her childish features were drawn, making her look like a caricature of a very old person. Her hands were clasped tightly around a bit of carved ironwood held before her.

Zakri crossed the room quickly to kneel beside her. Everyone stared at this strange Cantor and the little haloed girl.

Mreen, what is it? Why do we need Cantor Theo?

She put out her hand to him, and he took it in his own. Her fingers were small and soft, but they gripped his hand with a strength she should not have had. He found himself awash in images, a flood of ghostly scenes that flowed through his mind with frightening power. He did not see how her child's mind could bear them.

Do you see? she sent, begging with her eyes.

I see them. He released her hand, and stood to address Magister Mkel.

"It would be best," he said aloud, "if we speak privately."

Mkel looked about as if for counsel, and Nikei bent toward him. Without compunction, Zakri listened as Nikei sent to Mkel, *I do not know what the child sees, but as you know, hers is a strange Gift. It would be better to work this out without the audience of these Lamdon folk!*

Mkel nodded, and gave his mate a subtle sign with his hand. She squeezed his shoulder, and then urged everyone but the Singers out of the room. "Come to the great room, all of you," she said comfortably. "You'll feel better for some refreshment, and then a bath, I'm sure. We have such nice hot water here, because our students practice on it!"

With evident reluctance, the Housemen and the two

couriers followed Cathrin, Berk with a lifted hand to Zakri. The three teachers, Zakri, Jana, and little Mreen remained behind, and Mkel waved them all to chairs.

Mreen put the carving on the table, and then clambered into the chair nearest Zakri. Her hand found his once again, but no nightmare visions came with it this time. He wondered why she had sought him out, in particular.

You are the one, she sent, her eyes clear now, looking up at him. *You knew my mother, and you can help me.*

Help you do what, Mreen?

Help me call Cantor Theo, and Cantrix Sira.

Mkel and the others watched them in amazement. *Mreen,* sent Mkel. *Will you tell us why you came here today?*

Mreen's round eyes were solemn, her little nimbus steady and bright. *I heard the man, the sick man, calling.*

Jana and Zakri exchanged a glance. *Do you mean Cantor Izak, child?* Jana sent.

Mreen nodded. *Yes, Cantor Izak. He was calling, and I went to find him.*

I did not hear him calling, Jana sent, shaking her head.

But I did, Mreen assured her. *And I found him, and he gave me that.* She pointed her short finger at the carving lying now on the table. *And when I touched it—* She shuddered slightly, and Zakri held her hand tighter.

She saw things—pictures of battle, very like the one we have already experienced at Soren, Zakri sent to them all.

Mreen nodded. *And the man—Cantor Izak—sent me to Zakri. Zakri knew my mother!* she added, and Magister Mkel smiled a little at her. She went on, *And Zakri, I mean, Cantor Zakri, will help me. We need them. We need them now.*

How do you know that, Mreen? asked Magister Mkel.

She looked back at the little carved ironwood panel before her, but she did not touch it. *That told me,* she sent slowly, almost dazedly. Her face was round and plump, meant for smiles and dimples, but now solemn. Her eyes narrowed, with an expression as old as the mountains themselves. *That is for a* filhata, she sent to Mkel, *but if the carver is not stopped, there will be no more* filhata, *no more*

Gift, no more Singers. We need Theo, and Sira. And Zakri.
Her eyes glazed again, and her body went slack in her chair.
And me, she finished. Zakri gripped her hand, hard.

"Mreen!" Nikei said sharply.

Mreen shivered, once, and then her eyes focused on her
teacher's face. *Yes, Maestro Nikei.*

"Let it go now, Mreen," he said, firmly, but gently. "Clear
your mind." To the others he sent, *It is too much for her. Too
strong—*

But she is right, Zakri sent. *She has had a vision, and she
is right. We will need Theo, and Sira. I must go after them.*

You have to take me, too, Mreen told him. *Because you
cannot reach so far, and I can.*

Zakri took a deep breath. *So I will, then, Mreen, with your
teachers' permission.*

Cantor Zakri . . . is there no other way? Nikei asked.
She is so young!

I know of no other way, he answered. He looked down at
the tiny girl, radiant in her baby *quiru,* and he marveled at
how much she looked like her mother, and how strong and
strange her Gift must be.

Tears stood in Jana's eyes, and Mkel looked as if he could
hardly hold up his head from weariness. Nikei frowned deeply,
his arms folded across his chest. But Mreen smiled now,
looking up at Zakri. She released his hand and scrambled
down from the big chair.

All right, she sent calmly. *I must go back to practicing
now.*

They all watched her small figure go tripping out of the
apartment. Mkel asked, *Can we be certain she will be safe?*
No one had an answer.

CHAPTER FIFTEEN

SOOK'S ONE RESPITE FROM CONFINEMENT WAS HER DAILY visit to the *ubanyix*. It was a relief to walk the corridors, even though one of Cho's itinerants was with her at every step, and most of the House members she encountered turned away with frightened eyes. The itinerant, Bree, was not happy about the job; she stared defiantly at everyone they met, as if daring them to approach. When they reached the *ubanyix* she said briefly, "Wait here," and Sook had to stand in the hall while three other women were banished from their bath. They passed her on their way out, and their glances were sympathetic, without resentment. "Now," Bree ordered, and Sook followed her inside.

"O Spirit, it's good to be away from that room!" Sook exclaimed.

The itinerant sat on the bench with her legs crossed, her arms folded. Sook looked out at the vast, empty ironwood tub as she drew off her boots and tunic and trousers, and she sighed. "I don't see why I can't have company, at least to bathe."

"It's your own fault," Bree said sullenly. "You think I like acting as your serving woman?"

"My fault?" Sook asked. She gave the binding of her hair a sharp tug, and her scalp stung. "Am I locking my own door then? Turning away everyone who wants to talk to me?"

"You're a troublemaker, just like he says! Believe me, I'd be just as happy to see you go back to the kitchens where you belong."

Sook piled her soiled linens on the bench that encircled the room. Fresh ones, cleaned and folded, were waiting. She knew Mura had put them there especially for her. Naked, she stood facing Bree with her hands on her hips, her hair a black curtain around her. "I have an idea, Bree," she said. "Why don't you and all those other itinerants go back to your own business, get out and earn a living? Then he won't have any power over me, or anyone else!"

Bree shifted her weight, and turned her eyes away. "Cho wants what's best for us, for all of us!"

"Does he indeed! Living as prisoners in a House that gets colder every day? We have no visitors, we're running out of paper and cloth and metal! There's hardly a speck of fruit or vegetables from the nursery gardens because they're too cold to grow—it won't be long before we're down to nothing but meat on the table!"

"Cho will see to all of that!" Bree said.

"When the Glacier melts!" Sook retorted, and turned her back.

"Get on with your bath," Bree answered. "I want to get back upstairs."

Over her shoulder, Sook said, "So you can stand around outside his door waiting for him to give you something to do?"

"It's better than this," Bree muttered.

Sook ignored that, and stepped down into the big tub. The water was tepid and looked greasy in the dim light of the tattered *quiru*. She gritted her teeth and immersed herself anyway. It took more than just warming the water every day to have a fresh tub to bathe in! How would these lazy

Singers feel if the kitchens cooked their food in filthy water?

She was just reaching for a bar of soap when the door to the *ubanyix* swung open, slowly and cautiously. Mura and Eun looked around it, then stepped inside, bringing Bree swiftly to her feet. She stood in front of them, barring their way.

"Not now," she said. "No one comes in here now."

Sook bit her lip, but Mura winked at her. Eun held a cup, covered with a bit of napkin, out to Bree.

"What's this?" the Singer demanded.

"Just a bit of a treat for you, Singer," Mura murmured. Her sweet tone made Sook want to giggle. Eun pulled aside the cloth, and Bree sniffed the brimming cup, not letting it touch her lips.

Bree eyed Mura suspiciously. "You told Cho we had no more wine. I heard you!"

"We certainly don't have enough to go around," Mura told her. "I thought you might enjoy this last bit of it—but if you don't want it . . ."

Bree hesitated, her eyes sliding to Sook. Sook held her breath and looked down at the dark water.

"Don't worry," Eun put in timorously. "We won't tell anyone! We'd be in more trouble than you would, anyway. Just let us bathe with Sook, just this once. She's had no company for weeks!"

Bree gave them a sour smile. "She's got Cho for company," she said. Mura snorted derisively, and Bree chuckled a bit herself. She reached for the winecup. "All right," she said, "just this once. But if Cho finds out, we'll all be sorry!"

Mura and Eun hurried to shed their clothes and step down into the tub. Mura gave a grunt of disgust when the lukewarm water lapped her thighs.

"Singer Bree!" she called. "Couldn't you do something about this bath? It's as cold as glacier water in summer!"

Bree set the cup down carefully, and came to the edge of the tub, stooping to dip her fingers into the water. She snickered. "It's refreshing, don't you think, Cook?"

"Ship and stars! I don't know what good it is having Singers underfoot everywhere when we can't at least have a hot bath!" Mura snapped, sounding much more like herself. Sook smiled behind her hand. Mura's temper was perhaps the one thing in the House that hadn't cooled.

Bree pulled a battered *filla* out of her tunic, and held it up. "Suppose I heat the water for you," she said, "what will you do for me?"

Eun was indignant. "We already do for all of you!" she protested. "It's not easy making meals with nothing but meat and ancient dried fruit and no grain to speak of! What else would you have us do?"

Bree gave a shrug. "Well, I surely have a taste for some bread, but if there's no grain, I suppose that's out."

Mura said impatiently, "*Keftet* without grain is not to my taste, either, but that's all we'll have to eat before long. Tell that to your Cho!"

Eun sucked in her breath. "Mura, be careful!"

Bree laughed. "Oh, yes, Mura, be careful! Or you'll end up like Sook here, a prisoner of her own big ideas."

"Singer Bree," Sook said quickly. "No one needs to know any of this."

Bree rolled her eyes, but she brought her *filla* up. She played a *Doryu* melody to the end, and then began again at the beginning. Three times she played it through.

Sook had heard Singers and Cantors do their work all her life, but she had never listened critically, never analyzed what they did. Now she was struck by the thought that Bree's playing was a simple matter of the same melody, with the same rhythm, over and over and over again. The water began to get warmer, which meant it was fulfilling its purpose. But the melody seemed meaningless. Before she met Singer Zakri, she would not have noticed such a thing. But when Zakri played, the music changed every time. His melodies were living things, growing, developing, building lives of their own. They were more than just patterns of notes. They touched something deep inside a person, even a simple cook like herself. Or perhaps, she thought, it was just because he was Zakri, and nothing he did was ordinary.

Sook doubted that the pool of warmer water reached much past their own end of the tub. Maybe when all the Singers bathed together . . . she remembered with longing the hot baths that Cantrix Elnor had always provided, the steaming water that made her muscles limp and her cheeks hot, beads of moisture gathering to roll down her face and into her eyes. She was sure Singer Zakri could do the same. How wonderful it would be to be really warm again! Baths these days were more penance than pleasure. Still, the water was nicer than it had been. She said, "We thank you, Singer."

Bree grunted and went back to her bench and the waiting winecup. Sook washed her hair every day, to make the bath last longer. Mura now took a much-used cake of soap from the nearest niche and slid closer to her, ostensibly to help her with it. Under cover of lathering and scrubbing, she asked softly, "Sook—are you all right then? He hasn't—"

Sook looked up at her from beneath a cloud of foam. "No," she whispered back. "He hasn't. I don't think that's what he wants from me. Nori still—well, Nori comes to see him, and she's willing." She made a face. "I'm certainly not!"

"What does he want, then? Why does he keep you?"

Sook rinsed her hair, and wrung the water out of it. She wrapped it in a loose thick coil on her shoulders, glancing up to be certain that Bree was enjoying her wine and paying little attention. She kept her voice low. "I think it's about Zakri—Singer Zakri," she told them. "Cho knows I caused that ruckus in the carvery just so Zakri and his friend could get away."

"Right enough," Mura muttered. "But why keep you locked up?"

Sook rubbed the chilled skin of her shoulders. The water was still not really comfortable, but she was loath to leave it. Life as a prisoner was sometimes frightening, but mostly it was tedious, with nothing to do but stare out the window at the white peaks and forests of the Timberlands, or listen through the closed bedroom door as Cho and his itinerants talked and talked, endlessly, pointlessly.

"I think," she said slowly, "that Cho is afraid of Singer Zakri. He's afraid Zakri will come back, and he won't be able to fight him. And he thinks Zakri cares about me!" She pictured Zakri's sweet face and tall, slender figure, and she smiled fiercely. "He's right, too!"

"Oh, Sook, be careful," Eun said. "Don't tell him that!"

Sook shook her head. "I don't tell him anything. But I heard him talking, after that Cantor was here—the one from Lamdon. I heard Zakri's name. And I know—" She splashed her small fist into the water. "I know Zakri will come back! Then we'll—"

"That's enough," Bree called from her bench. "Surely you're clean by now!"

"Just a bit longer," Eun begged.

Bree set the emptied winecup on the bench, where it teetered and then clattered to the floor. She grabbed for it. "No, now!" she called. "Cho will wonder where you've got to . . . I don't need him angry at me."

"I'm coming," Sook answered quickly.

"Sook!" Mura said. Her round face showed real concern, and there was urgency in her voice. "Listen, I think Singer Zakri—I wouldn't want you to be disappointed if—"

"Let's go!" Bree said again, stumbling slightly as she got to her feet.

Sook stood, too, dripping and shivering, but she still smiled at the thought of Zakri. She breathed, "He's coming back, Mura, I know he is! And I'll be waiting for him when he does."

Bree came to the edge of the tub and threw a towel to Sook, cutting off Mura's answer. Sook was shuddering at the cold air on her wet skin, and she dried herself quickly. She dressed in the fresh clothes, and Eun climbed out to help her bind her hair. She looked back at Mura as Bree hurried her out, saying goodbye with her eyes.

Mura looked grim, staring after her. There was something she had wanted to say, something else she needed to tell her. Sook could only wonder what it might have been.

*   *   *

Cho was leaning into the window casement, his back to the door. Two of his itinerants sat at the long table with their legs stretched out, empty teacups in front of them. When Bree and Sook came in, Cho turned his head just enough to show them a thin smile. "So there you are at last, little Sook," he said lightly.

Sook took a step toward her room, and Cho's eyes narrowed, looking past her at Bree.

"Bree?" he said slowly, his smile growing wider. "Have you been up to something?"

"No—no," Bree stammered. "Just the *ubanyix*."

Cho straightened, and fixed her with his black-ash eyes. Bree stepped backward until her heels met the door. "Gone a long time, weren't you?" Cho asked. He pulled the thin plait of his hair through his fingers, over and over, and took a slow, almost languid step toward them.

Sook heard Bree groan, ever so slightly, and she knew Cho was doing it again, that strange and cruel thing he did to the Gifted. Whatever it was, it turned them sick and pale and had sent more than one of them racing for the chamber pot, to bend over it heaving and gagging. She put herself between Bree and Cho, lifting her head to meet his eyes.

"I like a long bath, Carver," she said swiftly. "What would you have her do . . . leave me all alone in the *ubanyix*? Where I might actually enjoy myself for a few moments?" She tossed her head, and tried to step past him to go into the bedroom which had been her cage all these past weeks.

Cho seized her arm with a strong hand. He pulled her close and leaned over her to put the point of his long, curved nose against her hair. "Mmm," he said. "Doesn't little Sook smell nice?"

She tried to pull away, but his grip was as hard as the ironwood he used to carve. Behind her, the door to the apartment clicked, and she knew Bree had made her escape.

Cho's thin body pressed against hers. Her cheek chafed against his tunic, and she smelled the scented oil normally reserved to the ruling classes, an upper-level tang that was as alien to her as the Magister's apartment had been before her imprisonment here. She turned her head away, as far as she could.

Cho laughed and released her arm, but he slipped his hand around her waist and held her fast against him. With his other hand he lifted his long braid of hair and tickled her face with it, drawing it back and forth across her eyes, her cheek, her lips. She twisted her head from side to side, but she could not escape it. He squeezed her tighter and put his mouth close to her ear.

"Wouldn't you like to know me better, Sook?" he whispered.

She shuddered at the feel of his breath against her skin, and she put all her strength into a shove, her fists against his chest, her legs braced. She fell back away from him, staggering against the edge of the table as he suddenly let go.

"Leave me alone!" she cried. Behind her the chairs of the two Singers scraped as they stood up and moved uncertainly away.

Cho gave a sharp gesture with his head, and the itinerants hurried from the apartment, the door closing sharply behind them. Sook backed away from Cho, around the table, stumbling again as her foot caught on a chair left in her path. His smile was mocking, a twist of dark, narrow lips.

"And where are you off to?" His tone was ice, chilling her very bones. He narrowed his eyes as he stared at her.

She did her best to glare at him, to warm herself with fury. "Your tricks don't work on me, Carver," she said as stoutly as she could. "I'm not Gifted in the least!"

"Well, small one," he said. "You may not be Gifted, but you have your own fine qualities." He moved around the table, toward her. "Those black eyes, for instance . . ."

Sook cast a longing glance at the door, but she knew there were only enemies beyond it, Gifted enemies who were vulnerable to Cho, and who would do anything to avoid one of his attacks.

Cho reached her, and she felt the wall at her back and his long arms on either side of her, pinning her. His long-nosed face was too close, descending on hers like a *ferrel* swooping down on a defenseless *caeru* pup.

"So my tricks, as you call them, don't bother you?" he murmured. His lips hovered over hers, and when she tried to evade him, his arm prevented her.

She thought of Zakri, so fair and so clever, and so strong. She prayed for strength. Then she closed her eyes as if in acquiescence.

As Cho bent to her, Sook dropped. She went straight down between his outstretched arms, crouching and then wriggling quickly away. As she went, she snatched the *obis* knife from its scabbard at his belt.

She reached the door to her bedroom, and she held up her prize in her closed fist. "If you come near me again," she declared, proud of the firm ringing of her voice in the big room, "I swear I'll stick this between your ribs!"

She panted with exertion, and with triumph. Cho laughed, and narrowed his eyes.

To Sook's dismay, the *obis* knife leaped from her hand and skittered across the floor. It felt exactly as if he had slapped it from her fingers, and there had been nothing she could do to stop him. Helplessly, trying to conceal her fear, she pressed her back against the door and waited, watching through wide eyes.

Cho bent to pick up the knife. He dangled it in his fingers and smirked at her. "Never mind, little Sook," he said softly. "Rape is not my idea of fun. Not now, anyway. I have more use for you . . . intact, as it might be!" He thrust the knife back into its scabbard. "You just remember . . . Gifted or unGifted . . . I have all the power here."

He walked around the table and opened the door to her bedroom. "Except," he added softly, "except perhaps for the power of those eyes!" He traced them with his finger, and she shivered.

She pulled away and slipped through the door. Cho smiled at her as he shut it. She heard him shoot the bolt, and she hurried to her solitary cot to collapse, weak with relief and anger and fear.

"Damn him," she whispered. "Damn him!" She rolled over to pull the furs around her, to shut out the cold of the air, to shake off the chill of her fear. "Just wait until Zakri returns!"

CHAPTER
SIXTEEN

MREEN BEHAVED AS IF THE TRIP TO OGRE PASS WERE A holiday, with nothing more serious to think about than which *hruss* she would ride. She took turns, riding up behind Jana or Zakri, keeping up a stream of mental chatter for hours on end. Sometimes, leaning against their backs with her cheek buried in their furs, she would fall suddenly asleep, lulled by the *hruss*'s swinging gait, comfortable on the wide saddle skirts. She would waken suddenly and completely, and resume her merry conversation where she had left off. In the evenings, she practiced her *filla* under Jana's watchful eye, and then she played, climbing on irontree suckers, packing snow into interesting shapes, climbing into her bedfurs upside down and pretending she couldn't find her way out.

Zakri felt old and careworn, watching her. His concern for Sook was never far from his mind, and he had added several other worries since leaving Soren, not the least of which was Mreen's safety. Berk, however, was Mreen's fast friend from the beginning.

On their first night out from Conservatory, Berk and Mreen struggled for a way to communicate.

"This isn't fair," rumbled the huge man. He was kneeling by the fire, looking down at the tiny girl. "You can understand me, but I don't have an idea what you're thinking!"

Mreen dimpled up at him, her halo twinkling. Berk was trying to bank the cookfire while Mreen teased him for more softwood to burn. She had delighted, as he cooked their evening *keftet,* in being the one to feed the twigs into the fire, clapping her hands in glee as they caught the flames and blazed up under the pot.

Now she snatched a twig from the bundle in Berk's saddle pack. *More fire,* she sent. Berk pretended to shake his head no. Mreen made claws of her hands, and exposed her little white teeth in a pretend growl. *The* tkir *might get us!* she sent.

"What? What's that?" Berk demanded. He wrested the stick from her, and held the pack at arm's length, far out of her reach. She danced around him, grimacing silently and pouncing upon him with her make-believe claws. He obliged her by falling backward into the snow, making a supine mountain that she immediately leaped upon with her soundless laugh.

"She is a *tkir,*" murmured Jana. "You are about to be devoured, Houseman."

Mreen dug her hands into Berk's furs and pretended to bite him. He yelped in falsetto. "Ouch! ouch! I'm being eaten! Someone, please, build up the fire!"

Triumphantly, Mreen scrambled across him and retrieved her softwood twig. She plunged it into the banked fire and watched it blaze up, whirling to smile wickedly at Berk where he still lay in the snow. *There!* she sent dramatically. *I have frightened away the* tkir!

"The beast is gone now," Jana said under her breath.

"Oh, thank you," Berk said to Mreen. "But is it too late for me? I have terrible bites all over me!"

Do not worry, Mreen sent. *Just lie still! I will heal you.* She reached into her tunic for her small *filla. Now close your eyes.*

Jana was about to relay this, but Mreen ran her palm over Berk's eyelids and he obediently closed them. She sat cross-legged beside his head and played a short *Iridu* melody. *There,* she sent.

"You are quite well now," Jana told Berk. He opened his eyes and sat up.

"Thank you, Singer," he said to Mreen, bowing. She bowed, too, and her dimples flashed.

Zakri sat in silence, watching. Jana caught his eye. *Are you all right, Cantor?* she asked.

He nodded to her. *I am,* he answered. *Only worried by what is to come.*

Jana held his gaze for a moment. Zakri noticed that she was considerably thinner than she had been when he first saw her at Lamdon, and he reflected that she must be fearful, too, for different reasons. She would be concerned about Izak, of course . . . and then there was Observatory.

Are you anxious, Cantrix? he asked.

She nodded, smiling a little. *So I am,* she responded. *It is foolish . . . but all I know of Observatory is what the legends say . . . and it is all frightening.*

What do they say?

She gave an embarrassed shrug. *Oh, it is so silly. It cannot be true!*

Tell me.

Jana looked across the fire to where Mreen was waving her hands about and making faces, trying to tell Berk something. Berk was laughing aloud, Mreen silently. *There is an old song,* Jana began.

Sing it, then.

She thought for a moment. When she began the song, it was with an air of apology, and she kept her voice low:

Beware the Watchers! You cannot see them.
They descend from their mountain,
They plunge from their cliffs,
They hide behind boulders to seize the unwary.
They disdain the cold and the cries of their victims,
They seize all the Singers and eat all the rest.

BEWARE THE WATCHERS! YOU CANNOT SEE THEM.
WATCH FOR THE WATCHERS!
FOR THEY ARE WATCHING YOU.

Zakri chuckled. *Sira would say it is all imagination,* he
sent. But Jana was not looking at him. He saw that Mreen
had come to stand by his shoulder.

It is not all imagination, Mreen sent, staring at Jana with
wide eyes. *They do Watch, you know.*

Of course, Mreen, Zakri answered. *But the Watchers do
not eat people.*

They did once, Mreen sent bluntly. Jana shivered.

Mreen! Zakri protested.

Her eyes left Jana and turned to him. They were very
dark, and something ancient looked out from their depths.
*Cantor Zakri, it is true. When there was nothing else. People
died, and there was no other way to make the* keftet. She
lifted her hands expressively. She looked like a tiny old
woman at that moment, her mouth turned down, her nimbus
shaded. *But that was a hundred summers ago.*

Jana was trying to swallow her revulsion, remembering
that Observatory, after all, had been Mreen's home. *How
can you know such a story, Mreen?*

It is not a story, the child answered. *I saw it when I picked
up an old cookpot, thrown away on the waste drop.* She
smiled suddenly. *It had a hole burned right through it,* she
sent brightly, as if that were the most interesting part. *My
whole hand went in! And then I saw the pictures.*

Berk had of course heard none of their conversation. He
was sitting on his own bedfurs now, pulling off his boots.
"That's a pleasant song for bedtime, Cantrix," he said wryly.
"Don't you know some more?"

"So I do, Houseman." Jana smiled. "And I will sing one
for you. But first, I think, a certain Conservatory student
should make ready for her bed."

Mreen sent, *No!* and scuttled backward to hide behind
Berk, making him laugh again.

"I understood that well enough," he boomed. "Be off with

you, and no more nonsense! I'm quite out of patience with you, little one!" But no one believed that, least of all Mreen.

Sira heard Mreen's call just as she was stripping off her boots, ready to go to bed. She froze with one boot in her hand, listening. The child could not possibly be any closer than Ogre Pass, yet the call sounded clearly, if faintly, in her mind.

Wait, she answered, standing with one foot bare, reaching for her *filhata* on its shelf. *Wait, Mreen!* She tasted fear in her mouth as she tore the leather wrappings from the instrument. Theo had returned days before, and they had been trying to accustom themselves to Observatory without Mreen's small haloed figure in their class, in the halls. She could not imagine a circumstance that would have brought Mreen to the Pass, certainly none that was auspicious.

Without bothering to tune the strings, and with her unbooted foot feeling the chill of the stone floor, she launched into a simple air in *Lidya,* one that her fingers could play automatically, that needed no concentration. She opened her mind as completely as possible.

Mreen? What is it? Are you all right? Why are you there? Her psi spun out urgently over the long distance, seeking answers. She reached down Observatory's mountain, skimming above the cliff road and the boulder-strewn slopes, stretching a fibril that grew ever thinner as it extended to its utmost limits, to touch at last the mind of her student. Her former student, who should at this moment be safe within Conservatory's walls!

Mreen had no *filhata* of course, would not have earned one for years yet. Still, her thoughts were as clear to Sira as if they were in the same room, face-to-face, as if she had leaned close to press her forehead directly to Sira's, a thing children sometimes did when they were learning to hear and send. *We are in the Pass,* she sent. *Cantor Zakri and I. And Cantrix Jana.*

But why? Why did you leave Conservatory?

They needed me, came the simple answer. *For this.*

Mreen, what is happening?

There was a pause. Sira played the *Lidya* melody, over and over, her fingers automatically seeking the right strings, the right rhythm. She sensed Theo come into her room to stand with his arms folded, leaning against the wall, supporting her extended psi with his own strength. She did not feel the ache of the cold in her bare foot. Her eyes were tightly closed, her mind as focused as she could make it, and Theo listened through her.

Cantor Zakri says to tell you it is Soren, and the Singers there. People are hurt, and people need help, and . . . Another pause, while Sira's fingers played on and on, repeating the familiar patterns. In the silence, the distance between herself and Mreen seemed insurmountably long and empty.

Then the child's sending came again, a small, crystalline, delicate voice. It was, in fact, all the voice Mreen had. *Cantor Zakri says he needs you, and Cantor Theo, too. Cantrix Jana will go up to Observatory. Cantor Zakri says, send Morys.*

It was an unbelievable request, with far-reaching implications. Mreen, of course, could hardly be expected to understand, but Zakri would know exactly what he was asking. She had faith in his judgment. He would have thought everything out as clearly as possible, but . . . She opened her eyes and met Theo's. He gave her his crooked grin. *I would never argue with that child,* he sent, shrugging.

We will be there tomorrow, then, Sira sent. Her back had begun to ache, and her fingers to tire. *Tell Zakri—* The image of Zakri was clear now between Mreen and herself, and Sira felt a rush of pleasure at the thought of seeing him again. And to be riding once more on the roads of the Continent . . . *Tell Cantor Zakri we will be there tomorrow.*

She broke off her melody, and the contact with Mreen. She straightened her back, holding her *filhata* upright on her knee, and flexed her arms and her weary fingers.

Do you have any idea what is happening? Theo asked.

She shook her head slowly. *I must think, try to remember. It is so odd—Jana, Cantrix Jana, was assigned to Lamdon. I cannot think what brings her here.*

But Mreen is well. Theo pulled up a stool to sit close to Sira.

Of course he knew her worry for Mreen, the frightening dreams she had. He knew all her thoughts and fears. She smiled a little at him, appreciating his calm, and the immediate way in which he had sensed her need and come to her when Mreen had called. *She seems perfectly well.*

Theo took the *filhata* from Sira and wrapped it again in its leather covering. She watched him, but she was thinking of Soren. *What is it?* he asked.

It is Soren—did you hear her mention Soren? Where the carvery is . . . I remember a rumor, something Singer Iban told me.

Singer Iban? He was your apprentice master.

She smiled again. *So he was, and a very fine one. He has eyebrows that dance on his forehead like ferrel wings—you would like him.*

And about Soren?

Sira narrowed her eyes and rubbed her temples with her long fingers, trying to remember. *He said—there was something about the itinerants, and they were gathering at Soren. . . .* She spread her hands in a helpless gesture. *I simply cannot remember, or else he never told me more.*

We had better see Pol, Theo sent, always practical.

He will not like this, she answered, making a wry face.

Theo laughed aloud. *No, Pol does not like surprises! But as they say, even the ironwood bends if the wind blows hard enough.*

Hm. I thought it might have been the one about the Glacier changing its course, she answered. The tension eased in her, and she became aware of the bite of the cold in her bare foot. She bent to put her boot on again.

You think you know me! Theo teased. *But I promise you, I have any number of proverbs you have not yet heard.*

Sira looked up at him, savoring the crinkling around his eyes, the twinkle that so often caused her to thank the Spirit for creating him. *You seem to be pleased enough about this . . . whatever it is.*

It has been a long time since we had an adventure, he

answered. Briefly, he laid his big hand over her thin one. *And together, at that.*

She only arched her scarred eyebrow, disciplining her own feelings, but she did not pull her hand away. *You will meet Zakri at last,* she told him.

He lifted his hand, and winked at her. *Ah, the trouble-maker,* he sent. *In the thick of it once again!*

So he is, she answered thoughtfully. *So he is.*

CHAPTER
SEVENTEEN

★ THE HALLS OF OBSERVATORY WERE HUSHED AND DARK when Sira and Theo emerged from her room. The two Watchers of the night had already made their brief ceremony and climbed the narrow stairs to the limeglass bubble that was built into the very top of the House. There they would spend the hours of darkness searching among the stars for a sign of the Ship.

Sira called to Trisa as she and Theo went side by side up the staircase to the upper level. *Trisa, are you asleep?*

The answer was drowsy, but immediate. *No, Cantrix Sira. Could you dress, please, and meet Cantor Theo and me in Magister Pol's rooms?*

There was only a slight hesitation, a swell of surprise and curiosity quickly shielded, before Trisa answered. *Yes. I will hurry.*

Moments later she came flying up the stairs, still tugging her tunic down over her trousers, her unbound curls tumbling around her shoulders. She caught up with them as Pol opened his door to their knock.

The Magister had just come from seeing the Watchers off

to their duty. An open ledger and inkpot on the table behind him showed he had been working. A flickering and odorous lamp, necessary in Observatory's dim nighttime *quiru*, cast a narrow circle of hazy light over columns of figures. He lifted his bushy gray eyebrows at his visitors, and his rough voice was hoarser even than usual. "Cantrix Sira? Cantor Theo?"

Theo said, "We need a word with you, Magister."

Pol's small hard eyes swept the little group. "I can guess this will be no pleasant surprise," he rasped.

Theo grinned without remorse. "Sorry," he said. Sira flashed him a look, registering the distinct lack of sincerity in his tone. He blinked innocently at her.

Pol took a step back to usher them into the gloom of his apartment. He had to clear chairs for them to sit in, moving bridles and torn saddle packs to a corner, pushing back a stack of papers that teetered at one end of the table.

"You look busy," Theo commented.

"It's been a long winter," Pol said. "I have to keep close track, because everything's running low. But in the summer—" He reached to the center of the table for the precious pouch Theo and Morys had carried from Conservatory. He lifted it, feeling its weight, and held it up for them to see. "This summer, we're going to make an expedition to the Continent. I'm going to go myself!"

Theo saw Sira's astonished look, and he felt no little surprise himself. "Have you ever been to another House, Magister?"

"No living Observatory member has," Pol said shortly. "No one. But Conservatory has made it possible now." He nodded brusquely to Sira. "You made it possible, through the little girl." He tossed the pouch in his hand once, nodding at the solid clinking of the metal bits, before returning it to its place of honor.

Sira inclined her head, accepting the tribute without comment, but Theo sensed her deep feeling at the sight of the little leather bag. Only he knew that the gifts from Conservatory meant more to Sira even than to Pol. When she had unwrapped the three small *filla* meant for Jule and

Yve and Arry, her eyes had grown bright, the stern lines of her features easing. She had picked the little instruments up, one by one, sliding her fingers over the their intricate *obis*-carved surfaces. She had held each of them in her hand, staring at it for long moments as if it had something special to say to her, some message from her past, from Magister Mkel or from Conservatory itself, something only her sensitive fingers could understand.

Trisa looked from Pol to Sira to Theo, making an intense effort to control her curiosity. She neither sent nor spoke, but she wrapped her arms around herself and bounced in her chair, up and down, back and forth. Her lips were pressed tightly together, holding back the questions that bubbled up inside her. She looked, Theo thought, exactly like a kettle about to boil.

Sira had not yet spoken. She sat down for only a moment before she got up again and went to the window, leaning against the frame to gaze out into the night. There was little enough to see beyond the faded glow of the *quiru* except the jagged peaks that surrounded Observatory. They rose like apparitions against the dark sky, reflecting starlight from their snowy flanks.

"Trisa," Theo said softly, "could you brighten the *quiru,* do you think, just here in Magister Pol's apartment?"

Trisa quickly unwrapped her arms and reached inside her tunic for her *filla*. Theo nodded his approval at her being prepared. It would have been an easy thing to leave it in her room, forgotten in some other tunic or pocket. He hoped his other students would learn from her example. She played a short *Aiodu* melody, quickly increasing the light and the warmth to a daytime level. She played just enough, grace-fully but not dramatically, which might have been consid-ered excess. The room brightened, its corners and high ceiling fully lighted, but Theo had perfect faith that beyond its walls, the *quiru* would be unaffected. Sira turned from the window and regarded Trisa gravely.

Indeed, she sent to Theo, *our young protégé is a model of discipline and skill. Observatory will surely be safe in her hands for one day.*

All you have to do, he sent back dryly, *is convince Pol of that.*

So I do. She broke her silence then. "Magister, the girl we sent to Conservatory—Mreen—is down in Ogre Pass."

Pol folded his arms and grunted. His head was lowered, and he regarded her from beneath his heavy brows.

"There is a great crisis on the Continent," she went on, looking from Pol's frown to Trisa's eager face. "One of Lamdon's own Cantrixes is also in the Pass, with Mreen. She is waiting to be escorted here, in exchange for Theo and me."

Trisa's eyes went wide, and her fingers whitened where they gripped her *filla.* Pol growled, "Why you? Are there no other Singers on the Continent, that they need the ones from my Cantoris?"

Theo leaned forward to answer. "They need me, because the crisis concerns the itinerants. I was an itinerant Singer for three summers, as were all of my family for generations past remembering. I know the itinerants and their business. There is some sort of rebellion, an uprising, and it sounds serious."

"It is hard to understand exactly," Sira added, "because our information came through Mreen, and she does not really comprehend all of it. But the only way they could reach us was through Mreen."

"They? Who? Who is with her?"

"When I first returned to your House, I told you about Zakri, who is now Cantor at Amric."

"I know him!" Trisa burst out, her first words since coming into the room.

Sira nodded to her. "Yes, I know you do. The situation must be grave, because he has left his Cantoris to come asking for us, and I do not believe he would have done that if it were not necessary. He is a strong Singer, with a great Gift, but only Mreen and I can reach so far, can send over the distance between Observatory and Ogre Pass."

Pol measured Theo with a cold glance, and then Sira. "Why both of you? They're asking a lot of my House!"

Sira answered Pol's look with one of her own. "Zakri

knows my strengths. If he says I am needed, you may be certain it is so."

There was a short silence. Pol rose to pace the long room while Trisa watched openmouthed. Her nervousness and her excitement made her shiver in her chair, and she hugged herself again, trying to be still. Theo caught her eye and winked at her.

From the opposite end of the room, Pol barked, "Do I have any choice in this matter?"

Theo pushed away from the table and went to stand next to Sira. "Magister Pol, your House will be safe. Singer Trisa is perfectly capable of performing the *quirunha* alone for one day. And on the second day, the Spirit willing, the other Cantrix will arrive to act as her senior in our absence."

"Observatory is rejoining the Houses of Nevya," Sira said slowly. "It is a great work, a noble accomplishment. You are part of the community of the Continent now."

"This is a high price to pay for it," Pol grumbled.

"But not to pay it," Theo said, "would be unthinkable."

"My father would have turned them away in a heartbeat," Pol mused, half under his breath.

Sira stared hard at him, her scarred eyebrow arched high. "Your father," she said, "was content to rule a cold House and hungry people. But under your leadership, Observatory flourishes, and the Gift fills it with life. You are a very different man."

Pol stood a little straighter, and a light kindled in his small, shrewd eyes as Sira spoke. He did not exactly smile, in fact Theo could not remember ever seeing him smile, but the set of his shoulders and the lift of his head spoke of his pride.

Pol nodded to Trisa. "Singer? Do you agree with all this?"

Trisa looked to Sira and to Theo, and then answered with grave dignity, her trepidation well hidden. "If my teachers say I am capable, then I am." But she sent privately to Sira, *Who is it that is coming?*

Sira smiled a little, looking down at her student. *She is*

Cantrix Jana, a classmate of mine. Do not worry, Trisa. We are confident of your skills.

Trisa turned back to Pol. "A Singer serves where she is asked," she said stoutly.

"Commendable, I'm sure," Pol growled. "So, when does all this trading and shifting take place?"

"We must wake Morys now," Theo told him. "And fill our saddle packs. We will ride at dawn."

It was possible, of course, to make the trip to Ogre Pass and back in one very long day. The riders from Observatory had done it when they first brought Sira and Theo to the House as prisoners. But it was far riskier to leave the House when it was still dark, to ride down the cliff road in the uncertain light of early morning. And it would be hard enough, Sira knew, for Jana to have to ride that terrifying path above the chasm. She wanted her to have the advantage of full day when she did it.

She herself had no qualms about the road. At the bottom of the mountain, in the Pass, were Zakri and Mreen, and her heart was light, soaring on the knowledge that soon, very soon, she would see them both.

The sun was high, its light filtered through thin clouds, when Morys led Sira and Theo around the concealing jumble of great rocks at the end of Observatory's road. They rode their *hruss* out into the open, pausing on a lip of stone overlooking the Pass, and Sira felt a beating at the base of her throat as she looked down and found the *quiru* perhaps a half hour's ride away. Its strong yellow envelope glowed vividly against the snow, reaching as high as the tops of the towering irontrees. The figures of the travelers were motes of darkness moving within its light.

There was still a twisting, complex path to negotiate as they made their final descent into the Pass. Sira wanted to urge her *hruss* forward, coax it into its lumbering trot, but she restrained herself. She stayed behind Morys, riding next to Theo, but she felt the muscles of her thighs strain forward, as if she could move them all faster with her own efforts. The travelers heard them coming, and they stood waiting, peering out of the *quiru* at the approaching riders.

Sira was the first to dismount. She tossed her reins to Morys and paced impatiently into the *quiru*, putting back her hood as she went.

It was Jana who bowed to her first. *It is good to see you again, Cantrix,* she sent formally.

Sira bowed in return. *And you, Cantrix. I thank you for your sacrifice.*

It is an honor. Jana smiled at her, and Sira was surprised to see how she had changed. She was thinner, and her face had grown brown in her travels, but she somehow looked happier than she had the last time they had met. There was a brightness, an aliveness, to her face. Sira thought it suited her.

Jana stepped back, and Zakri came forward.

Sira's breath caught at the sight of him. He had grown taller, and his shoulders and chest had filled out. His hair was as fine as ever, cut short now to curl about his ears and neck. His eyes, the clear soft brown she remembered so well, glowed with pleasure. Although he bowed as formally as Jana, his sending was different.

Cantrix Sira, he sent. And with mischievous humor, *Maestra.*

She had started to bow, but interrupted it to send, *You must not call me that! I have told you before.*

His eyes twinkled as he straightened, and he offered no apology. *I see you are as changeless as these mountains!*

She had to smile, a full smile of joy at seeing him well, tall and straight and strong. Her throat was tight, and she doubted she could have spoken aloud. *You, Cantor Zakri, are much changed. You are . . .*

Bigger? he finished for her.

She shook her head. *That, too, of course, but . . . you are different. Older.*

He laughed. *I have almost five summers!*

It is so good to see you. I have— Sira caught herself. She dropped her eyes to the snow, powerless to disguise the emotion that moved her. She had to control it, to stop herself from touching him, putting her hand on his cheek or stroking his hair. She composed her face before she looked back at him. *I have thought of you often, Cantor Zakri.*

He grinned, answering, *And I of you, Maestra.*

Before she could remonstrate again over the title, Theo was beside her, Mreen already hugged tightly in his arms. He and Zakri bowed to each other.

Cantor Theo, this is Zakri—Cantor Zakri.

Zakri was carefully respectful. *It is an honor to meet you, Cantor.*

Theo shook his head, chuckling. *No need to be formal. I am just an old itinerant with a new job. In fact, you and I have a lot in common,* he sent. *We are two leaves from the same tree!*

Zakri laughed at that. *Does she let you call her Maestra? Not a chance.*

Sira shook her head in exasperation and turned to greet Mreen. She did touch the child, just a light pat of her hand. Zakri and Theo, like old friends, went to the cookfire to assemble a meal. Morys and the huge Houseman Berk, who Sira remembered well from her days at Amric, had the *hruss* well in hand, and Mreen danced around them, underfoot, a sunny nuisance. Sira turned again to Jana.

Can you tell me what is happening?

Jana nodded, and gestured to two rolled bedfurs they could sit on. *It is bad,* she sent. They sat side by side, watching the activity. *There is a carver at Soren—*

Is his name Cho?

It is.

Sira nodded, remembering now. There had been a little bowl, too small to be useful, but breathtaking in its delicacy. She had admired it, years before, when Iban had been her master. And Iban had warned her then.

Jana sent, *Cho has gathered every itinerant on the Continent into his service, and those who would not join him he has coerced, or killed.*

Their Cantor? Or Cantrix?

Jana could only lift her hands helplessly.

Zakri, with his usual lack of regard for convention, had

been listening. He came to kneel beside Sira, looking into her face.

Cantrix Sira, he sent gently. *The Singer Iban—our master—is one of the dead.*

Sira had to close her eyes, and her mind, to hide her pain. Not Iban, surely. Iban dead? It did not seem possible that someone so full of life, so generous, so merry and good, should be gone. Iban had been her mentor, her teacher. She pressed her hand to her breast. *What happened, Zakri?*

This Cho is very strong, and untroubled by conscience. I do not yet know how he did it, but he killed Iban. And he holds the entire House of Soren hostage to his search for power.

Sira opened her eyes, looking into Zakri's and finding strength and courage, the courage they would need. *And this is why you came for us.*

He nodded.

Have you told Theo?

Zakri nodded again. *This will not be easy,* he sent. *Cho was one who tested for Conservatory, but failed, and he has never forgotten it. He hates Conservatory, and his Gift is lethal, out of control.*

Sira put her chin in her hand, and thought for a long time about Iban, and about the Gift. Once again she felt the tides of change swirling about her, tugging at her. But she did not fully understand, did not recognize the pattern, even when Jana told her how ill Magister Mkel had seemed when she was at Conservatory, how weak and pale and vague he had been. Sira asked worried questions, about Mkel, about Cho, about Soren and Conservatory, but still she did not see the road that was opening up before her. She knew the Gift was pulling her, but she did not know where it led. It did not matter, of course. She did not need to understand. She would follow regardless.

CHAPTER
EIGHTEEN

SHOUTS AND SLAMMING DOORS AND RUNNING FOOTSTEPS outside Sook's little prison brought her to her feet. She jumped up from the window seat and went to press her ear to the door. Loud voices called, and Cho and one or two others answered, but she couldn't make out the words over the noise of chairs scraping across the stone floor. She strained to hear. Something was happening, but she had no idea what it might be.

She was sure no one new had come to Soren; she would have seen them. Her narrow window looked out over the courtyard, right above the great double doors at the front of the House, and she had little to do these days but gaze out over the snowy landscape, passing long dull hours in solitude. In recent days there had been no movement at all in the courtyard, not even hunters riding past with their itinerant escorts. Sook welcomed any diversion.

The outer door to the apartment shut with force, and a crash followed, making Sook pull back and rub her ear. Silence followed. She waited for a breathless moment, straining her ears, before she tried her door. It was unlocked, and she pulled it partly open to peek out. "Bree?" she called softly. When there was no answer, she opened the door wide and stepped out of her bedroom.

The big central room had been abandoned. Teacups and pens and paper cluttered the long table, and the chairs were pulled out every which way. An ironwood pedestal, over-turned by the banging of the door, had pitched a carved vase to the floor, smashing it into sharp fragments. Sook picked her way around them and found the outer door also left unlocked in the Singers' haste to be away. She took a tentative step into the hall beyond.

The motley group usually camped outside Cho's apart-ment were charging away down the corridor, forgetting all about her. They surprised her by turning right at the end of the hall, not left down the stairs. Sook went after them, hanging back so that she could duck into the doorway if they stopped. Her feet were soundless in her furred boots, and her breath came quickly.

Around that corner, she knew, a staircase was set into the connecting corridor. It was narrow, a set of steps that led only to the attics where the carvers stored their finished work for future use or barter. But in a dormer room on that floor, the itinerants had locked their other, more important prisoner: Cantrix Elnor. She had not been seen outside her room for months. Some House members feared that, like her senior, she was dead. Mura prepared trays every day, to be carried to the Cantrix by one of Cho's men, but she had no way of knowing who really ate from them; she knew only that they returned empty.

Sook reached the corner in time to see a clamoring knot of people pouring down the staircase and into the corridor. It was not Cho at the center of the group, but someone else, someone shorter. Sook couldn't see. Was it—could it be Cantrix Elnor? That would mean at least she was alive! Would they free her at last, allow her back into the Cantoris? Warmth, light—hot baths, comfort! Sook indulged herself for a moment in wishing it were so.

She shrank back into the meager shelter of a doorway, but no one looked in her direction. There was nothing gentle in the way the itinerants were hauling their captive about, the whole lot of them yelling and cursing as they dragged whoever it was downstairs. Sook couldn't believe that even the Singers would treat Cantrix Elnor in this fashion. They descended the staircase with headlong speed, in noisy disorder, and Sook ran to bend over the banister and peer into the lower corridor.

The din below her diminished, then abruptly dwindled to nothing. A crowd of House members collected in hushed dread as the band marched their captive into the carvery. Only one voice rang out. "You bastard! What gives you the right?" It was cut off sharply by the crack of flesh against flesh.

Nori was at the foot of the stairs, staring after the itinerants, her hands pressed to her mouth and her eyes wide.

"Nori!" Sook hissed. "What is it? What's happened?"

Nori's eyes slid up to her, and filled immediately with tears. She took a step backward, as if she would run. "It's Yul . . . he was in the attic, where Cantrix Elnor . . . He shouldn't have gone there! It wouldn't have done any good!" she sobbed.

"What? Nori, what about Yul? What do you mean?" But Nori buried her face in her hands and wouldn't explain.

Sook felt her neck prickle under the heavy coil of her hair. She crept down the stairs, a tread at a time, until she could see the carvery door. No one noticed her, neither Singer nor Houseman. All eyes were on the end of the corridor, all ears straining.

Just as Sook reached the bottom of the staircase, Mura came running from the kitchens, her hands wringing a towel. Her eyes flicked over Sook, but she didn't stop. She pushed her way through the people. "Let me by! Let me through!" she cried roughly.

Quickly, Sook pushed herself through the crush to follow Mura. When people recognized her, they pulled back, making room, as if she were dangerous, or as if she were one of the Gifted they dared not touch. She understood it, and she knew there would be some penalty for her brief freedom, but she didn't care. She caught up with Mura, and they reached the carvery door together.

Sook stood close behind the older woman, gripping her shoulders. The carvery was brilliant with light and hot with tension. Yul, Mura's son, was just getting to his feet with the aid of two other carvers. He touched his lips with his fingers. His mouth was already swollen, and the mark of a hand showed clearly on his face, imprinted in red. When he took his hand away, he reached above his head to the row of *obis* knives, and snatched one from its hook. He pointed it, black and gleaming, across the room.

Cho leaned against a workbench on the opposite side of the carvery. His plait lay across his shoulders, and his own knife remained in its scabbard. His companions fell back, wary of the sickening psi that was sure to come.

"Yul? Don't!" Mura cried. Her voice echoed against the high ceiling amid the soft jangle of the swinging *obis* knives.

Her son lifted his free hand to acknowledge her, but his eyes never left Cho. The long, slender blade of the *obis* knife trembled in his hand, catching the light. Yul held it before him with the blade out, his forefinger braced against the choil as if he were about to make the first cut into some raw chunk of ironwood. Only the Gift, wielded with the *obis* blade, could separate the fibers of the irontrees, force their unyielding bonds apart. It was the special province of the carvers to do that work, and they served long apprenticeships learning their craft. They had a discipline and tradition all their own.

But this knife was pointed at a man's heart. Cho, who had been a carver himself, stood with one hip against the workbench, his arms loosely folded before him.

"Do you think you can do it, Carver?" he breathed.

Yul was shorter than Cho, and had to tip his head back to meet his gaze. His lips were drawn back from his teeth, and his face was so suffused with anger and fear that Sook hardly recognized him. "We've had enough of you!" he shouted. The veins in his throat stood out in ropes, painful to see. "Singers loafing around the House, nursery gardens half-dead, darkness, cold!" He gestured wildly about him with the knife, and the carvers near him stepped hastily away.

"Yul!" Mura cried again.

Cho flashed her a brief cool glance. "Ah, the cook," he said. "You should have taught your son obedience when you had the chance, Housewoman." His thin body in the dark tunic snapped suddenly straight, looking like a blade itself. "It didn't work, anyway, did it, boy?" He gestured around him to the people watching. "You didn't get away with it, did you? Maybe these honest Housemen and women like their freedom after all!"

"Get away with what?" begged Mura.

Yul looked to his mother, looked around at all the faces in the carvery and crowded into the corridor beyond it. "Cantrix Elnor is alive!" he exclaimed. "I heard her voice, and I tried to get her out of there! She's shut up like an animal, like—"

One of the other carvers stepped up to Yul again, cautiously touching his arm. "Yul, be careful! There's no point—" but Yul shook him off. In a much lower voice he said, "It's time. Time to fight back." He shifted the ironwood hilt of the knife in his hand, the nib pointing up, the haft in his fist. He whispered miserably, "I never thought to use my Gift in such a way."

Cho sneered at him. "You and your sacred Gift! What good is it if you don't control your own destiny?" Languidly, he lifted his braid and dropped it back over his shoulder. Then, very slowly, he unfolded his arms and opened them, spread them wide like the black wings of a *ferrel* gliding on the wind. He completely exposed his chest to Yul. It was unutterably insolent. It was both invitation and challenge. Sook felt as if the stone floor were dropping away beneath her as she watched.

The knife in Yul's hand quivered with the strength of his psi gathering around it. It seemed to take on a life of its own, vibrating, glowing faintly from within. Mura moaned her son's name, once.

Yul took a deep breath and pulled his arm back. With a graceful, swift motion, he threw the knife directly at Cho.

Someone in the hallway shrieked, and Sook knew without turning her head that it was Nori. The knife flew toward Cho, aimed with psi, thrown with muscle. It sang through the air, describing a precise arc toward its goal. For one splendid moment it seemed to the House members that it would succeed, that it would reach its target and free them at last from the tyranny that was destroying them.

But its path changed as they watched. As it neared Cho the arc became an angle. The knife lifted high, its hilt trailing, and then descended, blade down, whistling as it fell. Its sharp point struck straight into the floor and the blade sank a thumb's length into the stone. The haft quivered as its energy dissipated uselessly into the air.

An agonizing silence followed, so absolute that Sook thought she could hear the faint ring of the *obis* blade shuddering against the stone. Then Cho smiled, his narrow lips pulling up just at the corners. "So," he said softly. "You couldn't do it." He lowered his arms, taking a long time about it.

"But someone will!" Yul said loudly. He made no attempt to get away, but stood stalwart, hands hanging loosely, facing his fate. He knew, and so did everyone there, what was coming. A tear sparkled briefly in his eye and was gone, blinked away as he thrust up his chin and waited.

Sook felt Mura tremble under her hands. Cho looked down his nose at Yul, and began to narrow his eyes.

The Singer Bree cried out from behind him. "Cho! It's not necessary!"

His hand snapped around, finding her behind him, glaring coldly at her. "I think it is," he hissed. "Or shall I waste time defending myself whenever one of these *hruss* decides to challenge me?"

Bree faltered, swaying on her feet. The itinerants around her moved as far away from her as space allowed.

Cho swept the crowd with his eyes. "Anyone else?" Only Mura moved, one step into the carvery, and that didn't concern him. "Good," he said clearly. "You'll all remember this."

Mura cried, "No!" Nori sobbed from the hallway. Those were the only sounds as Cho's eyelids lowered until his eyes were only slits of darkness. Yul sank to his knees and then slumped to the floor, his eyes rolling back, his mouth open.

Mura's scream turned Sook's stomach to ice. As Mura ran to bend over her fallen son, Sook was close behind her. They knelt beside Yul on the stone floor, chafed his wrists and rubbed his cheeks, called to him, cradled him in their arms, but it did no good.

Mura turned her wet and livid face up to the other carvers. "Get him!" she shouted. "All of you, at once, you could do it! He's killed Yul! He's killed my son!"

The carvers looked at her in utter misery. One woman wept, the others huddled together in fear and revulsion and shame. Behind her Cho laughed aloud.

"You see, Bree?" he called. "That's why it's necessary. None of these will try me again."

Mura jumped to her feet. "I will!" she shrieked. "Give me a knife, someone! His cursed Gift is nothing to me!"

Sook's eyes were on Mura, and she didn't see Cho come for her. She felt her arm twisted suddenly, savagely, and she was jerked to her feet with a painful wrenching of her shoulder.

"And is this girl nothing to you?" Cho's voice was as sharp and light as a knife edge. He had Sook's arm tight in his hand. She felt the skin break under his nails, and drops of hot blood slipped down to her elbow. "Do you want to attack me now?" he taunted Mura, leaning over her so that drops of his spittle struck her cheek. He gave Sook a shake that jarred her teeth and loosened the binding of her hair, spilling her heavy tresses over her shoulders.

"Let me go!" she cried, and despite the pain in her arm, she tried to pull away. He laughed again, and wrapped his other arm around her, holding her like he might a sack of oaten grain or *hruss* fodder. She kicked and struggled, but she was too small, too light. When she gave it up, panting, she saw Bree bent to her knees, clutching her head, and she knew the Singer had tried to interfere.

Cho backed out of the carvery. The people in the corridor stepped on each other's feet in their haste to get away from him. Sook's toes could not reach the ground, and now her ribs and stomach hurt with the pressure of his arm. She couldn't draw a deep breath, and her vision blurred. When he finally set her feet on a stair, two treads above his own, she gasped for air and sagged against the banister. A drop of her blood fell out of her sleeve to the stone, leaving a small pitiful mark.

Cho held out his hand to Nori, and she came to take it, her head lowered, looking sidelong at the people she passed. "I always repay loyalty," Cho murmured, smiling.

Sook stared in speechless horror. Nori—Nori had betrayed Yul!

The people in the corridor gasped, and one or two made sounds of disgust. Nori's head dropped lower yet, but she let Cho draw her up the stairs nonetheless, and he prodded Sook to make her precede them. Slowly, pressing her fingers to her bleeding arm, she climbed the steps. The most eager of Cho's followers came after them, resuming their posts at the door as Cho thrust Sook into the apartment, and he and Nori followed.

He took Nori into his own bedroom, the large one. Just before closing the door, he looked back at Sook with a thin smile. The gleam in his eyes made him look as she thought a *tkir* must look, feral, ferocious in its hunger, heedless of the destruction it left in its wake. She felt as small as a *wezel* before his power.

"Your turn will come, little Sook," he said lightly. "Just be patient."

He shut the door between them, and Sook turned with dragging feet to her own room. Before she closed her door, she heard Nori cry out, twice. She knew Cho had hurt her, taking his pleasure, if pleasure it was, without regard for her pain.

Sook shut her own door sharply, and leaned her forehead

against it, sick with fear and grief. My turn, she thought. If my turn comes, I'll kill him. I swear it!

She went to the window, looking out over the snowbound hills, and wished with all her might for Zakri to come.

CHAPTER NINETEEN

"BETWEEN US, WE ARE STRONG ENOUGH TO DEFEAT HIM," Zakri said, aloud for Berk's benefit. "The trick will be to get to him without one of us being hurt."

"Can we not simply go in, and force him to leave?" Sira asked. She looked at Berk. "Surely we have the authority?"

Berk was just shedding his furs, and combing out his hair and beard with his fingers. He shook his head. "Cho doesn't recognize authority," he said. He eased himself down with a groan to rest his back against an arching ironwood sucker. It had been a long day of riding, pushing south through Ogre Pass. They had left it behind at last in the late afternoon, and had found the road to the southeast. The way led through irontree groves so thickly grown they sometimes meshed above their heads into a canopy of dark green needles.

"You know, these gray hairs of mine are reminders to you all that my bones are old!" Berk grumbled.

Mreen scrambled up from feeding softwood twigs to Theo's cookfire and trotted to Berk. She bent over him, looking into his eyes and patting his grizzled cheeks with her small hands. *Cantor Theo,* she sent, *please tell Berk I will heal his bones for him.*

"Mreen says she will work on those old bones," Theo said, grinning at the courier.

Berk grunted, trying to shift into a more comfortable position. "She must be some healer, if she can make old bones young!"

He has to sit still, Mreen sent. *And Cantor Theo, you have to tell me what mode to use!*

Theo chuckled. "This could be interesting, Berk. You have to hold still, and she does not know which mode to use, so it could take a while!"

"Being still sounds fine to me," the big man rumbled. "I can use the rest." He tapped Mreen gently under her chin with a thick finger. "Take as long as you like, little one." He leaned his head back against the great root and closed his eyes.

Mreen, I suggest Lidya, Theo sent. *Your patient is more tired than ill.*

Theo went on with the *keftet* preparation while Mreen played a *Lidya* melody on her *filla.* With nothing to resonate against, the notes were clear and dry in the violet of the evening, fading to nothing almost before the ear could catch them. Sira nodded her approval.

You have been practicing, she sent when the little melody ended. *Your fingerings are much improved.*

Mreen's nimbus glowed, and she hopped from one foot to the other, as full of energy as Berk was drained. *Oh, yes!* she bubbled. *Cantor Nikei is very strict.*

So I remember him! Sira answered.

Mreen danced to the cookfire and knelt beside Theo once again. *Cantor Theo, will you ask Berk if he is better?*

Theo did. Berk opened his eyes, and then closed one in a wink at Mreen. "Much better, child, thank you. Now, you just do that every night, and this old carcass might make it through the journey." The travelers laughed, and the *hruss* lifted their heads, their long ears turning to follow the voices.

As Theo put the finishing touches on their meal, Zakri

warned Sira, "You must not underestimate Cho's strength. His Gift is crude, but he has no conscience. His psi is like a kick from a *hruss,* nothing fancy, but it can do a lot of damage. He can ruin an unshielded mind in a moment. It is better if we combine our shields, as Jana and I did when he attacked Izak."

"And his own shields?" she asked.

Zakri held up his hands, palms outward. "Do carvers even learn to shield? We just do not know."

"And if we attack him? Then what happens to his mind?"

Zakri shrugged. "I have given that no thought," he answered. "I am not likely to care, either!"

Sira's lips pressed together, and she dropped her eyes. Zakri saw Theo give her a sharp look before he pulled the *keftet* from the fire, ready to spoon it into their bowls. Mreen stuck her finger into the pot and licked a dollop of *keftet*, smacking her lips and then silently laughing. Theo tousled her hair. "What Singers does Cho have around him?" he asked.

"I know hardly any names," Zakri told him. "There is a man named Klas, and one named Shiro. Those are all I met, though the House is crowded with Singers. I was only one among many. I know several of the House members, though . . . the cooks."

"Ah! So I am not the only one who is changeless," Sira observed.

Zakri laughed and tossed his carved spoon into the air, catching it and holding it up in a jaunty salute. "I promise, Cantrix Sira, my appetite is only that of a healthy grown man!"

"Indeed," she said. "We will see."

"My father knew Klas v'Soren," Theo said as he handed them their filled bowls. "Called him a thief and a sneak, not to put too fine a point on it. He traveled with him once, and he warned me never to make the same mistake. Singer Klas came poorly supplied at the beginning, so he helped himself out of my father's saddle packs—then took more than his share of the metal at the trip's end."

"Not a strong Singer, though, I think," Zakri said.

"Probably not, or he would not have been a thief," Theo agreed. He came to sit cross-legged on his furs next to Sira.

They were all quiet for a moment, enjoying the excellent *keftet*. It was fragrant with Observatory's spices and rich with good grain. Zakri could have smacked his lips like Mreen, and he eyed the pot to see if there was more.

"What I would like to know," Theo went on after a time, "is why the Singers, and so many of them, follow someone like Cho? Klas I can understand, but the rest of them—I knew many a fine itinerant Singer, honest and hardworking men and women. Where are they all?"

Zakir swallowed a large mouthful before he could answer. "I suspect there are a number of them who have second thoughts about the whole thing, but Cho wastes no time in punishing anyone who challenges him. His talent is for controlling the Gifted. They are all terrified, and rightly so."

"And the House members?"

Berk put his spoon down and looked around at each of them. "You have to understand, before we go into this situation, that Soren's House members are helpless now," he said. "Their Magister's gone, with all his family. Their Cantor's dead, and by now their Cantrix could be. They're dependent on the itinerants for their warmth and their light, such as it is. Cho has them trapped, just as he does the Singers. They can't see a way out."

"And I was told there is a Gifted child, ready and willing to join Mreen's class at Conservatory," Zakri added. "But Cho will not allow it."

Sira's eyes flashed darkly at that. It was a look Zakri remembered well. "How could things have gone so far?" she demanded. "Has the Committee done nothing?"

Zakri shrugged. "Lamdon did not know until we told them, and there was no evidence, except that the Singers from all over the Continent were disappearing. Iban was trying to reach Amric . . . to warn me, I believe. He almost made it . . . he came so close."

Sira laid her bowl aside, her meal unfinished, and turned her gaze beyond the *quiru* as if she were at that moment wishing Iban safe passage beyond the stars. Watching her, Zakri felt the icy pain of their master's loss once again, renewed by the freshness of Sira's grief.

Theo felt it, too. *We will set it right, Sira. I promise.*

The Spirit willing, Sira answered. She met Theo's eyes, her face open and vulnerable in a way Zakri had rarely seen. He was surprised to see Theo touch Sira's knee, and to see that she did not pull away, but even laid her fingertips briefly against his hand.

Would the Spirit dare will anything Cantrix Sira does not? Theo sent lightly.

That made Zakri laugh, startling Berk. "I am sorry, Berk," he chortled. "It is this Cantor Theo and his jokes. I will make him say them aloud from now on."

Berk smiled wearily. "I'm half-asleep anyway, and no decent audience." He bowed to Theo. "Cantor Theo, if you could save me a joke for tomorrow, I'd appreciate it."

Theo spread his hands in a deprecating gesture. "I am not so funny, I fear. Your Cantor Zakri is too easily amused."

Zakri smiled at Sira. "So I have heard, and often." He won a slight smile from her in return, though her eyes were shadowed.

Theo collected the *keftet* bowls, frowning over the bits Sira had left in hers, and stepped to the edge of the camp to scrub them out with chunks of snow. Sira took Mreen outside the *quiru*. They came back quickly, shivering. Despite Mreen's protests, Sira made her sit still while she undid the binding of her hair and helped her pull off her boots and her trousers. In just her tunic, Mreen quickly wriggled down into the bedfurs. Zakri saw Sira touch the little girl's cheek with the backs of her fingers.

Sleep well, child, she sent.

One song first? Mreen begged.

Zakri joined in. *Yes, Cantrix Sira! One song, please!*

Sira shot him a look. *You are still listening to every conversation around you!*

He gave her his most winning smile. *It has been a most useful habit,* he answered.

She sighed in mock exasperation, but she sat back on her

heels at the edge of Mreen's bedfurs and thought for a moment. *One song, then,* she sent to Mreen. *A very old one.*

Mreen dimpled and snuggled deep in her furs. The layers of the *caeru* pelt, yellow on the outside, creamy white in the soft depths, tangled with her red hair, encircling her sleepy face. Zakri's heart warmed at the sight. He could understand, just now, the look Sira sometimes turned on him. Occasionally he had caught her watching him, her angular features softer than usual, her eyes brighter. She always averted her glance if their eyes met, but the expression on her face was a mystery to him. He felt a bit sad, thinking of it. He closed his eyes to listen to her sing, and to sense the gentle *cantrip* for sleep she wove into the lullaby.

> LITTLE ONE, LOST ONE,
> SLEEPY ONE, SMALL ONE,
> PILLOW YOUR HEAD,
> DREAM OF THE STARS,
> AND THE SHIP THAT CARRIES YOU HOME.
> LITTLE ONE, SWEET ONE,
> DROWSY ONE, LOST ONE,
> THE NIGHT IS LONG,
> THE SNOW IS COLD,
> BUT THE SHIP WILL CARRY YOU HOME.

Mreen's drooping lashes made delicate shadows on her cheeks. Berk murmured quietly so as not to wake her, "Lovely. It's so good to hear you sing again, Cantrix. We've missed you at Amric."

Sira inclined her head to him. "You are kind, Berk. I thank you."

Mreen's eyes opened again, resisting. *More,* she sent sleepily. *One more song.*

Zakri chuckled. *I will sing you one,* he sent to her. *I am no Cantrix Sira, but I sing a little!*

Sira smiled at him. "It would give me pleasure to hear you," she said. "It has been some time."

"There is a song my mother taught me," Zakri told

Mreen. "My mother was a Singer like yours. Not a Cantrix, though—an itinerant Singer."

Mreen's green eyes opened wide, thinking about this. *Is she dead, too, like mine?*

Zakri looked across the banked fire at her. He saw her mother in her eyes, laughing Isbel of the beautiful voice and auburn hair. *Yes,* he answered, and he sent Mreen a picture of his own mother, as best he could remember her. She gave a little nod of understanding. "Now, I will sing this song, but then you must go to sleep. Promise?"

She nodded, heavy eyelids struggling against the effects of Sira's *cantrip.* Zakri turned his own eyes up to the stars blanketing the night sky above their *quiru.* It had been a long, long time since he had thought of his mother.

THE *CAERU* HAS PUPS, AND THE *FERREL* HAS FLEDGLINGS,
THE *HRUSS* HAS ITS FOAL, AND THE *WEZEL* ITS KITS.
THE *CARWAL* HAS WHELPS, THE *TKIR* HAVE THEIR CATLINGS,
AND I, MY SWEET DARLING, HAVE YOU.
THE *URBEAR* HAS CUBS THAT PLAY ON THE GLACIER,
THE *TKIR* LETS ITS BABES RUN WILD IN THE SNOW,
BUT THE CHILD OF MY HEART TUMBLES HERE ON THE FLOOR,
WAITING FOR SUMMER, WAITING TO GROW.

Sira, still kneeling on the edge of Mreen's bedfurs, looked up at Zakri, and he saw with shock that there were tears in her eyes. *I am sorry, Cantrix,* he began, but she shook her head.

No, Zakri, do not be. It is a beautiful song, and a beautiful thought. I only thought of your mother . . . it touched me.

Mreen was sound asleep, and the whole camp was quiet, ready for the night. Sira got up and went to her own bedfurs. The men made a quick trip out of the *quiru,* and Zakri made a last round of the *hruss,* making certain they were settled in for the long night. Their heads hung low to the trampled snow, but their ears swiveled back and forth, back and forth, following the sounds the people made.

When they were all in their bedfurs, ready for sleep, Zakri

leaned on his elbow, looking across the coals of the cookfire.

Cantrix Sira, why did that old children's song upset you?

It did not upset me, she sent firmly. *I was moved. That is all. It is nothing.*

But something upset you, earlier. I saw it.

Sira sat up in her bedfurs, tracing her scarred eyebrow with her finger. Theo sat up as well, watching her.

You were talking about carvers, and whether they learn to shield. Zakri nodded. She put her arms around her upraised knees and leaned her chin on them. *Long ago, I hurt someone, and I am loath to do it again. Perhaps I cannot do it again. And I fear this whole crisis comes about because of the way we treat the Gift, measuring it, testing it as if it were an absolute. For this carver, only Conservatory could have satisfied his ambitions. Theo felt much the same, but his parents would not allow it . . . they insisted he follow in their traditions. If there were only more choices for the Gifted, other paths for them to follow, this tragedy might have been averted.*

Theo put in, *Remember, Sira, the irontree sucker cannot force the treeling to take root.*

Sira shook her head. *I remember the proverb, but . . .* She shrugged, and Zakri laughed quietly.

I do not get it either, he sent.

Theo sent, *Cho is responsible for what he has become. You are certainly not, Sira, nor even, I think, the Committee or Conservatory.*

She hugged her knees tighter. *Just the same, I am fearful for the Gift. Will they listen, now, when we tell them about Observatory? That we have so many, while the Houses of the Continent have so few? And what awful things will we have to do at Soren?*

At the least, Theo assured her, *we will save the little one there. One task at a time.*

Sira took a deep breath, rubbing her eyes as if to banish her dark thoughts. *Why, Theo, no proverb for that?* she asked.

He chuckled. *Too tired, my dear,* he sent, and yawned to

prove it. *Much too tired.* They both lay down, pulling their bedfurs close about them.

Zakri followed their example. For some time he lay staring up at the stars past the *quiru,* thinking. He was afraid of what was to come, fearful for Mreen, for himself, for these others. But he was very glad to be here, to be with Sira and with Theo. He was grateful for the choice.

CHAPTER
TWENTY

✦ SOOK, STANDING ALONE AT HER WINDOW, SAW THE travelers cresting the ridge above the House. They trooped down toward Soren in a colorful wave of *hruss,* some carrying riders, two laden only with bulging packs, two with loaded *pukuru* sliding behind them over the snow. She pressed herself against the window and counted them. Twelve people, and sixteen *hruss*! Never had she seen so many riders at one time. With trembling fingers, she brushed and rebound her hair, and straightened her tunic, her eyes never leaving the scene. Surely, surely this meant Zakri was here at last!

Sook hoped perhaps Zakri could even see her, standing in her narrow window. She clasped her hands beneath her chin and watched a large *quiru* bloom about the traveling party, just beyond the edge of the courtyard. It towered against the dull gray of the sky, a wide inviting column of warmth and light. Housemen set about making the camp comfortable, unpacking a table from the *pukuru,* two high-backed chairs, several stools. They ranged bedfurs in a long row at the edge of the camp, and tethered the *hruss* on the other side. Sook stared into the brilliant light, trying to make out the faces of the people.

She could not find Zakri. There were two tall, slender men, but neither was he, and they both behaved like servants. They bowed often to two shorter men, one plump and dark, one even plumper, the fattest man Sook had ever seen, and pale as the snow on the hills around them. Those two were quickly seated in the tall chairs, and two others near them on stools. One of the Housemen started a cookfire and the seated men soon were holding cups of tea, looking up at the House, but making no move toward it. Two burly Housemen took up positions at the very edge of the great *quiru*. They wore long knives prominently strapped about them, and they stood facing out toward Soren, their arms folded, faces impassive.

Sook's hopes thinned and faded away like curls of smoke. She lowered herself into the window seat, feeling suddenly weary. She gazed out at the newly made camp, and the men in it, and she understood all too well who and what they were. She had never been to the capital House of Nevya, in fact had never been away from her own House in her life, but she knew that such an exhibition of riches could come from only one place. It wasn't Zakri who had come, but Lamdon. Lamdon! Cantors and Magisters and Committee members. What did such people know of real trouble?

In the outer room of the apartment, she heard the itinerants talking and Cho's light voice in response. She heard him clearly. "It's just what we've been waiting for," he pronounced. "Call all the Singers into the Cantoris, and you, Klas, give the carvers one last chance to be a part of this. Our goal has come to us!"

Someone asked a question Sook couldn't hear, and Cho's answer was as clear and sharp as the icicles that drooped under Soren's eaves. "It's Magister Gowan, and that dark man with him is Cantor Abram himself. Just where we want them."

Sook leaned forward, putting her forehead against the cold limeglass. The men from Lamdon were being served a meal, not a simple bowl of *keftet* but several different dishes spread out around them. She imagined what there might be for them to eat—grain for sure, dried fruit, perhaps nutbread with oil to dip it in. Her mouth watered, and a spasm of craving knotted her stomach. She wrapped her arms around her middle and stubbornly set her jaw. They must not give in, neither she nor Mura nor the carvers nor the House members! They must stand on their own, and together. And they must warn those soft men from Lamdon! Didn't they realize Cho could strike at them even as they sat over their meal?

Two short raps sounded at her door, and the bolt slid back. Bree opened the door and looked in.

"Sook," she said. "I'm sorry, but no bath today. You probably saw?"

Sook jumped to her feet. "I saw—what's going to happen?"

Bree's plain features twisted. "We're having a meeting in the Cantoris. I don't feel good about this . . . that's Magister Gowan out there!"

"So I heard," Sook answered, staring out the window once again. "Which one is he?"

"The white one," Bree grunted.

"Spirit!" Sook exclaimed. "Did you ever know a man could grow so fat?"

"A few weeks at Soren, and he'd be skinny as a *wezel*," Bree retorted. "Like the rest of us. Anyway, I have to go. Sorry about the *ubanyix*."

"Bree, wait!" Sook cried. "Could you just—just forget—about locking the door? I promise I won't say a word. And with all this excitement . . ."

Bree looked back over her shoulder. The apartment was empty, but she hesitated. "I'm still in trouble for trying to help you the last time," she muttered.

"I know," Sook said softly. "But if he fails, and you've been kind to me—I know Singer Zakri will stand up for you!"

"Zakri?" Bree squinted at her. "You know, Sook, I have to agree with Mura. You put a lot of faith in a man you don't really know. And he's not even out there!"

Sook stiffened her back and stuck her chin out. She was still a head shorter than the older woman. "He will be! And I know what I need to know."

"They all say the same thing," Bree said sourly.

"Bree—just for me, then? I'll be so grateful, and if he finds out I'll tell him I unlocked it myself!"

Bree shook her head, muttering, "Six Stars! I'll probably be sorry for this. Just remember, if he puts someone else on this duty, you may not get any favors at all!"

Sook gave Bree a brilliant smile. "Thank you, thank you! Hurry to your meeting, now, Singer," she said. "I'll be back before you are. They'll never even know I'm gone!"

Sook found Mura and Eun and most of the carvers gathered around the long scarred table in the kitchens. They gave hushed cries of joy at seeing her, and then drew her quickly into their whispered conversation. She glanced around to see that Nori was conspicuous by her absence, and that one or two carvers had also not come. She could hardly blame them for being afraid, but she was elated at the chance for action, at the possibility of being released from her prison. Surely something would happen now!

Yul's death had aged Mura. Sook came to stand close to her, and Mura's glance at her was bitter, her eyes under their wrinkled lids dark with grief. "We're going to send someone out," she said, "someone to tell them what's happening. That's the Magister of Lamdon out there, come at last!"

"Have you seen him?" Sook asked. "Any of you?"

No one had. "He's short and fat . . . and old. I don't think he's a match for Cho and these Singers!"

"But he's the Magister of Lamdon! Of the whole Continent!" one of the carvers protested. "How can the Singers oppose him?"

"This is just what Cho wanted," Sook told him. "I heard him say so."

"Surely he won't attack Magister Gowan!" Eun said faintly.

Sook thought for a moment, her fingers on her lips. "I don't think it's Magister Gowan he'll attack," she said. "The

Magister of Lamdon isn't Gifted, only the Magister of Conservatory. Right?" She looked around the group for confirmation. "So the one he'll attack is the man with the Magister. The Gifted one."

"But who's with him? Who came as his Singer?"

"Not just his Singer. Cantor Abram, senior Cantor of Lamdon." Sook put her hands on her hips. "He's a fool, sitting out there on a great chair like he was up on the dais, nice and safe in his own Cantoris! Cho will make *keftet* out of him in a heartbeat!"

Mura snorted. "That would serve him right," she said, "but maybe if we hurry we can prevent it. We were just deciding who should go."

"I'll go!" Sook cried immediately.

"No, you won't," said the carver. "They watch you too closely. You'll go back where they expect you to be. One of us will go."

"But," Mura said, "it shouldn't be one of the Gifted. He knows just how to hurt you."

"Then who?"

Mura stared at them. "I'm going to do it."

"Mura, no!" Sook protested. "Not you. Someone else, someone younger."

"She's right," the carver put in. "It should be someone who can run, who can get there quickly in the dark. In the cold."

"Me, then," Sook said again.

The heavy door to the kitchen swung open, and Bree's weathered face showed in the doorway. "Sook!" she hissed. "They're done! You need to hurry!"

Sook hugged Mura quickly, and lifted her hand to the carvers. "I'll have to go," she said. "But, Mura . . ."

"Please!" Bree said urgently.

Sook cast an imploring glance back at Mura, but she ran. She knew what could happen to Bree, and she had promised. Taking the back staircase, she hurried up to the upper level and into Cho's apartment, closing her bedroom door behind her with some moments to spare before the itinerants came back. Sook listened to the sounds of them returning, the thudding of resettled furniture, the brush of their boots against the floor, murmured conversation. She knelt in the window seat once again, and for most of the long afternoon she stayed there, staring into the large *quiru* across the courtyard.

Raised voices roused Sook. She startled, her eyelids flying open, and realized she had fallen asleep, curled in the window seat. Her neck was stiff from tilting her head awkwardly against the wall. She groaned, and massaged it with both hands.

"Impossible!" came an imperious cry beyond her door. "The Magister will never agree, nor the Committee!"

Sook stumbled to her feet, bending to rub one ankle that tingled unbearably. A glance outside showed her that the Lamdon party's *quiru* now shone in a sky grown dusky. The sun was already gone, and long fingers of shadow, cast by the unusual light beyond the courtyard, stretched across the cobblestones.

"That's what we want, and that's what we'll have," she heard Cho announce, his high-pitched voice carrying easily to her ears, although he didn't speak loudly. "Freedom to fix our own prices, whether itinerants or carvers; Soren as a base, without interference from the Committee; and the same rights Cantors have, private apartments, full privileges, and our own leader."

The Lamdon courier sputtered angrily. His voice did not carry so well, and Sook hobbled to the door on her stinging foot to press her ear to it.

"Are you prepared to make the sacrifices Cantors and Cantrixes make, then? To serve as they do?"

Cho's voice was cool and even. "But, courier, we do serve. We've served you, in fact. Did you drink from a carved teacup out there, in your great *quiru*? Did you eat from an ironwood plate? Use a spoon? A cookpot?"

"It's hardly the same," the courier shouted. "You're insane!"

"I?" Cho laughed and Sook heard the scrape of his chair on the floor. She could picture him in his usual pose by the window, leaning against the frame, drawing his long black plait through his fingers. "I think it's you and your Magister—and perhaps your Cantors, out there—who aren't sane. You have no power over me."

"But what you're doing to these people, to this House—" The courier grew shrill in his frustration.

Cho laughed again. "Do you see them trying to escape, to run across that courtyard to join you?"

"Well, that's nothing! We could hardly carry the whole House back to Lamdon, and they know that!"

"But they see you out there, you and your pale Magister and your weak Cantors. They see you eating and drinking like you were at some great feast, they see you fat and comfortable as they never are, and they understand even more why we need to do this."

"But—"

A bang, as of a fist on a table, startled Sook away from the door. "No more talk!" Cho said, very loudly this time. "Go back and tell them. If they don't leave, and carry our message to the Committee, they'll regret it. I can make it very painful for them—if they need a demonstration, I'll give them one!"

"You're going to be sorry about this, Carver!" the courier said. Sook heard, even through the door, the futility of his protest.

There was a moment of silence, and when he spoke again, Cho's voice was light once more. "You have it wrong," he said with a laugh. "The regrets will be all yours, and your masters', if they don't listen to me."

"Never!"

Footsteps sounded across the floor, and a door was flung open and then closed, banging against the wall, and again in the doorjamb. Sook ran back to her window to see the courier march across the dappled courtyard, past the two guards, and into the light of the *quiru*. The two younger Cantors rose to meet him, but the Magister and the senior Cantor remained in their chairs, not deigning to look at the House, but only at their courier. Sook made a noise of disgust.

A knock at her door heralded the arrival of Bree, supper tray in hand.

"Bree! Did you hear all that? What's going to happen?"

"You'd better just keep out of it," Bree said dourly. "And that's what I plan to do, too."

"But how can you? You're a part of it!"

The Singer's lips pressed into a thin line. She set the tray down and pointed to the bowl and the cup on it. "Look at that!" she said in a low tone. "*Caeru* stew, tea. No fruit, no grain, no bread. We can't work, we can't travel, we can't eat. This isn't the way it was supposed to be."

Sook came closer to Bree, leaning forward to look up into her eyes. "Bree—it doesn't have to be this way. You can fight back. We all can. You can help, talk to the others. . . ."

Bree turned her face away. "Ship knows I'm in it now, and of my own will, too. I was all right with it—until Yul."

"But now?" Sook prompted her quietly.

Bree's eyes were bleak when she turned back to meet Shook's. "Never mind. Eat your meal. I'll get the tray later."

Sook sat down on the bed and picked up her spoon. The stew was Mura's usual rich brown, and it smelled as spicy as ever, but she could see without touching it that it was only meat and broth, and it didn't appeal to her. "I'm not hungry," she said.

"Best eat it anyway," Bree said from the door. "It's all there is."

Sook said, "Bree . . . are you sure? Sure you don't want to—"

Bree put up her hand abruptly, cutting off her words. "Don't even say it," she said. "A taste of his—discipline, he calls it—was enough for me, that day in the carvery. You don't know what it's like."

Sook sat with her hand in her lap, holding the spoon. "What is it like? What does he do?"

Bree leaned the back of her head against the door and closed her eyes. "I'll tell you," she said grimly. "It's like having your brains cut apart. It's like dying, only you're afraid you won't die and it'll go on forever. It's more than losing your Gift, which is bad enough; it's like losing yourself."

Sook shivered. "I'm sorry, Bree. I guess I'll never really understand."

"The Spirit willing, you won't," the Singer answered. "Now you eat your stew, and I'll come back later."

But when she had left, Sook ignored the tray and went back to the window. The Housemen in the *quiru* were serving another meal to their Magister and the three Cantors. Sook was sure the Magister was drinking wine, although of course the Cantors didn't. It had been a long time since she tasted wine. Even worse, she knew it had been a long time since any of the itinerants had had any, and there was the Magister of Lamdon drinking it right out in front of them.

She stood with her hands on either side of the window, and pointed her small chin at the fat man. "Magister or no," she muttered, "you're a great fool!"

Sook was wakeful when the rest of the House was bedding down. Her forced inactivity made it hard to sleep through the long nights. She went back to the window seat when her meal tray had been removed to watch the darkness fall over the Timberlands and the stars come to life above the Continent. She watched as the Housemen beyond the courtyard fed their *hruss,* laid out the bedfurs, banked the cookfire. Thus it was that she saw Mura try to reach Lamdon's *quiru.*

Mura had left the House through the stable doors and slipped around to the front, skirting Soren's ragged *quiru,* aiming for the bright one. She never reached it.

The guards who had stood watch all day were already in their bedfurs, and two new ones had replaced them. The other Housemen had gone to bed as well, leaving the Magister and the three Cantors sitting around the table. Mura was a slow-moving figure heavily muffled in borrowed furs. As she drew near the light, one of the younger Cantors stood to meet her. He came to the edge of the *quiru* and reached out his hand to her, right out of the warmth and into the cold and dark. But before their fingers could touch, he reeled and fell back on his heels, stumbling, tripping over a stool. He went down on the packed snow, and lay without moving. The other Cantor ran to kneel beside him, and then turned an ashen face, mouth working, up to the House.

Sook looked down to see that the double doors directly beneath her stood open to the night. Cho was on the steps, just at the edge of Soren's fragmented light. He raised his long arm, pointing and calling something out into the courtyard. Mura whirled, trapped in the darkness between the two *quiru*.

Magister Gowan came to his feet, with Cantor Abram beside him. He made a gesture, and one of the Housemen snatched up his heavy furs and ran, pulling them on as he went, toward Mura. Sook found that her knuckle was between her teeth, and she was biting on it, hard. She watched helplessly as Cantor Abram pressed his hands to his temples and bent double, and the other Cantor, the one kneeling by his colleague, cried out and slumped forward. Cho shouted again.

The Magister called out sharply and the Houseman on his way to Mura stopped in confusion. He looked from his Magister to Cho, taking in the condition of the Singers, waiting in the darkness for interminable moments for some decision. Sook knew there was no decision to be made. There was no choice. Without their Singers, they were all dead. Even the great Magister of Lamdon could not keep himself warm in the deep cold. Cho loomed in the open doorway, both arms out, his head tipped far back so that Sook could see the curve of his long nose.

The Houseman backed away from Mura, taking slow and reluctant steps until he was within the circle of the *quiru*'s warmth. Cho lowered his arms, and Cantor Abram straightened, shaking his head and rubbing his eyes. Magister Gowan shouted something, but there was no answer. The double doors below Sook were closing.

Cho meant to leave Mura in the courtyard, in the cold. He had attacked the Singers of Lamdon, and he would do it again if they tried to help her. Mura had become his demonstration, his sacrifice. With a cry of fury, Sook ran to her door.

No one had forgotten this time. The door to her bedroom was secure, the wooden bolt driven home in its socket, turned and braced in the locking slot. She couldn't get out.

Back she flew to the window, pounding on the limeglass with her fist. "Mura!" she shrieked. "Mura! Run to the stables, go to the stables!"

It was impossible for Mura to hear her, but she looked up at her window nonetheless, and Sook saw the faint flutter of her eyes. She was already feeling the cold. Sook gestured wildly, pointing, to indicate that Mura should go back the way she had come, try the stable door.

The cook lifted and spread her hands. She mouthed, "Too late." She touched her heart, once, and then raised her fingers to Sook. She was saying goodbye.

"Mura, no! Try!" Sook screamed over and over until her throat ached, and the itinerants coming into the main room of the apartment banged on her door and demanded quiet. She ignored them, calling and crying to Mura until her voice grew hoarse, and then she sobbed in misery, kneeling on the window seat with her forehead pressed against the icy limeglass, staring at the macabre scene.

Mura walked slowly to the broad steps that led up to her House. She turned and seated herself, drawing the furs about her. Her back was straight, her head up, and Sook could imagine the glare she turned on the Lamdon contingent. They stared, as Sook did, unable to believe the dispassionate savagery of Cho's reprisal.

Even Sook's tears spent themselves eventually, but still she knelt at the window, her hands and her forehead pressed against it.

The end was not long in coming. Mura's rigid back curved slightly, and then she slumped, almost imperceptibly, within the inadequate shelter of the *caeru* furs. Irrelevantly, Sook wondered whose they were. They belonged to the stableman, perhaps, or to one of the Housemen who serviced the waste drop. They would come back into the House, those furs, and their owner would always know that

Mura had died in them, frozen to death in the deep cold only a few steps from warmth and safety. Sook felt as if the cold had reached right inside the House, into her own breast. It made her heart ache unbearably.

Hours later, when all hope that Mura might have survived was past, Sook heard the outer door of the apartment open and close, and steps pass by as Cho and someone with him went into his bedroom. Not long after came the sharp cry of a girl's voice, a cry of pain. Nori, or some other House-woman, Sook was not sure.

She rubbed the last vestiges of tears from her cheeks and whispered promises to herself. "I will not cry again," she vowed. "Not one more tear. He'll pay for this, Mura, for you and for Yul. I swear by the Ship!"

For the rest of the night, Sook kept vigil at her window, her eyes and throat as dry as stone. She gazed down at the figure of Mura, slumped on the steps, and at the impotent figures of Magister Gowan and his Cantors. Over and over, through the long hours, she prayed for Zakri to come.

CHAPTER
TWENTY-ONE

✴ MREEN LEANED AGAINST SIRA'S BACK AS THEY RODE, lulled to drowsiness by the *hruss*'s swinging gait. Each of the travelers was isolated in his own thoughts as they pressed on through the long day. No one had spoken for hours. Only the rustle of an intermittent breeze stirring the irontree branches filled the silence. A faint grating broke the monotony late in the afternoon, making Sira lift her head and thrust back her hood.

She turned her head right, and then left, straining to hear it again. There—it was a scuffing, a scraping sound, the sound of bone runners sliding over stone left bare by the worn snow of late winter. Mreen wriggled, awakened by Sira's sudden tension.

Do you hear it, Mreen?

The little girl pushed her own furs away from her ears, but she shook her head.

Riders, Sira sent. *Many* hruss, *and* pukuru. She called to the others, "A traveling party is ahead of us, a big one— coming this way, I think."

Zakri put his hood back and listened. "I do not hear them," he said, "but I will take your word for it."

Theo reined in, dropping back until all of them were within three arms' length of one another. "Until we know who they are, better to ride close." He spoke calmly, but Sira heard the undertone in his voice, the slightest huskiness. "Sira and Mreen, stay in the center," he directed. "Berk, there, to Sira's right. Zakri on the left."

I hear them now, Mreen sent. She tightened her arms around Sira's waist. Sira would have liked to reassure her, but it was clear the child was aware that, soon or late, they were riding into danger. She found Mreen's small hand, almost lost in the thick furs, and stroked it.

I am not afraid, Mreen sent stoutly.

No, I know you are not, Sira answered. *You are as brave as your stepsister.*

Do you mean Trisa? Is Trisa brave?

Sira patted her hand. *Indeed she is. Do you not know the story?*

Tell me!

And so as they rode forward, unsure of who was coming toward them, Sira distracted Mreen with the tale of Trisa's misery at Conservatory, her determination to run away, and her final success in accomplishing it. Mreen listened intently, smiling at Zakri and Berk's part in the adventure.

When Sira finished the tale, Mreen sent, *Trisa was brave, but she was so silly! Who would want to leave Conservatory? It is the best place to be on the whole Continent!*

Yes, it is, Sira agreed. *For you and for me, it is. But what is true for one Singer is not always true for another.*

Theo spoke aloud, keeping his voice low. "Here they are." They all lifted their eyes to the approaching riders.

"Ship and stars!" Berk muttered. "Somebody's emptied their stables right out."

"Not quite," Zakri murmured. "Look who rides with them! Only one man I know of could fill furs that size. And the senior Cantor himself, out of Lamdon at last. But the capital House has *hruss* and Singers still to spare."

"So," Theo said. "Do they have him?"

Zakri scanned the riders. "I do not see him," he said. "But there is a man in a litter, there on the *pukuru*." He gestured to the left with his chin, keeping his hands on his reins. "I cannot see his face." And then he added swiftly, "Shield yourselves, and very carefully. I will extend my shields around Mreen."

Mreen protested energetically. *I am shielded already!*

Good, Zakri sent back. *Then you will be twice protected.*

The man at the head of Lamdon's entourage kicked his *hruss* into a lumbering trot, hurrying to meet them in advance of his party. He lifted his hand, and called out when he was within range.

"Greetings from Magister Gowan v'Lamdon! What travelers are you?"

Theo raised his own hand, but he answered only, "Theo v'Observatory."

Zakri nodded approval of his caution. Indeed, Theo hardly looked like a Cantor. His hair curled at his nape, cropped like any itinerant's, and his shoulders were immense in his *caeru* furs. He looked like what he had been for more than three summers, an itinerant Singer accustomed to life on the roads of the Continent.

The Lamdon man drew closer now, and his *hruss* slowed its heavy gait, jolting to a halt a few steps from Theo. The rest stopped, too, facing him. Sira and Zakri's shields were linked with Mreen's, twined together like the interlocking roots of the forest around them. Theo's own defenses stretched around them all, not precise, delicate Conservatory shielding but his own stubborn, stony wall of protection, toughened by experience. Sira felt Zakri's probe reach out past that barricade to touch the Lamdon rider's mind.

No Gift in this one, he sent, and they all relaxed a bit.

"Theo v'Observatory?" repeated the rider. He looked them over. "I've never met anyone from Observatory, although I've heard some stories."

Theo grinned. "I probably told most of them," he said. He shifted in his saddle, sitting sideways with one foot dangling free of the stirrup, ready to chat. "You say you have Magister Gowan coming up there behind you?"

"So I do," the man said. "And Cantor Abram to boot. We've had a nasty time of it down at Soren."

Berk urged his *hruss* forward a step or two and spoke. "I'm Berk, courier for Amric," he said, letting his gruff voice carry over the snow, meaning it to reach to the rest of the Lamdon party. "Why don't you take my respects to your Magister, and we can all make our camp together. I've had some experience with Soren myself, and I'd like to hear what's happening there."

"But first," Theo put in, "tell us who else is riding with you. Other Singers? Anyone from Soren?"

The man shook his head. "No one from Soren, that's for sure, though we tried. Two other Singers besides Cantor Abram, but one's hurt, pretty badly, they say. He looks all right to me, but he can't speak, can't ride."

It was told matter-of-factly, almost offhandedly. The cold horror of it turned Sira's stomach. She looked ahead to the riders coming on, the litter whispering over the snow behind them.

The rider said, "Strange business, that. All our Cantors look like they've seen an *urbear* in their bedfurs. Scared half to death."

"Do they, indeed?" Theo answered. "We will hear the whole story at the cookfire, no doubt."

The rider nodded assent, and turned his mount, thumping its flanks with his heels until it resumed its heavy-footed trot back toward Magister Gowan. Theo pointed to a broadening of the road that lay between the two parties. "We can make camp there," he said. "There should be room enough."

Berk still stared up the road, watching as the rider bowed to Gowan, pointed back at their own troupe, bowed again. "We'll hear no good news this day," he said. "But I'd guess we've nothing to fear with this lot. It might be best if they know who and what we are. We could use some authority behind us when we settle this little matter."

The Singers agreed. They followed Theo to the spot he had chosen, and by the time the Lamdon party reached it Zakri had raised a substantial *quiru* and Berk's cookfire was crackling nicely. They stood in formal ranks to meet

Magister Gowan and Cantor Abram. Mreen hid behind Sira and Theo, peeking from behind their legs. Sira sent to Zakri, *I hope this will not be unpleasant. My last encounter with Abram was not even civil.*

He laughed under his breath. *Mine was downright offensive. I undid his hair for him.*

Theo cast them both a wry glance. *Wonderful,* he sent. *He will be so pleased to see you both.*

Two Housemen helped Gowan from his *hruss*. It was no easy task to provide him with a dignified descent from the high saddle. His great weight made both of them grunt and stumble, but soon enough he was standing on his own feet, his furs draping generously around his massive figure. Abram dismounted with only slightly less fuss, and both dignitaries came forward on saddle-stiff legs to meet the newcomers.

It was evident immediately that Abram was a changed man. He bowed, and when he straightened, his eyes were shadowed and dull, with deep lines graven around them. Sira doubted the lines came only from the weathering of this journey.

"Cantrix Sira, I believe," he said heavily. "And Cantor Zakri v'Amric. Is this coincidence?"

Their answer was forestalled as a Houseman lugged a chair forward for Magister Gowan and helped him into it, arranging his furs, setting a carved footstool beneath his boots. Gowan eyed their group with eyes reddened by snow glare. His white hair lay limp and oily against his scalp, and he seemed shrunken, as if his abundant flesh had diminished, leaving his pale skin to lie in limp folds about his neck and chin. He did not speak.

"Cantor Abram," Sira said, "you will have guessed our purpose in being here. We will explain everything, but first I would like to present to you . . ."

She turned to Theo, ready to introduce him as Cantor for the first time outside Observatory. She saw his eyes crinkle and his lips twitch, ready to grin at Lamdon's reaction. Her own mood suddenly lightened, and the weight of her worries lifted. So much of her work she had done alone, but now they were together, she and Theo, and that meant they were stronger, more resourceful, more able than either of them could be on their own. Beside her stood her other student, Zakri, young and fine and capable. She was proud of them both, and proud of her work with them. Nothing Abram or Gowan might say could change any of that, and whatever challenge was to come, they would meet it together. She smiled at Theo, and turned back to Abram.

"Cantor Abram, Magister Gowan. This is Cantor Theo v'Observatory. He has served in the Cantoris these six years."

Theo bowed. Abram stared at him, and then at Sira, saying nothing for a long, painful moment. When he spoke at last, his plump features barely moved. He said only, "Greetings, Cantor."

Sira's scarred eyebrow arched high. She had been prepared for criticism, denial, objections, but not this drab acceptance, this colorless acquiescence. The senior Cantor's confidence, his self-assurance, were gone. She experienced an unwilling surge of sympathy for him, which she pressed down quickly. Surely nothing could be more humiliating to him than pity.

Mreen edged between Sira and Theo then, taking their hands in hers and gazing up at the dark man and the pale fat one. Abram caught sight of her and exclaimed, "In the name of the Spirit! What is this?"

I am Mreen, the child sent immediately.

Abram frowned deeply at her. Before he could remonstrate, Sira said, "Mreen is a Conservatory student. She sends because she cannot speak."

"Not at all?" They were Gowan's first words. "Is she always silent?"

"Always," Theo said with a chuckle. "A mixed blessing."

"And that—that light around her?" Gowan demanded. His voice was thin and querulous, and his jowls wavered as he looked from one face to another.

Sira said only, "Mreen's Gift is very intense," and left them to make of it what they could.

Abram still frowned, but he bent his head to look more closely at Mreen. "How did she come to be this way?"

"She was born so," Sira answered. "As best we can tell. She has never uttered a sound."

The senior Cantor straightened and lifted his head. With a hint of his old arrogance, he asked, "Why is the child not with her class then, where she belongs?"

Berk stepped up beside Sira and bowed briefly. "We'd best tell you everything from the beginning," he said. His shrewd eyes assessed the Lamdon party. "I'd guess you have a story for us as well."

Once again the animation left Abram's face. "Indeed." He sighed. His shoulders bent as he turned away to signal to his Housemen. Zakri sent privately to Sira, *He wants to forget it all.*

She flashed him a look. *Suppose you wait for him to tell us about it before you eavesdrop on his private thoughts?* He smirked at her, and she shook her head in exasperation.

There were eight of the Lamdon Housemen, and they worked with speed and efficiency. In moments they transformed the campsite into a creditable simulation of a Magistral apartment, with chairs and stools ranged around a table, cups laid out, and meal preparations begun. Berk, Gowan, and all the Gifted but one had seats facing one another. Mreen climbed into Theo's lap and sat watching the strangers with one finger between her lips. The light around her sparkled faintly. Abram moved uncomfortably in his chair as she turned the full force of her green gaze on him.

Zakri nodded toward the litter. "Someone is injured," he observed. The Housemen had laid the litter on a pad of furs near the cookfire. Its occupant was still, his head turned away, eyes staring blankly out into the dusk gathering over the Southern Timberlands.

Sira felt Zakri reach to touch the man's mind, and then withdraw. He gave a slight, almost imperceptible shrug.

"He was attacked." Abram's voice cracked as he spoke. "At Soren."

Magister Gowan leaned to one side, resting on the arm of his chair as if he had not the strength to support his own weight. His pale eyes flickered from one face to another. "They have no respect for me," he quavered. "Nor for the Committee. They wouldn't talk to my courier, and then . . ."

Lamdon's courier stepped up to the table. He alone looked energized, angered by what they had seen. "Have you been to Soren?" he demanded. "Do you know what they're doing there?"

Zakri's answer was mild. "We did try to tell you," he reminded Gowan and Abram.

Gowan's folds of flesh trembled. "They locked her out," he whined. "In the cold."

They looked at him, mystified. "Who?" Theo asked, but Gowan ran on without hearing him.

"I sent my Houseman to help her, but then my Singers . . . he was hurting my Singers! What could I do? I told him, I ordered him to stop, to let her come in, but he wouldn't listen!"

"Who was it?" Zakri asked sharply. "Who did they lock out?"

Abram lifted one shoulder. "I do not know her name . . . a cook, I think."

Zakri's face blanched white, and then flamed. "Old? Young?" he snapped.

Abram shrugged again. "I have no idea. Have you felt it? What that man can do to the Gifted?"

"Yes," Zakri said shortly. His clenched fists were motionless on the table. Flashes of light glinted on his cheeks and hair.

Sira asked, "Will your Cantor recover, do you think?"

Abram shook his head wearily. "I do not know. How did you know he was a Cantor?"

Zakri struck the table a sharp blow with one fist, and the glimmers around him intensified. "We told you! There are no itinerants left outside of Soren!" He took a shuddering breath, and Sira felt his struggle to control his emotions. He was angry, but even more, he was afraid, not for himself, but for someone else. Abram and Gowan were staring at him. When he had quelled the outbreak of light, he spoke more quietly. "Cho did the same thing to Cantor Izak. Izak is recovering, at Conservatory."

Abram's eyes brightened. "Recovering? Completely recovering?"

"He can talk, and he can walk. But his Gift, no. At least I do not think so. Cantrix Jana and I did all we could."

"Poor Jana—is she all right? Is she with him?"

"She is fine," Sira told him. She felt Theo's wry glance at her. She hesitated, and then plunged in. "Cantrix Jana is at Observatory," she said bluntly

"What? What?" Abram sputtered. He glared at her, and then at all of them.

Gowan's courier broke in, his voice loud, almost frantic. "How is this possible, any of it? You are Conservatory, all of you! How can a mere carver—a weak Gift, half-trained Gift—how can he have such power over you?"

"What is Cantrix Jana doing at Observatory?" Abram burst out. "She should be—"

Gowan moaned, "Everything is coming apart, I have no control. No one will listen, no one has any respect. . . ."

Sira put out her hand and laid it on the table, palm down. Everyone fell silent, looking at her hand, and then at her face. She spoke first to the courier, keeping her voice even. "You should never refer to the Gift in that way," she said. "Mistakes have been made, perhaps in testing Cho's Gift. But his training has been thorough, and it is exactly that which he is using against us."

"I do not understand you!" Abram cried. "He has no training!"

Sira glanced at him. "But he does," she said. "He is trained to guide an *obis* knife with his Gift. It is as precise a skill as raising a *quiru*."

Zakri said levelly, "It is the perfect weapon against the Gifted. He assaults minds the way he wields an *obis* knife, and you may thank the Spirit for our own training, that makes it possible for us to protect ourselves."

"But Jana?" Abram asked.

"Cantrix Jana is serving in Observatory's Cantoris," Theo said. "It was her choice to—"

"Her choice! Hers? It is my duty to assign Cantrixes!"

Cantor Abram's face grew red, and his eyes shone as if he would weep.

"There was no other way we could be free to come here," Theo said calmly.

Sira spoke again. "We intend to put an end to this, now. In our own way. We could not wait for Lamdon to make these decisions. People are suffering. We mean no disrespect."

Gowan whispered, "They locked her out. She sat on the steps and died. Froze to death in the cold, and we had to sit and watch. . . ."

Next to Sira, Zakri took a deep, shuddering breath.

"We will do all we can," Sira said.

The Housemen began setting bowls of fragrant *caeru* stew before them. They laid platters of nutbread and dried fruit in the center of the table, and served wine to Gowan and Berk. There was a spicy brown tea for the Gifted. Sira sat with her chin in her hand, watching the elaborate service.

Might as well enjoy it, Theo sent to her privately. *Gowan certainly is.*

It was true. Only the Magister's appetite, it seemed, was unaffected by his experience.

More to the point, she answered Theo, *we will need all our strength.* But still she did not pick up her spoon. She glanced across the fire at the fallen Singer on his litter, and she felt the terrible emptiness where his Gift should have been. She looked at tiny, shining Mreen, perched on Theo's knee. Both Theo and Mreen met her eyes.

Sira, eat, Theo commanded.

It is good, Cantrix Sira, Mreen urged. *Try it.*

Sira smiled a little at them, and looked to her left, to Zakri. He joined in, forcing a smile to his own lips. *Eat, Maestra!*

She did as she was bid.

Mreen was right. The food was delicious. But the ugliness of what had happened, and what was yet to come, spoiled her taste for Lamdon's riches.

CHAPTER
TWENTY-TWO

SOOK WAS KNEELING IN THE WINDOW SEAT WHEN THEY rode over the rise above Soren. She saw a tall, lean woman who sat her *hruss* easily, leaning back in her saddle and scanning the House from the crest of the hill. Her *hruss* turned its broad head back and forth, ears working, while the woman stared at Soren as if she could see right through its thick walls and into its troubled heart. Sook cupped her hands against the glass to shut out the glare, and squinted against the light, but she couldn't make out the woman's features inside the muffling circle of her *caeru* hood.

It was mid-day, and a tray rested untouched on the table behind Sook. She had heard the bolt secured after Bree had left. Cho and his itinerants—and the carvers who had changed allegiance and now were at Cho's side every moment—had gone to the great room for their meal.

The stranger on the hill swept her furs away from her face as Sook watched, revealing short-cropped dark hair and an angular face, sharp planes of cheekbone showing clearly in the harsh light. A hint of white marked one of her eyebrows.

Sook was breathless with excitement. There were stories—

stories she had heard from travelers eating at the long table in the kitchens. They told of a Singer, a Conservatory-trained Cantrix who had abandoned the Cantoris and had done heroic things—and that Singer had a scarred eyebrow, marked with white by a *caeru*'s claw!

The bolt in her door rattled sharply, making her jump. She hadn't heard the carvers return. The door crashed against the inner wall, and Cho staggered into the room. His mouth was strangely twisted, and he peered at her as through a thick fog. He grabbed for her, missing her arm and taking instead a painful, clumsy grip on her neck beneath her coil of hair.

"What is it?" she cried. "Let me go!" She struggled in his grasp, managing only to pull the hair at her nape more sharply. The sting of it brought tears to her eyes.

Cho only grunted. His dark skin was slippery with sweat, and he almost lost his hold on her as he dragged her by force through the apartment and down the corridor. The tears burned her cheeks and she screamed her outrage. "Stop it! You're hurting me!"

At the top of the stairs two rebel carvers met them. Cho let her go, but the carvers took her arms and half dragged, half carried her down the stairs. She kicked at them, catching one a glancing blow on his shin. He swore, and she turned her head to spit in his face, winning a brief moment of satisfaction from seeing her spittle drip down his cheek. He dared not release her to wipe it away. "Shame!" she hissed at him. His skin burned red, and he avoided her eyes.

Behind them Cho stumbled and made a gagging noise deep in his throat. Sook thought he might actually retch as they rushed down the staircase. She could only guess what it all meant, but surely, surely it had to do with the tall woman on the *hruss*.

Two itinerants, their eyes stretched wide in pale faces, threw open the double doors as they approached. The carvers hauled Sook outside, and for a moment she thought she was to suffer the same fate as Mura. The cold hit her like a fist; she had only her tunic and trousers on. Cho and the carvers hadn't taken time to put on furs either.

Cho came from behind to seize her by the hair, tearing the

binding loose, thrusting her forward and holding her as he might dangle a cleaned fish over a cooking pot. Her neck was twisted to one side, and she lost her footing. When she found her balance again, she looked out past the courtyard to the top of the rise.

The tall woman was still there, and now three other *hruss* had come up beside hers. Sook's heart leaped and her pain and tears receded. Even the bite of the cold seemed to lessen as she saw that one of the riders was slim and tall, his furs pushed back to show his light hair and his fine features. This rider she knew for certain. It was Zakri, it was indeed, Singer Zakri come at last! Sook smiled fiercely through the cloud of her tangled hair.

Cho panted as if from a physical struggle. Holding Sook took almost no effort—something else was pushing him right to the edge of his endurance. He groaned, and swallowed noisily. Sweat dripped from his arm onto Sook's neck. He took a deep breath and shouted, so close to her ear that it hurt.

"Stop!" he cried in a shrill voice. Sook knew as surely as anything that he was frightened, and she exulted. "Stop it now, or else this one—" He yanked Sook's hair so hard she thought her spine would crack. "This one will suffer the—"

He gasped, and swallowed again. He jerked Sook right off her feet.

The tall woman raised her hand then, and Cho let out his breath in a rush. He let go of Sook and she fell, bruising both her knees on the icy step. She scrambled to her feet again, and looked up the hill, full of hope.

Sira had broken another's mind once, and she remembered it well. Too well, in truth: the power of it, the rush of energy, the sickening sensation that was like pushing someone off a cliff. It had been an irrevocable act, with irreversible consequences. It came back to her in her nightmares, the exhilaration, the violence, and the guilt that overrode everything and lasted forever. It made her hold back when she exerted her power over Cho. She wielded her psi with restraint, with caution.

Cho's Gift was less sophisticated, less refined, and far less vulnerable than that other's. She did not know for certain that she could break him, and she did not try. With Zakri and Theo lending her their strength, and Mreen under strict orders to keep her mind closed and apart, Sira applied her psi like a hook, a tether, taking hold of Cho and pulling him out of his lair as surely as he had pulled that poor girl by her long hair.

He was a canny opponent, and he resisted her with a stubborn strength. He held her off just long enough to drag his hostage out with him, although the effort was a costly one. She felt Zakri's shielding waver, and the rush of his relief and then his renewed fear. She believed Cho was capable of breaking the girl's neck before them all. She raised her hand to make certain Cho understood that her action was deliberate, and then she released her grip on his mind.

Cho let go of his victim. The girl collapsed on the steps, but she got quickly to her feet again.

"Sook!" Zakri breathed. "Thank the Spirit!"

Berk rumbled, "Clever bastard."

Cho's high-pitched voice carried across the courtyard and up the slope of dirty, much-trodden snow. "It won't work!" he called. Sira heard the forced bravado that made his voice almost a shriek, and she glanced at Theo with her eyebrows lifted.

He grinned. "Scared him," he murmured.

The group on the hill sat motionless, looking down at the thin dark man with the long braid, the girl before him, and the carvers and itinerants behind them. Through the open doors they saw others, House members, putting their heads around just far enough to see what was happening.

"He's right enough," Berk muttered. "It's a standoff. We'll have to try something else."

"They must feel the cold by now," Zakri said. "If they do not get Sook indoors, she will freeze."

Cho shouted again. "Get away from my House! You have no business here!" He grabbed at Sook again, jerking her backward and holding her in front of him with one arm tight around her. Her head reached only to his chest. Her loosened hair fell over her shoulders and her eyes, long and dark, were fixed on the riders on the hill.

"Who is she?" Sira asked.

"She is one of the cooks," Zakri said through clenched teeth. "He would not stop at killing her."

"We will not let that happen," Sira assured him. "But he is surprisingly strong. And someone is helping him, the same way you and Theo were supporting me."

"They're learning," Berk said.

"We will have to teach them a different lesson," Theo said calmly. "But perhaps not right at this moment."

They reined their *hruss* around, retreating from the hilltop, backtracking to a shallow clearing they had passed earlier. There they dismounted, Theo lifting Mreen down with a passing kiss on her curly head. They set about making their camp in silence.

Sira untied the bedfurs and pack from her saddle. As she set them down, she found Mreen standing beside her, her face tense. *Cantrix Sira,* she sent. *There is a child in that House.* Her little nimbus shifted around her, flecks of darkness disturbing its light. *There is a boy—a Gifted boy—and all this fighting is making him ill.*

Sira looked around for Theo. *Did you hear that?*

So I did. He came to kneel by Mreen. *Mreen, you must not open your mind to everything that comes your way. There is great danger here. This is a time to practice your shielding.*

I was careful, she sent. The green of her eyes had darkened almost to black. Strange lines were graven around her mouth and eyes. *You were all linked with that man, and I heard the boy. He is scared, and he hides in his room with a pillow on his head, but he cannot shut it out.*

Zakri finished the *quiru,* a modest one just large enough to encircle the people and the *hruss.* He came to join them, replacing his *filla* inside his tunic. *I am sure he could not hear the boy and Mreen,* he sent. *He was too busy with our Maestra.*

Nevertheless, Theo repeated. *It is not safe for her.*

But the boy needs us! Mreen insisted. *He is so scared and sick.*

Aloud, Sira said, "Yes, Mreen, and no wonder. We will do our best, but we must protect you, too." To Berk she explained, "Mreen hears the Gifted child in the House. He is suffering from the psi being used—Cho's psi."

Berk fairly growled in his beard. Theo, too, set his jaw, the muscles flexing into knots. "I am going in there," he said. "To get the child out. I do not see another way."

Sira found a flat rock at the edge of the *quiru* and sat down on it, stretching out her long legs, massaging her calves. "We cannot protect you at such a distance," she told Theo. "It was all I could do to force him outside. There is a wildness to his psi, an abandon, that I have never felt before. He has no compunction at all."

"Zakri handled him," Theo pointed out.

"It was not easy," Zakri warned. "And he did not have help then. I am not so certain I could handle him now."

"Please, Theo, let us think of something else," Sira said. He did not answer and she sighed with a deep fatigue.

Berk and Mreen worked over the cookfire, side by side. Mreen's little halo glowed peacefully now as she fed softwood twigs to the flames, always her favorite chore. Berk said, "That's enough, little one. We don't want smoke to show them where we are." She dropped the last bits of wood into her pocket.

None of them felt hungry, but Berk made tea, "to help us think." Mreen served the tea, dimpling at each of them as she delivered the brimming cups, spilling only a few drops into the snow.

They sipped their tea and listened to the rustling of the irontree branches around them. In the Timberlands that sound never died down. The trees grew so closely that it was hard to tell, looking up, which branches belonged to which trunk. Above their clearing clouds gathered, and the lazy snowflakes of late winter drifted through the *quiru*, making miniscule sputtering sounds as they dropped into the fire. Mreen sat cross-legged on her furs, rolling tiny balls of snow and tossing them into the fire to hear them hiss.

Berk said, "You're going to put out our nice little fire, Mreen."

She looked up hopefully, and he chuckled. "Yes, you can put in a few more sticks."

She stood and plunged her hand into her pocket. When she drew it out she was holding Cho's bit of carving in her hand, the little panel Izak had given her. She stared at it, her nimbus burning bright around her. When she looked up, her face was pinched and white.

Very clearly, she sent, *We must all go in. All at once.*

All the Gifted gazed at her, openmouthed. Berk looked around in consternation, and Zakri whispered, "She says we must all go in together." Berk, too, opened his mouth, and then closed it, shaking his head.

Theo went to Mreen and squatted beside her. *It is a brave idea,* he sent, *but I do not think we will be allowed inside Soren. Cho is very powerful, and he is a very bad man. All the House members do what he tells them, because they are afraid he will hurt someone. There is no one inside the House to help us get in.*

There is a Singer there. He is afraid of her, Mreen responded. Her eyes were as clear as new limeglass, and there was neither doubt nor hesitation in her sending.

Mreen, Soren is full of Singers! sent Zakri. *And they are all terrified, every one of them.*

This one is locked up, she answered. Her sending was so precise, so lucid, that Sira imagined even Berk could hear her. But the big man only watched, forced to wait until someone explained.

Zakri suddenly snapped his fingers, making them jump. Their eyes turned to him and he grinned. "Of course!" he cried. "Cantrix Elnor!"

Sira blinked. "Mreen," she said. "Could you hear her, too? Cantrix Elnor? Is she still alive?"

For answer she held out the carving. *She was alive when he gave this to Izak.*

"I will try to reach her," Sira said.

"It might be the answer," Theo put in. His arm was around Mreen, the sleeve of his coat alight in her glow. "But now, Mreen, put the carving away." To Sira he sent, *I am worried for the child. This is too intense for her.*

Sira nodded, but she felt a fresh energy and a renewal of hope. Mreen obediently dropped the little panel into her pocket. Berk began preparations for a meal, and Mreen crouched beside him, dropping her bits of softwood into the fire, laughing her silent laugh as they burst into little stars of flame.

When they had eaten, Theo and Mreen scrubbed out the bowls and the cooking pot. Zakri measured out handfuls of softwood leaves for the *hruss*. Sira went to sit alone on the flat rock. She took out her *filla,* turning it for a moment in her long fingers, thinking and gathering her forces. Then she lifted the instrument and began an *Iridu* melody, slowly at first, and then increasing the tempo until it was as bright and merry as the child playing by the cookfire. She cast her mind out, with the careful precision learned over years of Conservatory training and practice. With perfect discipline, letting nothing distract her, she sought the mind of the older Cantrix.

CHAPTER
TWENTY-THREE

⭐ *WHO IS THERE?*

The sending was clear, but faint, from weakness or caution Sira could not yet tell. She answered, *I am Sira. Cantrix Sira v'Observatory, formerly v'Bariken.*

She paused, waiting for an answer. There were slight rustlings as the others prepared for bed, but Sira's focus was so narrow that she heard nothing but the feeble voice in her mind. Her *Iridu* melody ended and began again. The old Cantrix's voice, despite its frailty, was as precise as the touch of a fingertip. It tingled delicately in her forehead, a familiar and distinct sensation, the unmistakable signature of Conservatory training.

I know your name, Sira, Elnor sent now. *I am glad you are here, but this is dangerous for me. He hears everything.*

Sira opened her eyes and signaled to Zakri. "Do you think you could occupy Cho, distract him so that Elnor and I can talk?"

"Is she alive, then?" he asked. He came to sit beside her on the flat stone, and Theo followed to stand behind him. At the fire, Berk offered Mreen a handful of dried fruit from his saddle pack.

Sira said, "She is alive, but her sending is weak."

"She is rather old, after all," Zakri said.

"And she must be frightened," Theo added.

Sira nodded. "She has good reason. I have no doubt Cho controls her by threatening her people."

"It is imperative that he not know, then." Zakri took out his *filla* and looked at it, then smiled and put it back. "I think I can deal with our friend Cho," he said. "I am in just the mood for a game of knuckle and bone. Any wagers on the winner?"

Sira looked to Theo. "Will you follow, just at a distance? I do not know what will happen . . . his abilities are so odd, and now he has help. Zakri . . ." Her voice trailed off.

Theo smiled down at her. "I will follow," he said.

"And no heroics," she warned. Theo chuckled, and winked at Zakri, but they both promised.

She put her *filla* to her lips to resume the *Iridu* tune. She played through it once, giving Zakri a chance to begin, before she sought out the captive Singer. *Cantrix Elnor? I think it will be all right now, at least for a time. Are you well?*

Again the thread of Elnor's thought was thin, but perfectly intelligible. *No one in this House is completely well,* she answered. *It is cold, and we are hungry. Our nursery gardens no longer grow.*

Your filhata?

They took it from me, and my senior's, too. He is dead.

Yes, I have heard. I am so sorry.

Elnor was silent for a few seconds. When she sent again, it was like listening to someone whisper. Sira's brows drew together as she poured all her strength into listening. *Are you here to help us?* Elnor asked. *What can I do?*

Sira explained their intentions. The Cantrix was quick to grasp their plan, and eager to do her part. Sira wanted to ask her more, but Theo touched her arm in warning, and she broke the contact.

"What is it?" she asked.

Zakri and Theo exchanged a look. "He knows we are here," Theo said. "He was at his evening meal, and at first he was not sure anything was taking place, but at the end—"

"He knew me," Zakri said. "He has grown much stronger. He cannot actually send clear thoughts, but he hears a great deal. I tell you, I hate feeling his mind anywhere near mine! It is like putting your hand into something rotten. And he is expecting a fight. As soon as he knew I was there, those others were there, too. Carvers, I am sure. Their psi is similar to Cho's—that sort of wide focus . . . strong, but dull. The way they use it—it is rather like trying to cut bread with the side of your hand, sort of plowing through instead of slicing it neatly."

Theo gave a short laugh. "A colorful turn of phrase, my friend, but it describes the sensation well enough."

"Theo—now you have felt their power—do you think we can do this?" Sira asked.

"We can do it," he said quietly. "We must. But there are none too many of us."

I want to fight, too.

All their eyes turned to Mreen, kneeling by the fire with Berk. She looked back at them, her chin up, her eyes dark.

"Mreen," Sira began. Berk looked around, startled.

"It is not safe for you, little one," Theo said firmly. "If you were listening, then you heard what Cantor Zakri said. This is an evil man, and he would not hesitate to hurt a child."

He is already hurting one, she sent.

"Let us not put another at risk, then," Theo told her. "Cantrix Sira and I will help Cantor Zakri, and Cantrix Elnor will do what she can. Your job is to help Berk with that *keftet* before we all starve!"

Mreen turned obediently to the fire again, but her face was grave. Sira missed her dimpling smile. She rubbed her forehead with a weary hand.

"We will make it work, Sira," Theo assured her. "Between us, and Elnor. We will free Soren, and the little Gifted one. By this time tomorrow, it will be done."

"By the will of the Spirit." She sighed.

Theo patted her shoulder. "Exactly."

The task of getting into the House by way of the waste drop fell to Zakri. He crept around the frozen mound of offal and refuse, moving on silent feet past the inner wall of the eastern wing. It was early, and the narrow door was in near darkness. The sun had risen above the mountains, but the space behind the House, between the two angling wings, was still in shade. Zakri shivered in his furs. Soren's inadequate warmth did not reach past the frigid walls. There was no spill from the *quiru* to warm him.

Theo came to the stable door at the same time, leading two *hruss*. They reasoned that even if the stableman recognized him, it would be from his early years, when he was himself an itinerant Singer. The stableman might be surprised, but hardly alarmed. Theo would stay with the *hruss* while Zakri slipped inside.

When they were in position, Sira walked boldly up the front steps and pounded on one of the tall double doors with her fist. Theo was bent over one of the *hruss*'s feet, ostensibly looking for a stone. His forehead pressed against the shaggy flank, his eyes closed as he listened. Zakri, inside the House now, flattened himself against the corridor wall, also following Sira with his mind. Cantrix Elnor was joined with them, the thread of her psi as fine and slender as a single hair of a *hruss*'s tail. Together the four of them spun a web of power, wove a snare for their prey. Zakri thrust away his doubts, and tried to believe it was enough.

Cho himself came to meet Sira in the hall, as they had hoped, but he was flanked by three others. Sira judged they were carvers, since they, like Cho, wore long *obis* knives slung about their waists in slim leather scabbards. Two itinerants hovered on the stairs. All five were men, their faces rigid with tension. Since the day before, Sira was sure, they had known something was coming. Their fear was a presence, a cloud like the patches of darkness that marked the corridors. Nevyans were born and bred with a deep reverence for a fully trained Gift, and they already understood what Sira was.

Cho had no such misgivings. He sneered at her, and said lightly, "Well, Conservatory. You've got nerve, coming into my House alone."

Sira lifted her head high to meet his eyes, confident that hers were as cold and hard as his own. She flicked a glance over the carvers, and then the itinerants. "Are these your converts, Cho? Your faithful?" She spit out the words as if they tasted evil in her mouth. One of the carvers dropped his gaze to his feet, and the itinerants glanced at each other. Cho's laugh was too high, a snicker like that of an adolescent boy. His voice had almost no lower register, and it offended her ear.

"So they are, Cantrix—" He smiled. "Is that what I call you? Or is it Maestra?"

"It matters nothing to me what title you use." Sira's tone rang through the hall, and the itinerants shifted their feet, recognizing the power of it.

Cho shrugged and stroked the long thin plait that hung over his shoulder. "Fine—I'll just call you Conservatory, then. We'll go up to my apartment, and you'll be treated just as any courier might be, coming from one House to another. But remember . . . this is my House. I rule here."

Sira took a long and measuring look around her at the fractured *quiru*. She looked back at Cho with as challenging a glance as she could muster before she started up the stairs on her own, her long legs spanning two at a time. The itinerants jumped back hastily, to get out of her way, and she stopped, straddling three steps. "Do you really think," she asked them, "that I would indulge in the kind of abuse that your leader does?" She spoke over her shoulder then, to Cho. "But I suppose fear is a potent persuader—if you have no other."

He only laughed again, a titter as thin as his braid. He followed her up the staircase. At the top, he strode past her, leading the way. The carvers and the itinerants followed at a cautious distance.

Inside the apartment, a plain woman with graying hair lay

stretched on a couch. She leaped to her feet when they all trooped in, and Sira eyed her.

"This is Bree," Cho said. "Gifted, like yourself."

Bree flushed, and bobbed her head in a semblance of a bow. Sira turned away without responding and looked about her. "The *quiru* is little improved, even in your own rooms," she commented. "It looks to me, Carver, as if you have serious need of Conservatory."

Cho's smile faded, and he flipped his braid over his shoulder with an angry gesture. "You have nothing we want."

Sira pulled out a chair and sat down, stretching her legs out before her. "I wonder if your House members would agree," she murmured, and raised her scarred eyebrow at the others in the room.

Cho went to the window to lean against the casing. He tipped his head back to sight down his long nose at Sira. "I should warn you," he said with a smile. "My aides are ready this time, so none of your tricks . . . your Conservatory tricks."

"We call it training," Sira said. "Discipline."

He shrugged. "Call it what you like. Much good it does you now."

Sira folded her arms. "I have come for the child," she told him. "And for Cantrix Elnor."

"You can't have them."

"Since when on Nevya have innocent people been imprisoned?"

"Cantrix Elnor is sworn to serve Soren."

"But you are not allowing her to perform her duties."

Cho pulled a chair out with his foot. He sat in it and leaned far forward over the table until his face was level with Sira's. "She is there to serve if we need her. When I say. If I say."

Sira met his eyes without flinching. "Ah—so you do not have faith in this patchy mess of a *quiru*."

"Certainly I do," he said, leaning back in the chair. "Just now, we are learning how to do things—many things—our own way, not Conservatory's way, not Lamdon's." He glanced around at his uneasy troupe. "It's a question of cooperation, isn't it, my friends? Teamwork."

"Indeed," Sira said dryly. "And the child? The little Gifted one?"

"He doesn't know what is best for him."

"And you think you do?"

"So I do."

Sira pushed back her chair and stood, her hands on her hips. The itinerants and carvers who leaned against the walls or waited in the doorway watched her warily. "Do you all want to live this way?" she demanded of them. "Is this what you want, your House cold, your freedom gone—"

"Gone?" Cho shrilled. "Their freedom isn't gone! They're just winning it now!"

"Truly?" Sira strolled around the table, and leaned forward to look into Bree's eyes. "Tell me, Singer. What freedom do you have now that you did not have before?"

Bree's plain face creased with misery. "Cantrix . . ." she murmured. "I'm sorry. . . ."

"Oh, no need, believe me. This will all be ended soon." Sira stepped to Bree's right, to address a man standing next to her. "And you? A carver, are you not? Much call for your skills just now?"

"Don't say a word!" Cho snarled from behind them. "Nobody says anything!" The carver dropped his eyes to stare at the floor.

Sira went to the next, a heavy man with dark hair. "What is your name?"

His eyes pleaded with her, and she felt the tremble in his mind. "Ah. You are a Singer," she said. He nodded. "Your name?"

He began, "I'm Klas, Cantrix—" and then broke off. He sagged against the wall behind him, and his knees began to bend. His face went utterly pale, sweat beading quickly on his fleshy cheeks. Sira whirled to look at Cho.

Cho was standing, and his eyes were narrowed and fixed on Klas. "Stop it!" Sira ordered. When Cho did not respond, she widened her own shielding to stop his attack on the itinerant. Cho turned the full force of his assault on her.

She was shocked by the strength of his psi, the brute force, the sheer power of it. Meeting it with her own was like being shoved headfirst into a stone wall. She stiffened her shields with an effort that made her head ache and her vision blur. It was no wonder these itinerants were cowed into submission.

Theo, who had followed everything, joined his energy to hers, and Zakri and Elnor did, too. Together they broke off Cho's onslaught. With a gasp and a flaring of his thin nostrils, he gave it up. His eyes flew wide and he stared triumphantly at Sira.

"So!" he exclaimed. "Conservatory didn't come alone, after all!"

Zakri! Theo! Sira sent swiftly.

On my way, Theo sent immediately.

And I, from Zakri.

Cho heard both. Before Sira understood his intent, he lunged for a door at one side of the room, thrusting back the bolt and going inside. Sira thought he was fleeing, and she was about to reach out for him with her psi, to attempt to force him out as she had the day before, when he appeared in the doorway, holding the girl Sook by the arm. He caught her close to him, at the same time pulling his long knife out of his belt with his free hand.

"Cho, no!" the Singer Bree exclaimed. Sira heard the terror in her voice, and her own anger flared again.

"If you do anything to harm this girl," she snapped, "I will break your mind like snapping an icicle over my knee, and the pieces will never mend!"

"I don't think you can do it, Conservatory," Cho answered. "But you're welcome to try!"

Cries and pounding feet from the corridor heralded Theo's arrival. He burst through the door, a crooked grin on his face, a cringing itinerant Singer dragged behind him. "Sorry to be late," he said breathlessly. "I had to pick this one's brain to find out where you were."

The itinerant pulled away, rubbing his arm, and casting fearful glances at Cho. "I couldn't help it," he whined. "I don't know how to shield myself!"

"Get out!" Cho commanded. With his eyes on Theo, he brought the long knife up to rest on Sook's breast, a handbreadth from her slender throat. Despite the nearness of the black blade, the girl's dark eyes shone with a sudden flash of joy. Zakri had just appeared in the doorway.

"Singer Zakri!" she cried, and Sira's heart turned over at the poignancy of her welcome. The girl did not know, did not understand.

"Let her go," Zakri growled. His voice was lower, older than Sira had ever heard it. Both Theo and Zakri took two steps closer to Cho.

The knife moved up, just under Sook's chin. The haft of it pressed into her skin, and her eyes widened. She made no further sound.

"There's nothing you can do," Cho said, very softly. "Before you can get to me, this blade will do its work."

Sira held up her hand. She commanded, "Enough! Enough have died in this House. We will not attack you. Lower the blade."

With agonizing slowness, Cho dropped the knife to Sook's breast once again. Sira felt Zakri's power building beside her, felt his overwhelming urge to slap the knife from Cho's hand with a burst of psi. The carvers came to stand on either side of Cho, and she felt the wall they built, the frightening power of combined kinetic psi they possessed. In truth, Lamdon and Conservatory vastly underestimated the Gift in these artisans.

Zakri, wait, she ordered.

Theo joined in. *Sira is right. This is too dangerous.* Cho smirked, hearing their thoughts.

Zakri breathed out hard, and was still. The three Singers faced the four carvers in a tense tableau, the dark-haired girl, the focus of their conflict, holding them apart. The scene froze for the space of several heartbeats, and then Sook herself broke it.

"I don't care!" she cried, her voice breaking. "Let him kill me, Singer Zakri! Then you can get him!"

Cho laughed. "Feisty little piece, isn't she?" He brought

his hand up from Sook's waist and gripped one of her small breasts, making her wince.

And then he broadcast a picture, very clearly, of Sook in his bed with his hands on her body. His lip curled as he projected the image. None of the three carvers with him could receive it, but it flamed in Zakri's mind, and Theo's and Sira's, all too clearly. It was a fabrication, but it was detailed and obscene, the foul fantasy of a twisted and violent sexuality. Zakri tensed like a *tkir* about to spring, and Sira put her hand on his arm.

"Liar!" Zakri hissed.

"Maybe not," Cho said softly. "I'm perfectly capable of it, and she knows it." He laughed. "She's heard things, haven't you, little Sook?"

Sook's cheeks flamed, but her eyes on Zakri never wavered.

"If you don't leave, and now," Cho said, "I'll show your little friend here"—he jerked her hard, so that her head fell back against his chest—"such a time as she'll never forget. You won't want her after that, will you?" At that, Sook closed her eyes.

Zakri's control broke. The air around him burned, brilliant sparks firing about his face. His psi gathered, that old involuntary surge that had so tormented him in his youth. It lashed out, striking at the *obis* knife in Cho's fist, to fling it across the room.

The support of the carvers had made Cho fearfully strong. The knife quivered, and moved in his hand, but it did not fall. He laughed and thrust it up under Sook's chin again. Zakri shuddered under Sira's hand, and his breath came fast. She felt his effort, and slid her hand down to grip his.

Let it go, Theo sent swiftly. *He will do it.*

I know. Zakri made a supreme effort that both Sira and Theo could feel. The sparks disappeared, and his mind closed. Cho relaxed his grip slightly on Sook, and lowered the knife once again. One tear slipped from her eye to make a lonely track down her cheek.

"And now," Cho said with a casual air. "You will leave,

all three of you, or someone here will—lose his mind, shall we say?"

There was an audible intake of breath around the room. Theo touched Sira's back lightly with his hand, and she gave a slight nod. She turned to look at the frightened itinerants. "This is the future you have chosen, then!" she said to them. "Spirit have mercy on you."

With icy dignity, her back arrow straight, she left the apartment, Theo and Zakri behind her. They made their way down the staircase, listening as they went. There was no sound from the Magisterial apartment except the sudden rush of feet when the itinerants were released from Cho's presence at last. Too angry even to speak, the three Singers strode down the corridor to the stables to retrieve their *hruss*. The stableman looked at them with eyes that were fearful and without hope. There was nothing they could tell him.

CHAPTER
TWENTY-FOUR

★ "THE ONLY WAY IS TO GET HIM ALONE," ZAKRI SAID. THE Singers squatted or sat cross-legged around the cookfire, facing each other. "I truly thought that if we went in together, he would be no match for us. But he uses the psi of those others as if it were fuel for his own fire."

Berk, standing by the pile of tack, stretched out his massive arm and flexed his fist. "Perhaps physical force is what we need, and not psi force. I'm ready!"

Sira shook her head. "He holds them all hostage. If he is threatened, the Gifted around him will suffer. The itinerants especially are frightened of what he might do to them. He does not care how many minds he ruins—but he knows we do, and he uses it against us."

"If they could only get themselves organized . . ." Theo said thoughtfully.

"They did try, once," Zakri told them. "A carver died. And now he holds Sook because of me. Ah, Spirit, I wish I had his neck between my two hands right now!"

Sira ran her hands through her hair, and then looked down at her fingers, long and dark and supple, made for the strings of a *filhata*. She said slowly, "This is yet another lesson in the Gift. I have been lecturing Lamdon, and Conservatory, trying to get them to consider new possibilities—but I, too, have much to learn. Such a painful way to learn it . . . I have been arrogant, overconfident. Maestra Lu would have pointed out that my strength is also my weakness."

They were silent for some moments. Mreen was leaning on Theo, her curly head on his shoulder, staring into the fire. She gave a small sigh, and her little halo blurred and darkened, its light dimming to a pale shadow in the afternoon sunlight. Theo watched it change in response to the somber mood around her. Suddenly he leaned forward, startling her. "I am sorry, little one," he said swiftly. "But listen, my friends. What is Cho's weakness?"

"Does he have a weakness?" Berk asked.

"Indeed he does," Theo answered. "He has one great weakness." A slow grin began on his face. He gave Mreen a squeeze. "It is in his Gift. His Gift, like all our Gifts, has its flaw."

They stared at Theo. Mreen's halo sparkled and brightened as she absorbed his excitement, and she wriggled in his arms. "Our friend Cho," he pronounced above her head, "is a most capable carver. But he cannot make *quiru*."

The white slash of Sira's eyebrow rose. Zakri said, "But, Theo, I do not see—"

Theo tousled Mreen's curls, and she laughed silently, her small white teeth gleaming and her dimples twinkling. "You show them, Mreen," he urged her. "Show us what your Gift can do!"

Mreen smiled around the circle, making sure she had every eye before she scrunched her eyes closed, and pinched her lips tight with effort. Her nimbus began to darken, to fade. The sparks that danced through it slowed, dimmed, and went out completely. She repressed her energy until her halo was completely quenched, and she stood in ordinary daylight, without the least gleam of *quiru* activity showing about her. They watched, holding their breath. Her eyes flew open to see their expressions, and she dimpled. The light around her began to shine again, and they laughed aloud to see its aureole flare, as welcome and expected as the morning sun blooming above the eastern peaks.

"The *quiru*!" Zakri exclaimed.

"Indeed," Theo chortled.

Berk slapped his knee and roared. Even Sira, for whom a full smile was a rare thing, grinned until her cheeks hurt. It was the perfect weapon, aimed against the one vulnerable spot in Cho's defenses. It would not be an easy thing to accomplish, but it would be devastatingly effective. For some minutes they laughed together, enjoying the moment. When they sobered, they began to lay their plans. Mreen followed everything with grave attention.

At the very end Sira brought out her *filla* to try to reach Cantrix Elnor. They would need her. They would need every bit of strength they could draw upon. Before they left the campsite, Zakri made the *quiru* as strong and bright as he knew how, to last through the night.

A second time they approached the House in unison, just as the long afternoon began to shade into twilight. This time, though, they did not go in. Sira took up her position to the north of the House, just at the edge of the courtyard. Theo went in from the west, through the door of the stables. He nodded to the stableman, one finger on his lips, as he passed the *hruss* and the tack room. The stableman watched him go in a hopeful silence. Theo moved into the corridor that led to the House, and found a private corner in which to work. On the south side, Zakri once again made his way around the waste drop. This time he sat down on the cold stone step of the rear door.

Cantrix Elnor was ready, too. Her sending had been more frail than ever, but she assured Sira she was all right, and looking forward to meeting them all face-to-face.

They knew Cho heard them come, but spread out as they were, he hardly knew which of them to assault first. They intended that by the time he had called the carvers around him and organized a sortie, their work would have begun and his support would be eroded . . . all his support. Sook was the one at risk; but the swiftness of their attack was meant to occupy Cho, prevent his reaching her before they could. He would be on the defensive, trying to stop them, busy repairing the damage they were about to do.

Zakri began first. In his early years, this very phenomenon had been part of the curse of his untamed Gift, the wild and unpredictable talent that had earned him banishment from House and master more than once. He remembered with painful clarity what it had felt like, seeing the *quiru* die around him. He knew how to do this.

He had no need of his *filla*. He bent his head, and closed down his hearing, his sight, his sense of warmth or cold. He drew in his thoughts, folding them in upon themselves like rolling up his bedfurs. He concentrated and reduced his Gift until it became a void at the back of the House, a black engulfing shadow that drew away every bit of light and heat from the nearby apartments, the corridors, the carvery.

In the west wing, Theo drained the *quiru* that sustained the kitchens. He had to thrust aside his repugnance, the fear every Nevyan was born with. Grimly, he repressed every nearby patch of light and warmth. They darkened and cooled with fearsome speed.

Cantrix Elnor, with a strength born of desperation, drew the light and the heat away from the upper corridors. Vestiges remained here and there, like puddles of melting snow, but the dark and the cold that lurked outside every Nevyan House, that haunted every Nevyan's dreams, began to spread.

Sira advanced then across the courtyard to stand with her arms outstretched on the broad steps. Her Gift was the strongest of all, the most highly trained. She was a full Cantrix, a Singer in her prime, at the peak of her abilities, and she threw herself into the battle with all her resources. She slowed the tiny particles of the air around her in an utter reversal of the techniques she had learned so painstakingly years before. She felt the light fade from the great room, the Cantoris grow chill and dank as if the limeglass windows were thrown wide. She focused her mind so fiercely that the cries of alarm from within the House hardly reached her. Her body grew cold, but she did not feel it. Not until her work was done did she feel the stiffness of effort in her neck and shoulders.

The cries from the House became wails, and then shrieks. Children screamed with terror as shadows they had never known crept around them. Sira shut out their fear. She knew all too well that these people would never forget this night, this moment when the dreaded darkness fell over their House.

She could not regret that now. She shielded herself, closed her mind to their suffering in the old manner. Zakri, too, had to brace himself against the emotions that poured from the House members. Theo, always vulnerable, found his face wet with tears, but still he held. Cantrix Elnor suffered the most, because she was weakened by hunger and age and grief, and because this was her House, her people. But even she did not relent, not for an instant.

The House grew cold between them. Cho stormed out of his apartment and raged about the corridors, ordering the itinerants to play, to work, to bring back the heat and the light.

Some tried. Fragments of melody sounded here and there, but the power of the two Cantors and the two Cantrixes was too great. The Gift was turned inside out, darkness drinking in light, a terrifying revocation of the great work of all Singers. It was a nightmare made real, and against the overwhelming fear of the cold, even Cho's awful weapon paled. Any light that began to swell around the itinerants soon dimmed and died. Their fear made them tremble, and the cold itself defeated them.

Vaguely, Sira became aware that Cantrix Elnor was no longer with them, no longer mirroring their work from her attic prison. She searched for her with her mind. She found Cho and two others, the Singers Klas and Shiro, bursting into Elnor's room, carrying her bodily down the stairs from the attic and then down the main staircase. Through the ruckus of psi and fear and the din of frightened people, threaded Elnor's cry for help.

Sira, she sent, *they have me . . . they . . . .*

Sira threw open the double doors and strode into the hall.

Cho and the itinerants were hauling Elnor into the
Cantoris. The Cantrix was weak, her limbs trailing, her head
falling back. A third man was halfway down the stairs, one
hand sliding across the elegant banister, the other clutching
a wrapped *filhata*.

Sira ordered, "Stop right there!"

The man threw her a wide-eyed glance. His feet were still,
but he was poised to flee, up or down. "Please, Cantrix," he
whined. "The *quiru*—"

Cho appeared in the doorway of the Cantoris, his thin
body rigid, his features twisted with rage. "Bring me that,
man! Hurry!" he commanded.

The itinerant put one foot on a lower tread. Sira snapped
at him, "Do not move, Singer!"

He froze again, trapped like a *wezel* between two preda-
tors. Cho's eyes narrowed, and he hissed, "If you don't get
down here, I'll wipe your idiot mind as clean as any *obis*
blade!"

The man gasped, and sagged against the banister. Sira
sent swiftly, *Zakri! I need you here!* Then she set her jaw
and stretched out her shields to encircle the itinerant.

Cho's blow struck her an instant later. He must have
known, have sensed what she was doing, and how it would
weaken her. Protecting the itinerant taxed her strength to the
utmost. She struggled for breath through a surge of nausea,
fighting to focus her mind under the pressure of his attack.
She saw nothing, heard nothing, but grappled desperately
with the reckless force that was Cho the carver. She threw
her inhibitions aside and struck at him, trying to break his
hold on her and on the itinerant.

She failed. Her knees bent, and she grew dizzy, the floor
tilting beneath her feet. She flung out her arms to orient
herself.

Cho was too strong, and she was stretched too thin. Her
shielding wavered, and she sent frantically, *Oh, Theo! I
cannot hold. . . . I am sorry. . . .*

But before she broke, her groping hand found Zakri's
shoulder, and her mind melded with his. Their shields
joined, firmed and thickened, twining like the irontree

suckers to make a whole that was greater than their individual strengths. It was Zakri who fired a burst of energy at Cho, as strong a volley as he could muster. Cho's attack collapsed under it, and Sira's head abruptly cleared.

The itinerants Klas and Shiro flanked Cho in the doorway to the Cantoris. Cho's lean face was wet with sweat, but he was unhurt, and his eyes dazzled black with fury.

"You can't do this to me!" he hissed through the murky darkness.

"We are doing it!" Zakri exclaimed. "Look around you! It is as dark as night in this House. Give it up, Carver!"

For answer, Cho paced to the staircase and reached up past the banister to seize the *filhata* from the itinerant. The man cowered back, shrinking from Cho as if his very touch might be the end of him.

"Elnor will sing," Cho snarled, "or she will die!"

Sira took two steps toward the Cantoris, keeping her wary eye on Cho. *Cantrix Elnor? Are you all right?* There was no answer. Cho moved behind her, and Sira hurried to reach the doorway before he did.

Elnor slumped on the dais where the itinerants had left her. She had fallen from the stool, and her hair spread in gray wisps on the floor about her head. She was not moving, and she sent nothing. Sira caught her breath.

The sound of *filla* came again in the upper corridor and in the hallway, threatening to undo their work. Theo still struggled from the west wing, but it was too much for any one Cantor to hold his own against the itinerants.

We must stop them! Sira ran into the Cantoris and leaped onto the dais, leaving Zakri stationed in the hall. Sira knelt beside Elnor, and began again, drawing in the light, fighting back the efforts of the Singers to repair the *quiru*. Zakri did the same. They drew in their shields as well, keeping them close and strong. Cho flailed at Zakri, and then at Sira, but it did him no good.

The House members had fled to their own apartments to wrap themselves and their children in thick layers of fur, hiding under rugs in a last attempt to stave off the deep cold. The various sounds of the itinerants' *filla* faltered and died, and they, too, ran for the slender shelter of furs and rugs in their own rooms.

Cho swore foully, and raced up the staircase.

Sook felt the cold seep into her little room from the top down, as if someone had lifted the roof right off the House. She had no furs, but she threw her bedfur around her shoulders and ran to the window seat to look down into the courtyard.

Below on the steps she saw Sira spread her arms, and saw the faint glow of *quiru* light around the walls of the House dim and vanish. Sook's lips stretched in a furious smile. "At last!"

She flew to her door and pounded on it. "Bree!" she cried. "Bree! Let me out! I want to see this, oh, please—Bree!"

The bolt rattled on the other side, and she pulled the door open to see Bree, her lips and nostrils white with fear, on the other side. "We're all going to freeze to death!" she moaned, and ran back out of the apartment before Sook could answer.

Sook was close at her heels, seeing the darkness closing in on the House, the corridors dim and treacherous, the stones of the floor already frigid with the loss of warmth. Sook laughed aloud, triumphantly. She ran to the staircase and looked down.

Bree passed Cho on his way up. She glanced back once, hesitating a moment, but her fear was too great, and she fled toward her own room. Cho's lip curled when he saw Sook, and he moved more quickly up the steps toward her. The glitter in his eyes was the only light in the corridor.

"Well, little Sook," Cho cried. "Now it's just you and me!"

Her heart fluttered in her throat, but she stood as straight as she could. "It doesn't matter, anyway," she cried. "Singer Zakri will see that you get what's coming to you!"

"Singer Zakri? Singer?" Cho laughed and seized her arm. "You're a fool! That's no Singer at all! Your Singer Zakri is a full-fledged Conservatory Cantor!"

Sook felt suspended in the darkness, with nothing to hold

on to. She staggered under his hand. "What?" she whispered. "You lie! You're a liar!"

Cho tittered, peering down at her face through the gloom. "I have no problem with lying," he said softly, squeezing her thin wrist, wrenching it upward. "But there's no need. You think he's for you, don't you, my girl? For you, a cook?"

"Zakri—Zakri's not—" She faltered.

"Oh, yes!" he crowed. "Zakri is! Zakri is Cantor Zakri, and no mate for you or for anybody!" His braid swung across his chest, and he threw it back, out of his way. He dragged her back down the corridor to the apartment, opening the door with his free hand. "So we'll just see how he likes this!" he exclaimed. He forced her across the room, flinging her into his own bedroom, slamming the door and shooting the bolt from the inside.

Sook stumbled over a small stool and fell her length on the stone floor. Her head snapped back, striking the edge of the bed frame. A rushing filled her ears and she sank into a gray fog of unconsciousness.

When she came to, Cho's body pressed hers into the soft furs of his bed, and he breathed sour gusts into her nostrils. His head lifted slightly, and his eyes narrowed. They were directed at her, but not seeing her. She knew that look—the itinerant Singers had suffered when he had that look. But she had no Gift to feel it! What was he doing? Who was he trying to hurt?

His hand gripped the collar of her tunic and he ripped it from neck to hem.

"O Spirit!" Zakri cried. He was still in the hallway, leaning against the wall, his eyes closed, his shields strong. Cho was sending him an image, a powerful scene that no shielding could shut out. Sook was on his bed, Sook with her head lolling, her face pale. Zakri tried to evade it, to disbelieve it, but Cho was in his mind, fastened to it with a tenacious strength worthy of a *tkir*. He was the *tkir,* Cho was, just as in Zakri's dreams. And he had Sook in his claws, tearing her tunic away from her body. This was no imagined deed, no empty threat. The sharp edge of reality made it vivid. Zakri gritted his teeth and his breath came fast.

He sent to Theo, *Theo! I need your help! It is Sook—in Cho's apartment! We must hurry!*

Zakri ran, ignoring the cries and shouts from all over the House. He leaped up the stairs as fast as he could go, skidding at the top on the cooling stone. He raced down the hall toward Cho's apartment, bursting into it with a crash of the outer door.

The inner door was closed and barred. Zakri pounded on it with his fist, and then pulled back his booted foot to kick it in. He heard Sook cry out in fear and pain, and he struck out with a blow of psi, hoping Cho was too occupied to block it. It was a broad swipe, fully intended to do as much injury as possible.

His strike met a parry of shocking strength. Cho had learned fast. Instinctively, Zakri shielded his own mind. He would be no good to Sook if his mind were ruined before he could get to her. He kicked at the door instead, using all his strength, and felt it crack slightly under his heel, but it did not give.

Cho shouted, "Cantor Zakri! I'm going to do it right now while you beat on my door, and I'm going to let you see and remember every moment—to entertain you in your lonely Cantoris!"

Zakri tried to close his mind to the image, but he could not escape it. Cho tore at Sook's tunic until only the drape of her hair fell over her bare skin. He made Zakri watch, and feel the sinister pleasure he took in it. Zakri battered at the door again as Cho reached for Sook to thrust her back. He took a fistful of the fabric of her trousers and ripped it.

Zakri could bear it no more. With a convulsive thrust of energy, he broke the psi contact. He was kneeling by the door with his head in his hands when Theo dashed in, out of breath.

"What is it? What has happened?"

Zakri found that there were tears on his face as he looked up at the older Singer. "It is Sook—my friend—" He pointed to the cracked and splintered door. "She is there! You must help me, please!"

The bedroom lay in deep shadow. Only the fading daylight from the window gave it any light, and that hardly reached to the bed. Sook blinked, thinking the blow on her head was still affecting her sight, and then, feeling the chill air strike her bare skin, she knew it was the dying *quiru* that made it hard to see. Cho leaned above her, and ripped her trousers from waist to knee with one hard jerk. She bared her teeth at him and he grabbed her hair, forcing her head up and back.

"Make plenty of noise, now, you little bitch," he panted. "We want your Zakri to hear everything!" He pushed her down with his weight.

He was too heavy, and too big, for her to resist. She felt as small and weak as a *caeru* pup, pinned by his body, with no purchase for her hands, nothing to push against or pull on. His long body covered hers, one hand in her hair, the other reaching for the tatters of her trousers.

Her left hand battered uselessly on his shoulder. Her right grasped at the bedfurs, searching for something to hold on to, something to fight with. She moved it desperately, seeking, searching . . . and at last, finding.

The hilt was in her hand, the haft smooth and worn under her fingers. The scabbard, slim and black and hard, was pressing into the flesh of her hip, and would leave its mark in a long bruise when this was over. It was almost over. She was all but naked, and Cho was fumbling with his own clothes now.

Sook pulled the blade free of the scabbard and gripped the hilt in her right hand. With her left she found the long braid that lay on Cho's shoulder, and she pulled on it with all her might. His head twisted to her left, and he cursed with the pain of his pulled hair. When he lifted his arm, stretching to reach his plait and jerk it from her fingers, Sook did not hesitate. Just so had she spread the ribs of a *caeru* carcass, to carve the meat from the bones. When she thrust hard with the knife, it glanced upward, to his heart.

Cho gasped, and his body went rigid. His face above hers paled to the texture of glacial ice, and when he released the breath, red, hot heart's blood gushed out over her hand. She screamed, not in fear but in rage and triumph.

At that moment, with Theo helping to guard his mind, Zakri used his special talent, his kinetic psi, to shove back the bolt that held the door, and he and Theo burst into the room.

CHAPTER
TWENTY-FIVE

"MREEN? MREEN? CHILD, WHERE ARE YOU?"

She heard the call, and her soft little heart gave a twinge, but she could not stop now. She had waited for just this moment, when Berk was occupied with tack and *hruss,* to make her dash for the House. The boy's misery was an ache in her mind, an insistent pull she could not ignore. Terrible things were happening in that House. She thought the boy might not survive them.

The thoughts and emotions of all the Gifted poured from the House, washed over the snow in a roiling deluge. She had to shield herself as strongly as she knew how, or find her own mind submerged in the flood. Much of what penetrated her shields was incomprehensible to her five-year-old mind. There was violence, that much she knew, and fear. And then there was the boy, whose own Gift was so undeveloped she could not even discover his name. He huddled in his room, weeping, shouting, anything to block out the chaos around him.

Boy! Boy! she sent, trying to attract his attention. *Hold on. I am coming. Boy, listen!* But he could not sort her small voice from the cacophony, and she feared for his mind in the sea of uncontrolled psi.

There was no path where she cut through the irontree groves, and in places the snowdrifts were too deep for her short legs. She had to wade through them, sometimes having to get on all fours and crawl over the top of the snow. She grew hot and damp under her furs.

Slowly she made her way up the hill, reaching the crest just as Soren's *quiru* began to collapse. Twilight blanketed the surrounding hills in a violet haze, and Mreen shivered in her furs, watching it, although she was not really cold. She cast a glance behind her, hearing Berk call her name again and again.

I am so sorry, she sent to him, though she knew he could not hear her. *I will be back soon.*

She hurried on. By the time she had forded the deep and crusted snow to reach the beaten snowpack of the courtyard she was breathless. She ran just the same, as fast as her aching short legs could carry her.

Soren lay in a muddy darkness. Mreen shuddered to see one of Nevya's great Houses without any gleam of *quiru* light shining from its windows, no comforting glow crowning its peaked roofs. It was an apocalyptic vision, the realization of the deepest fear of any child of Nevya. Mreen lowered her eyes, avoiding it. She clenched her small fists and raced over the unswept cobblestones and up the broad steps to the front doors.

One of the doors was ajar, left open by someone in a hurry. Mreen hesitated on the step, hating to put her foot into the dark hall. The swirl of psi around her, around the entire House, had not abated, but intensified. Somewhere, on the upper level, she sensed that the final confrontation was taking place. Her mind shied away from that conflict as her hand might pull back from a hot flame. She sought the boy instead, closing her eyes and concentrating, calling out for him, although she supposed he still would not understand.

Boy! Boy! Where are you? I am trying to find you!

"What in the name of the Spirit—"

Mreen opened her eyes and looked up to see a large man with black hair looming above her. She took an involuntary step backward.

"Who are you?" he demanded.

Mreen's nimbus, the only *quiru* light in the hall, shone brilliantly in the gloom. There was no other light. She was luminous, a lamp for the darkness. She gasped as she realized it, and took another step backward.

I am Mreen, she sent, but the man did not seem to hear her, although it seemed to her she could feel his mind, the anger and the fear in it. Surely he had the Gift. But he bent forward and reached with his meaty arm to take hold of her thin one. She knew perfectly well that no Gifted person touches another without permission.

"Looks like you've got the only light in the House," the man growled. He hauled on her arm, and she winced with pain. No one, in her entire life, had ever laid a hand on her in that way. If she could have screamed, she would have, in sheer fury. "You're coming up to see Cho," he said, and pulled her toward the stairs.

Mreen fought him. She kicked, and scratched at his thick hand with her nails. Black hairs covered his arm and his hand, and she tore at them. He cursed, some word she did not recognize, and bent down to take her around the waist. His forearm was just close enough. She sank her small white teeth into it, with a shudder at the taste of his skin and the texture of the coarse hairs that covered it.

For good measure, she focused on the spot of the bite, and made the broken skin as hot as her abundant psi energy could make it. He yowled with pain. He dropped her as he might have dropped a *caeru* cub that got its claws into him. She turned and ran, in the only direction she could, back out through the open door and into the night.

"Six Stars, girl, when I catch you . . ." he swore. He lumbered after her, out into the cold and dark.

Her halo was brilliant in the darkness, a clear beacon for her pursuer to follow. She ran to the edge of the courtyard, and then she stopped, bending down to huddle on the cobblestones. She forced herself to focus, to draw in her light until it faded to nothing, leaving her invisible in the darkness.

It was almost more than she could bear. This was nothing like the demonstration she had made at the campsite. Everyone feared the dark, of course, but Mreen, in all her five years, had never seen true darkness. Light had always emanated from her like the twinkling of a star. Now there was no light to reassure her, not her own, nor that which should come from the Cantoris, nor even the cheery small flames of one of Berk's cookfires. She was shocked to find herself growing cold, a sensation she could not remember ever experiencing. A silent sob escaped her, and her teeth chattered. How, oh how, she wondered wildly, did other people bear it? She felt bereft, desolate, and oh, so very cold. Her feet were numb already against the frigid stones, and the icy air burned in her chest when she breathed. She struggled to stand upright. She knew, if this awful man did not give up the chase, that she could freeze to death, right here in front of the House, and no one would know until morning.

The man was struggling against his own fear. He called out twice, and then stepped back into the dark House, where at least a semblance of warmth remained. But he remained in the doorway, peering out into the night, looking for her. She watched his sinister bulk, a shadow of menace in the doorway, and she despaired. She was too cold to cry, but her breath caught in painful spasms of shivering. She knew instinctively that she must not get caught; if the bad man in this House had her in his control, nothing Cantrix Sira could do would be enough.

It was when she thought she could no longer control herself, when she thought she would have to surrender, give in to her need for warmth, that his footsteps at last retreated, and she thought she saw his dim form moving up the staircase, but she could not be sure. She waited, shuddering with cold, hugging herself inside her furs.

The moments passed. When she began to feel warm, she knew she had waited as long as she dared. She let out her breath all at once, and her nimbus flared around her, its consoling light and soothing warmth feeling like strong arms about her.

Mreen raced back to the open door and peeked cautiously inside. No one was in the hall, although she heard voices and running feet everywhere above the stairs. She bit her lip and then trotted away down the nearest corridor, calling *Boy! Boy!* as she went. From above her, on the upper floor, there was a ruckus of shouting mixed with a tide of psi. She tried to shield herself, but it was vivid and violent, with horrible images, the more terrible because she did not understand them. She was afraid she might be sick, right in the hallway. And then she heard him screaming.

"Stop it! Make them stop! Mama, Mama!"

She was in the wrong corridor. She heard his voice dimly, through the cries and wails of the other House members, and then only because his Gift lent it carrying power. She tried to fasten on it, to follow it.

Mreen looked behind her. No one had seen her light, and the man had not returned.

She could hear the boy clearly now, feel him. He was crying, sick and frightened, and screaming out for his mother to help him. She retraced her steps, and ran frantically down the opposite corridor, all the way to the last apartment. Other people passed Mreen, running, calling each other's names. Some stopped to stare at her, but no one offered to touch her again. Their fear was as powerful as the darkness overtaking the House.

Mreen reached the closed door and heard the boy sobbing inside. There was another voice, a woman's, pleading and crying. Mreen wasted no time in knocking, but lifted the latch and pushed the door open.

The boy was perhaps five or six. He knelt on a couch in a muddle of bedfurs and pillows, his hands over his ears, his eyes squeezed shut. Tears and mucus ran down his face. A thin woman knelt beside him, trying to hold him as he rocked back and forth, wailing. "Oh, please, Joji, please," the woman cried, over and over. "Joji, stop! Joji, listen to me!"

Mreen shut the door sharply behind her and the woman

looked up in alarm. "What is—who are you?" she exclaimed.

Mreen went to the bed, touching her silent lips with her hand and shaking her head, trying to explain that she could not speak. She gazed intently at the boy, but his mother pulled him back, farther away from her, shielding him with her arm.

"What is it? What do you want?"

Mreen ignored her. *Boy!* she sent. *Joji! Can you not hear me now?*

"Who are you?" the mother repeated.

Joji! Mreen sent, as loudly as she could. Her own shields were still young and untried, but she extended them as much as she knew how, trying to shut out some of the noise from the boy's mind, wary of leaving herself too vulnerable. She felt the mother's suspicious gaze on her as she concentrated. Her halo sparkled vividly around her, intensified by her efforts.

The boy's sobs subsided little by little as the noise in his head diminished. He wiped at his eyes, and his mother produced a bit of cloth from her pocket to clean his face. He sniffled, and then sat up.

"Is it over? Is it—" His eyes stretched wide, sniffles forgotten, as he caught sight of Mreen. "Mama! Who's that?"

"I don't know," his mother said. She looked down at Mreen, who stood still beside the bed, powerless to explain herself.

Mreen stamped her foot in frustration. *Boy!* she sent, sharply. *Joji! I am trying to help you.*

"Oh!" he cried. "I can hear her, Mama—I hear her in my head!" His eyes grew bright and he put out his hand to Mreen.

Mreen drew close to the bed, and reached up with her small hands to pull his head down. His mother gasped and pulled him away again, but Joji wriggled free of her. "It's all right, Mama, she only wants to talk to me!" He crawled forward on his knees through the tangle of the bedfurs. "What is it?" he asked Mreen.

She put her hands on his shoulders, bringing his head down to her level, and touched her forehead to his. Carefully, as clearly as she knew how, she sent, *I am Mreen. I came to take you away.*

Joji stared at her. He was dark, with soft brown eyes, and painfully thin, thinner even than his mother. He shook his head. "I can't do that," he told Mreen. "I can't leave Mama."

"Joji!" his mother exclaimed. "What are you talking about?"

He turned his head to look at her. "This is Mreen, Mama. She's Gifted."

The woman stared at Mreen in consternation. "Where did you come from? Why don't you speak?"

Mreen felt her shielding begin to waver, and she grasped Joji once again. *We have to hurry,* she sent urgently. *I am shielding you from all the psi, but I cannot keep it up. We have to leave before they catch us!*

"Then I have to take Mama," he said.

Mreen shook her head. *No, no. Tell her we will be back for her. . . .* She drew a deep breath. *Tell her I promise.*

Joji stared at her for a long moment. Mreen was growing tired from the effort of keeping her shields up around them both, and she wavered. He gasped as the noise rose again on the periphery of his mind, and then he turned to his mother.

"Mama, I'll be back for you. Stay here! Stay right here!"

His mother's tears shone in the reflected light of Mreen's nimbus, and she clasped her arms about herself. "Oh, Joji, I don't even know who this is! And where are you going?"

"She's Mreen, I told you. She's shielding me, but she can't keep it up too long." He jumped down from the bed, turning back to pat his mother's arm. "We'll be back, Mama, we'll come back for you." He glanced at Mreen, and then repeated, "I promise."

His mother put out her arm as if to stop them. Mreen turned her green eyes on her, fixing her with the intensity of her gaze, and the woman shrank back, her hand to her lips. *Tell her,* she sent to Joji, *that it will be all right.*

Joji frowned, not understanding completely. Again Mreen

touched her forehead to his. *Tell your mama it will be all right. Cantrix Sira is here.*

Joji smiled at her, and turned to smile at his mother. "It's wonderful, Mama! I can hear her, clear as anything! And she says don't worry, Cantrix Sira is here."

The woman stared at him. "Joji—I don't know who that is, either."

He shrugged. "Me, neither, but I know Mreen!"

Mreen tugged at his hand. She was getting very tired, and thought if they did not get away soon, her shields would fail. Joji followed, looking back only once at his mother.

In the corridor, they ran, hand in hand, to the front doors and out into the dark. Joji pulled back suddenly, tearing his hand from Mreen's, when he saw that night had fallen over the snowy hills. He whirled, turning back to the House as if even the misery inside it was better than the terrors of the cold and dark outside. Mreen gripped his hand and pulled him close to her.

They slowed to a walk when they were down the steps. Mreen relaxed her shields and poured her energy instead into her own tiny *quiru*. It had lighted and warmed her since her earliest memory. It was much easier for her to intensify it now than it had been to quench it earlier. It bloomed full and bright about both her and Joji, and in relative comfort, hands tightly joined, they made their way across the courtyard.

Mreen was tired, exhausted by her trek down the hill and the effort required to shield Joji from the psi that buffeted the House. Her legs felt as heavy as *hruss* legs, plodding and thick.

A sudden hoarse yell from the House made her heart thump hard in her breast. She glanced over her shoulder and saw that the hairy man had spotted them, and was coming out of the House and across the cobblestones.

Joji, hurry! Run! she sent. If he could not understand her sending precisely, he sensed her alarm. He yelped in fear, a small, pitiful sound, and they ran, together, racing for the shelter of the ironwood grove on the hill.

The big man's legs were much longer than theirs, and he

could not be half so tired as Mreen was. She heard his feet slapping against the cobblestones, and she and Joji ran as hard as they could, striving for the trees, not daring to separate for fear that Joji would be left in the cold. Mreen's breath came shallowly, and her short legs burned with effort. At the edge of the cobbled courtyard, she fell headlong from the stones to the snow.

The man exclaimed in triumph. She struggled to her knees, but her legs were too tired, although she tried.

Then Joji, fresh and energized by his fear, pulled her to her feet. "Come on, Mreen," he cried, "you can do it! Come on, a few more steps!"

He tugged at her, and she came, the two of them running together, Mreen staggering, Joji insisting. The man behind them cursed, and stumbled in the darkness. The children reached the shelter of the thick irontree grove, and the man swore again as their little halo of light disappeared among the trees.

Mreen and Joji did not stop, struggling on through the obstinate snowdrifts, until the House itself was obscured by the thick trunks of the trees. Only then did Mreen collapse on a huge sucker, sobbing soundlessly with what little breath she had left. Joji clung to her, terrified of the dark, amazed at his own daring in coming out with her, casting wide eyes back the way they had come to make absolutely certain the man could not see them.

For long minutes they rested, Mreen with her cheek against the rough bark of the sucker, Joji gripping her hand as if it were his only chance. When they could breathe again, and Mreen's legs felt stronger, they began the climb up the slope toward the campsite.

It was heavy going. Mreen tried to find her own path, to retrace her footsteps, but her nimbus did not give enough light to make it easy. The snowpack was frozen stiff by the deep cold, slick on the surface, deep and spongy when they broke through the crust. Twice they fell, together. Once Joji rolled away, out of Mreen's halo, and his terror when he found himself in the deep cold was a painful thing. Mreen had learned that fear herself not long before. He began to sob immediately with the shock of it. She clambered over the snow on all fours as fast as she could, to embrace him once again in her light, and they snuggled together, shivering, like two *caeru* pups lost in the drifts.

They wound slowly up through the trees, relieved when they saw at last the flicker of the *quiru* and the small steady fire within it. Mreen's heart ached to see Berk slumped beside the fire, his head in his hands. She must have been gone for hours. She pulled at Joji, rushing him, forgetting her exhaustion, hurrying into the light and warmth Zakri had refreshed before going down to Soren. Once they were safe in its circle, she dropped Joji's hand and flew to Berk.

She reached out her small hand and patted his grizzled cheek. His head flew up with a cry, and he swept her up in his massive arms. She hugged him back, hard. He buried his face in her shoulder and squeezed her until she thought she might never breathe again. When she could look into his face, she saw tears of relief standing in his eyes.

"You rascal!" he said hoarsely. "I thought you were gone! I—" He caught sight of Joji and broke off. "By the Ship! Who's this, then?"

Joji dropped his head, and stared down at his boots.

"Mreen!" Berk exclaimed. "You could have frozen, the two of you. It's dark already—the cold!"

Mreen dimpled up at him, and he drew a ragged breath and hugged her close once again. "You kept him warm, didn't you, you little darling? You got him out of there, and you kept him warm! O Spirit, yours is a strange Gift!"

Berk held out his hand to the little boy. "Better come on over here by the fire, young man," he said. "And you'd better tell me your name, since this one can't—you can speak, can't you?"

Joji took a hesitant step closer, and then another, and reached out to put his hand in Berk's. "I can talk," he said shyly. "My name's Joji."

"Joji, is it," Berk said. "Well, Joji, you've had quite a time of it. But it's nice to have your company. Hungry?"

Joji nodded, and a smile brightened his thin face. "I'm really hungry," he said.

"Well, then. You just sit here and watch while Mreen and I make the *keftet*. We're good at it, aren't we, Mreen?"

Mreen nodded briskly, and ran to the saddle packs for softwood. Berk watched her go, shaking his head, muttering to himself. He gave a shaky sigh, and looked down at the little boy she had rescued. "Ship and stars," he muttered. He patted Joji's shoulder and ruffled his hair before he went to fetch the cooking pot.

CHAPTER
TWENTY-SIX

✶ CHO AND SOOK LAY IN A HUDDLE IN THE HALF-LIGHT.
Only the dull shine of Sook's bare shoulders and
the river of darkening blood flowing between them were
distinguishible to Zakri and Theo when they thrust the door
open. Zakri froze in the doorway, afraid to know whose
blood it was that stained the bedfurs. Theo pushed past him
to reach for Cho and pull him away from the girl.

The carver was limp and heavy, a deadweight in his
hands. Theo grunted, lifting him up, turning him faceup on
the bed. The knife was still buried in his ribs and it caught
on the tangled sheets and furs. Sook looked down at it, and
then at Cho's sightless eyes, and turned her head away.

Theo pulled a sheet free of the bedfurs and wrapped it
around her nakedness. She searched his face as she accepted
his ministrations, her eyes gleaming in the dusk.

"Is he dead?" she asked in a small and breathless voice.
"Did I kill him?"

Theo put his fingers under Cho's jaw, and then slipped his
hand beneath the loosened tunic, feeling with his palm just
below the juncture of the ribs and the breastbone. There was

no movement of heart or breath. Sook clutched the sheet around her shoulders and wriggled as far away from Cho as she could get, stopping only when she bumped against the wall. Theo thought she looked very young, surely not older than four summers.

"You must not blame yourself," he told her gently. "He gave you no choice."

Her protest was no more than a whisper, barely audible. "No, no!" Her tension constricted her throat, and her hands, holding the sheet, were stiff. "Tell me! Have I killed him?"

Theo had to tell her. He tugged on the sticky bedfurs, pulling them up and over Cho's inert body. "Yes," he said quietly. "He is dead."

Her small fist pounded the wall next to her once, sharply, making Theo's nerves jump. "Thank the Spirit!" she exclaimed.

He stared at her for a moment. He understood now the expression that burned in her eyes. He had seen it often enough in his youth. He had guided hunting parties, and had seen the faces of hunters standing over their fresh kill. Sook wore the same expression the hunters had. It was the hot flush of victory, the blaze of triumph. There was no regret in it.

Zakri found his feet at last and moved close to the bed. He glanced briefly at Cho's sightless eyes, swallowed hard, and looked away. "Sook? Are you all right?" he asked. His voice cracked.

"Zakri!" she exclaimed. "He's dead. Cho's dead. Look at him—"

Zakri looked back at Cho's face. It was waxen, the narrow lips and thin nostrils white. The black eyes that had struck terror into so many were now unmoving and dull, fixed forever on the view beyond the stars. His long braid lay twisted around his neck as if to choke off his last breath. But the knife still protruded from his side, blood drying on the hilt. There was no doubt about what had happened.

Sook had done it. Alone. Zakri could hardly take it in.

She came to her knees, the sheet bunched under her chin. Her stiff muscles now trembled violently. "I'm not sorry," she said, speaking too fast through dry lips. "I had to do it. He was an awful man, and he was going to hurt me! I'm not sorry, I'm not!"

Zakri stared at her, speechless. It was Theo who reassured her. "Of course you are not," he said quietly. "You did what you had to do. But it was a hard thing, and a frightening time for you. You need some water, and some fresh clothes. We can call a Housewoman to help you."

Sook crawled on her knees to the edge of the bed, keeping her distance from Cho's body. She glanced over her shoulder at it, and her face blanched as if indeed it had been her own blood that had been spilled. "See—" she began. She found the floor with her feet and stood up, clutching the stained sheet about her, and took one step toward Zakri.

Her legs collapsed. He caught her just in time to stop her falling to the floor. He swept her up in his arms as he might pick up Mreen. Sook's head lolled back and her eyes rolled. Her loosened hair cascaded over his arm to brush the floor. Theo exclaimed, and came to put his hand under her neck, to support her head until they could reach the couch in the outer room. They lay her there and covered her carefully with the sheet.

"Stay with her," Theo told Zakri. "I will finish with— with what has to be done."

Zakri nodded, and knelt beside Sook, pulling a fur from the back of the couch to tuck around her. Theo returned to the bedroom, where Zakri could see him arranging Cho's long legs, straightening the bloody bedfurs. Theo hesitated briefly with his hand above Cho's face before he closed the staring eyes with his palm. At last he pulled the bedfur all the way up over the body, leaving a long, narrow, lifeless mound.

Theo closed the bedroom door firmly and came back to the couch as the room began to brighten around them. Sook stirred and sighed.

"What . . ." she whispered. "Where is . . . ?" She struggled to sit up, and her eyes went wide as she remembered. She gasped, and cast a horrified glance back at the door to Cho's bedroom.

"It is all right now, Sook," Zakri said. "It is all over. See, the *quirunha* is going on even now."

He put out his hand, clearly visible now as the light intensified. The room was warmer, the chill being pushed back as if swept away by the warm, bright air that replaced it. Sook looked from Zakri to Theo and back again. Her chin began to tremble.

"Oh, Zakri," she cried. "I—I killed Cho, didn't I? I took his knife, and I—"

Zakri repeated, "It is all right, Sook! It is over now."

She stared at him, shaking her head. She tried to speak again, but her words dissolved in a torrent of tears. He knelt helplessly before her as she sobbed.

I do think, Cantor Zakri, Theo sent to him, *that it will not compromise your Gift to comfort the girl. She has had a terrible experience, and there is no one else here for her.*

Zakri cast Theo a grateful glance, and then gingerly put his arms around Sook. She sobbed the harder, throwing both arms around his neck, weeping out all her loneliness and fear and horror. He held her, patting her shoulder, stroking her tumbled hair. The House warmed around them and the sounds of shouting and running feet in the corridors died away. By the time Sook's tears were spent, Soren was as bright as morning, and warmer than it had been for many months.

Theo left the apartment, returning just as Sook was wiping her face and trying to reorder the mass of her hair. "The House members have seen to the rest of them," he said obliquely.

Zakri stood up. He bent to rub his knees, which had grown stiff on the chill stone of the floor. "Are we needed, then?"

"Not for that. Sira would like us to come to the Cantoris—Cantrix Elnor is there."

"Good news," Zakri said. "Sook, shall we fetch a Housewoman for you?"

She shook her head, still shuddering slightly with the aftermath of weeping. "I have clothes, in there," she told him, pointing to the little bedroom which had been her prison. "I just need a moment. But I don't want to be alone!" She gave an involuntary glance at the closed bedroom door. "Will you wait for me?"

"Of course we will," Theo assured her.

When Sook had gone into her own room, Theo and Zakri went to the window and looked out into the night. The unkempt state of the courtyard was made clear by the generous spill from Sira's *quiru*.

What have they done with the others? Zakri asked.

They have rounded them up like wild hruss *and stabled them in the carvery,* Theo sent. *No one else was hurt.*

Do they know about Sook? About Cho?

I told them only that he was dead.

Sook's door opened, and she emerged dressed in a brilliant scarlet tunic and fresh trousers, her hair brushed into a fresh binding. She had scrubbed her face, but her eyes and lips were swollen and red. Still, she tossed her head as she looked back at the little bedroom. "I never want to see those walls again," she said. Her voice was shaky, but growing stronger. "I've had enough of being a prisoner!"

Theo bowed to her, smiling. "So be it," he said. "May you live the rest of your life as free as the *urbear* on the Glacier!"

Sook managed a tremulous smile at him.

Together the three of them left the apartment and walked down the corridor to the broad staircase with the beautifully carved banister. The weeks of poor heat and light had left their mark in pockets of creeping mold and mildew that festered in corners and crevices. It had been impossible to clean the House adequately in the weak *quiru* light. Dust and dirt lay everywhere. But the House members, pale and thin though they were, smiled and chattered to each other, lively in their relief. They waved to Sook, and bowed to Theo and Zakri as they passed.

Zakri looked to his left when he reached the foot of the stairs. The carvery door was closed and bolted on the outside, and several House members stood guard before it. There were decisions to be made, reparations and punishments to be decided upon. He hoped those functions could be left to some other authority. Now that Sook was safe, and

Soren free of its despot, he wanted only to return to his own House as soon as possible. He suddenly missed his own Cantoris, Cantor Gavn, even the sour Cantor Ovan, with a sharp pang that surprised him.

In the Cantoris, Sira was still on the dais, a borrowed *filhata* in her lap. Cantrix Elnor, slight and gray-haired and weak, sat on one of the benches, facing her. A number of carvers were seated around Elnor at a respectful distance. They had broken into the locked attic at the first sign of the collapsing *quiru*, and had carried their Cantrix bodily down the two flights of stairs and into the Cantoris. They now sat, smiling, but keeping a watchful eye.

The *quiru* was complete. Sook, Theo, and Zakri walked together up the aisle to the dais. Sira's brows rose at the sight of blood on Theo's clothes. He winked at her and sent swiftly, *I will explain it all later.* She nodded and stepped down from the dais.

She bowed formally before the elder Cantrix, and said aloud, "Cantrix Elnor, I present to you Cantor Theo v'Observatory." Theo bowed also.

Elnor inclined her head. Her neck trembled slightly, and there was no color in her wrinkled cheeks, but she smiled. "I am glad to meet you, Cantor," she said. "And I thank you from the bottom of my heart for coming to the aid of my House."

"Glad to be of help," Theo responded. "And pleased to see you well."

She shrugged delicately. "Well enough. I will be better soon."

"And this," Sira began, holding out her hand to Zakri. "This is Cantor Zakri v'Amric—"

She was interrupted.

"No!" Sook burst out. "It's not true!"

Zakri turned to her, stricken. "Sook! I could not tell you before—it was not safe, but—"

Sook's eyes blazed and her cheeks turned pink. "How could you let me think—let me feel—oh, be damned to you!" And she whirled and ran from the Cantoris, leaving the Cantors and the carvers to look after her, dumbfounded.

Sira and Theo stared at Zakri. His cheeks flamed, and then paled.

"What have I done?" he begged them. "And what am I to do now?"

Sira had no answer. Theo said, "My friend, I think you had better go after her. She is hurt, and angry, but she needs to hear your explanation just the same."

Zakri looked at Sira, and at Cantrix Elnor, who watched the scene in confusion and consternation. The carvers around her exchanged glances and shifted uneasily in their seats. One of them rose as if to follow Sook, and then sat down again.

Cantrix Sira, Zakri sent desperately. *I had no intention of deceiving the girl. I meant only to protect her.*

Sira's answer was sympathetic. *I never doubted you, Zakri! But you must tell her that.*

Zakri bowed to Elnor and to Sira, and hurried up the aisle after Sook. Theo watched him go with a wry grin. *There is always one more surprise,* he sent to Sira.

Even for you, she answered.

Oh, yes? He looked at her, folding his arms and cocking his head to one side. *I can hardly wait.*

CHAPTER
TWENTY-SEVEN

✴ ZAKRI FOUND SOOK WHERE THEY HAD FIRST MET, IN THE kitchens. She had served him tea then at the long, knife-scarred table under Mura's strict eye. But now Mura was gone, and Sook showed him only her back, her face turned to the window and the darkness beyond. He would have sworn she had already wept herself dry, but her shoulders quivered, and no Gift was needed to understand she was struggling not to cry.

"Sook," he said softly. "I did not mean to deceive you. I would never want to hurt you! It just did not occur to me that—I mean, for a Cantor—"

Her arms were wrapped tightly around herself. She shook her head hard.

"Sook, please. Will you not speak with me, let me explain?"

A tiny sob escaped her. Unshielded, he felt what she felt, the pain and the despair that made her heart ache. The air around him showed random flecks of darkness as he sought to control his own emotions. "Oh, Sook, listen to me," he pleaded, and was horrified to hear his voice shake. He gulped and began again. "Listen! We are friends, are we not?"

When she spoke, her voice was full of tears. "We were friends. You deceived me!"

"I did not mean to."

"You let me think—you let me believe you were an itinerant, a Houseman, one of us!"

"I protected you. It was not safe for you to know what I was."

"I would have kept your secret! You knew that!" Her voice rose and broke, and she bowed her head and pressed both hands to her face.

"Sook, I know you would not have deliberately betrayed me—but Cho heard all kinds of things he was not meant to hear."

"But I'm not Gifted!"

"Just the same, he might have picked up all sorts of things from your mind. Berk and I decided at the beginning that the fewer people who knew what I was, the better chance we had of getting away, of getting help."

Zakri felt suddenly weary beyond bearing. He flung himself into a chair and buried his head in his hands. Sook glanced over her shoulder at him, and fresh tears welled. She stammered, "You see, I thought—I hoped that you and I would be—" She sobbed, and turned back to the window, unable to finish.

"I see that now," he said sadly. "But I did not understand it before. You see, I do not—I never think of myself in that way. I never have. The Cantoris—the *filhata*—these are my life. To give them up, after working so hard to earn them, would be a sacrifice I could never bear."

He looked up to see her straighten her shoulders and brush back errant strands of her hair. She sniffed and wiped at her eyes. "All those weeks, when he kept me up there, all that time, I dreamed of you coming back to Soren. Sometimes I thought I couldn't stand it another moment, but then I would imagine you riding over the hill, coming to rescue me."

"Oh, Sook," he said miserably. "I meant to do just that. And now I have failed you after all."

She shook her head again, hard. "No, Za—Cantor Zakri, you have not! I am so grateful to you and your friends. It's just that—" Another sob made her voice break.

"Sook!" Zakri stood and took a step closer to her, but she kept her face turned away. The curve of her cheek and the line of her slender neck tormented him. "Please hear me," he said. His voice was low and intense, and he knew by the lift of her head she was listening.

"If I were not what I am, things could be different. But I have a difficult Gift, difficult even now. If Cantrix Sira had not trained me as she did, no one could have lived with me, not you nor any other person. My Gift was wild, out of control. I was a danger to everyone around me."

She made no answer.

"But, Sook—if there were ever to be anyone—if it had ever been possible—it would have been you! I . . . I admire everything about you . . . do you understand that?"

He waited for some response, but none came. After a moment he backed away from her, going slowly, still hoping. Sook steadfastly stared out the window, her back straight, her small shoulders squared. He reached behind him and opened the door. "Goodbye, Sook. Please forgive me." He went out, and closed the door softly after him. Faintly, through it, he thought he heard her speak, but he could not be sure. He almost went back, to find out, but he thought better of it. His sacrifice had become hers, and there was nothing he could do to change that. He went back to the Cantoris with heavy heart and dragging feet.

The Housekeeper of Soren, a frightened woman who seemed still stunned by the events of the long day, opened an empty apartment for Sira and Theo and their party. She produced clean bedding, but fresh clothes were not available from Soren's depleted stores. Apologetically, she explained that there was no soap, and no spare linens. At least the apartment was large and comfortable. There were bedrooms enough for Zakri and Berk to have one, Sira and Mreen another, and a long couch in the main room that Theo claimed. It was late, and there was more work to come in the morning. The moment the door closed behind the House-keeper, Theo threw himself on the couch with a great yawn, propping his feet on the carved arm. Sira stood by the long window, looking out, not yet ready to rest.

Well? he demanded. *My surprise?*

Her narrow lips curved upward ever so slightly and she cast him a sidelong glance. *Mreen was here,* she sent.

He sat bolt upright. *Mreen! When?*

Sira came to sit beside him. *When the* quiru *was down,* she answered. *She came and found the little boy . . . Joji, his name is. And she took him away, back to the camp.*

Theo stared in disbelief at Sira's face. *How—by the Six Stars, how is that possible?*

She pointed her long forefinger at him in mock admonition. *You gave her the idea, you and your* quiru *games. She got him outside, and then she expanded her light to protect them both. They had quite a climb, from what she sends me, and she frightened Berk half to death, but they are safe now, with Berk at our campsite. I must find Joji's family and reassure them.*

Theo fell back on the couch, one hand pressed to his heart. *This is too much for an old Singer! That child will be the end of us all.*

More likely, Sira sent, *that child is the future of us all. Her Gift is beyond my understanding. She must have some great purpose in store for her.* She looked thoughtful, tracing her scarred eyebrow with her finger. *I only hope it gives her joy.*

Just like you, Maestra. You, too, have a great purpose. Has it given you joy?

She stretched out her hand to touch his cheek. *My dear,* she sent. She did not smile now, but her eyes glistened, reflecting the *quiru* light. *No greater joy is possible, while we are together.*

Theo caught her hand in his and held it for a moment until she pulled it gently away. He shielded himself. He did not want her to hear his thought, his fear, that her purpose might carry her away from him yet again.

Mreen and Joji and Berk arrived at Soren's doorstep before the next morning's meal was served. The little boy was alight, full of chatter about Mreen, about snow and irontrees, and especially about sleeping outdoors in bedfurs. His mother hugged him, and held his hand tightly during all of the introductions that had still to be made, but when they went in to the meal she would not sit at the center table. She backed away, going to sit at a table by the wall with other House members. Joji stayed with Mreen and the Cantors, his small chest puffed with pride at his newly elevated status.

The great room hummed with talk and movement as House members hailed each other in celebratory fashion. Sira and Theo sat side by side, with Cantrix Elnor across from them. The Magister's seat they left empty. Many House members glanced at the carved chair at the head of the table, the same Cho had sat in for months, and their faces were grim. Sira wondered if there were no one at all to grieve the carver Cho's passage beyond the stars.

Sook herself served the central table. Her small body was straight, her face composed. "Good morning, Cantor, Cantrix," she said calmly as she placed bowls of *caeru* stew before them. "There are no vegetables or fruit at all yet. We've had to make the best of it, but we hope you'll come back when our nursery gardens have fully recovered."

Sira nodded to her. "Thank you, Housewoman," Theo said. "We will try to do just that."

Another Housewoman came after Sook with a pot of tea. This one kept her eyes averted from the empty chair, pouring tea with a nervous motion that spilled drops around every cup. Sira arched her brow.

Zakri, is this one afraid of us?

Zakri watched the girl's hasty retreat from their table. *That is Nori,* he sent. *She may be the only person in the House to be sorry Cho is gone.*

Do you not think those in the carvery are sorry? Theo asked.

No. I think by the time we arrived, everyone was so frightened of him that they are mostly relieved. Except now they have to face the Committee!

But they are Gifted. The Committee will be lenient with them—they will have to be! The shortage is still their main concern.

Sook looks fully recovered today, Sira put in.

Zakri sighed, and Theo reassured him. *She is a strong young woman, Cantor Zakri,* he sent. *She will be all right, in time. She has made up her mind to it.*

"Excuse me, Cantrix Elnor?"

An itinerant bowed to Elnor and to the rest of them. He smiled rather nervously, and bowed again. "I'm wondering . . . that is, a lot of us are wondering . . . can we go now, go back to our Houses, get back to work?" He gestured behind him to a table full of Singers. "We'd all like to know, actually."

Elnor lifted a tremulous hand. "I do not know," she said. "I will leave these decisions to you, Sira."

Sira and Theo exchanged a glance, and Theo nodded. "Yes," Sira told the itinerant. "It is time. You may all go as you see fit, and we wish you safe journey."

"Thank you, Cantrix." The Singer bowed again, and then he smiled broadly. "Tell me—does anyone want to send a message north? I'll be on my way to Manrus first thing tomorrow!"

Zakri said quickly, "Yes, indeed, if you will be riding by way of Amric!"

"So I will, Cantor," the Singer said.

"You have a long ride ahead of you," Theo commented.

"And I can't wait!"

There was laughter, and the itinerant bowed once more before going back to his own table. A burst of excited chatter and more laughter greeted him there, and the Cantors looked at one another.

"Things will be back to normal very soon, Cantrix Elnor,"

Sira said. "I am sure you will have a Magister, and a new junior, before the summer."

"I do hope so," Elnor said softly.

"Of course we will stay until you do," Sira added.

"Thank you, my dear. I am not sure I am strong enough to manage just yet."

Theo looked around at the House members. None of them looked strong, in truth, but he was certain that when their gardens were revived, their health would improve rapidly. Perhaps by summer, they could put all of this behind them. But for himself, and Sira, he could only guess what the summer might bring.

He had not shielded his thought, and Sira heard it. *Do you not think we will be back at Observatory by summer?* she sent.

Something is still to come, he answered. *But I do not know what it is, or where it will take us.* He pressed down his suspicion that it was not his own future that was in doubt, but Sira's. He had known for years that some great service still awaited her, and his instinct, or his Gift, told him it was near. She watched him, knowing he was hiding some thought. He smiled at her, and gave a slight shake of his head. *Nothing to worry about now,* he sent.

"Well, then," Sira said aloud. "I believe it is time for the *quirunha.*"

They all rose to go to the Cantoris. They planned a special *quirunha* for this day, a ceremony of music and thanksgiving. The second missing *filhata* had been found and tuned, and with its mate it awaited Sira and Theo on the dais.

Berk, Zakri, Mreen, and Joji followed them to the door. Elnor, leaning on her Housewoman's arm, preceded them across the hall to the Cantoris. Sira was following her, but she stopped suddenly in the doorway, making everyone else come to a halt. Theo sent, *What is it?*

Look.

At a table beneath the window, a man had fallen forward, and the woman next to him was pulling him upright again. She propped him against her shoulder, and tried to get him to take a mouthful of *keftet.* As they watched, the meat and broth fell from his slack lips to splash back into his bowl. Patiently, the woman wiped his chin with her hand, and tried again.

Zakri stepped up next to Sira. *That man was one of Cho's demonstrations,* he sent. *He has been like that since I first came here.*

Did you try to help him?

No. There was no opportunity—and I believe his mind is past retrieval.

Sira and Theo looked at each other, and he nodded. "Mreen, Joji," he said, holding out his hands to the children. "Let us go on to the Cantoris and make sure everything is ready for the *quirunha*. Joji, are you strong enough to lift chairs and move stools about?"

Joji hurried to him. "So I am, Cantor Theo," he asserted. "I'm very strong, Mama always says so."

Theo led them across the hall to the Cantoris while Sira turned aside, with Zakri and Berk, to go to the man and woman by the window. As they approached, the woman looked up. She was of middle age, weathered and brown, and her eyes and face were worn now with exhaustion.

"Forgive me for not standing, Cantrix," she said. "If I do not support Karl, he falls."

"I see that, Singer," Sira answered. She pulled out a chair across from the two and sat down. Zakri and Berk stood close behind her. "Can you tell me what happened to him?"

The woman eyed the three of them, and then shrugged. "I guess it hardly matters now," she said. "I couldn't say before, or I'd get the same as Karl, and then I don't know who would have taken care of him—or me, for that matter."

"What is your name?" Sira asked.

"I'm Ana," she answered. "Ana v'Perl, it used to be. I don't know if they'll have me now." A flash of spirit showed in her eyes. "Karl wanted to come here, to follow Cho. I didn't, but he—" Her eyes grew dull again. "He's my mate, Karl. I had to go where he went, didn't I?"

Sira nodded gravely. "I expect you did. And I believe all the Houses will be delighted to have their Singers return. I am sure you can return to Perl when you wish."

Ana managed a tired smile. "Thanks, Cantrix. I hope you're right."

"Can you tell us, then, Singer?" Berk asked.

She looked up at the big man. "I wanted to tell you before, when you were here. You're the courier from Amric, aren't you?"

He nodded.

"I didn't dare talk to you," she said. "It was that Singer, the one from Trevi."

Zakri caught his breath. "Iban!" he whispered.

She glanced at him. "Yes, that was it," she said. "Singer Iban. The thing was, Karl here was supposed to make sure Iban didn't leave Soren, but then he got away, along with his relative. Escaped. Cho didn't care about the other one, Clive I think his name was, because he wasn't a Singer. But Clive couldn't get home without Iban to make his *quiru*. So one day they just disappeared—they weren't anywhere to be found."

Her mate's head lolled, and she replaced it on her shoulder with a gentle hand, as if she had done it a thousand times and knew she would be doing it a thousand more. She went on, "Cho was furious. He kept saying if there was even one exception, his plan would be ruined. Every Singer had to be here, by will or by force. And so he made Karl go after Iban, to bring him back."

She paused to try to coax another spoonful into Karl's mouth. Sira prompted her. "What happened then? What happened to Iban?"

"I only was there because Karl and I always traveled together." She looked down at her mate's vacant features. "Always," she repeated sadly. "It's a long ride to Amric from Soren, and they were riding hard, but so were we. On the third day we caught up with them. I told Karl we should just let it go, just let Iban go where he wanted, but Karl wouldn't hear of it. He said—he said Cho was depending on him!" The last words were said bitterly. "And then Cho used him, he used Karl, and this is what's left to me!"

"What do you mean?" Sira asked her. "How did he use him—how could he, at such a distance?"

Ana looked at her mate's hands lying useless on the table. Tears formed in her eyes, and she wiped them away with her sleeve. "Karl was a good Singer," she whispered. "A strong one, the best. That's why Cho picked him." The others waited while she collected herself. When she could, she continued, "Cho used Karl's Gift to kill Iban. He struck with his own psi through Karl's, like . . . like calling out in a canyon, and hearing your voice echo off the far wall. Like skipping a stone across the Glacier. I don't know, because I couldn't have done it, but I was watching Karl when it happened. At first he smiled a little, like with pride or something, but then he looked sick, and then—afterward, he couldn't move or speak. I managed to get him back here . . . I didn't know where else to go. I thought at the time that maybe because Karl's mind broke, Iban got away after all, but then you came asking about him. Karl—" She turned her hopeless eyes to Sira. "Karl was a strong Singer, but Cho's psi was so awful. None of us could resist it. Karl's been like this ever since."

Berk rumbled something deep in his throat, but Zakri had no anger left. "So this is what happened," he said with great weariness. "Iban—our master—was brave to the end, and it cost him his life."

"But had he not come to you," Sira reminded him, "Soren might have been lost forever. Cho grew stronger every day."

"Nevya must know about Iban," Zakri said. "It is all we can do for him now. He must be remembered as a hero."

"A hero indeed," Sira said. A shared memory of Iban, his expressive face and bright gray eyes, sprang up between them. *We will always remember,* Sira sent to Zakri. *But we have no time now for grieving.*

I know, he answered. He looked at Karl's blank eyes and drooling mouth. *At least,* he sent, *our master did not have to finish his days like that.*

They said goodbye to Ana and her mate, leaving them to struggle on through their meal. They went across the hall to join Theo and Elnor in the Cantoris, to perform the one task that every Cantor or Cantrix must fulfill every day, without fail. Their personal feelings must always take second place to their duties. But Iban was present for them that day, as if he had been with them in the Cantoris. It seemed once or twice to Zakri, as he listened to Theo and Sira spin out their melodies from the dais, that Iban was at his shoulder, his eyebrows dancing, his eyes sparkling in the old way. Safe passage, he thought sadly. I wish you safe passage beyond the stars, Singer. We will always miss you.

CHAPTER
TWENTY-EIGHT

✦ THE HOUSE MEMBERS GATHERED IN SOLEMN ROWS WHEN the prisoners were taken from the carvery. Housemen and women lined the corridor in stony silence, holding their children by the hand or in their arms. The three carvers and six itinerants marched past, eyes averted. The whisper of their fur boots against the stone floor was the only sound. Saddled *hruss* stood waiting for them in the courtyard. Two itinerant Singers and six of Soren's strongest riders were already mounted and ready to begin the long ride to Lamdon. There the rebels would face the judgment of the Magistral Committee. Sira and Theo had debated this move; it would not be an easy trip. The number of riders was large, and available supplies were limited. They had decided to outfit the group one way only, and trust Lamdon to supply them for the journey home.

Theo stepped forward at the double doors. He held out his hand to each of the itinerants as they passed. One by one, Klas, Shiro, and the three other men dropped their *filla* into his palm.

Bree came last. Her neck burned with shame, and she

stared steadfastly at the floor. She pulled her *filla* from her tunic and held it out between two fingers without looking at it. Theo took it carefully, not touching her hand, and dropped it with the others into a leather pouch. It would be up to the Committee to decide if and when the *filla* would be returned. Bree swallowed and turned to the open doors with the three carvers trudging behind her.

"Wait!" Sook came running down the corridor from the kitchens, a towel still in her hands. "Wait, please!" she called.

She was breathless when she reached Bree, and put her small hand up to grip the Singer's shoulder. Bree looked into her face, and then quickly away, shaking her head. "It's no use, Sook," she muttered.

Sook turned to Theo, and then searched past him for Zakri. Zakri, with Berk and Sira, stood by the doors of the Cantoris, Mreen and Joji flanking them, ready to see the travelers on their way.

"Cantor Zakri," Sook said.

Zakri glanced once at Sira, and then came forward. "What is it, Sook? What can I do?"

"We have to help Bree," Sook said. "She helped me more than once. She took me to see Mura, she unlocked my door, she brought me food. She even tried to stand up to Cho! I don't know what might have become of me if she hadn't been there."

Theo gave Bree a hard look. "Singer," he said. "Do you have something to say for yourself?"

Bree lifted her head to meet Theo's eyes. "I'm getting what I deserve, if that's what you mean, Cantor," she said. "I helped Sook when I could, yes. But I was part of this from the start. It's just that—when I saw what was happening—I couldn't take it anymore. I should have done more . . . but it had gone too far." Her plain features were bleak.

"She doesn't need more punishment," Sook insisted. "She helped me, and she needs my help now." Her great eyes flashed at Zakri. She put out her hand as if to touch his sleeve, and then jerked it back, remembering. "Please, Zakri. Make them let her go. For me."

Zakri lifted his hands in an appeal for understanding. "What can I do, Sook? These are not my decisions!"

"You have to do something," she said. "Please, do something!"

Zakri flushed under the intensity of her gaze, aware of every eye upon them. "Cantor Theo," he murmured. "Is there anything we can do? Can you help me here?"

"Lamdon has to deal with them," Theo answered. "They are Gifted, and therefore subject to the highest authority. Sook could send along a letter, perhaps, some message asking for leniency in Bree's case."

Zakri looked hopefully at Sook. She considered for a moment, biting her lip. She glanced at Bree, and her chin lifted. "I'm going to go with them!" she declared. "I want to be there for the judgment."

Behind her the Housekeeper exclaimed, "But, Sook! Who will run the kitchens if you leave now?"

Sook put her hands on her hips and glared at the assembled House members. "Surely someone can manage during my absence so I can make this journey!" The House members looked at each other. "You all ate when I was locked up for those weeks, didn't you?" Several put up their hands, about to speak, but Nori forestalled them. She came from behind the crowd, her cheeks pink. She cast a shy glance at Zakri as she passed him, and came to stand before Sook and Bree.

"I can do it, Sook," she said. "I want to."

Sook tossed her head. "Good. Then it's settled."

Zakri opened his mouth to protest Sook's plan, to remind her that this would be no pleasant journey, but then he closed it without speaking. He had no say in this matter, either.

Theo smiled down at Sook. "Well, Housewoman, you have your way, it seems. Now you had better hurry, or the travelers will leave without you!" he said.

Sook gave him a brilliant smile, and flew down the corridor toward her own apartment. Zakri stood at Theo's shoulder as the rest of the offenders were ushered out into the courtyard to mount their *hruss*.

"Do you think they will listen to her?" he asked. "I fear the Magistral Committee will tear her to pieces."

Theo chuckled. "I think, Cantor Zakri," he answered, "that your young friend will not rest until the Committee hears her out! She will be like a *wezel* in a *caeru* den . . . she is small, but she is persistent, and when she gets those sharp little teeth into something, she will not let go until she is good and ready."

"I suppose you are right," Zakri said shakily, and laughed a little under his breath. "But I worry about her."

Theo clapped him hard on the shoulder. "My friend," he said. "You had best worry about the Committee—they have no warning!"

Within ten days of the restoration of the *quiru*, the gardens of Soren began producing vegetables once again. Limp, yellowing leaves turned green and firm, and sagging stalks straightened under the warmth and light that poured daily from Sira and Theo's *quirunha*. Cantrix Elnor grew stronger, too. Like the plants in the nursery, she stood straighter and her color improved. When she joined them on the dais, her voice was unsteady at first, her intonation uncertain. But before many days passed she was singing securely, her voice high and clear. In due time she took a turn with one of the *filhata,* and on that day, she pronounced herself ready to welcome a new junior and take responsibility for her own Cantoris.

Messages flew between Soren and Lamdon, Lamdon and Conservatory, Conservatory and Soren. Sook returned to Soren in the company of a courier from Lamdon, bearing the news that the offenders had been censured and fined one hundred bits of metal, which should keep them busy for many summers. They had been released to go and earn their freedom, with the proviso that none of them ever visit Soren again. Only two, the Singers who had escorted the Magister's party and then allegedly abandoned them, received the ultimate sentence. Those two would be exposed in the

Mariks, left to the elements as they had left the Magister and his mate and children to the deep cold.

Bree's fine was reduced to twenty bits of metal because of Sook's testimony in her behalf. When Sook told the story of the Committee meeting, her eyes flashed and tendrils of black hair flew about her face. Her cheeks had grown brown from the long days of riding, and her gaze was direct and confident. Zakri watched with pride, as if she were a treasured little sister. Theo watched them both, hiding a smile.

The carvers had been banished from Soren, from their home, in perpetuity. Their family members would have to decide for themselves whether to join them, whether to become members at whatever House might agree to take them in, or to forgo seeing them ever again.

I wonder if they know about Observatory? Theo sent to Sira, grinning at her.

I should imagine you will tell them, she answered.

Certainly. Observatory could do with some carvers of their own. And I doubt Pol would have any difficulty disciplining that lot!

The courier's greatest news for the House members was of their new Magister. The younger brother of the Magister of Arren was to be appointed in due course, and would arrive in the summer with his mate and their children and a retinue of servants. A search party had gone looking for the vanished Magister of Soren and his family as soon as there was a Singer available, but as yet no trace had been found. The courier's features were stoic when he described the Committee's feeling that when the summer came, the melting snow would reveal their remains. Those around the meeting table glanced at each other, shaking their heads.

Finally, the courier said, "Had Carver Cho not died in the battle for Soren, the Committee would certainly have had him exposed. As it is, they ruled that his body should be left in the hills, not to be buried when the thaw comes."

Sook, seated at the table with the dignitaries of her House for this one special meeting, kept her head high and said nothing. Theo caught her eye and tapped his temple, reminding her that she had done what she must. She gave him a small nod of gratitude.

"And a Cantor?" Elnor asked at last. "Or a Cantrix? Is Conservatory going to send me a junior?"

The courier bowed to her. "Yes, of course, Cantrix. Your new colleague should arrive any day. Conservatory is providing his escort. And Conservatory requests that Cantrix Sira return with their riders."

Sira stared at him. "I? Go to Conservatory? Why is that?"

He bowed again. "I don't know, Cantrix," he answered her. "I'm only the courier. They don't tell me everything."

Theo said, "It is a lot to ask, it seems to me. With no explanation!"

The courier spoke carefully, bowing yet again. "I'm sorry, Cantor," he said. "It's what they told me to say."

Zakri grinned across the table at Sira. *What have you done now, Maestra?*

Sira arched her white-slashed brow at him. *Do not call me that! And I have no idea what this is about. I may not even go.*

Theo chuckled. *Oh, I do think you will go, Sira. And so will I! Who can resist a chance to visit Conservatory? Besides, we need to take Mreen back—and Joji.*

Sira regarded him thoughtfully. *You are right, as always. And it has been a very long time since I have walked down the halls of Conservatory.* She ran her fingers through her dark hair, and turned her head to look out the window. The first melt was beginning to pare away the snowpack. The dark green of the irontrees was already brightening, promising summer. *Would it not be lovely,* she mused, *to be in the open when the Visitor first rises in the east?*

Theo sent, *Indeed it would, my dear.* Zakri, listening as usual, quickly withdrew from their conversation. He smiled to himself, watching Sira and Theo exchange a warm glance. Sira's eyes were bright, and the sharp planes of her face were softer, the lines of weather and worry smoothed away. She looked very young just then, Zakri thought. For a brief span she looked no older than Sook.

The moment passed, and Theo turned to Zakri.

"Cantor Zakri?" he asked aloud. "Will you be coming with us?"

Zakri looked at both of them, and reluctantly shook his head. "I think it is time I went home—my home, which is Amric. Gavn has been alone with Ovan a long time."

Sira sent privately, *It will be hard to say goodbye to you.*

Zakri had to press down the sudden fear that he might not see her again for years, perhaps ever. He forced a smile to his lips, and sent, *And to you, Maestra!* He could not push away the thought that Observatory was a long, long way from Amric, no matter how he reminded himself of his duty.

Theo sent to him, *Zakri. Conservatory is not more than a day's ride out of your way. Do come with us at least that far!*

He is right again, Sira sent. *Let us all ride together, one more time.*

Zakri laughed and gave in. *So I will!* he sent. *I see there is no resisting you two!* The air glimmered before him as if full of ice crystals catching the sun. He allowed the sparks to dance around him for a full minute before he quenched them.

The evening meal began in a festive mood. There was wine for the first time in months, a gift from the Magistral Committee, sent from Lamdon as a sign of encouragement and unity. Sook, for the first and only time in her life, sat at the central table to be served like the upper-level House members. Her bright tunic was a flame among the coal-dark colors of the others. Theo made certain everyone spoke aloud throughout the meal, for her sake.

The Gifted were served their tea, and the wine was measured out for the House members, poured into small ironwood goblets that were carved into charming shapes, no two alike. Sira admired the one at Sook's place. "Such a wealth of beautiful things here," she said.

Sook nodded. "It's a wonderful House," she said. "At least it was."

"It will be again," Theo assured her. "Just look around you."

Indeed, the great room was bright and warm, bustling

with the talk and activity of a lively community. The mold that had taken root in the ceiling corners had been eradicated by much scrubbing, and the last bits of grime that had lain hidden in the darkness had been scoured away. The limeglass of the windows gleamed, and the stone of the floors shone smooth with polishing. Only the scarcity of fruit on the tables gave testimony to the time of hardship.

Will it be summer soon, Cantor Theo? Mreen asked.

Indeed it will, he told her. *And we will all be at Conservatory soon.*

Mreen leaned close to Joji, to touch her forehead to his. *Joji, summer is coming, and we are going to Conservatory!* He wriggled in his seat, bouncing as if it were all he could do to stay in the chair. Mreen frowned at him, and lifted one chubby forefinger. Joji froze in his place, and Theo, watching them, roared with laughter.

"What is it?" Sira asked. He tried to answer, but as soon as he drew breath, he laughed again, helplessly. Sira tapped the table with her fingers and looked around at the others. "Does anyone know what is wrong with Theo?"

"I think," Zakri said, also chuckling, "that you have an imitator!" He gestured with his thumb to Mreen.

"What do you mean?" Sira demanded.

"Never mind," Theo finally sputtered. "At least she chose a good model." He wiped his eyes, and lifted his teacup to Sira. "To our Maestra!" he cried. "May summer find you disciplining Conservatory as you have disciplined all of us!"

Zakri and Mreen laughed with Theo, and lifted their cups. Sira shook her head at them all, but she was smiling, and her eyes glistened in the rich yellow light of the *quiru*.

"We will see about that," she said softly. "It very well may be the other way around." She lifted her cup, and every House member did the same, whether tea or wine. "To Soren!" Sira said, and the cry was echoed around the room. "To Soren!"

CHAPTER
TWENTY-NINE

★ THEY SAW NO REASON TO HURRY AS THEIR PARTY MADE its way northeast to Conservatory. The weather was warming, the air fragrant. Joji and Mreen crowed with excitement at every new scene they passed. Mreen gave up her treasured post behind Theo to Joji, and rode behind Sira or Zakri through the long days. In the evenings, they all lingered long by the embers of the cookfire, looking up into the clearing sky. They found the Six Stars, and Conservatory's star, and then they slept gloriously late in the mornings, lulled into laziness by the sweet air that foretold summer.

Sira woke one morning to an insistent little hand on her cheek. *Cantrix Sira!* Mreen sent, bending close and patting her face softly. *Cantrix Sira! There it is!*

Sira sat up, blinking. Mreen's smile was enormous, her dimples flashing. She pointed, and Sira followed the direction of her chubby finger.

The sun had risen above the eastern horizon, and below it, trailing it like a distracted child, the Visitor traced the outlines of the Marik Mountains. Together, the two pale stars dissolved the early morning clouds into tatters of pink and gray. Sira caught her breath, and drew Mreen into the circle of her arm. The little girl knelt beside her, tucking her curls beneath Sira's chin.

That is the Visitor, is it not? she asked. *Summer is here, is it not?*

Indeed it is, dear one, Sira sent, hugging the warm small body close to her own. *Indeed it is.*

Then I have two whole summers now!

Sira chuckled. *So you do.*

Shall I wake Cantor Theo and the others?

Sira smiled down at her and traced her round cheek with her finger. *In just a moment, Mreen. Just one more moment.* She looked back at the two suns shining above the distant peaks. Just there, she thought, just below the Visitor, is Observatory. They will be out in the courtyard today, looking up at the sky, celebrating, expecting our return. And in one more day, I will ride up to Conservatory. My true home. Every Singer's true home, as Mkel always says. And it may be the last time ever, for me.

It was a sobering thought, and she tried to thrust it aside. *Wake the others now, Mreen. They will want to see the Visitor.* Mreen dashed away to each of the others still dreaming in their bedfurs, and Sira reached for her boots. Summer at last! It was a time to rejoice. It was no time, she scolded herself, for dark thoughts.

A large company awaited them on the steps of Conservatory. Sira's heart lifted at the sight. House members, students, and teachers waited in formal ranks to receive her and her two students, the two Cantors who had never attended Conservatory. The two suns, shining together, gave luster to the colorful scene, the red and yellow and blue tunics of the House members, the deep colors worn by the upper levels and the Gifted, the bared heads of all the people. Mreen and Joji were welcomed in a flutter of the youngest students. They looked like a flock of *ferrel* fledglings, circling their elders, swooping down on their new classmate and flying away with him. The *hruss* and all the gear disappeared swiftly and efficiently, and Sira, Zakri, Theo, and Berk bowed to Maestro Nikei, Maestra Magret, Cathrin, and the others. It was a joyous reunion, but Sira knew in a heartbeat who was missing from the ceremonial gathering. Magister Mkel was not present.

Maestro Nikei? she began. He nodded, intuiting her query before she could form it.

That is why we sent for you, Sira, he sent. *Mkel is very ill, worse since we sent our message.* He glanced at Cathrin, who was bustling about shooing everyone indoors, making much of Zakri and Berk and Theo in her usual cheerful fashion. *Cathrin is being brave, but even she knows it will not be long now.*

Is there nothing we can do? Sira strode up the steps, formalities forgotten, to stand close to her old teacher. Maestra Magret came to join them, and they stepped aside, out of the flow of people.

Nikei has done all he can, Sira, Magret assured her. She patted Sira's arm in maternal fashion. *But Mkel wants to see you, and you can judge for yourself.* Sira nodded and turned to hurry indoors. *Sira!* Magret sent. Sira stopped in the open doorway to look down at her senior's lined, gentle face. *Be prepared,* Magret warned. *He is very ill indeed.*

Sira felt her throat tighten. She took a deep breath. *Thank you, Maestra. I will.* More slowly now, she went into Conservatory. As she passed, she laid her hand flat against the carved wood of the door, as if greeting an old friend. The ancient plaque hung above her head. She cast her eyes up to read once again the familiar words:

> Sing the light,
> Sing the warmth,
> Receive and become the Gift, O Singers,
> The warmth and the light are in you.

Those lines, she thought, were carved as deeply into her heart as into the ironwood of the plaque. Despite the sadness that awaited her, she savored this moment, in which she entered Conservatory as an honored guest and alumna, no longer an outcast, no longer in disgrace. Her eyes filled with unaccustomed tears as she thought that she was, however briefly, truly home. She blinked the tears away and found Theo at her side.

What is it, Sira? he asked, standing close but not touching her. His blue eyes were dark as an evening sky. *What is wrong?*

She gave him a rueful shrug. *It is everything,* she answered. *Mkel is ill, and I am worried about him—but I am home, and all I can think of is how much I would like to stay!* More tears burned behind her eyes. She frowned and pressed her lips together to compose herself.

Theo sent, *My dear, you look as fierce as that* tkir *that haunts Zakri's dreams!*

She sighed a little. *I know. But it is better than weeping like a first-level student in front of all these people.*

They were following Magret and Nikei up the wide stairs then, their feet slipping easily into the worn spots of the treads. Sira looked around her, tasting the rich air of Conservatory, breathing in its essence. There were almost no adornments of any kind in the House. The arches of the doorways, the simply carved furniture, were of the simplest and most graceful designs, and the stone floor was devoid of rugs. In fact, rugs were never necessary at Conservatory. It was perfectly warm, perfectly and evenly lighted. Indeed, even now fragments of melody floated from the practice rooms, and with them came warm drafts that seemed infused, almost scented, by the music.

Yes, Theo agreed. *It is a magnificent place. The best place. I have always envied you your years here.*

At Mkel's apartment, Maestra Magret looked once, intently, into Sira's face. Sira nodded to her, indicating that she was ready. Nikei opened the door, and stood back for her to enter.

Sira was grateful for Magret's warning. Had this not been Mkel's own apartment, in which he had lived since her student days, and had she not expected to find him changed, she would have doubted her own eyes. He had always been well fleshed, with thick hair that had been gray since she could remember, and lively eyes that saw and understood almost everything. But his illness had emaciated him, wasted him to a husk. He was so thin she wondered that he still lived. Only wisps remained of his hair, and his eyes fluttered, the lids falling as if he had not the strength to hold them up.

Is it Sira? Sira, are you here? he sent. She sensed that he had no breath to speak aloud. Swiftly, she moved to his bedside and knelt beside it.

Yes! Yes, Magister Mkel, it is I, she sent. *I am here. I am terribly sorry to find you so ill.*

He moved his hand from side to side, a negating motion. *That no longer matters,* he sent. *I only thank the Spirit you are here at last. I have been holding on to this life only . . . only . . .* It seemed he might be too weak even to finish his sentence. She waited, and finally heard, faintly, *. . . until you could come.*

Sira broke with custom by taking the spotted and wrinkled hand in her long smooth ones. *Why should that be, Mkel?* she asked, forgetting his title in the intensity of the moment. *Everyone here loves you, you have Cathrin, and Nikei—why should you need me to speed you on your journey?*

His fingers slipped against hers, trying to grip them. She did it for him, holding his hand tightly, wishing she could hold his spirit as well.

Sira, my dear . . . you will find out soon enough. But thank you for being here. Watch out—watch out for Cathrin, will you? Remember she has always cared for you . . . looked out for all of you. . . .

Sira turned her head to find Nikei, near the door. She whispered, "Someone should fetch Cathrin, and quickly!"

Theo said, "I will do it, Maestro Nikei," and was gone in an instant.

Sira looked at Mkel once again, but his body was so wasted, his features collapsed and vacant, that she closed her eyes. She held his hand and saw, in her mind, the old Mkel, the vigorous man who had led and taught and set an example for all the Singers who had passed through Conservatory during his tenure.

Take care of them. . . . he sent feebly, very weakly. Sira heard the door open and close, and she felt Cathrin's warmth beside her, reaching for Mkel's other hand. Sira was distantly aware that Cathrin was weeping softly. But for Sira, the moment was one of pure psi contact, and the physical world receded into shadows.

What can I do for you, Mkel?

His breath rattled in his chest, and she thought for a moment it was over. Then she heard in her mind, very faintly, like a melody barely remembered, *Receive . . . receive the Gift.* . . .

Sira did not know what it meant, but she accepted it as Mkel's farewell to her. She sent to him, *Safe and swift passage, Mkel,* but she believed his mind had already slipped away. A moment later his hand in hers went limp. Cathrin was sobbing brokenly, and Nikei came near to murmur comfort to her. Sira opened her eyes to see that Cathrin had pressed her face against Mkel's chest. It no longer rose and fell with his breath.

"Cathrin," she said gently. "Mkel's last thoughts were for you."

Cathrin lifted her tear-stained face to look into Sira's eyes. "Oh, no, Sira," she said, shaking her head. "Oh, no, they were not. I know better."

Sira began to protest, but Cathrin shook her head again. "Never mind, my dear," she said, wiping away tears that were quickly replaced with fresh ones. "I know what Mkel's thoughts were, and they were for Conservatory, just as they should have been. I'm so very grateful you came! He's been waiting."

Sira stared at Cathrin, and then at Nikei, mystified. Theo came to help her to her feet, and they stepped back to give Cathrin and Nikei time to say their own farewells.

What did he say to you, Sira? Theo asked privately.

He said he had been waiting for me, she sent. *And then—it was so odd—he said, Receive the Gift.* She felt stunned by sorrow and confusion, and she put her hand in Theo's, needing the warmth and the strength of his touch. *I do not know what he meant. I do not understand it at all.*

Theo pressed her hand. *He was so close to death,* he sent. *Perhaps he did not know what he was saying.*

But why should he be waiting for me? He is surrounded by friends!

Theo had no answer for her.

The summer warmth caused the ground to thaw quickly. Within a week of summer's arrival, Nevyans hurried to inter their dead while it was possible. The bodies, which had lain frozen by the deep cold, were retrieved from their winter resting places and buried among the flourishing softwood shoots that sprang so quickly out of the softened tundra. It was good luck to be buried in a softwood grove, to return to the ground during the reign of the two suns.

Mkel's burial ceremony was a grand one. The senior Cantor of Lamdon came himself. All of Conservatory, House members, Singers, teachers, riders, and a number of itinerants gathered to bid the Magister farewell, trooping on foot from the courtyard in a long column, trudging after the *pukuru* which bore Mkel's body to its burial site. Cathrin had chosen the place carefully, on a slope overlooking the House, where, she said, Mkel could look down and see that Conservatory's work was properly carried on. Cathrin and Nikei and Magret were dignified and composed. Only the very youngest students wept. Joji and Mreen were wide-eyed and mystified by the whirl of events of the last weeks.

Sira kept an iron control of her feelings. Theo stayed close beside her, and although they sent little, she knew he understood very well her grief and confusion, mixed with her joy at these precious days in her old home, these last days with Mreen and with Zakri.

When the solemn rite was over, a quiet meal was served in the great room. Cantor Abram called all of the Gifted into the Cantoris the moment they were finished, leaving the House members to drink a commemorative glass of wine. Only Cathrin joined the Cantors and Cantrixes, the teachers and students, and the visiting itinerants who came to stand in rows facing the dais.

It was not a *quirunha,* and no *filhata* were in evidence.

Abram stepped up alone to the dais and bowed to the assembly. They all bowed in return, and he gestured for them to be seated.

"We will speak aloud out of respect for our guests," he said, nodding to the itinerants who sat in a cluster far at the back. "And for Cathrin, of course, who has our deepest sympathy at this sad time." He bowed to Cathrin, who sat on the first bench with Maestro Nikei and Maestra Magret on either side. Sira and Theo were on Nikei's left, and Mreen crept close to sit in the circle of Theo's arm.

"My friends and colleagues," Abram went on. "The last years have seen great changes on the Continent. We at Lamdon have spent many hours discussing the challenges all Nevyans are facing—"

Theo's elbow dug into Sira's side and she flashed him a look.

Abram said, "The shortage of the Gift has been of especial concern, and it is Lamdon's feeling that in the next years we must examine the causes and possible remedies as closely as possible. We are particularly pleased by the renewal of trade and exchange of information with Observatory, and we . . ." He rattled on for several minutes, never saying anything in two words if five would accomplish the same.

Sira tried to keep her attention on the speech, but a strange sensation distracted her. She heard in her mind, but clearly, as if with her physical ears, the old song:

> Sing the light,
> Sing the warmth . . .

She almost looked behind her to see who was singing in the Cantoris, singing even while Abram droned on. Of course, she knew there was no one, but the song was so vivid!

> Receive and become the Gift, O Singers,

Surely even Theo could hear it! She glanced at him, and then at Magret, and Nikei, but their eyes were politely fixed on the dais. Then she looked down, and saw Mreen's round green eyes opened wide, and staring at her.

Do you hear it, Cantrix Sira? the child sent.

Sira caught her breath and nodded. Mreen heard it, too. Where did it come from?

THE WARMTH AND THE LIGHT ARE IN YOU.

The melody faded away. It was achingly familiar, that song. Sira had learned it as a first-level student, and had sung it before an erudite audience at Lamdon when she had just four summers. She had taught it to Theo, and to Zakri, and last, to Mreen. It echoed in her mind now, and she sighed. It was as if it was sent from the Spirit, from beyond the stars. It was Mkel's farewell.

Abram talked on.

"We feel that the choice of Conservatory's next leader is a crucial one. It is always an important decision, of course, but in these difficult times even more so. After much weighing of possibilities, Magister Gowan, the Committee, and I, your senior Cantor, have decided to accept Magister Mkel's own nomination for his successor."

Nikei and Magret and Cathrin looked at Sira, and she arched her scarred eyebrow. They seemed very calm, she thought, considering the importance of this announcement. Probably Nikei or one of the other teachers—doubtless they already knew Mkel's choice—

Abram's chest swelled and he stepped to the edge of the dais. He raised his voice and announced in ringing tones, "My friends and colleagues! I present to you Conservatory's new Magistrix . . . Magistrix Sira v'Conservatory!"

He turned to her and bowed very low.

CHAPTER
THIRTY

✦ SIRA FOUND HERSELF IN A DREAM. AT ABRAM'S AN-
nouncement, she rose to her feet very slowly, as if
trying to stand in deep water. She felt every vertebra in her
spine, every joint of hip and knee and ankle flex and expand
to lift her upright. Her feet carried her to the dais without her
being aware of making a conscious decision to go there.
She saw herself bow to Abram, and then to the assembly,
but she seemed to have left her real self still standing at
Theo's side. Nikei and Magret's smiles were serene, Cathrin's tearful. The entire body of the Gifted rose to bow to the
phantasm of Sira on the dais, while the real Sira, the essence
of her, watched in shock.

The assembled people erupted in applause liberally mixed
with exclamations of surprise. Not a few expressed dismay.
The true Sira saw only Theo, registering the amazement that
made his eyes wide, and then the immediate freezing of his
features as he reined in his emotions. His usually open face
became a closed mask. He bowed with the others, and when
he straightened, although his eyes were open, she could
neither see into them nor hear his thoughts.

Several moments passed before the dream Sira and the real Sira, reluctantly pulled from Theo's side, fused into one. Her face felt stiff, her body awkward as she bowed once again, and then looked over the faces in the Cantoris, trying to take in the import of what had happened, what had been said. Abram was saying something to her, and she nodded, but his words had no meaning. Nikei and Magret stepped up on the dais, to stand beside her as bulwarks against the tide of thoughts flowing around the room. She nodded to them as well, and it seemed she spoke, but none of it was real. Every detail was unutterably trivial . . . except for Theo's unmoving face, his eyes blue black, fixed on a point beyond her head.

Abruptly, Sira had to be away, away from the Cantoris, from the noise, both mental and audible, from the crush of people. With a muttered apology, she left Magret and Nikei standing with Abram on the dais. She glanced once at Theo, and then she fled, striding up the aisle on her long legs. She was not aware until she was already in the corridor, on her way to the old haven of the nursery gardens, that Mreen was with her, trotting frantically to keep up.

Mreen flashed a pleading glance, and Sira slowed her steps. The little girl, panting, took Sira's hand. *It is going to be all right, Cantrix Sira,* Mreen sent firmly. The words were sent as one adult might send to another. There was no doubt in them. Mreen's childish features shone with confidence. *You are the one. The Gift decided it.*

They reached the gardens, and Sira pushed open the door. Inside, the air was rich and heavy, the farthest walls invisible in the nourishing haze of moisture and glowing *quiru* light that protected the plants. Sira and Mreen were alone. All the House members were still in the great room, all the Gifted were left behind in the Cantoris. Hand in hand, Sira and Mreen walked between the flats of seedlings, and then the raised beds of root vegetables, on to the rows of tiny fruit trees that were kept close by the inner wall for warmth. Sira's legs grew suddenly weak, and she sat down abruptly on the nearest ledge. Mreen stood close by, stroking her arm.

Sira looked at her closely, seeing her, and everything, clearly for the first time since Abram's startling announcement. *Mreen! What is that in your hand?*

Mreen was holding a little *filla,* an old-fashioned one with tiny fragments of smooth metal worked around the stops. She held it up to Sira.

You remember this, do you not? Mreen asked, still in that strangely adult way. *This was Mkel's, and it was given to him by his own Magister, who had it from his Magister.* Her eyes glazed and grew distant, but there was no fear or passion, only a pleasant dreaminess, in her expression. *So many hands,* she sent, shaking her curls. *So many Singers.* She dimpled at Sira. *And now you, Magistrix. You must have this.*

Mreen handed the little instrument to Sira, who took it with weak fingers. *Mreen—why?*

Because that is why Mkel gave it to me. Mreen suddenly laughed with her familiar soundless mirth. She was free of her burden, all at once, and the adult look faded from her face. *You will have to give me yours! Now I have no* filla *at all!*

Sira stared at her, and then at Theo, who had come up behind her. *Theo—I am so glad you are here. Look what Mreen has given me!*

Theo looked at the little *filla,* and he bent to sweep Mreen up into his arms. *I see that,* he sent. *So this is why he gave it to you, little one.* He hugged Mreen, and the look he turned on Sira was warm with love, but the old crooked grin was absent.

Yes! Mreen answered. She bounced in his arms. *Now let me go, Cantor Theo, please. I have to go to my lessons!*

He set her on her feet and she bowed to both of them, her nimbus as bright as the Visitor itself. She turned and ran up the path toward the distant door of the nursery gardens, and then whirled and trotted back. She stopped in front of Sira, and sent with a little shrug, *Magistrix, it is true—I have no* filla *now.*

Sira reached into her tunic and brought out her own *filla,* which was hardly less worn than the one Mreen had just given her. She handed it to Mreen, and the child bowed, dimpled, and ran off once again, leaving Theo and Sira alone.

Sira met Theo's eyes, and then dropped her gaze to the *filla* in her hand. She turned it over and over in her long fingers. Theo's shielding was a wall between them, a barrier to their usual closeness, and it hurt her to feel it. "You are unhappy," she said aloud.

"I am proud of you," he answered. He sat beside her on the wooden ledge, and picked up a crumb of the rich soil of the bed behind them, rubbing it between his fingers into black dust. "You will be a wonderful Magistrix."

"Do you think so?" she whispered. "I am frightened half to death."

"I think that is natural," he said, with an attempt at a chuckle. "There is no more important job on the Continent, if you ask me."

"When we rode up to Conservatory," Sira mused, "I wanted nothing more than to come in and stay. And now—now that I will be staying—maybe for always—I do not know how to feel. I am torn in pieces!"

His face was close to hers, and he met her eyes, but he did not touch her. "You are thinking of Observatory," he said, "and our school."

"And of you, Theo." Her throat closed.

"I know," he said softly. He watched her tears spill over and roll down her face, but he did not reach out to wipe them away. She supposed it was because she was now Magistrix, and that made the difference.

He shook his head. He had heard her thought. *No, Sira, it is not that.*

What then?

Theo stood up, stretching his arms over his head, rubbing his hands through his thick hair. She knew he was giving himself time to discipline his own emotions. He turned to face her, and the pain in his eyes was almost more than she could bear.

Sira, this is the destiny that has driven you all along. You are the reformer. You will restore the Gift to the Continent, and make our Houses safe. I— He managed a wry grin then, shrugging his broad shoulders. *I am only an old itinerant. It is my destiny to love the Magistrix of Conservatory. We have been apart as much as we have been together. Now it looks as if we might be apart forever.*

Sira stood, too, and faced Theo. They were not any great distance from each other, but she felt that a chasm yawned between them, a gulf with no bridge. She hoped he would not ask, and he did not. Then suddenly she wished he would, and she chided herself. Of course he would not ask, because he knew perfectly well she would refuse. He knew her heart and mind as well as she herself did.

You know that I love you, too, Theo.

I know that very well.

But the Gift—

He held up his hand. *Shall I say it for you, Sira? Do I need to tell you that you would not be yourself if you made any other choice? Or even that I would be disappointed in you if you made another choice?*

She shook her head, and now he did smile at her, fully and generously. He dropped his shields, and she stepped forward, of her own volition. They came together, their arms tight around each other, for a precious and fleeting moment. She pressed her lips to his cheek, once. When they parted, his eyes burned fiercely, and Sira found fresh tears on her own face.

CHAPTER THIRTY-ONE

✦ SIRA'S INVESTITURE AS MAGISTRIX OF CONSERVATORY was to take place in three days. In the meantime, a thousand details were brought to her attention, needing her judgment, her decision. She had no time to contemplate what had happened, how her life had changed in a single stroke of fate. Questions about the House, about the students, about her plans, rolled about her until she thought she would have no peace at all. Cathrin had already removed all of her personal things from the Magisterial apartment, although Sira protested her hurry.

Cathrin smiled at her. "This is what it is to be a Magister's mate, Sira."

Maestra Magret was there, and Maestro Nikei, sitting with Sira at the long table, helping to ease her into the demands of her new position. Magret and Nikei looked up sharply at Cathrin's words, and Nikei looked away quickly. "I think perhaps I will excuse myself now," he said hastily. He picked up the books he had brought with him and bowed quickly to the women before leaving the apartment.

Sira stared after him in confusion. "Why did Nikei leave like that? You would think an *urbear* was after him!"

Cathrin laughed a little. Magret said delicately, "We have been waiting, actually, Magistrix, for a moment to speak of this with you. Nikei feels this is a discussion to be held only among women."

Cathrin put down the stack of linens in her hands, and came to sit close to Sira. "When it was Mkel's turn, you know, Magistrix, all the women left the room."

"Oh," Sira said faintly. "I see."

Magret said, "Of course you are aware that the Magister of Conservatory, traditionally, takes a mate."

"Yes," Sira said.

"There has never been a Magistrix before, at least not in our memory," Magret went on. "Nikei and I, and the others, would like to know your wishes in this matter."

The two older women waited, watching Sira's face, in a polite and respectful silence. Sira looked down at her hands, and out the window, and then at Cathrin. "Cathrin, I would never want to say anything to offend Mkel's memory, please know that."

Cathrin nodded, searching Sira's face with her eyes.

"It is just that I want to use my Gift. It is not enough for me to simply oversee the school, and the training of the students." Sira smiled a little, ruefully.

"I believe Maestra Magret already knows that when I first left Conservatory, I burned with ambition. I wanted to sing for great audiences, to hear the acclaim of my colleagues, to prove that I was the best! The Spirit taught me, through all of the strange turnings my life has taken, that what is truly important is to sing, no matter for whom. The work, the music, is everything. I need to teach, to sing—to perform *quirunha*. Otherwise, the tasks of this office would be eternal punishment."

Magret nodded quickly. "I felt certain you would say exactly that, Magistrix." She rose, adding, "I will let the others know for you, shall I?"

Cathrin stopped her. "Wait, please, Maestra!" Magret turned back in surprise.

"Sira," Cathrin said, very softly. She paused, searching for the words she needed. "You know, being mated made Mkel's job all the easier. It's an enormous duty you have taken on, and it can be exhausting. Wouldn't you like to think about it, to consider?"

"So I have," Sira said quickly. "There was no decision to make, truly."

"But," Cathrin insisted gently, "your special friend, Cantor Theo. Wouldn't you like to have him by your side, to help you to bear the load as I helped Mkel over the years?"

There was a silence. Sira could not sit still any longer. She pushed away from the table and went to stand by the window. She looked out over the summer-green hills, where the softwood shoots were already half as tall as she herself. For one fleeting moment she wished she and Theo could simply ride away, out under the sky that was the same blue as her dear friend's eyes, away from all the problems and decisions and responsibilities. But she could not turn her back on this call, and she knew it. All her life she had answered the call of the Gift, and she would not change that now.

She turned back to Cathrin and Magret. "I would, Cathrin," she said softly. "I would so like to have Theo's support, his help and his companionship, here at Conservatory. But I will never mate. It is not in me to make that compromise with my Gift. And how can I ask Theo to stay here, to abandon his work at Observatory? In truth, I am not sure he would want to do so either way, mated or unmated. He is Cantor Theo v'Observatory, not Magistrix Sira's mate!"

"I should tell you, Magistrix," said Magret, "that Lamdon believes you will move your school at Observatory here, bring those Gifted children to Conservatory to be trained."

Sira's chin went up. "I will not," she said. "That would be throwing aside all that the Gift has been teaching us at Observatory. And if that is why they chose me, they were mistaken, and they will have to choose another."

Magret laughed. "Oh, they cannot choose another! Despite Cantor Abram's fine speech, Magister Mkel chose you, and they were bound to respect his wishes. But they did hope that your appointment as Magistrix would simplify things. You are such a puzzle to them all!"

Sira came back to sit again in the tall chair that had been Mkel's. "I believe I am to meet with Cantor Abram this morning," she said. "After the *quirunha*. I will explain to him, and to all of you, my plans for Observatory. But, Maestra, I hope I will have advice from you, too, you and Maestro Nikei and all the others. It is important to me, and to Cantor Theo, to hear everyone's voice."

Magret bowed to her. "Magistrix, we will give you every support we can."

Magret was right. Abram's smug expression crumpled into an angry one when he learned that Sira and Theo had no intention of moving their students from Observatory. Sira was Magistrix already, though, despite the fact that the ceremony had not taken place, and he could not give vent to his feelings as he had when she was simply a rebel Cantrix without a Cantoris.

"Surely, Magistrix," he pleaded, his plump features pinched by his attempt to control his temper. "Surely it is better if all the Gifted are trained in one place."

Sira knew very well the power of her new position. It frightened her in the long night hours, but at this moment she understood it was her job to use it. She trusted to her instincts. "Cantor Abram," she said levelly. "Why do you think Observatory, small House that it is, has seen such a flourishing of the Gift?"

Abram stared at her. "Does anyone know the reasons for such things? Those are the mysteries of life on the Continent!"

Sira met Theo's eyes and he winked at her. "I believe I do know," Sira said. She abruptly rose and paced the room, to the window and back, to stand behind her tall chair, the Magister's—no, the Magistrix's—chair. She gripped it with her hands. The teachers and Cantor Abram, Theo, Berk, and Zakri were ranged around the meeting table. She swept them all with her glance.

"I am sure Cantor Theo would say that the *ferrel* builds more than one nest," she began. Theo grinned. "The way we have trained the Gift, and the way in which we have used it on Nevya, has grown more and more narrow over the years. It is natural to try to control that on which we are dependent; but we have tried too hard, we Nevyans. We have set such a price on the Gift, misused our Singers, isolated them. For some, discovering their Gift is tantamount to a punishment, and therefore, the Gift does not appear."

"What punishment?" sputtered Abram. "I do not understand you! The Gift has to be disciplined!"

"Yes, it does," Sira said, nodding. "But discipline does not require ancient rules that have outlived their time."

"What rules, then? What rules do you wish to break?"

"Only the artificial ones," she said mildly. "The ones that say the Gift can only be trained in one way, in one place. The rules that ignore realities, such as those that touched Trisa's life, or Zakri's, or Isbel's, or—" She held out her hand to Theo. "Or Cantor Theo's."

Abram was silent, shaking his head. Maestro Nikei said quietly, "Mkel came to believe, in his last years, that change was necessary, and that Magistrix Sira was sent by the Gift to effect the change. And when Mreen arrived, this child that is purely of the Gift, nurtured at Observatory and brought here by as revolutionary a figure as Cantor Theo—"

Theo chuckled aloud at that. Nikei smiled at him. "Indeed you may laugh, Cantor," he said. "When the Gift has you in its current, you must simply float on the tide. I doubt any of the great revolutionaries set out to be so. I doubt that Magistrix Sira set out to be a reformer."

Sira smiled at him. "You know I did not, Maestro Nikei," she said. "If I am, as you say, a reformer, then it is the work of the Spirit. I am no visionary." She paused for a moment, surveying the people around her. Very softly, she finished, "I am only a Singer, like each of you, willing to work hard and to listen to the Gift when it calls."

There was a silence, and Theo's eyes smiled at Sira, clear blue now like the sky above the hills.

Abram said wearily, "What do you want, then, Magistrix? What are we supposed to do?"

Sira opened her hands, a gesture to include them all. "We will work," she said. "We will study and teach and practice as we have always done. Observatory's school will go on, with Theo and Cantrix Jana if she is willing. We will be open to surprises like Theo, here, and like Cantor Zakri. We will be more open in general, in fact, since I have learned from Theo that our healing can be much improved by being more open."

Abram shook his head. Sira saw Zakri staring at him, and she suppressed a smile. No doubt later Zakri would tell her all that Abram had been thinking! She would scold him, but it would do no good. And she would not, in truth, mind knowing.

"I do not know what will happen," Abram muttered.

"No, Cantor Abram," Sira agreed. "Nor do I. We will simply have to try, and trust. It is all we can ever do."

The day of Sira's investiture as Magistrix of Conservatory dawned bright and warm, the two suns brilliant in the sky. The Housemen and women, the young Singers, all the teachers, and the many visitors spent most of the morning bathing, planning what to wear and what to say, preparing to celebrate the ceremony and enjoy the feast afterward. Only Sira, with Theo and Nikei, was working, seated once again at the long table in her apartment.

"But if you leave yourself open," Nikei was saying, "how can you bear the illness, and still do your work?"

"If you are closed," Theo answered him, "how can you know where the illness is?"

"You will have to show me, I think, Cantor. . . ."

They were interrupted by a knock on the door, and Theo opened it to find a young Housewoman standing with her hands on her hips. "Yes?" he said.

"If the Magistrix doesn't come and bathe soon, there won't be any time!" she said sharply.

Sira stood quickly. "Cantor Theo, please meet Ita . . . she is my new Housewoman."

Theo bowed to the girl, and she bowed in return, properly, but quickly. "Truly, Magistrix," she insisted. "It's late. You must come now! I won't have you looking like some kitchen worker—"

"All right, Ita," Sira said hastily. She arched her brow at Theo as she passed him. "I am coming."

Theo and Nikei listened to Ita scold Sira as they went down the corridor together. "It's really too bad about your hair, Magistrix," she was saying. "But there's nothing we can do about it now—I suppose it will grow, in time."

Theo laughed aloud then. "I wish her luck with the hair," he chortled. "But it seems Sira will be obliged to obey someone, after all!"

It was a grand and colorful event, the investiture of Magistrix Sira v'Conservatory. The dark tunics of the upper levels and the Gifted gave way, through the ranks of the assembly, to the brilliant hues of the Housemen and women. Magister Gowan's white hair and face contrasted sharply with Sira's tanned, lean figure on the dais. Magister Pol attended, on his first trip outside of Observatory. Sira's parents, too, Niel v'Arren and his mate, were there. She had struggled to find something to say to them; they were almost complete strangers to her. But they did not seem troubled by that; their pride made them almost speechless in any case.

Mreen made Theo hold her up in his arms so she could see. Between them, Magister Gowan and Cantor Abram made the succession of the Magistrix of Conservatory official. The rite itself was short, but the congratulations and the cheering of the House members were long, cut off in the end only by the announcement of the meal.

Conservatory's kitchens had spared no effort, and the feast laid out in the great room was the richest Mreen had ever seen. She sat with her class, of course, but she watched Magistrix Sira at the central table with all the teachers and the dignitaries from Lamdon. She thought she looked wonderful, tall and noble, as if born to be a Magistrix.

She watched Cantor Theo, too. He had a special place at Sira's right hand, and Mreen saw them glance at each other often, and she sensed the pain between them. It was wrong, somehow, that pain. Her own halo darkened when she felt it. Little shadows flitted around her despite her pleasure in the day. There was only laughter and vivacity around her, but Mreen was distracted from the rich *caeru* stew, the nut-bread, the sweets she loved. At last she could bear it no more, and she ducked under the table to scamper across the great room to the very center.

She tugged on Theo's sleeve, and he grinned down at her. *Well, hello, little one,* he sent. *Is the food at your own table not so good?*

She dimpled. *The food is wonderful!* she answered.

Then what are you doing here, with the old folk?

I know you are worried, you and Ca—I mean, Magistrix Sira.

Theo patted her cheek. *You know, even when we are happy, we each have our special sorrows, dear heart. Mine is that I must say goodbye to Magistrix Sira tomorrow . . . and to you as well!*

But, Cantor Theo, she sent urgently. *You are coming back!*

He looked at her quizzically. *Well, I suppose one day, Mreen, but . . . I am certain to come for a visit someday. Perhaps when you sing your first* quirunha!

She shook her head, her curls bouncing, her nimbus sparkling with energy. *Oh, no, Cantor Theo . . . very soon!*

How can you know that, Mreen?

She grinned at him, laughing her soundless laugh. *You are everywhere in Conservatory,* she sent. *I feel you in the classrooms, even in the practice rooms.*

Mreen, he sent carefully. *I have never been in any of those places.*

The little old woman peered out from behind the child's face again, in a way that had become almost familiar. *You will be, Cantor Theo. You will be.* Her nimbus shifted, dark and light together.

Mreen looked up to see that Sira, Magistrix Sira v'Conservatory, was listening to what she sent. Theo and

Sira looked into each other's eyes, and they smiled. The pain between them evaporated like morning fog under the light of the two suns, and Mreen's halo frothed, glimmers and sparks of light doing a wild dance about her head, her red curls floating. The ancient expression vanished from her plump features, and her dimples flashed.

Suddenly, she was ravenous. She hurried back to her own table, eager for the lovely treats that awaited her there.

Praise for *Sing the* 12/19

$2.00

"Louise Marley is a fine new writer with [...] career ahead of her as a fantasy writer. I recommend her."
— Anne McCaffrey

"Louise Marley's knowledge of music and story make for a stunning combination of talent."
— Greg Bear

"The subject . . . is full of beautiful ideas and the feeling for place is real, specific, substantial."
— Geoff Ryman

"*Sing the Light*—a highly crafted science fiction tale that makes authentic use of the author's extensive musical background."
— *Bellevue Journal American*

"Marley makes her writing sing."
— Everett Herald

"First novelist Marley shows a real feel for the elements that make fantasy (and science fantasy) popular."
— *Locus*

Ace Books by Louise Marley

SING THE LIGHT
SING THE WARMTH
RECEIVE THE GIFT